O9-BTZ-091

"Sam?"

Rachel jumped when the small back door banged shut. Her husband had probably just stepped out after he sent Andy back to the house, she reasoned, so he couldn't hear her. He'd come back in now.

But he didn't.

Her stomach clenched. As she walked onto the broad threshing floor past the enclosed granary and peered into the shapes and shadows of both full haymows, the whole barn seemed to heave a huge sigh. High above the shingled roof, Rachel heard the horse weather vane creak as it spun atop the cupola. The metal track that winched the hay fork across the peak of the barn rattled. Yet the familiar smells of the place comforted her—grain, hay, dust and pungent animal smells—even in such a clean barn. But she smelled raw animal fear, too, and wondered if it were her own.

Rachel ducked as something brushed her face and cap. One of the pair of resident barn owls must have come in low instead of through the drop-down haymow door. The hair on her neck prickled.

"Samuel Mast!"

She saw him then. Her scream cut through the shriek of wind. The horses banged their stalls as rain began to beat against the lofty roof.

"Karen Harper delivers unforgettable romantic suspense."

—*Romantic Times*

Also available from MIRA Books and
KAREN HARPER

THE BABY FARM

Watch for the newest novel of romantic suspense from
KAREN HARPER
Available June 2001

KAREN HARPER

DOWN TO THE BONE

MIRA

If you purchased this book without a cover you should be aware that this book is stolen property. It was reported as "unsold and destroyed" to the publisher, and neither the author nor the publisher has received any payment for this "stripped book."

ISBN 1-55166-589-1

DOWN TO THE BONE

Copyright © 2000 by Karen Harper.

All rights reserved. Except for use in any review, the reproduction or utilization of this work in whole or in part in any form by any electronic, mechanical or other means, now known or hereafter invented, including xerography, photocopying and recording, or in any information storage or retrieval system, is forbidden without the written permission of the publisher, MIRA Books, 225 Duncan Mill Road, Don Mills, Ontario, Canada M3B 3K9.

All characters in this book have no existence outside the imagination of the author and have no relation whatsoever to anyone bearing the same name or names. They are not even distantly inspired by any individual known or unknown to the author, and all incidents are pure invention.

MIRA and the Star Colophon are trademarks used under license and registered in Australia, New Zealand, Philippines, United States Patent and Trademark Office and in other countries.

Visit us at www.mirabooks.com

Printed in U.S.A.

"There is no past we can bring back by the longing for it, there is only the eternally new now that builds and creates itself out of the elements of the past."
—Johann Goethe

This novel is dedicated to the two people who have most given me a precious past and a happy now. Don, my husband, and my mother, Margaret.

Prologue

Clearview, Ohio
September 18, 1997

The wind whined around the corner of the farm-house, and loose straw scuttled across the yard. Rachel Mast wiped her hands on her long apron and looked out the kitchen window, frowning at the gray, clotted clouds. She'd had to light the kerosene lamps early. As soon as Sam came in from unhitching and feeding the horses, she'd serve the hot dinner she was holding. You might know, she thought, bad weather for her twenty-fifth birthday, though they'd be all snug and warm tonight. She'd heard Sam trying to teach the twins the happy birthday song, but she'd still act surprised.

Behind her, kneeling on a chair to set the table as he'd been asked, her son Aaron sneezed on the freshly cut bread. Rachel would have scolded him, but she was worried about what was taking Sam so long. Then she saw Andy, her other three-and-a-half-year-old, through the window. He was not in the barn with his *Daadi* as he was supposed to be, but squatted looking at something just outside it. Why didn't Sam keep an eye on him? If the wind picked up more, that old door could break loose and crack him good.

"*Mamm,* I dropped a spoon," Aaron said as it all too obviously clattered to the linoleum floor.

"You stay right here and don't touch the stove," Rachel told him, swinging him off the chair to the floor. "I'm going to get Andy and *Daadi.*"

The wind bucked the back door as she went out. "Andy, come here!" she called from the porch. He looked up but didn't budge. A gust whipped his straw hat off and spun it away. He didn't so much as glance after it. Last week it had been so warm for mid-September that she had not yet made the boys change to their broad-brimmed black hats.

"Look, *Mamm,*" Andy called in the German dialect all Amish folk spoke to each other. "The barn owl ate heads off the moles again."

To her dismay, he picked up the brown, furry scrap of death, extended it at arm's length and started toward her.

"Put that down! You get in the house and wait till I wash you up good. Where's your *Daadi?*" When he glanced at the gaping barn door, Rachel started toward it, pointing to the house.

"He said run tell you he's near ready," the boy shouted back. Of the two boys, Andy had talked first and better, sometimes as if he had to interpret for his brother. He was the older of the identical twins by about an hour and the leader of the pack, as Rachel sometimes thought of the two of them. No one but she and Sam could tell the freckled redheads apart, and even Sam had to look real close unless Andy was ordering or dragging Aaron around. But besides being the leader, Andy had a slightly rounder face.

"If *Daadi*'s ready, where is he?" she asked, her voice on edge.

Evidently thinking he might get a smack on his trousers when she kept coming toward him, Andy finally dropped the beheaded mole and ran for the house.

Rachel strode faster toward the barn. Not only were her chicken and mashed potatoes cooling inside, but she didn't want to leave the boys alone. What was keeping Sam?

Though the barn was painted a soft, faded red with black trim, all seemed gray now as the early dusk and storm closed in. When she reached the doors, latched to the outside wall with the big antique hooks, they shuddered on their hinges. From just inside, she heard a muffled shuffling, a deep snort and thud. Chester, the huge, blond Percheron gelding who led the work team, stepped out past her. Startled, she jumped back, then reached up to grab his bridle. Sam hadn't even gotten that off yet?

Clucking to the big beast, Rachel turned and pulled him back into the barn. Sam had evidently not lit a lantern. She waited a moment for her eyes to adjust, but it was dark as the devil's heart in here, she thought with a shudder.

The Mast barn on Ravine Road just outside Clearview, Ohio, was a pioneer building showing its age, but they had been thrilled to find such a large, beautiful one. Several other Amish families new to this fading farm community had bought places with houses much worse than this one just to get a sturdy barn.

"Sam, you here? Chester got out."

Unafraid of Chester, for Rachel loved horses, be they buggy trotters or the draft-bred, she pulled him into his stall next to the two others which were unhitched and unharnessed. In the far bay across the threshing floor the two buggy horses shifted and stamped. Rachel called out to calm them, "*Sehr gut,* Bett. *Sehr gut,* Nann."

The horses seemed to sense the approaching storm. Even the massive Percherons snorted and sidestepped against the walls, the whites of their eyes showing. Rachel slipped Chester's harness off and smacked his rump before she closed and latched the stall door behind him.

"Sam?"

Rachel jumped when the small back door banged shut. He'd probably just stepped out after he sent Andy to the house, she reasoned, so he couldn't hear her. He'd come back in now.

But he didn't.

Her stomach clenched. As she walked onto the broad threshing floor past the enclosed granary and peered up into the shapes and shadows of both full haymows, the whole barn seemed to heave a huge sigh. Thank God, it was a bit late for tornado weather, because the wind was almost that bad. High above the shingled roof, Rachel heard the horse weather vane creak as it spun atop the cupola. The metal track that winched the hayfork across the peak of the barn rattled. Yet the familiar smells of the place comforted her—grain, hay, dust and pungent animal smells—even in such a clean-kept barn. But she smelled raw animal fear, too, and wondered if it was her own.

Rachel ducked as something brushed her face and cap. One of the pair of resident barn owls must have come in low instead of through the drop-down haymow door. The saw-toothed edge of their wings let them fly silent as a moth to kill their prey, but she'd felt its stealthy, soundless presence. The hair on her neck prickled.

"Samuel Mast! *Wo bist du?*"

She saw him then. Her scream cut through the shriek of wind. The horses banged their stalls as rain began to beat against the lofty roof.

One

"A whole year, a whole year," Rachel whispered to herself as she squinted through bright sunlight at the barn. "I miss you, Sam, but I had to work this place to hold it for our boys."

At first after Sam's freak accident, she'd dreaded going into the barn but, with help from the Amish brethren, she had kept the farm going. Now, she'd made peace with the place where he'd died, though it had pretty much taken her this whole year.

On the day of her twenty-sixth birthday, Rachel Mast tried not to think of finding Sam's bloody body on her last one. Though birthday gifts were worldly, she was giving herself one today: an hour of silence before she walked across the pumpkin field to fetch the boys from her friend's house. Just as she did years ago at home, she was going to climb into the fresh hay in the mow. She was going to read again yesterday's letter from her sister Susan in the big

Amish community of Maplecreek across the state from which the forty-one-member Clearview Amish had come three years ago, seeking affordable farmland for themselves and their sons. She was going to rest and dream.

Rachel removed her deep, black bonnet and tiptoed barefooted into the barn as if it were a sacred place. Her hat and shoes were off only because she wanted to hold on to summer. Today the depths seemed empty and not just because Sam had died here. Her fine team of Percherons were gone, being used and stabled by other plain families who in turn helped work her fields. At least the buggy horses, cats and cooing pigeons were here to keep her company. The pigeons and barn swallows had returned after the owls had left the night Sam died.

Hanging her bonnet on a row of pegs by the door, she spoke to the buggy horses, Bett and Nann, then petted the new litter of kittens lapping milk from the bowls she'd left out. They were safer with the owls gone, too.

Though Sam had always insisted that barn cats were not pets, Rachel favored the mother of the kittens, a butterscotch tabby who was whisker-deep in the biggest bowl. The cat dragged one crooked back leg which had been injured when Sam had fallen on her. Rachel had named her Mira, for miracle, since the cat had survived Sam's gruesome death. Mira, Rachel reasoned, had been with Sam at the end when she herself had not.

Rachel leaned a moment against the wooden ladder to the east haymow above the empty Percheron stalls. With her forehead resting on a well-worn rung, she momentarily clung to the sturdy ladder. She had to admit, despite how busy she kept herself, she missed Sam not only in the fields, barn and house but in bed. Yet memories of him were muted now, even those of his quick, callused hands along her bare skin under her nightgown, the feel of him against her, in her.

True, she admitted, Sam had not been the love of her life, for she had lost *him* early and tragically, too. But she had known Sam nearly forever, as he was reared on the adjoining farm. He was so solid, so sure he loved her that agreeing to marry him had seemed the right thing to do. Besides, most of her friends were wed, and she was getting up there at age twenty after teaching in the Amish school for two years. Though she loved those kids, she knew it was time to be having her own brood. And the fact both twins were boys and would need their own land to farm someday was one reason she and Sam had left home. For that reason and others, there was no way she was going back. *This* was home now.

She sighed, climbed the ladder, and flopped onto the loose hay. She stretched and wiggled her toes, but tensed again when she heard hoofbeats. Guiltily, Rachel hoped the buggy would go past. No Amish places lay out farther from town than hers on this road, but she was not expecting anyone. She clambered through the deep hay to the rim of stacked bales and looked out at the huge square of sky.

Through this high, drop-down haymow door, shuttered in the winter, the new-cut bounty had recently been hoisted up from wagons. The heavy grappling hook still hung from its track along the peak of the roof. Rachel shuddered, uncertain if the cause was the hook or the hoofbeats.

Without her glasses on, she had to squint to see. "Oh, no," she muttered when she realized who was probably in the black-topped buggy.

As most Amish, Rachel could read which family owned even identical buggies from the size and gait of the horse. She could only hope it was her friend Sarah Yoder who had come calling and not Sarah's father, Eben, the bishop of their small community of souls. Not today, not alone, and in a buggy the size the young men used for courting.

Her first instinct was to hide here until Eben left, but the back door of the house was open, and he'd probably worry that some judgment of God had befallen her. Besides, it never did to hide from things. They eventually caught up with you and had to be faced, anyway.

Everyone in the Church here, even some back home, expected Rachel Mast to marry Eben Yoder. Just as when she'd wed Sam, it was obviously the "right" thing to do. It would solve a lot of problems, people whispered, and that was true. Amish adults needed to be matched to their own kind. Marriage to Eben would cure her financial woes and no longer necessitate the others helping her when they were busy enough with their own places and kids. Eben was alone with six children, and Rachel's two were a real handful. She and the boys could move to the Yoder dairy farm a half hour's trot away, and some other family from back home—one with a man as proper head of the household—could buy this place and join their little community.

But Rachel didn't want to marry Eben Yoder or anyone else now, even if it was the *right* thing to do.

She squinted again to make the black blur become

clearer. Her heart fell to her feet when she saw she was right. It was Eben, and he was alone. Slowly, leaden-footed, she climbed down from the loft to greet him.

Eben Yoder was forty-two but felt and looked ten years younger. His sandy head of hair was holding its hue and shape, though his beard was flecked with gray. Pride in all things was bad, but he knew he was a good-looking man, well-muscled from farm chores, disciplined by milking cows on schedule all his days. And since Eben Mary had been gone nigh on three years—gone the week after they came here to Clearview—he felt it time to wed again. He'd made no bones about that. And now he wouldn't have to go back to Maplecreek for quick courting, even if his boys and neighbors could pitch in with the milking.

He wanted Sam Rachel badly for his helpmeet and for a mother to his five who would still be at home after his eldest, Sarah, wed. He and Sam Rachel could have more youngsters of their own. He would take those twins in hand, take Sam Rachel in hand, too, when she'd changed her name to Eben Rachel Yoder, for it was custom to call Amish women by their man's name, too.

Eben's practiced eye skimmed the Mast farm with its two deep side fields and one behind, then the small woodlot stretching nearly to the train tracks. Eighty acres, it was. The barn was weathered but sturdy, its original slate roof patched in places with brown shingles, and every board still stained with its original reddish pioneer paint, at least on three sides of the big barn.

Unfortunately, the side that showed itself to this

road from town bore one of those painted-up ads that tempted one to taste the world's sins. On a yellow background was painted in white letters with dark shadowing Mail Pouch Tobacco, and smaller, below those bold words, Chewing Serves to Settle the Nerves.

Eben Yoder snorted and snapped the reins. Nothing about Sam Rachel had settled his nerves this past year as he'd waited to court and wed her. Even when he and Sam Mast served as leaders of the splinter group that migrated here to buy affordable farms and to duck the crowds of tourists in Maplecreek, he had kept his eye on Sam Rachel.

The white farmhouse, Eben noted, was still unpainted, but the vegetable and flower gardens were neatly kept, especially for early fall when everything ran riot. Sam Rachel had fought hard to keep the place up. She'd put in a field of pumpkins for extra cash, but Eben didn't approve of that since she'd done it with a worldly neighbor who had no man, either. The fact Rachel had overstepped more than once to do men's work and mix with the English was a bad sign, but that would be over soon, he'd see to that. No way in all creation his second wife would be a fence-jumper like his first.

Brushing straw from her black skirt and white apron, Rachel came out of the barn to greet him. She was barefooted and bareheaded but for her small white cap, ripe for plucking. As for no bonnet, women didn't wear them inside among the people, but outside the lack of it made her seem almost undressed. His pulse beat faster. He braced his feet hard against the buckboard as if that was the break for the buggy.

Grateful to be off the slanted berm where buggies kept to avoid passing cars, he turned up the short, gravel lane and reined in. Though it was the inside of folks that mattered, Sam Rachel Mast's outside was pretty good, too. She had a fine, oval face, even if she'd gone a bit too skinny lately. He quickly pulled out his pocket watch and clicked its face open. Good time. He'd made it here in twenty-six minutes. The boys would be starting with the milking in a half hour. He considered reminding Rachel that he would miss overseeing it this afternoon so she'd know how momentous this visit was for him.

"A beautiful Indian summer day," she said by way of welcome.

"*Ach,* that it is."

Rachel had molasses-brown hair with highlights that shimmered red in the sun. Her eyes were green as grass. When she wore her spectacles to read the Bible or hymnbook, her gaze reminded him of the pond on his property. Eben hadn't gone swimming since he was a boy, but he'd like to swim in those eyes.

"Sam Rachel," he said, wrapping the reins and climbing down, "got some good news."

"I can always use some of that."

"I gave Jacob Esh permission to enter into wedlock with Sarah, sure did," he said with a nod. "Our first wedding for the Clearview Church, uh-huh."

"That's wonderful. They've waited a long time. But if they wed before next summer, you'll have to buy the celery."

"Well," he drawled, relieved she sounded happy now when she didn't look that way a minute ago,

"January is the month, so I'll just have to spring for two hundred stalks at the SuperMart."

They shared a quick laugh. Creamed celery was a traditional wedding dish, and the leafy stalks were used in arrangements on the bridal table.

"Jacob waited real patient for Sarah these years she had to help with the *junge leit* their mother left behind," Eben said, clearing his throat. "So I approve of their marrying soon. They've known each other a goodly while. That helps make a sound match, I think. No use waiting if the couple is mature and sure."

When Rachel only fidgeted and nodded, he remembered he'd brought her a gift and reached back in the buggy for the sack. "Some of Sarah's bulb starts to plant in the fall, enjoy in the spring," he said, extending the bag to her. Their fingers touched briefly. "Crocus and those sweet-smelling ones near knock your socks off."

"Hyacinth," Rachel said as she took the sack and they walked up to the front porch. No need for words like *thanks* or *please* among the Amish, as such was understood and not expected. It was the same for not saying *"Best wishes"* for a betrothal or a wedding.

Rachel indicated he should take the larger rocking chair. Eben noted it was dusty, but he sat anyway without remark or swiping at it. She asked him if he'd like a cool drink or some *snicker-doodles*, but he wanted to get this part past so he said no.

"The boys not here?" he began, shifting in his chair and making it creak.

"Over next door. I need to go get them before supper."

"*Ach*, you don't see the dangers there, do you?"

She frowned at him, probably without knowing it. "Jennie's tending her two grandsons, and they play together fine with the twins," she said. "I don't pay Jennie Morgan but bake and can fruits and vegetables for her."

"Sarah used to tend the twins," he said, his voice so serious.

"But that's a half hour each way and now, obviously," she protested, "Sarah's going to be even busier than she's been."

"The Troyers or Lapps could help."

"That's a real buggy ride, too. This is working out for now, Eben."

He settled his broad-brimmed black hat harder on his head and planted his feet firmer. "For *now* is right, Rachel. I think there ought to be some changes, I sure do."

She, too, sat up straighter. Her nostrils flared as if she scented the wind. Eben had hunted enough to know that look, that alert, wary stiffness, waiting, listening. Getting ready to bolt, she was. But no matter what, he was closing in for the kill real soon.

Rachel almost panicked. No way could she misconstrue what was coming. Eben had arrived alone during milking time in a courting buggy he'd probably borrowed from Dan, his oldest boy. He'd brought her a gift, even if it was flower bulbs and not flowers. He'd dressed if not in his best crowned hat, in a good one, and he'd pulled on a black *wamus* coat over his clean broadfall trousers, white shirt and distinctive X-shaped suspenders that marked all the Clearview Amish men. Worse, he'd called her just "Rachel" when women, even widows, were always referred to by their husband's names attached to their own.

"You all right?" he asked, leaning so far, elbows on spread knees, that he seemed to career toward her. "You look all stirred up."

"Just thinking about Sarah again," she said, though that was a bit of a lie. "I'm happy for her. She loves Jacob, and she's ready to wed. That makes all the difference in the world."

"The world, ha," he said with a single shake of his head. "We don't do things like the world, aren't in the world. And marriage is a good woman's rightful state."

"*When* it's the right state for her."

His brow furrowed, and he gripped his hands together so hard his knuckles whitened like sausages. "I'd like permission to court you, Rachel, looking toward marriage soon, maybe right after Sarah and Jacob. My intentions can't be much surprise to you. It's been a while since Sam died—"

"A year today," she cut in. "Exactly."

"I didn't figure. Today? Then it's your birthday, too."

"I thought that was partly why the gift..."

"You're twenty-six then, Rachel, more than a quarter century, old enough to know what's what, what's best. For you and your fine boys."

"And for you, Eben?"

"Yes," he said with a vigorous nod. "For me, for sure. Best for all our folk here."

Rachel knew Eben was a man of few words, and he had shared many here so far. Though he was the bishop of their community, it had fallen to him by holy lot, not because he was a good speaker, though he had gotten better with practice. He was a man of duty, discipline and dedication.

All these things were good, but they were not what she wanted when she agreed to be courted or to wed. There had to be something more than economics, family necessity or community approval. Rachel had been a good wife to Sam, and they had been friends, when they were not arguing over how to handle the strange rebellions of their little boys. She supposed she had never really loved Sam wholeheartedly, but they had been a good team, pulling together and usually comfortable, like the horse teams. But even then, she had known there had to be some new depths or heights to a relationship, something more than mutual respect and shared bodies.

Rachel stood. Eben rose, too, just staring now as if he'd run out of words. Their chairs both rocked as if ghosts sat in them.

"Eben, I am honored, but I can't agree to that. I have too much on my hands and on my mind here to—"

"Woman, I want to take things off your hands and off your mind! I just surprised you, overwhelmed you. I'll fetch you and the boys Saturday at nine to go into that estate sale near town and," he added hastily, holding up a hand when he evidently saw she would protest, "you can help Sarah plan for her big day."

But even that will not get me in the mood for mine, Rachel thought defiantly as she let him have the last word for now. She waved to him as he walked off the porch and drove away with just one frowning glance at his pocket watch and then at her.

Rachel crumpled back in her rocker and watched Eben's black box of buggy shrink to nothing on the road.

After Eben left, Rachel was still shook, but she marched right back to the barn and her plans. She lay flat in the haymow, watching sunbeams and dust motes dance in the shadows of the soaring expanse above her. Her starched cap was smashed flat and got all creased so she took it off, too, only to snag her heavy hairpins in the hay and have one big braid spill free. For now, she let it go.

An Amish woman's hair was never cut and was her glory, only for her husband's eyes. As for a cap coming off, back during the time called *rumspringa,* the young folk had always said if a girl took off her cap for a boy she'd sleep with him. Thank the Lord she had only had her bonnet off when Eben had come calling.

Still, Rachel remembered, as she toyed with her loose braid, she had always said if her heavy hair gave her headaches like it had her mother and started thinning at age forty from all its weight, she'd hack some off. She pictured herself cutting some of it, just a bit, clip, clip. She was so tired and sleepy. Was that another buggy on the road? Clip, clop. If so she wasn't getting up again.

A lazy, buzzing fly had become caught in a gilded web as the sun sank lower. Its rays caressed the patina of hand-hewn beams and boards with their unique grains, knots and whorls. Though she'd never told anyone about it, just as in a calendar picture or in the clouds, she could see things there, full-blown roses, ponds, faces. Waves licking at a sandy beach.

She had always wanted to see the ocean—or at least Lake Erie.

She was floating, maybe sleepwalking as Aaron sometimes did before he woke and screamed out what her friend Jennie called night terrors. Now Rachel saw Sam standing over her, his hand outstretched, beseeching her about something, his head and back bloody, his body pierced like the old martyrs of Germany that had made the Amish flee to America...

She startled instantly awake. Were those footsteps on the hollow threshing floor below? Someone—a man—cleared his throat, then called out in English, "Anybody here?"

Her heart galloping, Rachel crept over and peered down. Her gasp gave her away, and the stranger looked up.

"Sorry if I startled you, ma'am," the man called up to her. "I knocked at the house to ask permission to look around, but no one answered."

Rachel nodded mutely. She realized she had been so sheltered she had never faced an *Englische* man alone before, not even in the days she'd delivered *Mamm*'s quilts back home. This man was tall, big-shouldered and square-jawed. He wore black jeans and a plaid shirt in forbidden red, rolled up to show strong forearms. Instead of suspenders, a worldly belt cinched in his waist to emphasize his ribs, broad chest and narrow hips. He looked as sun-browned as an Amish farmer and wore work boots, but the similarities stopped there. Many Amish men were short or medium height and this man looked real big.

Rachel thought all this in but an instant, yet the look seemed to last forever. She knew she should properly glance away from his intense brown, assessing eyes, for such a common stare was worldly and intimate. But it was his thick, *verboten* mustache over his firm mouth and his clean-shaved face that really rattled her. It was the opposite of Amish men with beards but no mustaches, not to mention that Amish men wore their hair cut collar high and this one's raven hair was clipped about an inch short.

The impact of him, strong and bold, standing in her barn with his legs slightly spread, brought back those stories of Amish-hating ogres, the soldiers who tracked down and arrested the faithful in *The Martyr's Mirror* to haul them off to captivity, torture, even death. Never in her life had she imagined such tumultuous, jumbled feelings for any man, let alone an *auslander*.

"This is my farm and my barn," she said, her voice both loud and firm. "Are you lost? What do you want?"

His smile made his eyes narrow and his teeth look so white in the dimming light. "I *may* be lost," the man said in a deep voice, "but actually, I want your barn."

Two

"You want my barn?" Rachel echoed the stranger's words. Her pulse began to pound even harder. "It's not for sale, and it goes with the farm. You mean you're looking for a farm to buy?"

Both annoyed and intrigued, Rachel started down the ladder, careful not to show more of her bare legs than necessary. She rued the fact her shoes were in the house, and that it was too late to retrieve her smashed cap and stuff all her straw-filled hair up under it.

"Let me explain," the man said as she faced him at the bottom of the ladder. At least he kept his distance. "I buy and tear down barns, then make them into homes for people who will appreciate, even treasure them. In other words, I do barn rescue. See, here's my card."

Rachel took the white card he held out as he stepped forward, but she kept moving past him so he wouldn't stay between her and the door. Standing in the broad entrance, she read it in the sinking sun.

MITCH RANDALL
BARNS REBORN, REBUILT, RELOCATED
RESCUE OF DERELICT OR DAMAGED
BARNS

Rachel recognized his address as a rural road near Woodland, a tiny town to the northwest. The card gave his phone number and numbers and letters called e-mail and fax and web, as if he were some spider. She shuffled slightly farther away from him.

"This barn's not in need of rescuing," she told him, holding out the card stiff-armed to give it back. He took it, reluctantly, she could tell, and slid it in the pocket of his red shirt. "This barn is already appreciated and treasured," she insisted when he still stood his ground.

"But the thing is, ma'am, it's obviously historic and in need of some serious repairs," Mitch Randall said. "If they're not done soon, things will get worse."

Their eyes met and held again until she looked away. "I know the Amish need and care for their barns," he went on, his voice apologetic now. "I just thought, in this case, you might want the twenty-five thousand dollars it would bring to build a new one here. Not that the Amish want new things, but I know how important their barns are."

It took her mind a minute to wrap around the number Mitch Randall had given. "Twenty-five *thousand* dollars?" she said, gaping up at him. Even as he nodded, her mind did quick calculations. Back home prime farmland could be two thousand dollars and up an acre, if there was any available in the area anymore. Here, it was not even a third of that, and the brethren could raise a new barn just for the cost of the supplies. But that much of a fortune could go a long way to solving all her problems. Two different proposals from two very different men in the same day! she marveled.

"But this barn belongs here," Rachel protested, fighting her own covetousness for the money. "It's been here since 1838."

Mitch Randall's eyebrows lifted at that date. Eager to prove it to him, she led him outside down the long front of the building, moved the grain shovel leaning against the wall, and pointed to the inscribed corner-stone.

"Eighteen thirty-eight, indeed," he said, looking impressed. "I knew there were several pioneer ones remaining in this area, but I thought, with your Victorian cupola, the place was probably 1860s or 1870s, even though hinged doors like yours went out about 1850." He gestured toward different parts of the barn as he talked. "Your cupola," he said, looking up, "which needs some work, must have been added later. I should have read the signs everywhere else, though," he added, squatting to touch the incised numbers almost reverently with his finger before he stood again.

"What signs?" Rachel asked, before she could kick herself for her bursting curiosity.

Looking slightly down at her as he stood, Mitch ticked things off on his long fingers. "The horse trough is carved from an entire tree trunk, and I saw some tally marks on a beam inside where the flailers or threshers kept track of their counts. That grain shovel is from a solid piece of basswood and an absolute antique. You see," he added and smiled at her, "the Amish are pretty modern compared to the pioneers who built this place."

He peeked around the corner of the barn at the slanted wood doors to the root cellar. "Do you still use that?" he asked. "It looks all overgrown."

"We opened it when we first came here, but we never use it," she explained as he examined the door, greatly covered by mats of frost-blasted morning-glory vines. "That small cellar can also be entered through a trapdoor in the barn, but it's not worth it. I keep my turnips and potatoes in the house cellar."

Rachel started to walk toward the house, purposefully heading him toward his shiny, red truck parked in her driveway near the road. "Look," he went on, gesturing as his strides easily kept up with hers, "I know the Amish don't want their pictures taken, but would you mind if I come back just to shoot the barn—you know, a few photos? I'd be pleased to pay a fee. Should I ask your husband for permission?"

Rachel didn't want to lie, but she didn't want to tell him she was alone here, either. Maybe he'd think her easy prey for his sales pressure or picture taking. Mitch Randall seemed so intense, his brown eyes almost burning when he explained what he did. And he had a habit of searching her face for something—looking *all* of her over—in a way an Amish man never would.

"I can make decisions about the barn," she told him, concentrating on keeping her voice steady. "I suppose a picture or two would be okay. But its image is not for sale, and don't you go telling buyers the barn is, either. So how do you make a house from a barn?"

He looked startled at her change of topic, then relieved. "We either jack up the frame, put it on a semi—a truck—and roll it. More often we code each board and beam, we take them apart, power-wash them and reassemble it on-site. Of course, the frame needs lighting, plumbing, insulation, interior walls and some internal design work. In general, the hay-lofts become bedrooms, and stalls become kitchens or dens, maybe bathrooms."

Rachel nodded as he talked, trying to picture everything he said. Her gaze skipped to the family's well-used outhouse, though they had a perfectly usable bathroom upstairs. She hung laundry there in the winter and used it for an oversize linen closet. Their running water came from their own well, but all the Clearview Amish had paid to have their electrical and phone lines taken down soon after they'd arrived.

"I'd be happy to show you samples of barn houses I've resurrected if you like," Mitch added, his hand on the door of his truck. It was only then she realized he meant he'd take her to show her some reborn barns.

"In person, no pictures?" she said and stepped back. "No, that's not necessary. So you're used to assessing what barns need to fix them? Other than a new roof and the cupola you mentioned, what would you say about mine?" she asked, hoping she sounded nonchalant. She crossed her arms casually over her chest.

A hint of smile crimped the corners of Mitch's mouth, but he looked pleased she'd asked. "I'd need an in-depth look around," he explained, "but just from today, I'd say a few replacement timbers on support beams that have been exposed to weather.

Two of them are high up under the roof, the shoulder bones of the place, so to speak.''

"On the roof,'' she interrupted hastily. "You mean where the track for the hay grapple hook hangs?''

"It could affect that,'' Mitch admitted, "but I'd have to check. The threshing floor looks sound but the planks of the east bay—you obviously have horses there sometimes—need some work, though there's evidently been some patching before.''

Rachel nodded, trying to concentrate on everything he said.

"Tell you what, ma'am. In exchange for my coming back to shoot some photos, I'll do a real walk-through with you, point things out, even give you ballpark figures of what each project might cost.'' He looked so earnest, so intent. "Would that be all right?''

"I really don't need things done now,'' she said, to try to put him off. "It's not a good time with winter coming on and all.''

"It's the best time,'' he insisted, "before the rain rots things more or the weight of snow or even winds cause problems. I know that an antique barn, maybe the fact you're Amish, too, suggests things should stay the same, but not always. Change and progress can be good.''

"In the first place,'' Rachel said, realizing she was shifting the subject again, "it's just plain crazy to think some person would want to live in my old barn. Especially one with that Mail Pouch painting on the side,'' she protested, wishing she hadn't started this. They kept talking about barns, but it somehow seemed like much more.

"You'd be surprised how that would be a draw." He bumped his fist gently on the door of his shiny truck as he spoke, so maybe he was nervous, too. "A lot of people drawn to barn homes want them as backdrops for folk art, and that primitive, almost art deco painting would really be attractive to them."

Art deco? She'd have to look that one up if she ever got back inside the little Clearview Library again. A car went by and honked. Without looking away from her, Mitch lifted a hand in a half wave.

Rachel felt exasperated with him now, since she'd hoped he would leave, but he made no move to. She frowned at the door of his truck where the same information that was on his card was written in big white print. She caught her reflection in his rearview mirror and stepped back, feeling she was caught with him, by him. It had shocked her to be reminded she was bonnetless and disheveled.

"Primitive art, that's the way some people see the Amish," she blurted when she'd meant to just ask him to go.

"They're the ones who are crazy then," he said. "Amish barns have more in common with factories than with museums. They are living, breathing, unique and beautiful."

Their gazes snagged and locked again at close range. Mitch's eyes narrowed and his nostrils flared. Rachel was late to get the boys but she didn't budge. She became intensely aware of herself as the wind bumped her braid of hair against her cheek and chin when she had never had hair loose in the wind, never in her life. As she grabbed for it to throw it back over her shoulder, she realized that straw was stuck in it and the wild *struvvles* at her temples had come all loose. Finally, she remembered to talk.

"Okay, Mr. Randall, just a few pictures if you keep my place and name out of it."

"May I ask your name?"

"Rachel Mast," she said before she realized she should have said Sam Rachel, but then that might have only confused him or made him ask more questions. She could tell by the little frown that perched like crow's-feet at the corners of his eyes and mouth that something she'd said had bothered him.

"Mast," he said, frowning. "Last year...in the papers...a freak accident in a barn..."

"Yes," Rachel said hastily, not wanting him to go on, to say it, especially today.

"I'm sorry," he said, his voice and face sad now. "I didn't mean to pry about that, didn't know this was the place."

Glancing back at the barn, she nodded. Tears prickled behind her eyelids, but she blinked them back.

"I recall you have twin sons."

"I do, and this place and this barn is their heritage—fixed up someday, but never sold and torn down, not while I'm alive."

Mitch nodded. "I know you gave my card back," he said, "but please keep it. There's something on the back I use in advertising, but I really mean it. Thanks for putting up with me just crashing in like this, but I was—intrigued."

Mitch felt in his shirt pocket and dug the card out again. He pressed it into her hands and got into his truck. With a single wave, he pulled away. So much for her quiet time in the barn. Now she needed to pin up her hair and get her shoes and bonnet and close the house and barn doors before she ran across the pumpkin field to fetch the twins.

As she started for the barn, Rachel flipped the card over. It read, in real nice raised print on the underside, *"There is no Past we can bring back by the longing for it, there is only an eternally new Now that builds and creates itself out of the elements of the Past."*—Johann Goethe, 1749–1832.

Rachel bit her lower lip. Goethe sounded German. He'd died six years before her barn was built. But he spoke to her head and heart, just as that *auslander* named Mitch Randall had.

"Jennie!" Rachel called at the side door. "Sorry I'm late!"

"We're playing Indians in here!" her friend called out, her voice cheery as always. At least, Rachel thought, four boys under the age of five hadn't done her in yet. Besides the twins, Jennie baby-sat for her own grandsons Jeff, age four, and Mike, age two, her son Kent's kids. Kent managed the lumberyard in town which the Amish often frequented. His wife, Marci, the county sheriff's daughter, was what they called a stylist at the town beauty shop, The Hairport, where no Amish person ever set foot.

Rachel had to laugh when she saw Jennie's latest clever creation. In the room called the den, a card table covered with blankets had become a tepee, and a "fire" of kindling sat in the middle of the carpeted floor. Pieces of apple were stuck through with sticks which were supposedly roasting over the nonexistent flames, turning brown in the air as if they were cooking.

"Glad to see an a-d-u-l-t," Jennie said. Her girlish giggle lilted amid war whoops. The boys' chanting continued and little Mike kept beating a spoon on an empty box that must be a drum.

"Have they been good?" Rachel asked, stooping to kiss her two red-haired warriors, who sported paper headbands with real chicken feathers sticking out of them. They had some sort of war paint on their faces that could be anything from Jennie's lipstick to food coloring.

"Good as gold and all of them chattering in Indian talk I taught them. You know, *wampum* and *canoe*. I even showed them some of Kent's old arrowhead collection. You're not the only one who's turned those up plowing around here—Shawnee ones, sure as shooting."

"You're a great teacher because you always educate them as well as amuse them. I don't know what I'd do without you."

"You'd have more cakes and pies to eat on your own and you'd fill out more, that's what you'd do without me," Jennie insisted with a smile, patting both of her own full hips.

While Rachel watched in amazement, her friend darted over to flip the box Mike had pounded nearly flat on one side, then came back. She was lively and quick, especially for a fifty-two-year-old grandmother, but she said the kids kept her young. In her spare time, Jennie Morgan did many kinds of crafts, evidenced by the crewel and needlepoint pictures on her walls and the hooked rugs on the floor. Jennie was perpetual motion.

Yet she was as plump as an Amish matron and, more than once, had admitted to Rachel that she did what she called bingeing. But in Rachel's eyes, Jennie Morgan was a blessing. Not only did she care for the kids in exchange for the canned, baked and garden goods Rachel gave her, but she, too, was a woman alone—though her ex-husband lived just on the other side of town with his second wife.

"Come on, Indians," Rachel said, "you two red-haired ones, at least, we've got to go home before it gets dark."

"We're not scared of dark!" Aaron declared in English and stuck his head not under the tent flap this time but under the floor-length skirt of a chair Jennie had upholstered.

One big problem of having the boys cared for here, besides the disapproval of Bishop Eben Yoder and some other Amish, was that the boys were speaking just as often in English as they did in Amish *Deutsche*. Rachel herself had taught English and other subjects to school-age scholars before she married, but preschool age Amish kids only spoke German—except for Andy and Aaron Mast.

"Wait till I tell you about my two visitors today," Rachel told Jennie.

Despite the giggling going on as Jennie tried to pry Aaron out from under the chair, she turned her head up to Rachel and mouthed, "Eben?"

Rachel nodded and rolled her eyes. As far as she knew, Jennie was the only one who would sympathize with her not wanting to wed him. "And a man who wanted to either repair or buy the barn," she added.

"You're kidding," her friend cried.

"I'm not, but I don't think he'll be back."

"Let's talk about all that tomorrow. Come on out,

Rain Cloud,'' Jennie told Aaron while Rachel got Andy up to leave.

When Jennie hauled Aaron out by his legs, he was holding a picture in a gold frame. Her boys hardly ever saw photos as the Amish avoided such graven images, and Jennie had none here, either. The twins bent over it. Rachel could see it was a young girl dressed like the English did for church, smiling. Her face was wreathed by clouds of curly hair. Jennie snatched the photo and, without a word, put it flat on the top of the hutch where no one could reach or see it.

Silence crashed into the room. Rachel realized she'd finally glimpsed the face of her friend's long-lost daughter, Laura.

Kent Morgan drove into his mother's driveway to pick up his sons just as Rachel was leaving with hers. "Wait a sec, and I'll drop you off!" he called to her. "That pumpkin field's getting to be a vine-tangled mess. Don't want Clearview's best farmer to break her leg walking through it to get home."

She nodded and waved her thanks. Kent Morgan was a little older than Rachel and quite handsome, slim and tall with brown hair and hazel eyes. Like his mother, he always seemed busy and purposeful, but he resembled his father, whom Rachel had seen in town several times. Kent was patient with customers at the lumberyard and knew a little about a lot of things. And Rachel appreciated that, like his mother, he was great with her kids, though he rough-housed them—his word—a bit more than she liked.

Everyone in town knew and liked Kent. At Clearview Consolidated Junior-Senior High School, he'd been a basketball star. She'd heard his pictures were still up in the front hall of the school for going to the state competition. But now, for the first time, she wondered why Jennie didn't have Kent's photos around her house. The absence of pictures of Laura, she guessed she could understand. Maybe it was because pictures of Kent's achievements and of his kids would also remind Jennie of the life's blessings Laura had lost.

Kent came back out quickly. Rachel knew that, even with the four boys along, she probably shouldn't be accepting a ride from a worldly married man, but she was exhausted. She was sure going to sleep well tonight. Perhaps today's doings had taken more of a toll than she'd realized.

Rachel watched Kent strap his boys into the narrow back seat of the truck cab, Mike in his plastic, padded kid chair. In the front seat, she put Andy between her and Kent while Aaron sat on her lap.

"Mom's kinda quiet," Kent observed, looking in the rearview mirror to back away from the brick ranch, the only modern-looking house on this stretch of Ravine Road. "She feel okay?"

Rachel wondered why he hadn't asked her himself, but he was probably just in a hurry. His wife, Marci, worked late hours, the kids were hungry, and who knew what troubles people had.

"She feels fine," Rachel told him. "She's just a little upset because one of the kids pulled out a picture of your sister that was under a chair."

"One of my kids?" he asked sharply.

It wasn't what she thought he'd say, but at least he was always concerned about his mother. She should be so lucky with these two tornadoes when she was a *grossmamm* someday.

"No, sorry," she admitted. "One of mine."

"No problem. She just can't hack it—even the good memories."

"I'd never seen her picture before. Having pictures around would be one way to remember her, wouldn't it?"

Kent sped up and squealed the brakes so the truck spit gravel when he turned into her driveway. The three four-year-olds all squealed in unison.

"Oh, she's got pics of Laura, tons of mementos, believe me," he said, gripping the wheel, ignoring the noise. His left leg was bouncing hard and fast to some invisible beat. Rachel noted as she had before that his fingernails were ragged and bitten down. "She just doesn't want to share them with anybody and that's that," he added. He reached over to open the door for her when she fumbled with the lock and handle.

Rachel wasn't sure if *that's that* meant the end of the ride, the discussion or that topic for good. Someday, she vowed as she watched the boys jump down from the big step of the truck cab, she was going to ask someone what really happened to Laura Morgan ten years ago. She needed to know, and the Morgans weren't going to relive that nightmare for her. And she understood that, she surely did.

Rachel hustled the twins into the house before she looked back out the window and saw she'd left the barn door open. She thought she'd closed it, but she'd been in a rush to pick up the boys.

"Let's go out and close up the barn together."

They trooped back outside. Rachel couldn't help it, but she started thinking again, *A whole year ago.*

Both boys walked solemnly, silently for once. She was now sure she had closed and latched the big doors.

At the threshold, Rachel hesitated, peering in, thinking perhaps the Lapps had returned the Percherons, though they weren't due back for a few more days. Their stalls were empty. The buggy horses stamped nervously. Surely, Mitch Randall had not come back and looked around on his own.

Rachel recalled she had left her bonnet hanging here and had taken another one from the house in her haste, so maybe she hadn't closed the doors. Bett and Nann were just agitated because they knew it should have been closed, that was all.

Rachel turned to retrieve her bonnet from the row of pegs. It hung there, undisturbed, but another hat— an Amish rye straw man's hat—now hung next to it.

She gasped. Although Amish men's hats were much alike, Sam had always had the habit of sticking several nails in the band, in case he had repairs when he was away from his tools. Two nails protruded, one piercing the brim.

Rachel grabbed her bonnet down and smashed it between her fist and belly as her mind raced. She had saved some of Sam's clothes for the boys and given some to other Amish, but she would stake her life on the fact she'd taken all the nails out of his hats.

"I told you, Aaron," she heard Andy whisper behind her. "*Daadi*'s back."

Three

"Now I've told both of you more than once to-night that *Daadi*'s not coming back," Rachel told the twins as she tucked them in bed.

They had chattered endlessly about Sam's being in the barn, asking questions about the hat for which she had no answers. Now she sat on Aaron's bed and took a deep breath. "We all want *Daadi* to come back," she tried to explain, "but he can't. Life and death just do not work that way. It's not that he wouldn't want to be with us and—"

"—take care of the farm," Andy put in.

"Yes, but when someone dies, if they go to heaven, like *Daadi* did, they are very happy there and know that God will take care of his family and they will see him again someday."

"When?" Aaron asked, his eyes wide, his red hair splayed against the pillow like a burst of sunset.

"When we all get to heaven, too."

"When is that?" he persisted.

She wanted to tell him to stop the questions, but he so seldom asked them. Aaron's quietness compared to Andy's control was the way most people learned to tell them apart. Only lately had it become obvious that Andy was right-handed and Aaron a lefty. The fact that the hair whorls on the back of their heads grew in opposite directions was too fine a contrast for outsiders. To Rachel, they weren't so much identical twins as they were flip sides of the same coin. Andy was the heads of it, dominant and distinctly etched, while Aaron was more muted, smoothed-over and sensitive.

"Remember, *Mamm* told you," she went gamely on, "that most people don't die till they're old, so I don't want you to worry that something like what happened to *Daadi* will happen to you."

"I don't walk under that big hay hook, ever," Andy said, folding his arms over his chest on the outside of the covers, though it was chilly in the room tonight.

Rachel bit her lower lip. No way she was getting into a discussion about her deepest doubts and fears. Sam had obviously been in the midst of unhitching the Percherons when he'd suddenly sent Andy to the house, then walked under the grappling hook, which was halfway across the barn, hanging over the threshing floor. The sheriff's report had said high wind, weakened roof beams and the weight of the hook not properly secured on a rusted track had caused the tragedy, but it was the Amish who had insisted the case be closed.

Rachel kissed both boys' foreheads, then lifted the lantern from the table between their beds. She could not bear to picture Sam the way she'd found him or to doubt the wisdom of Eben and her Amish brethren when they'd wanted no part of a worldly investigation of a freak accident that was God's will. And she was not going to cry in front of the twins.

"The Lord keep and bless both of you this night." Rachel said her version of her mother's nightly fare-well. She left their door open so more warm air from the natural-gas stove in the living room downstairs would find its way in. Amish homes, even refur-bished ones, had no central heating. Then she re-membered that the floor opening in the boy's bed-room through which hot air could rise might be blocked by their shoes and clothes. Sometimes, not realizing it made the room cold at night, after she left, they dumped things there so they would be warm in the morning.

Rachel set the lamp at the top of the steps and tiptoed back. Two small forms were framed by the window as they looked out at the barn.

It was nearly nine when Rachel finally got the twins asleep, but by then she was even more unset-tled. She agonized about whether she'd closed the barn doors today, about how that hat could have ap-peared. And she began to rehearse in her mind what she would say to Eben tomorrow at the estate sale, something that would not insult or alienate him, but that would make him realize she would not marry him. He should go ahead and find a wife from back in Maplecreek since his choices among their own kind were limited here.

When Rachel's thoughts turned to Mitch, what he had said, the way he'd looked around the barn—looked at her, too—she got up, wrapped her flannel robe over her long nightgown and felt her way down-stairs in the dark.

No way, Rachel told herself as she lit a kerosene lamp by feel on the kitchen counter, was she going to waste time in bed if she couldn't sleep. She had plenty to do and wouldn't worry that she'd wake the twins if she did some laundry. They slept the sleep of the dead.

She shook her head at the way she'd put that. She understood more fully now why Jennie—Kent, too— did not want to talk or think about losing Laura. At least the sheriff, she'd heard, had done a lot of looking for the missing girl, even if they couldn't solve her disappearance. Worldly people no doubt demanded investigations and didn't squelch them.

"But we must accept," she repeated to herself. "Accept and go on."

When Eben first became bishop here, just after his wife had deserted their family, months before Sam died, he had preached a whole sermon on that topic. "Accept God's will," she whispered what she recalled of that message. "The fall of a sparrow is God's will, even if we don't understand our own falls or want to accept them."

Rachel sighed as she carried the lamp into the large, shelved pantry where she kept her washer in the middle of the linoleum floor. Part of her dowry, it was white enamel, barrel-shaped and sat on legs with the wringer perched above it like two rolling pins pressed together. One of the first things Sam did when he started to Amishize this house was to hook it up to a gas motor here instead of in the basement so she could keep an eye on her youngsters and do laundry at the same time.

Rachel unscrewed the cap to the motor and checked the gas level. Good, half-full. The washer's vibrating motor and the soft purr of the lamp would calm her nerves. Still, before she started, she went into the kitchen and heated some milk to settle her stomach.

All Amish kitchens in Clearview and back in Maplecreek were basically the same. They had modern appliances but only powered by gas or diesel, no electrical cords, wires or cables to link them to the world. The walls were plain white but the curtains at the windows were traditional cobalt blue. Bright green paper napkins, turned down over the edges of shelves, geraniums on the window ledge rescued from an early frost, a dark blue oilcloth over the big table and a farm calendar on the wall with outdoor scenes provided splashes of color. A framed, quilted piece her sister Susan had sent was embroidered with the words Work Makes Life Sweet. Rachel sighed again.

As soon as she drank her warm milk, she filled two big kettles with water to heat on the stove for the load of wash. Meanwhile, she sorted clothes—black or white were the major choices with just one of her blue day dresses. While she waited for the water to heat, to keep busy—and to keep from peering out through the curtains at the barn as she was itching to do—Rachel straightened the pantry shelves. She felt more secure to see the rainbow array of jars of peaches, pears, green beans, beets, grape and tomato juice she'd put up for the cold months to come.

Rachel toted the two big kettles of boiling water to the washer and poured them in atop the soap. Steam rose like mist. She added the white load and turned the switch. The motor began to vibrate, and the clothes swished, lulling her. Leaning her hips and thighs against the machine, she began to daydream about Mitch Randall again, to feel all tingly and needy.

She jumped back as if she'd been burned. Thinking about him was not good. The mere, brief memory of him was making butterflies in her belly and her face moist, though that was probably just the escaping steam, she reasoned.

While she waited for the washing cycle to finish, she straightened her bags and jars of herbs and spices on another pantry shelf. Merely moving them released delicious, mingled aromas of spearmint, sage, basil, garlic, even fresh-ground coffee. Such sweet, stimulating smells! She hadn't noticed things like that for so long.

After turning on the switch to start the wringer, Rachel lifted items singly from the still-hot water with an old broom handle, carefully feeding them through the automatic rollers, guiding them as they plopped into a tub of rinse water on the floor. She'd leave them there until tomorrow, run them through the wringer again, then hang them out to dry. It must be getting late, she thought, so maybe she could sleep now. She had to try, or she'd be even more jumpy and spent tomorrow.

Debating whether to dump the soapy water outside tonight or wait, she whipped opened the pantry curtain and glanced out.

The barn loomed large and black in the cold moonlight, throwing a hulking shadow toward the house. And then she was sure she heard a sound. A creak? A thud?

Hair prickled on the back of her neck. She left the

lamp in the pantry and padded in her wool slippers into the dark kitchen to peer out the back-door window. Nothing. But she had heard a thud, followed by hollow footsteps somewhere, and not from the boys upstairs.

Rachel darted around the house, peeking out unlighted windows into the darker night, realizing why English homes had outside lights. As she hurried toward the windows overlooking the porch and the road, a sharp rap rattled the front door. An ebony shadow moved from it to the window, peering in, both hands lifted to the face. The figure wore trousers and a loose, black frock coat, like Amish men. Hatless, but with hair collar-length, just like Sam...

Transfixed in a nightmare, Rachel could have screamed. She wanted to flee but her feet were lead. The figure knocked on the glass, gesturing her to the door. The face...

It was Jennie in her new navy blue pantsuit. She must have parked down the driveway, Rachel realized. That thud had been her car door, the footsteps her treading the wooden porch.

Rachel fumbled with the doorknob and lock. "I saw your light and knew it was late for you," Jennie said when they stood with just the screen door between them.

Her heart still pounding, Rachel stared out at her, then managed to say, "It's only that no one comes in the front door. You gave me a start."

"Sorry, but are you okay? I know you turn in early, and when I saw a dim light back here when I drove by, I was hoping the kids weren't sick. Or you," she added, her keen eyes searching Rachel's face. "I know today must have upset you."

"Sure, I'm fine," Rachel said, realizing Jennie didn't know the half of it. She stepped aside, relocked the door and led her friend through the dark house to the kitchen. She quickly fetched the lantern from the pantry and set it on the table. "Want some coffee or hot chocolate?" she offered.

"No thanks. I stopped with some others at the Country Kitchen after choir practice, so I'm fine. I repeat, are *you?*"

"Just couldn't sleep." Rachel debated whether to tell her Sam's hat had reappeared, but she didn't want her friend to think she had a bug in her bean.

"Actually," Jennie admitted, sitting at the table, "I've been dying for you to tell me about Eben's visit and your mystery man."

"He's not *my* man," Rachel protested, realizing too late her voice sounded strident. "Neither of them is, and I want to keep it that way." She put out a plate of sugar cookies, which Jennie seemed willing enough to help herself to. Rachel took one, too.

"You know, however much it looks to folks around here like you're fated to be mated to Eben Yoder, I'm on your side," Jennie assured her, covering Rachel's wrist with her hand.

"You're the only one. It might be tough on me when word gets around the church I won't marry him."

"Not—what's it called—shunning?"

"No, not for that, but you know how much our little community needs each other and how they've all helped me. It's cooperation, not good old American competition, that keeps my people going. Still, sometimes I'm sure I could almost farm without help if it wasn't frowned on for a woman to do heavy work—man's work. And if I'd get my work team back full-time.''

"In other words, sexual discrimination is alive and well in Amish country," Jennie groused.

"No, it's not worldly like that," Rachel denied vehemently. "Everyone works well in their roles as part of the whole. But no matter what, I don't want to leave this farm. It's for my boys, it was Sam's dream, and I'm sure I could keep it going if they'd let me—and if I still had you to tend the boys until they are in school half days next year. Then, eventually, the two of them can take on more chores."

"I'd miss you and the boys terribly," Jennie said, "but I can see why you might want to move to a bigger house like Eben's, maybe get a new start."

Rachel tugged her wrist free. "I thought you'd understand. I've already made the last new start of my life, and it was to leave my past and move here." She gripped her cookie so hard it exploded to crumbs, which she hastily swept up with her hand from the dark blue oilcloth.

"Okay, okay," Jennie soothed. "But then here comes this meddling barn guy. I think I've read about him in the paper. He rips barns down—rips people off, no doubt," she added, frowning. "I don't want to lose my best friend as my neighbor, or her twins I love almost as much as my own grandkids. At least you'd never sell him your barn, especially not after Sam..."

"Of course I wouldn't sell, but Mitch Randall offered me a pretty penny."

Jennie sat up straight against her ladder-back chair. "He actually quoted you a price already? A big one?"

"Twenty-five thousand dollars. And suggested some repairs, roof beams, floor patch, things here and there."

"Which he'd probably deduct from the price he quoted. You know," Jennie said, sounding madder by the minute, "I know a way to protect the barn from him and others. There are unscrupulous people who just look for old barns and tear out their timbers to resell, right under people's noses sometimes."

"I didn't say Mitch Randall was unscrupulous," Rachel protested, amazed her voice sounded angry now, too. "Just a little pushy and real interesting— and interested, I mean."

"Slick, more like it. I was thinking," Jennie plunged on, "you could look into getting the barn preserved and protected another way, a way that would keep outsiders out, once the deed was done."

"The deed was done?" Rachel echoed, leaning closer across the corner of the table. "It sounds like evil doings. What are you talking about?"

"I know a guy named Lincoln McGowan—Linc, they call him—who goes to my church. Actually," she said, also shifting forward in her chair, "he's a professor at a college in southern Ohio but he's on sabbatical. He used to teach history at the high school here. His mother's in the Clearview Care Nursing Home, so he brings her to church on Sundays, and he's started singing in the choir. He has a gorgeous baritone voice."

Rachel listened intently, nodding, not sure where this was going.

"But the thing is," Jennie rushed on, talking faster in her excitement, "Linc's done things with the State of Ohio Historic Preservation Department, and I could see if your barn would qualify. Once it gets designated as such, no one could tamper with it. They preserve things as they are—except, of course, for minor repairs you'd do to continue to work it.''

"It wouldn't bring a lot of visitors, would it?" Rachel asked. "One reason we left eastern Ohio was to avoid the onslaught of tourists. Sometimes it was like we were animals in a zoo, not that some of the brethren weren't taking advantage of tourist dollars.''

Jennie shook her head. "Besides Linc, you'd probably have a committee visit, but you'd be registered—protected—after that. None of us needs gawking tourists around here. The preservation people are not commercial like that Mitch Randall and don't take over.''

"It's a worldly thing to do, so I'd have to get permission," Rachel explained. "At least the Amish believe in preservation and live and let live. The preservation committee would have to understand that Amish barns are more factories than museums," she said, before she realized she was quoting Mitch.

Rachel heaved a huge sigh that seemed to deflate her, but just having Jennie here bucked her up, too. One of the things she had missed most about losing Sam was having him to consult and plan with, even though they'd sometimes argued about the boys.

"I can't give you an answer now, but I thank you for being a friend," Rachel said, blinking back threatening tears. Suddenly, exhaustion wrapped around her like a cold, wet sheet.

"Only a worldly friend," Jennie said with a dour look and a little shrug.

"A *good* friend. And that's the only kind that counts when times are tough.''

* * *

The Saturday-morning auction was awkward. Eben kept acting as if they were a family already, ordering the boys around and sticking like a burr on her skirts, while among the rest of the Amish, men and women went their own ways. The men stood in line for bidding numbers or huddled near the old farm machinery while the women clustered around household goods spread on the side and front lawns. Eben sent his son-in-law-to-be, Jacob Esh, to get his number and escorted her around. Rachel felt on display like some purchase Eben planned to make and had staked out.

More than one of the plain people had given Rachel a knowing wink or nod, and David Christina Zook had whispered some sort of tease about needing a double batch of celery. Rachel hadn't yet had time to explain to twenty-two-year-old Sarah, who was so excited over her formal betrothal, that she cared deeply for her and would help plan the wedding, but had no intention of becoming her stepmother. It was impossible to get time alone with anyone, not with Eben hovering.

The situation wasn't helped when both boys darted out of Eben's grasp to hug Jennie and Kent and chatter in English to their little friends Jeff and Mike.

"Linc McGowan's here, and I want you to meet him," Jennie called to her.

"Maybe another time," Rachel said, shaking her head. Jennie nodded quickly, evidently realizing her timing had been bad, then bent to talk to the twins and sent them running back to Rachel.

Eben looked like an Old Testament prophet preparing to pronounce doomsday. She was pretty sure things could not get worse. Then she saw Mitch Randall not far off. He was on the other side of a fence, near some propped-up doors and a carved banister, and she realized he'd been watching her.

Mitch turned back to the old, solid wood doors so he wouldn't seem to be staring at Rachel Mast, but he knew she'd seen him. He'd watched her arrive with a lot of kids and a stocky, sandy-haired man in a big buggy, so he wondered if she was engaged or even remarried. Or maybe that was her brother. No matter. No damn business of his.

He both hated and loved country auctions. They reminded him all too well of the ruination of another farm, but he needed to rescue what he could here. For starters, these doors could be stripped, sanded and refinished. But he glared at their fine, carved oak and saw another door, one his grandfather had slammed in a man's face nearly twenty-five of Mitch's thirty-three years ago.

"What did he say this time?" Mitch's grandmother had asked. She'd been just around the corner in the dining room with both hands tight on young Mitch's shoulders so he wouldn't bolt out to be with his grandpa.

"Called me a no-account old coot and cussed me out. He had a paper, an eviction notice about eminent domain," the old man had muttered. "He said if the state or country want this place, we got no rights and he'll get me arrested. I still wouldn't sign."

"What does that mean—eminent domain?" Mitch had asked, but his insides were already churning. His grandparents must have kept this terrible thing from him, must have thought he wouldn't be able to help.

They'd been whispering for weeks, and he thought he'd done something wrong. Now he pictured the cruel face of that man, their enemy, but it turned into his own father's face as he walked away and left him here.

"It means the government can come and make a son-of-a-bitchin', fancy new road cut through a man's land and his life," Grandpa had thundered. Mitch felt his grandma's hands clench tight when Grandpa swore, or was it that she was real shook, too?

"Russ, where you going?" she'd cried and run right behind him into the room that held mostly Grandpa's stuff. "What are you going to do with that?"

"Going to get justice the only way a man can, curse their papers and lawyers, just like he cursed me. I'm not just doing this for us, Ellen, not even just for Mitch. It's for other farmers the big-city boys think they can stomp down like those goose-stepping, jackbooted Nazis I fought once with a gun, too."

"No, you're not taking that rifle into town!"

A door slammed, followed by the sound of sobbing. When his grandpa came out with the long gun, he glanced at Mitch, and Mitch saw he'd been crying. He could hear more sobs from Grandma, too.

"Even when there's nothing a man can do, he's gotta do something, and don't you ever forget it, boy," he said. He banged out and slammed the back door and took the truck to town.

From that dreadful day on, especially through his grandfather's trial and his grandmother's final illness, Mitch had felt the burden of loss and the fear of losing more—losing everything—on his shoulders, on his back. First his mother in that car wreck, then his father deserting him, and then this…

He slammed his fist into the door and jumped when it banged into the next door. That brought him back to reality. He forced himself to look around at other people, at the here and now. The living nightmare that drove him segued to a sunny day with a growing crowd ready to devour another family's treasures.

He shook his head to clear it. After all, he tried to tell himself, the Amish, some local Mennonites, and people they called English mingled at the estate sale of just another local farmer who had not made it. The Blakes, who'd owned this place, had gone out more quietly than his grandparents had. A paralyzing stroke had sentenced this farmer to a convalescent center until he died, and the daughter was taking the unwilling widow to live with her near Chicago.

Yet Mitch felt torn in two, just as he had for years. He understood and accepted, even made his livelihood on these sorts of changes, but ripping down and tearing apart the past still galled him. Though most surviving farms were getting bigger, they used what Mitch called chemical-dependent farming: the farms and their produce were on drugs. One of many reasons he admired the Amish was that they used only natural lime and manure to boost soil output, and they got a greater yield than the so-called modern farms, anyway.

Mitch's feelings for the Amish in general was one reason he wanted to help that young widow, if she still was a widow, he tried to tell himself. It was really nothing personal. He walked toward the crowd clustered around the auctioneer, who was standing on the front porch of the farmhouse with a microphone set up. He passed piles of the past, the litter of a lifetime the heirs did not want. Sadly, eventually, they'd probably sell the site for a trailer park or a Kmart. The buildings would rot or be torn down piecemeal when the Amish would have quickly bought the place and made the fields fertile instead of fallow. Yes, he greatly admired the Amish—and that young widow for trying to keep her farm for her boys.

The auctioneer began his staccato patter in that distinctive rhythm like a stick dragging on the spokes of a turning wheel. Small domestic things went first—dishes, crocks, jars, linens. Mitch saw the man Rachel was with bid for glass canning jars and get them. Like the auctioneer, the Amish man had a ringing voice.

Next, they offered an old treadle sewing machine an Amish woman snapped up. Then furniture, mostly junk, a few antiques. Mitch bid on the banister and got it for a barn house renovation he was doing up in Wood County.

Mitch felt a surge of excitement from the Amish as some rusty, old farm machinery, not the more modern equipment on display out back, went up for bids. The press of people moved him closer to Rachel, who was standing with the man and a young Amish couple. The couple made no bones about holding hands, when Mitch knew the married Amish never showed affection in public, so they must be courting. He didn't know whether to be relieved or upset that Rachel and the other man were not touching.

The black-garbed Amish quickly bought a grain

drill, a corn planter and a spring-tooth harrow. They did not bid among themselves for long once several bidders were established, and he wondered if they shared the equipment. Mitch shifted so that he stood closer to Rachel's group, just one person away. They were speaking German to each other, so he had no idea what they were saying.

He realized the three wood doors had come up for bids. "Fifty bucks for the lot," he began the bidding, holding up the small wooden paddle with his bidding number on it.

"An a fifty for bee-oo-tiful old doors from number 27," the auctioneer worked into his never-ending spiel. "Do I hear a-fifty-five?"

To Mitch's surprise the man with Rachel called out, "Fifty-five."

The bidding between the two of them quickly climbed to seventy-five. Mitch almost began to lose track because Rachel, evidently recognizing his voice, or at least wanting to know who was bidding against her friend, had been shooting him quick, sideways glances. She had to turn her whole head because of her bonnet brim. She looked intense and unsettled about something. He wondered if those doors were for that old house she lived in.

They were certainly worth over a hundred bucks, and competition always got his blood up, but something made Mitch let them go. The Amish man got them for eighty-five and left Rachel to make his way toward the man at the money table. It was only when the people between them shifted away, too, that Mitch realized, by each hand, Rachel held to a red-haired boy, dressed identically. They were mirror images, probably not quite five years old, just the age

he'd been when his dad had left him with his grandparents and never came back.

Rachel turned her shoulders toward him this time,
though her lower body faced forward. Crowd noise
and the resumption of the auctioneer's rhythmic
rattle went on around him. Mitch stared into her clear
green eyes, then at her full mouth as she spoke, in
English now.

"They were for a new house. His daughter's getting wed this winter." She dipped her bonnet toward
the younger woman who was following the man.
"Nice you didn't run up the price on his pocketbook."

Mitch felt tremendously relieved. She didn't sound
married to the guy. "Sure," he said. "They're good
solid doors. You're welcome. About the pictures of
your barn. Can I come out—"

"Sam Rachel!" the stentorian voice interrupted
them. "Bring the boys, and we'll get the doors together."

"If you can't get them in the buggy and want them
delivered..." Mitch began, still addressing her. The
man evidently overheard them. As if defying him to
say more, he glared at Mitch, before he gave a civil
nod. Mitch nodded jerkily back.

"Oh, no. We'll manage," Rachel said as she
tugged the boys away. "We—I—don't need any outside help."

Mitch stared after her as she set sail into the bobbing sea of black bonnets and broad-brimmed hats.
He'd heard her hands-off message to him loud and
clear, but she was one of the most fascinating women
he had ever met—and he did want to see that barn
more up close and personal.

Four

Not Eben come calling again already, Rachel thought with dismay as she stood in the midst of the frost-blighted garden on Monday morning and squinted down the road. Yes, a courting buggy was heading her way, pulled by a Yoder horse.

"Who is it, *Mamm?*" Aaron asked.

She shaded her eyes in the bright, windy day, annoyed that she wasn't sure who was driving. She supposed she needed to wear her glasses full-time, not just when she read, but she hated them sliding down her nose, and she was always misplacing them. If it was Eben, he would ruin the entire week as he had last weekend. After church yesterday at the Lapps' place, he had preached her a private sermon about not mixing with the English and the world, yet he had stuck like glue again as if to tell everyone she was his when she most certainly was not.

"It's Sarah," Andy put in. "Keep pulling up those dead plants, *doplic*," he ordered Aaron.

"Don't you call your brother clumsy," Rachel scolded, still looking at the approaching buggy.

"We should have a sister," Andy muttered, "'cause little gardens is girl's work."

"*Are* girl's work," she corrected him. "And who said so?" She was relieved that she could now tell the visitor was indeed Sarah.

"Bishop Eben," the boy said defiantly, as if evoking that title and name settled things. How much he was like his father sometimes, she thought. Things were the way they were just because that's the way they were. And a man's word was law next only to the Lord's. And even at his age, the boy realized how much weight a church elder, especially a bishop, exerted on all their lives in this struggling community.

"Can you two at least keep pulling those up while I talk to Sarah?" she asked.

Andy just kept yanking them while Aaron nodded, wide-eyed, wanting to please.

She washed her hands in the washhouse next to the outhouse, then ran to meet the buggy as Sarah turned in. "What a nice surprise," Rachel called up to her.

Eben's oldest daughter was short, slightly plump, and very blond. She was a sturdy worker with a stoic personality, who had dutifully postponed her own family to care for her younger siblings. Her brother Dan was just two years younger and really on his own when Eben Mary had her breakdown and ran away, leaving her other kids in Sarah's care. But the same girl who had seemed so happy at the auction and church looked out-and-out somber today.

"Is everything all right?" Rachel asked, alarmed when Sarah did not even climb down. Rachel quit wiping her hands on her soiled apron and clutched a handful of it.

"I've got some things to buy in town, that's all. Got to meet Jacob there. This is his buggy." Once a betrothal was formally published in church, it was the custom for the future groom to move in with the bride's family to help prepare for the wedding. Rachel waited for her to say more, but Sarah kept chewing her lower lip.

"And..." Rachel prompted.

"And the bishop said to stop and tell you something."

Rachel's stomach clenched, and she pressed the wad of apron against it. A decree not from Eben the man but from the bishop. Sarah only called him that when she was angry with him. Rachel felt bad Sarah was being put in the middle of this.

Finally, Sarah blurted out, "He took the Percherons from Lapps' to our place, Rach. To rest and feed them up good, he said."

"But he told me your brothers would be here midmorning with them to harrow, then plant my field for spring rye," Rachel protested quietly, trying to keep her voice calm. "Are Dan and Ben all right?"

Sarah nodded. Something was going on here Rachel could not grasp. "He said," Sarah repeated as if by rote, "just trust him, rely on his decisions, and everything will get done right. Listen, I better get into town now."

"Sure, but you let me know when you're ready to start planning the wedding, all right? And can you come the day before the barn *danze* this weekend? Now it looks like the perfect way to end your *rumspringa*."

Rumspringa was the so-called running-around time Amish youth enjoyed in their teens. They could date, stay out late, and many even went further. They tasted forbidden things like movies, radios, smoking, drinking. These days, some even got into drugs. The plain people wanted to be certain when a member asked for baptism that he or she meant it and knew what fancy, worldly things they were "giving up," because to go back on those vows meant shunning.

But this momentous commitment also meant the church was eager to offer kids an occasional activity that was attractive to them and nearly unchaperoned. Just before Sam died, the Masts had suggested their barn for a sing fest and dance, though it had been put off a whole year. Recently, they had invited others from Amish churches within a day's trot, which, unfortunately, didn't include kids from home, though some might come in a hired car.

Rachel saw a smile light Sarah's blue eyes, though it did not quite soften her pursed lips. "Rach, you sure you're still up for it? In there?" Sarah added and glanced at the barn.

Rachel nodded determinedly. "Sam said we should do it to help our *junge leit* meet others for courting. I'm looking forward to it, especially seeing some of the Maplecreek kids again if they can get someone to drive them over. Even your father said it was okay."

At the mention of her father, Sarah's face clouded again. "Got to get going," she repeated and lifted the reins from her lap.

"Sarah," Rachel called after her, "did your father say *when* he'd send the boys with the horses? Only, today and tomorrow are supposed to be clear weather and then rain's coming."

But her voice was ripped away by the breeze or

drowned in the hoofbeats and crunch of steel wheels on the gravel as Sarah turned the buggy away.

Rachel stood forlornly, watching her friend head toward town. She looked out over the clod-filled field that needed to be harrowed and planted before she did final cleaning and preparation of all that barn-dance food. The barn had been empty of her and Sam's beloved Percherons too long.

Rachel spun back toward the boys, who were still pulling the corpses of tomato plants from the stakes in the garden. "Wash up now. We're off for Jennie's," she called to them.

"You said we'd be here today," Andy protested. "This now, then watch Dan and Sim work the team."

"I know what I said, but things can change. *Mamm*'s got to go get the Percherons back and harrow that field herself today."

"Can we go, too?" Aaron cried, jumping up and down.

"Only to Jennie's," Andy answered for her, "'cause when *Mamm*'s made up her mind, that's that."

Rachel had Bett and Nann harnessed and the boys dropped off at Jennie's in a half hour, then headed for the Yoders' dairy farm. She set out at the good clip that two horses allowed. Most Amish used one buggy horse at a time, but Sam had bought these two stallmates for the price of one and had always hitched both to keep them in shape. He'd had to explain to Bishop Yoder once why that was practical and not prideful. Besides, Rachel thought, she'd need two-horse power instead of one, leading her big Percherons home.

Eben was also leading her, she thought, testing her to see if she would submit to his will. Whether that entailed planting a field or planning her future, she was going to do what *she* thought best, though of course she'd listen to her Amish community's advice first.

By the time Rachel pulled into the Yoder farm's long driveway, she had steeled herself to face down Eben, but it was twenty-year-old Dan and sixteen-year-old Benjamin who came out of the farmhouse to greet her. So, she realized, it wasn't that they were extra busy or had some emergency that they hadn't come to do her field as had been promised. The necessity of 5:00 a.m. and 5:00 p.m. milkings of the herd of thirty-seven black-and-white Holsteins ran the Yoders' lives, but Eben had said the boys would have time between milkings. Now he'd gone back on his word, probably because he felt she had overstepped with Jennie and Mitch at the auction, not to mention she had not gone all blushing and delighted at his marriage proposal.

The Yoder farm was the largest and most impressive piece of Amish land in the Clearview area. It sat on a slight rise in a part of the state that was so flat compared to Maplecreek. Besides spacious grazing meadows, the Yoders had four large fields to till. Numerous outbuildings sat behind the L-shaped farmhouse with its clean white siding. Eben had the biggest family, so it was right he had the biggest, newest house and barn in their scattered Amish community. Besides, he was the wealthiest of them by far and didn't owe his own relatives or any other family for his land.

"I've come for my work team," Rachel told the boys flat out when she reined in. "I can rest them and feed them up at home. And they've got work to do. Besides, I've missed them."

They exchanged quick, alarmed looks. "Father's out in the back field with Joseph and Eli," Dan told her, naming his youngest brothers, aged ten and eight. "A calf broke its leg in a woodchuck hole, but I'll go fetch Father double quick."

"No need," Rachel said, wrapping her reins and climbing down. She watched where she stepped to avoid cow flops. "I can handle the team."

"Biggest and best around, leastwise west of Maplecreek," Ben said as he hurried after her. Dan had already sprinted through the wire gate, obviously heading for Eben.

Rachel did not break stride, passing the long, white building with the stanchions where the cows were still milked by hand. She hurried past the milk house with its cooling tanks. The smells of fermented corn silage and animals assailed her as she went in the stable door with Ben on her heels.

"There you are, my big boys," Rachel called to the Percherons, as the tall, blond trio picked up their heads and their ears. Chester and Gid were geldings and Cream a mare, but Sam had always called them "my boys." They were part of his heritage when he left home. His older brother, whom Sam had helped to farm, had split his team of six to give Sam and Rachel a team for their new farm. Now they shifted in their stalls and Chester, the lead horse, whinnied and tossed his head.

"You have to wait for *Daadi*," Ben said. "If you really want to, he can help you take them back."

Rachel wondered for a moment if that had been Eben's plan. To make her come to him, plead for his help, ask him to change his mind to give the horses back when they were already hers. And ask for help to harrow and plow. But she would do none of those things.

"*Gut, sehr gut,*" she told the draft horses as she pulled their gear down from hooks on the wall and began to harness them. Their collars were always so heavy. She lifted the first one off the post with a grunt.

"Here, I'll help," Ben said, jumping off the side of the stall. He probably figured his father would return to stop her and would be angry if she'd hurt herself or the team. Or else, perhaps he'd heard she would become his stepmother and he wanted to stay on her good side.

Rachel accepted his help to lift the collar over Cream's head. She had to smile because, when it was his turn, Chester bowed his head slightly to help her. He knew he was going home.

They had the team's cruppers and breast straps on, their bridles and reins set before she led them out. Their gear was clean but not freshly oiled the way Sam had always kept things. Snorting, the team followed her willingly, three big beasts behaving like babies. Cream kept playfully nuzzling Rachel's shoulder, nearly knocking her off balance. Ben darted ahead of her, keeping out of the way of the big buckets of twelve plodding feet.

Eben stood just outside the door of the stables, arms stiff at his sides, his hands balled to fists.

"Have you lost your mind, woman?"

She pulled the team to a halt. "Not yet. And I am grateful for how well you've taken care of my horses, but there's no reason to depend on your kind hospitality for them longer. I hear Dan and Ben are busy right now, and you, too, so I won't take more of your time."

"You can't take those horses back when you've got to drive the buggy," he insisted.

"They'll behave like lambs for me, so don't give it another thought. Giddap, boys, come on, *sehr gut,* Chester." The team snorted and stepped out again, clustered around her like protective tanks rolling into battle.

Bishop Eben Yoder had no choice but to get out of her way.

Blessedly, Eben did not get a buggy and follow Rachel down the road. Her own buggy and the five horses made a strange parade, and she tried to stay as far over on the berm of the road as she could. Route 197, which locals called Old Pike Road, would be the busiest part of her journey. She'd have to go into Clearview, then turn left at the town's only traffic light to get on Route 14, or Ravine Road, where she lived. It was a narrow two-lane road, but it had fewer cars.

Rachel prayed she hadn't overstepped, not only about standing up to Eben, but to try taking the team home on her own. The Percherons were used to putting their shoulders to the traces and pulling, not being led by the likes of two sleek horses with the buggy in between. She had Chester harnessed first, but the team obviously wanted to trot abreast, not strung out.

Every time a car passed, Rachel had to stand in the buggy to look back and call to the team to keep them settled down. Buggies always rocked and tilted in the best of times, but this was really bad, trying to stay far over with the team wanting to go their own speed. She hoped folks heeded her orange slow-moving vehicle sign and gave the Percherons a wide berth. Buggy horses were trained to keep calm in traffic, but draft horses were used to open fields and verbal commands.

A car tooted its horn before it passed her. The buggy horses didn't bob or budge, but the team snorted, and, as Rachel glanced back, Cream shied and tugged.

"Giddap, Cream," she called and blew the huge horse a loud kiss. Tossing her head, Cream edged back in line.

Rachel began to wish she'd asked Dan or Ben to come along, but maybe Eben would have forbidden it. And when she saw the Percherons now ran abreast, so close they almost nosed into the buggy, she realized she'd have to let them do it their way.

Hopefully, folks on the road would put up with this, but not everyone thought the Amish new to this area were quaint and charming. Bad feelings simmered about their not paying taxes or serving in the armed forces, about their pulling electricity out of their homes, and leaving horse apples on the roads. Like this bunch was doing right now.

Hoping she'd see someone in Clearview she could ask to drive her buggy back while she walked the team home, Rachel was disappointed. She knew most of the Amish families had been to town on Saturday, and this was only Monday. She didn't see one buggy and didn't want to stop with the heavy traffic. But she breathed a big sigh when she got the horses turned left at the light onto Ravine Road, even if it was another good two miles to her place.

Soon Bett and Nann picked up their ears and headed for the barn, so Rachel had to hold them back. But the work team scented home, too, and began to trot faster, their huge hoofs clomping on the asphalt behind her like distant thunder. Rachel had just grabbed the side of the buggy and turned to glance back again when a vehicle behind them blared its horn. Cream began to rear, settled down, then shook her collar and harness so hard the buggy jerked. Chester edged way out into the road.

"Chester, gee!" Rachel shouted. She bounced hard into her seat and inadvertently pulled back on the buggy reins. Bett and Nann halted while Gid hit his shoulder into the back of the buggy and actually peered in the berm side at her. The car behind her honked again and pulled abreast.

It was the kind of open car called a Jeep, with blotches on it in pale green and beige to make it hard to see in foliage. Two laughing men in gray-green uniforms of some sort sat in it. Their faces looked dirty with beard stubble. Her stomach cartwheeled at the leer the one in the passenger seat gave her.

"Hey, Amish honey, going to the races?" he shouted. "Where's your man? Listen, do us a big favor and take your bonnet off."

Not the type to reason with, Rachel thought. She had to get going. But they moved ahead and slanted the Jeep just enough to cut her off from passing them. A small ditch loomed on the other side of the road, not deep, but too dangerous to try. Surely someone else would be along soon, some *Englischer* who didn't act as if they should live in trees.

Another glance down into their Jeep scared her even more. They had two rifles on the back seat, big and bold as you please. It was deer-hunting season, but Rachel didn't like guns. A memory from childhood jumped at her: poachers had been on their woodlot and her father had taken all of them to cut wood right in front of the intruders to force them away. The hunters had taken shots just above their heads, spattering them with bark and sticks before they'd shouted curses and left.

"Let me pass," her voice rang out. "Other cars will be coming."

"I thought they called you folks plain. She look plain to you, buddy? She's a real looker, but I got to have that bonnet off to tell for sure."

"Or more than the bonnet," the driver said, and both snickered.

"Tell you what, honey. Take that bonnet off so's we can get a good look, and we'll be on our way."

"Less you'd like to have a beer with us. Those big studs you're pulling look like the Budweiser team, so you got the time, we got the beer."

"That's the Miller ad, you jerk," the passenger said and took a playful swing at him.

Rachel was tempted to get out of the buggy and pull all five horses and the buggy around on the other lane, but the men would probably just move to block her in again. Or worse, get out of that vehicle. *Oh, dear Lord, protect your own,* she prayed when the driver stood in the Jeep, leaned over the roll bar and looked back at her as if he might climb out.

"Cat got your tongue?" he goaded. "We too low to even talk to?"

Rachel saw a truck barreling down on them from the direction she was going. It was bright red and honking like mad. When she realized it was Mitch Randall, he had already hit the brakes, gotten out and was yelling at her harassers. She wanted to warn Mitch they had rifles, but he could probably see that and she didn't want to give anyone ideas. Besides, the driver was yelling back obscenities, but he was revving up his engine.

"She you're girlfriend, MR 409?" he shouted at Mitch. It took Rachel a moment to realize he was calling Mitch by his license number. "I'll fight you for her fair and square, MR. We'll be back..."

The Jeep roared away. Rachel would have liked to watch them turn tail, but the Percherons were snorting and pulling and the buggy was going to tip. She leaped down and ran to the team.

At the squeal of tires, the team had jerked. Rachel jumped free as the buggy went two side wheels into the ditch and tilted, pulling Bett and Nann backward to the edge. Rachel darted to grab Chester's bridle, backing him up so the rest of the buggy would not pitch in. It trembled and clung to the fringe of the berm.

She turned to see Mitch. He had moved his truck into the same lane as hers and had his warning lights blinking.

"You all right?" he asked as he took huge strides toward her. Rachel nodded. "I got their license, too, at least. Idiots from that paramilitary bunch that has weekend retreats across the county line, I'll bet. Bumper sticker said Guns, God and Glory. Now, what in heck do you think you're doing out here alone like this?'' he demanded, whipping off his sunglasses and jamming them into his black jeans-jacket pocket, where he thrust his hands, too.

''Trying to get my farm team home, and doing fine until they came along,'' Rachel said, but her voice broke. She kept unwinding traces and reins the Percherons had somehow scrambled.

''I suppose you should file a report against them,'' Mitch said, sounding reluctant.

Rachel turned to face him as the horses finally simmered down to mere snorts and shuffling. ''I can't and won't do that, Mr. Randall. It isn't our way,'' she explained when he looked surprised. ''The Lord—and you—took care of things.''

''You can't just let them off like that,'' Mitch protested. ''I'm not one to run to the police, believe me, but who knows what would have happened.''

''As I said, it's not our way. But, again, I thank you.''

Mitch expelled a rush of air, sounding more exasperated than the horses. ''I was at your place and saw you weren't there,'' he told her. ''I thought maybe I could take the photos, then look around more thoroughly and give you a detailed assessment of needed repairs in the barn, just for your future use, if you decide on them.''

''That would be fine, but not today. I've got to pull the buggy back up and get home. This afternoon and tomorrow morning I've got a lot to do,'' she added with a nod that bounced her bonnet.

"Okay, I see," he said as he reached up to pat Chester's flank.

Though Mitch wore his hair cut short, the stiffening breeze ruffled it. "I'll bet," he was saying, "the buggy can be righted with just one tug from these petite ponies."

Rachel laughed despite herself, then sobered as his eyes met hers and held. This time he looked away before she did. She watched his large, sun-browned hands tighten and tie the teams' reins better to the back of the buggy. Suddenly, all she could think of to say was, "The Percherons make all things look small."

"Except potential problems like those bast—idiots. I really think you should file a complaint. Don't worry about having to go to court or anything like that," he assured her. "The sheriff can just put them on notice to keep that from happening again."

"On the other hand," she said, frowning, "if I did file a complaint, who's to say they wouldn't try to get back at me for that? Best to forgive and forget."

"Do you believe that?" His voice rose, and he clamped one hand on her elbow before he evidently realized he shouldn't touch her and stepped back. A tingle shot up her arm as if she'd hit her funny bone there.

Rachel wanted to say yes, she believed it, but she knew it would be a lie. At least a lie about just accepting and forgetting Sam's strange death.

"It's what my people believe," she repeated. "But I won't forget your help today."

In two minutes the draft horses had the buggy upright on the road, and the parade headed for the farm again, this time with Mitch's truck bringing up the

rear. When they safely turned in the lane, he waved
and went on his way. Rachel was gratefully looking
forward to rubbing down, watering and feeding all
five horses before the afternoon's work. But what she
found in the barn made her wish she'd asked Mitch
to stay.

Jennie Morgan blessed the moment of peace and
quiet. Her four little charges had been so wound up
today she'd made them "camp out" before she fed
them lunch. So they'd stretched out on old blankets
she'd called their sleeping bags on the den floor and
had actually gone to sleep—all but Andy, who was
just playing possum, but at least he was quiet.

She went out into the kitchen to make macaroni
and cheese, then decided to take a little break for
herself. Just a few minutes with Laura.

Jennie tiptoed down the hall to the farthest door.
This 1970s-era brick ranch had once been her dream
home, hers and Mike's, but now it entombed a nightmare. Yet this room that was her private shrine comforted her. It was like coming to a grave to pray and
remember because Laura didn't have one she could
leave flowers.

She unlocked the door, went in and quickly, quietly closed it behind her. Only then did she click on
the light. It always smelled a bit musty in here at
first, like muted memories, but she didn't even open
the drapes or the blinds, anymore. Jennie wanted
everyone else shut out. She wanted this place just the
way it was before everything went so bad.

Jennie had read once that Queen Victoria of En-
gland had kept her dead husband's personal effects
laid out in his room, preserved just the way it was

when he died, tragically at a young age: slippers, hairbrush, his last newspaper. The queen had blamed her son for Prince Albert's fatal pneumonia, since he'd gone to visit their wastrel boy, and she'd never forgiven him. People had whispered she was eccentric, even crazy. But Jennie understood.

She leaned against the bed with its cluster of stuffed animals. Laura's childhood Barbie doll collection lined the top bookshelf. The chest of drawers and dressing table still bore her cosmetics, which Jennie feather-dusted almost daily. Laura's desk displayed her school pens and last pile of homework, her biology text on top. Jennie's eyes lifted to the mirror with a photo of Bruce Springsteen stuck in it next to the cheerleader pom-poms, even sales slips for their shopping trip for her sixteenth birthday to Southwick Mall in Toledo. The dress from that receipt was the one Laura had worn that last night.

Jennie sank to her knees on the faded pink carpet, her hands clutching the bedspread, her face thrust in the flowered pattern. For a moment she just listened to the wind, rattling a shutter outside. She began to sob silently, breathlessly, but then froze when she heard the doorknob turn. If only the door would bang open and Laura would bound in, full of fun and life.

Jennie stared transfixed as the knob turned and the door swung inward and Andy Mast's red head peered around before she shouted at him to get out.

Five

꘎

Leaving the hitched buggy outside the barn, Rachel
led the Percherons in. And stopped to stare.

Someone had filled all five horse troughs with
fresh water and had forked hay into the feed bins.
Fresh hay was also strewn on the floor, which had
been swept clean for several weeks in their absence.

"Is anyone here?" she called out in German, then
English. Still holding the reins, she glanced around
the lower bays, then upward into the lofts and spaces,
even craning her neck to squint far up into the cupola. Nothing but sun spilling through swirls of floating hay dust. So the filling of the bins had just been
done.

Mitch had said he'd stopped by, looking for her,
but he wouldn't know to do this. Surely, none of the
Yoders could have gotten here before she did, even
if they did have second thoughts about helping her
get home. Though the trouble on the road had de-
layed her, Eben or his sons would have had to pass
her to get here in this amount of time. Simeon Lapp?
Maybe he had stopped by to tell her Eben had the
horses or to explain the change in plans. But then

why wouldn't he fill only the buggy horses' troughs and feed bins?

Jennie, that was it! Rachel had told Jennie she was bringing the horses home, so she'd brought all four children over on one of her little field trips to give them something useful to do and to give Rachel a nice surprise when she got back.

The only thing that scared Rachel, then, was *how* it was done. The water was poured to the exact level and the hay humped up in the center precisely the way Sam used to do it. And the fresh hay forked on the floor for them in case they wanted to lie down— only Sam had done that.

Rachel spun around to stare at the straw hat she had not been able to make herself so much as touch. It hung there still, but on a different peg now, down at the other end of the row. Perhaps whoever had been here had seen it, moved it, or maybe it had blown off and been rehung. Chinks in the barn siding let air in when a stiff breeze was blowing.

Rachel quickly tied the horses outside their stalls where they couldn't reach hay and water yet. If they drank too soon after a workout, they'd get colic or the gripes. Besides, she had to know something now, fast, even before she rubbed them down. She snatched Sam's hat and took it outside into the windy, sunny day.

Still holding the hat, Rachel unlocked the back door of the house and went into the kitchen to get her glasses, then came back out into the brightness. Bett and Nann shifted nervously, apparently wondering why she didn't unhitch them now that they were home.

Rachel put her glasses on, leaned against the outside wall of the barn and closely examined the hat. It certainly seemed to be Sam's size. Sweat marks inside the rough woven straw attested to the fact it was well used, as Sam's always were before he'd get another one, at least for field work. The two nails stuck in the band were still there. But the one that had pierced the brim was now properly pulled up into the band.

Surely, this was just a hat Sam had left in the barn somewhere and it had blown out of its hiding place. Or someone here to help in that first blur of weeks after his death had found it, taken it home accidentally, then finally remembered to return it.

Rachel flipped it upside down and looked along the inside of the band. Yes, broad, sturdy stitches definitely done on a treadle machine, the kind the Amish used. And—she held her breath—one auburn shaft of hair was held there, glinting in the sun, shivering in the breeze. Surely Sam's.

Rachel closed her eyes and cradled the hat to her breasts. *I always tried to love you with my whole heart, Sam,* she thought. *And now I'm trying to love our Amish brethren, obey the elders, but I have to know what really happened to you. I can't accept you died from a freak accident, and I can't accept Eben as my husband.*

Bett whinnied and Rachel stared down at the hat again. Determined to ask some questions about it, the hay and water, she darted back into the barn to rehang the hat on the first peg. She closed the barn doors and climbed back into the buggy. Before she fed the team and began to work the field, she wanted to see that her twins were okay, to ask Jennie to bring them over to watch her work.

And she did not want to be alone here, not right now, not even out in the middle of a sunny yard or open field.

Despite her worries—Jennie had said she knew nothing about filling the troughs and bins for the horses—Rachel joyously worked her west field that afternoon, running behind the team while Jennie and the four boys kept her company.

The harrower had no seat but dragged its own weight on long, springy, steel teeth which dug deep to pulverize the earth. The horses were happy to be here and stepped sure and sprightly, their bucket-big feet helping to break up clods. Usually harrowing was done in April after spring rains, but this field needed it now to best benefit the rye seed she would plant tomorrow. Rachel could picture the green, supple stalks, swaying and bobbing nearly half a foot high next May, just like a field of winter wheat.

But it was autumn for sure now. The sun felt warm on her back, the breeze crisp on her face. Heading south, honking geese flew over in a perfect V, and bright red bittersweet edged the field. Today the train whistle made the roar of the double engines sound busy and not just lonely the way they did at night. It was so good to be alive, she thought.

As she made the turn at the corner of the field, Rachel noted the boys were standing on the blanket and pointing the distant train out to Jennie. Sam had walked them back to the tracks more than once to see it go by. Since his death, Rachel had forbidden them to go near a train, and not for Amish reasons that the huge machines were modern or linked them to the world. She'd known an Amish boy—her first, lost love—who had tried to hop a train only to be crushed beneath its wheels. God's will, just like Sam's death, she wondered, or caused by willful man's misdeeds and sins? Though she was working up a good sweat, a swift shudder racked her.

As she made the next turn, her shoulder and leg muscles began to ache, but it was a good ache. She could still make the payments on this place if it kept producing as it was. The profit she and Jennie would split from the pumpkins would help, too. Rachel was not afraid to work the farm herself but liked it. Sam was gone, and she owed money to Sam's brother Zebulon back in Maplecreek, but she had two fine boys to love and rear.

"They who sow in tears shall also reap in joy," she said aloud, and Chester picked up his ears.

It was then, at the next turn, facing the woodlot, Rachel had the oddest feeling. Not like a premonition, because she didn't believe in that, but a strange sensation that prickled the hair on the back of her perspiring neck and feathered down her backbone.

Her eyes darted around the fringe of the open field, even far back toward the train tracks. She did not break pace but glanced into the woodlot. The riot of colors on the turning trees distracted her at first, but then she saw a man's figure—dark clothes, no hat— jump back behind a tree. Someone had been watching her from her own woodlot.

To calm her panic, Rachel glanced back at Jennie and the boys. Aaron was waving excitedly, and Andy was throwing acorns at a fence post.

Rachel glanced at the woodlot again and almost tripped. All she needed was to fall flat in the soil and get herself dragged. Yet she looked again to see if the man was still there. The buckeye trees stood bare already, and she wondered if the black form she'd seen had been one of their dark trunks and not a man at all.

Rachel left the harrow out back and led the team toward the barn. While the twins and their friends ran ahead, Jennie brought up the rear, folding the blanket until Rachel slowed the team for her to catch up. She was as out of breath as the horses, anyway.

"When I was about half done," she said to Jennie, making sure the boys didn't hear, "did you see a man in the woodlot? You know me without my glasses," she added, trying not to sound overly alarmed.

Jennie frowned into the late-afternoon sun as she turned to face her. "In the woodlot? Don't you mean the guy on the road?"

More than one? Or the same man moving around for the best vantage point? she wondered. "Doing what?" she asked, her voice rising.

"Just watching, I guess. I didn't spot a car or buggy. I don't know," Jennie said, shrugging, "maybe seeing an Amish woman walking—actually running, you crazy girl—behind a team is pretty un- usual around here. Maybe he just wanted a picture or something."

Mitch, Rachel thought. "So he had a camera?"

"Not that I saw."

Rachel gritted her teeth. "I know it was from a distance, but can you describe him?"

"Mmm, black clothes, some kind of jacket or coat. Not sure about hair color because he wore a hat."

"Amish broad-brim, baseball cap, or what?"

"Rachel, I don't know! I couldn't pick out a style of brim from that distance, okay? What is all this?" Jennie demanded, hugging the folded blanket to her. "You're starting to sound like Perry Mason—oh, sorry, you don't even watch reruns. Listen, are you thinking those paramilitary guys might have followed you home?"

Rachel hadn't thought of that, though she probably would have, most likely in the middle of the night. "I'm overreacting," she said, pulling the horses faster again. "I just want things to be good now."

"God knows, you deserve it," Jennie said. "I didn't mean to sound angry."

Rachel gazed up at the big, hinged, drop-down haymow door, then peered into the dim barn before she led the horses in. Jennie paused just outside the door. The boys were already in the barn, petting poor, limping Mira who had appeared from the depths. Sam had once told the boys that the cats were barn police, on assignment to seek and destroy all vermin. A little smile crimped the corners of Rachel's stiff mouth. Good memories hovered here as well as the bad.

She dared to dart a look at the straw hat—same place, untouched. Yes, she'd been overreacting about being watched. Locals, not to mention visitors to the area, sometimes stopped to watch the Amish plant or reap. She might still ask around about who'd brought that hat back, but she had to calm down.

"It would be great," Jennie called to her, her eyes closed, her face turned up to the sun as she leaned against the barn door, "to have some happy times here. If you're still having the barn dance this Saturday, I'm willing to help."

"Offer accepted gladly and gratefully," Rachel told her as she began unhitching. "Besides our seven in their teen years from this church, I just got a letter that a vanload is coming from our relatives and friends in Maplecreek, and who knows how many from other Ohio communities. We can sure use the help at the dance."

"A dance?" Andy piped up. "Like a *danze?* Can we go?"

Rachel was going to tell him no, but the twins also needed good memories of this barn. "For a while," she told him. "If when I say it's time for bed, you go without an argument."

"I will!" Aaron declared and raised his hand as if he were answering a question in school.

Andy glanced over at Jennie. "I will, too. I won't go where I shouldn't be anymore."

Oh, dear, Rachel thought, he's been into Jennie's kitchen cupboards again. She'd have to talk to him about that.

That night Rachel slept like a rock, but suddenly awakened. She didn't know what time it was, surely several hours before dawn.

But what had waken her from such sound sleep? Five minutes later, though hearing nothing else, she still felt tightly wound. She kept no clock here and she'd put away Sam's pocket watch he'd kept under his pillow. She kept it now in the top dresser drawer, thinking she'd give it to whichever of the twins got married first.

She lay there, straining to listen. Night noises, nothing else. But she reached for the flashlight on the bedside table and got up, stuffing her feet by feel into her slippers and wrapping her robe around her long nightgown. She'd better look in on the boys, look out at the barn. All she needed was those doors opening and closing on their own again.

Rachel tiptoed down the hall and shined the light into her sons' room. Andy was asleep. Aaron was missing.

Her heart began to beat like a booming clock. Aaron sleepwalked, though he hadn't done it all summer. It had really gotten bad after his father died. He'd walk, wide-eyed, even down the stairs, never faltering, but then wake up and scream out his terrors. Rachel had been so sure he'd finally outgrown that, just the way the twins had outgrown the secret language they had used when they were younger.

She darted the flashlight in the other second-floor rooms, then hurried downstairs. He usually ended up in the kitchen. In the worst of times, she'd taken to removing the key from the back-door inside lock, fearful he'd actually go outside. Surely, he hadn't gone out to the barn.

He was not on the stairs, not in the kitchen, living or dining rooms. The back door was closed and locked from inside. Rachel wanted to stop to light a proper lamp, but she was starting to panic. She seldom called for him, not fearing that she'd wake Andy, but that she *would* wake Aaron and he'd begin to scream.

Now, his muted shriek sliced through her soul. With just the flashlight beam, Rachel followed the sound, thudding down the wooden steps to the basement into a darkness so black she almost went back up to light the lamp.

"Aaron," she called, "it's okay. *Mamm*'s here."

But she still didn't see him and only followed the sounds of now-muted whimpering.

Amid the piled hemp sacks of onions, turnips and potatoes, Rachel couldn't see him. He'd gone silent. She bumped her head into braided hanging garlic. A cobweb laced itself across her face, and she swiped the strands away. Her hair was wild, too, and caught on her flushed cheek.

"Aaron? *Mamm*'s here."

Her beam sliced across his huddled form. He was lying at the feet of the two old carved rocking horses Sam had made for the boys. They'd outgrown them but she hadn't wanted to part with them, so they'd ended up down here.

Aaron fought to open his eyes. At least it was *Mamm* here, not *Daadi*, 'cause he was scared of him now. *Mamm* sat on the cold concrete floor beside him. Balancing the flashlight on a lumpy sack of something, she pulled him into her lap and wrapped him tight in her arms.

"It's all right," she told him, rocking them. "It's all right now."

He wiped tears from his face, then cuddled closer. *Mamm* stayed that way a long time, humming to him. She said softly, "'When you lie down, you will not be afraid. Yes, you will lie down and your sleep will be sweet. Do not be afraid of sudden terror, nor of trouble from the wicked when it comes...'"

Her voice kind of broke and she stopped talking, but he didn't want her to. He liked how her voice hummed from her chest against his ear and filled the empty air. He'd better tell her now.

"He's back in the barn with the horses," he

choked out. "*Daadi* wants me to come out and help feed them, but it's dark out there."

When *Mamm* tried to talk, nothing came out but a squeak at first. "You just had a dream," she said, clearing her throat. "You saw *Mamm* plowing today, and you heard me ask Jennie if she fed the horses, and it just reminded you of *Daadi*, that's all. But that's a good memory and dream, Daadi in the barn with the horses."

Not wanting to upset her, he shook his head so hard against her, he bumped her chin. "He's mad at you, *Mamm*, 'cause you're doing his work. He's the boss here, not you."

She jolted but held him even tighter. "I—I know he told you that a long time ago, Aaron. But *Mamm* has to be the boss now that he's gone. And he's not just gone to the barn. I told you that, and I don't want to have to tell you ever again."

Rachel ached all over, probably not so much from huddling on the cold, hard basement floor cradling Aaron, but from working with the horses. After she got him back in bed, she heated two teakettles of water and carried them upstairs. Since Sam had died, at least in the winter she had used the tub but not the toilet in this modern bathroom he had not gotten around to tearing out.

Two kettles of water wasn't much, but Rachel mixed it with hot water from the tap—the pipes ground and groaned because she hadn't used them for months—and it felt warm enough. She'd ask Jennie to rub some peppermint liniment on her back muscles tomorrow if she still hurt after she drilled the holes and planted the rye seed.

Though the water only came up to her hipbones, she sank back in it and closed her eyes, lifting her heavy hair up and out of the way. Suddenly, this seemed so forbidden. She was seldom naked long, partly because she couldn't afford the time for a soaking bath and partly because it just wasn't the plain people's way to lie about like this. But this was medicinal, she told herself as she settled in deeper.

She sighed and drifted somewhere between consciousness and sleep where everything merged in the dark of jumbled thoughts. Right after Sam had died, she'd hated sleep, feared sleep, however much she needed it. Sleep was sometimes full of the demons of regret...

"If the twins talk to each other in their own speech, so what?" Sam had said, sinking onto the bed next to her so hard he almost bounced her onto the floor. "It won't last long."

"So what?" she'd protested. "They won't learn to talk to others then—to you and me—if they always have each other."

"It's just twin-baby talk, Rach. Do you have to question everything?" he'd demanded, pointing a finger in her face as if he were a teacher. "And I don't want to see any more worldly, psychology books about this like it's some mental disease, this cryp—crypt..." he stammered as he heaved her library book into the wastebasket next to their chest of drawers.

"Cryptophasia or cryptoglossia," Rachel put in. She'd dig that book out and return it when she could. "It just means a secret language."

"You and your book learning! Sure, when you were a teacher you had to read a lot and take those correspondence courses, but not all this far-fetched worldly stuff, uh-uh. You just take care of those boys, and they'll talk to you when they want or need to.''

"Sam," she said, grabbing his arm so he wouldn't get up and walk out, "it's wonderful that they have each other and that you are such a good father to them, but Andy's dominating Aaron. I suppose they will outgrow it, but it's stunting their growth now."

"Stunting? Sounds like some tree gone bad."

"Just hear me out," she implored him. "I want to separate them from time to time so they can't just whisper twin talk and act like master and slave and give us those looks when we try to tell them not to."

"Give *you* those looks, you mean," he said, tugging free of her touch. "Doesn't bother me. They know you're angry with them."

"I'm not angry with them. Just upset at the situation."

"Angry with me then, uh-huh, too full of answers about them, Rach, when they're just little boys. 'Seek and ye shall find,' sure, but not in worldly books about twin talk and whispering and looks. You better learn to listen to me more, even to Eben and the elders..."

The cooling water rustled when Rachel sat up and put her face in her hands. It scared her that she was still angry with Sam for how he'd refused to listen to her sometimes. But she had to let the dead rest, not keep letting him haunt her in more ways than she cared to count.

"You do realize, Mrs. Mast, that your barn is built in the English style and not the German," Mitch

Randall told Rachel the next afternoon. She caught the glint in his eye. He was teasing her.

"Then I guess there is *something* good the English did, compared to the *Deutsche,*" she countered, but she could not keep back a little smile.

They walked inside together. It was the safest she had felt in the barn for days. "Will it take you long to give me an idea on what will need to be done to keep up the building over the years?" she asked as he stopped in the middle of the threshing floor and looked around.

"About as long as it took me to get those great photos earlier," Mitch said as he pulled a ballpoint pen from a pocket and tapped it on his clipboard. He took off the cap of the pen with his mouth, reversed the pen to bare the point.

Rachel nodded. He'd spent a good hour with his camera in and around the barn while she had finished planting the rye this morning, then tended to the horses and washed up. She'd felt so exhausted when she had started, but the exercise had invigorated her, or else his presence had.

"This is one gorgeous, old barn," he said, craning his neck to look straight up into the cupola. "The fascinating thing about barns is that the inside—the skeleton, so to speak—is totally exposed to view, unlike with people. So, with a little know-how, it's not hard to diagnose the problems."

"It would be good if doctors could do that with humans," Rachel said, and he nodded. It excited her to think how well they understood each other, even if they were so different.

"Would you mind writing down things for me so

I have my hands free for some climbing?'' he asked, extending the board and pen to her.

''Okay,'' she said, but jumped back when their fingers touched. She covered her surprise by moving away and poising the pen over the paper.

Mitch climbed ladders and walked the haymows, calling down from the depths and heights comments about pegged joints and tie beams that needed work. He dictated the types of wood he found where: oak in the heavy framing timbers, hickory and maple in the pegs, maple and ash in the wood siding.

''Do you think the track the hay grappling hook hangs from looks strong?'' Rachel asked. ''Like maybe the roof leaks there a little?''

''I'd need to make a scaffold out of a couple of ladders to get a closer look,'' he said, ''but I can do that.''

''Oh, that's okay. Maybe another day. No problem. I don't want you to take a chance and fall.''

She watched him climb the little ladder to the interior of the cupola. ''Be careful up there!'' she yelled. ''I already know that needs some work!''

''You've got that right. And don't you be coming up here until you get it done.''

''It's tempting, though. The view is wonderful.''

Mitch leaned over to look straight down at her, propping his arms over his head. He had his feet spread for stability on the little boardwalk that circled a central open section. From the boards, you could look out through the broken louvers at fields and railroad tracks and beyond. Rachel could only imagine how striking the scene must be as this vibrant autumn began to don her colors, but he kept looking down, not out.

"It's wonderful all right," Mitch said, then straightened and peered out through the louvers. "Put down that the roof needs a little patchwork, since a new one would be prohibitive right now. It's sure at a steep slant, but that's probably made the snow slide off it all these years and saved it." His voice got louder again as he climbed partway back down. "It's amazing those old asphalt shingles have been blended so well with the original slate."

"Both are a little mossy in spots, slippery for workmen, I suppose. I don't know when that patch-work was done."

"Man, I love these old hand-hewn beams every-where," he said, standing at the edge of the haymow from which she'd first seen him. He had his hand on a big cross beam over his head, as if he could help hold up the barn. "You can still see the mark of the pioneer's adze. No one's used that tool for years and most wouldn't recognize it. Would you?" he asked, looking down at her.

"I have to admit I wouldn't. How do you think these floors are?" Rachel asked, suddenly nervous again when he jumped down to the threshing floor and clapped the dust off his hands.

"This center floor's good, but I'm sure these are two-inch-thick boards, and original floors like this wear like iron unless the roof starts to go." Mitch hunkered down to knock his knuckles against the boards here and there. "It's your bays where the an-imals and their wastes have been over the years that need a bit of work."

"We—I—keep the barn real clean."

"I've seen you do it, but we're talking over a hun-dred and fifty years of use. You ever wonder about those who had this barn before?'' he asked as they started to walk out. He stroked Bett's nose as they went by the horse stalls.

"Yes, but I only know about the elderly widow we bought it from."

"A widow, huh?" He took the clipboard and pen from her and skimmed what she'd written. "You surely have a neat hand, Mrs. Mast—your writing, I mean."

"I used to teach school—well, just two years."

He nodded and smiled as he looked up from the clipboard. The moment of silence stretched between them.

"Mrs. Mast, I'd like to make you a deal. No," he said quickly when she started to protest, "please hear me out, not for the barn again, not exactly."

Rachel clamped her hands together behind her back and kept silent.

"I'd like to offer to do some repair work here gratis, or rather, in fair exchange for your agreeing to let me use the photos I took today in my advertising and on my website."

"Oh, something commercial. I couldn't."

"I would completely protect your identity and location," he promised. "I would simply call it an antique Ohio barn, though most of my clients know I'm based in northwest Ohio. You and I could draw up a priority of the repairs. Cupola first, then the two support beams, later floors, would be done. Then I'd take photos of my work as I go and the finished product and use those to promote my business, too."

"I don't know," she floundered. "I might have the barn declared historic by the preservation people." She looked away and picked at some straw protruding from Nann's feed bin.

Mitch stepped closer, one hand on the stall rail close to her shoulder. "But that, or what I propose, doesn't negate that it would remain a working barn, and to work well it's going to need some help."

However much of a gift from heaven free repair work would be, Rachel knew she should tell Mitch no right away. Squelch this flat out before she had to ask permission for these unusual and worldly things from Eben and the other brethren. She'd even been dragging her feet about bringing up the historic preservation idea to them and had decided she'd wait until that Linc McGowan contacted her before mentioning it to Eben.

But when Rachel opened her mouth to say no, definitely no way, Mitch said, "You know, most people look at barn wood and say it's just old, or they might notice the graining or weathered patina." He walked over to a stretch of beam where the sunlight spilled in and touched the wood, his big hand splayed flat on it. His fingernails were cut short and very clean, his fingers long and flecked with dark hair.

"This may sound crazy," he said, his voice, which had boomed out to fill the barn, now low and almost raspy, "but sometimes I swear I can see patterns and pictures in wood like this—people or places, a map, maybe, clouds, or water like up on the lakes."

"The Great Lakes?" Rachel blurted, suddenly sounding inane to herself, but she was just trying to fill the vibrating air with words, something to keep between them. "I always wanted to see Lake Erie," she added before she could snatch the words back.

But Rachel had never heard anyone, certainly not a man, say something about imagining things in the wood. It scared her because that meant Mitch was, in his yearning, wayward heart, a lot like her. And an *Englische* man and Amish woman feeling the same things and having the same longings was not only ridiculous. It was absolutely forbidden.

Six

Mitch took his new field binoculars out of his locked toolbox in the back of his truck. Whistling that old song with the words *Take me home, country roads,* he had driven down a dirt road, now unused and overgrown, on the east side of Rachel's land closest to town.

He was in a soaring mood so why not try climbing that old apple tree to get as high as the birds? Rachel hadn't exactly said she'd let him work on the barn, or as he got ready to leave, that she'd go with him to see the barn home he was building, but he had hopes she'd visit with her friend.

Not only was her barn a rare one, but Rachel Mast was the most unique and intriguing woman he had ever met. She seemed fresh and unspoiled and yet, in her world, not naive. Unlike other women he'd known, Rachel was boldly herself with no pretense or artifice. He wished he could say the same for himself. He knew he'd not only built barn walls, but walls around himself so no one could ever hurt him again—maybe so no one would ever know him, either. But he'd really like to risk knowing Rachel Mast.

Mitch hooked the binoculars around his neck and climbed. This must have been a great orchard once, he thought, maybe part of Rachel's place, maybe of another farm. Now only a few rotting apples lay on the ground. He peered through the browning leaves to get his range and line of sight.

Steadying himself in a sturdy upper crotch to half sit, half lean in, Mitch lifted the glasses and adjusted the distance. Rachel's barn jumped into view, her yard, her porch. Perfect. He could see each separate shingle on the roof before he returned his sight back to her porch. He wished he could see into the woman herself. The Amish were so different, and yet he felt so drawn to her. He fiddled with the fine focus.

Mitch jolted when he saw her come out her back door, lock it, then put the key under a crock on the small porch. It was almost as if he was watching her on TV. She hurried around the house and disappeared toward the pumpkin field, probably walking over to get her twins from the neighbor as she'd mentioned.

As Mitch leaned forward, the limb under his left foot snapped. He grabbed at the trunk. Off balance, he swung, then dropped to the ground, hitting on all fours, then crumpling to his knees. His binoculars bumped against his forehead.

Damn, he thought, he could have broken a leg or his neck, and who would find him hidden back here but a stray hunter someday?

He brushed himself off, then started back to the truck before he realized he'd slightly sprained his wrist. Not bad, nothing to slow him down, he thought, gingerly flexing it. He'd work through the pain.

Mitch Randall had always worked through the pain.

Rachel felt so excited she almost skipped. Like a gift from God, she'd been offered free barn repairs. And she might get up the gumption to ask Mitch more about whether the track set in the peak of the barn could have let that hundred-pound grappling hook fall on Sam. But that would mean she had not accepted God's will as the brethren believed she must. A craving to know the truth, even forbidden truth, was eating at her insides.

Surely Eben, as bishop, and the two lay preachers from the church would allow Mitch to use her barn if he kept the location and owner anonymous. The Maplecreek Amish barns, houses and fields had been on calendars and even in published books. When Mitch had invited her to see his barn house, Rachel had told him, if she could bring Jennie along, she'd be there. After all, she ought to know if the man was any good before she let him get closer to her barn.

Rachel picked her way through the tangled pumpkin vines that stretched, clear to Jennie's yard, with the larger cornfield running parallel to it. Two early frosts had blasted the vine leaves to gray, limp shrouds draped over the twisted mass beneath. But the bulbous orange vegetables, all shapes and sizes, looked fine. Even in the cloudy, dimming day Rachel admired the bright-hued bounty of her and Jennie's bright crop. Soon they would set up a roadside stand with big pyramids of pumpkins on display. Pick

Your Own in the Field Or in Our Piles, the sign would say.

"Hope folks use them strictly for pies, but I know better," Eben had said after church last Sunday when the topic of crops finally turned to her huge pumpkin patch. "Bad enough to see all those fancy decorations worldly folk make with them, standing next to ghosts and witches on porches in town."

"We sure will use them for pies, bread, too," Ferd Ida Esh, soon to be Eben's in-law, had piped up. "What other folks do with them is not Sam Rachel's worry."

"I suppose," David Zook put in, "a lot of them will end up smashed on Amish front porches or thrown at the buggies like last year."

"'Least those weren't Sam Rachel's last year," Eben said. "I just can't abide they end up grinning demons faces for that ungodly Halloween."

"They call them jack-o'-lanterns," Rachel put in. "I try just to think of them as carved lamps, pretty in the night."

Eben had leaned over to take little Susie Zook's faceless Amish doll from her and hold it up. "No graven images even on our dolls and not on God's harvest bounty," he declared.

Rachel bit her tongue before she added that she thought carving a pumpkin might be a bit like making a pattern on a quilt.

"At least," Eben said, giving Susie's doll back and smiling stiffly at Rachel, "it will give you some money for keeping things going till you find a better way."

Now Rachel sighed and stopped dead in her tracks amid the pumpkin vines she'd been stepping over.

There was no way she could ever wed Eben. And she couldn't keep fighting through this mazelike field when she could just go walk through the alleys of corn shocks the brethren had put in for her last spring in the back field.

She walked a few yards to the corn and went several rows in to one that seemed slightly wider than the others. This field corn crop was nearly ready to harvest, tall, full of ears, its stalks and shocks gone dry and rustling. The shocks were thick, which meant a cold winter. And she'd seen a woolly worm the other day, more black than brown, which meant heavy snow coming. But she and the boys would be safe and warm. And if Mitch worked on the barn, all would be well there, too.

The field seemed to swallow her. Suddenly nervous, Rachel picked up her pace. Her bonnet bounced back off her head, but she just let it hang by its strings tied around her neck. How she had once loved to run through the corn back home. As kids, they'd played tag in the fields as soon as the green stalks got head-high. Trembling, ready for the reaper, this crop was a good half foot taller than her. Soon the shocks would be cut and hauled to the barn from which the ears would be sold or stored and the stalks chopped for fodder.

Rachel walked a straight path until the row bent to go around the contour of the woodlot. She walked even faster, then stopped, out of breath. She heard something behind her in the field, something more than wind. Someone else was walking through the corn, not far back, not quite in this row but close. A big body, maybe a deer. But usually, if a deer heard or scented her, it would not keep coming closer, not crashing through like that.

Rachel turned around, squinting down her row. She shoved through the stalks to look one row over. Hunters? She had heard the distant crack of rifles early this morning. If one had glimpsed her moving through the shocks and seen her black garb and white cap on her brown hair, he might think she was a deer. Maybe those two men who'd stopped her on the road yesterday had been hunting. They might have seen her, known it was her, alone out here today.

The rustling all around her rose like weird whispers. Or was it more a whacking sound? In the barn were several two-foot long, razor-sharp corn knives used to slice stalks down. Sam had used them the day before he'd died.

Rachel started to run, trying to angle her shoulders to get through, elbowing heavy ears out of the way. Shocks grabbed at her, ears bumped her shoulders and hips as if to pull her back. Panting, ignoring the stitch in her side, she plunged on. The day, already dim and windy, got darker, louder. Even over her gasps for breath, the sound of someone smashing through the shocks came closer. This row, the next? So near and yet she could not see a thing. She thought about screaming, in case it was a hunter who thought he'd flushed a deer, but her lungs were bursting. And she didn't want him—that unseen beast— to find her.

A wild thought leaped at Rachel. More than once, Sam had chased her through their families' adjoining fields when they were courting. He'd catch her and kiss her, but now the field was whispering, screaming at her...*Daadi's mad at you, Mamm, 'cause you're doing his work. He's mad at you, Mamm, mad...*

Gasping, Rachel burst out the other side of the field into Jennie's backyard. She had never been so glad to see her friend's house, though a strange car meant Jennie had company. She tore behind the garage, then peeked around the corner, waiting to see who else shot out from the corn, writhing in the rising wind.

But those were the only sounds now. No one running, thrashing through. No one exploded from the field as she had done. No one at all.

Rachel leaned against the back of the house, her hand lifted to cover her face. She *had* heard it. That was not her imagination. Yet it could be someone's prank, or just a deer, and she had fled as if Satan himself were chasing her.

Slowly, Rachel's breath quieted. She straightened her stiff white cap and replaced and tied her bonnet, then jolted at a scraping sound close by. Jennie had slid open the patio door and stepped out.

"What are you doing out here?" she called. "Are you all right? You look like you've seen a ghost."

Rachel wanted to tell her what had happened, but the twins came hurtling at her and she bent to hug them. "Just ran over to avoid the storm," she managed to say. "Got out of breath."

"It's coming. I'll run you home later," Jennie said, gesturing her inside.

"We'd better get going now then," Rachel protested. "Besides, I see you have company."

"The company," Jennie said, smiling, "is not just for me but for you, too. Come on in."

* * *

"Storm coming, Father," Sarah told Eben as she and her only sister, Annie, age fifteen, hauled in the last baskets of wind-dried clothes from the backyard line. They'd been nearly whipped to pieces out there.

Eben sat reading the weekly national Amish newspaper, *The Budget,* at the kitchen table and didn't look up. "Just hope and pray, girl," he said from behind the paper, "your big day in January's clear so folks from Maplecreek can get here, too."

Sarah let Annie go ahead to the workroom where the two of them would sort the clothes before they heated their irons on the stove. She put her basket down. "Father, I'll be needing to spend time with Sam Rachel this week to prepare for this Saturday's barn *danze.* I'm just hoping this rain gets through so they can get someone to drive them over from Maplecreek."

Eben looked up over the top of his paper, his brown eyebrows almost crushed together. "Get her and the boys over here to work things out for the dance then. You've got a lot of work to do on that wedding, too, so she can help you with that."

"Oh, I'm used to a lot of work," she said before she realized that sounded sassy. Quickly she added, "But it will be best if I go to her place."

Father crumpled his paper in his lap. Sarah steeled herself for a reprimand.

"I know it's been hardest on you she got so crazy and deserted us," he said. Sarah knew he wasn't speaking of Rachel now. Father never used her mother's name, and there was not one thing to be found in this house that was hers—except six children.

Sarah fiddled with her apron, fluffing it out in front. "I'm not complaining, Father."

"And if I've been hard on you, Lord forgive me, girl," he said, shaking a finger at her, "because the book says provoke not your children to wrath. But you just remember something else, too, in these days you and Jacob plan your future. 'An excellent wife is the crown of her husband, but she who causes shame is like a rottenness in his bones.' If I've been harsh, it's *her* fault, *her* doing."

"I—yes, Father." Sarah had almost defended her mother, but for what she was not sure. *Mamm* had acted so strange, then run off, and never written. Last month, Eben had her officially declared dead. The Church, not worldly government, had ruled on it, but then, he had refused to report her missing to the outside authorities in the first place.

Sarah bent to pick up the laundry basket. Sometimes she could almost grasp why her mother had run away, but she should never have left her brood. Only, as much as Sarah detested her for all that, she needed her so bad right now. Needed her not just to plan a wedding, but to tell her this secret and beg her to protect her, not from God's wrath, but that of her earthly father.

"Rachel, this is Linc McGowan I was telling you about," Jennie said, indicating an elegant-looking man who rose from the sofa in the den. He did not have a prematurely silver hair out of place, still had a summer tan, and his slacks, knit shirt and jacket in dove gray all matched his hair, even his silvery eyes. He was so perfectly groomed that he made Rachel, who had been taught it was prideful to worry about one's appearance, realize she must look like something the cat dragged in.

"I'm so glad to make your acquaintance," Linc said with a slight bow. He evidently knew better than to try to shake an Amish woman's hand, so that was good, Rachel thought. He seemed old-fashioned, and she liked that. Even his voice was soft and controlled the way Amish people were taught to talk.

Linc McGowan was not tall, but was lean and stood so straight he seemed tall. Without even looking, he smoothly put a pair of gold, wire-rimmed glasses in the case he had in his jacket pocket. The jacket was a felt kind of material, probably that expensive suede. His slacks were wrinkle-free but for the sharp single crease, and his shoes had a leather fringe.

It was only when Linc indicated she should sit that Rachel realized that Jennie had whisked the four boys out of the room to the kitchen. Rachel was grateful to her friend again. She had arranged this so Rachel would have an excuse to leave if she felt the need, yet she wouldn't be alone with Linc. And Jennie had penned in the kids so Rachel could really concentrate on what Linc had to say. If he had paperwork, though, she wished she'd brought her glasses.

"Jennie tells me you are considering having your barn registered as an historic site," Linc said. He tugged up each pant leg slightly before he sat, indicating she should sit, too. "I can only say, I think that is a terrific idea, and I'd be happy to guide you through the process, Mrs. Mast."

"I'm still undecided since I am planning on a few basic repairs," she explained. "That's what Jennie

thought I should be protected from—someone overstepping to change the barn too much. But I still
think registration might be a good idea so I'd appreciate your advice and information.'' She perched on
the far end of the couch from him but turned his way.
''I suppose you'd like to see it first.''

''Actually, I've been watching your barn for years.
Well, a slight exaggeration,'' he quickly amended
with a small shrug. ''I've driven past it for years and
was in it several times long before you owned it.''

''When the Bricker family was there.''

''Precisely. Your barn has a long, venerable history,'' he went on, obviously enjoying being the focus of her attention. ''And I've focused my life on
the study of Ohio history, and our barns are a big
part of that, like huge family albums, if you know
how to read them right. I'm on sabbatical now to
write, but I always tell my students that it was not
adventurers and explorers who tamed America, but
the farmer with his barn across the fruited plain.''

Rachel waited to see if he'd go on, but when he
looked her way for approval, she said, ''I'm sure you
are a good teacher and professor.''

''If dedication and passion make me one, I believe
so. After all,'' he went on, gesturing grandly, ''the
Egyptians have their pyramids, the Europeans their
castles and cathedrals, but America its barns.''

''And skyscrapers,'' Rachel put in.

That drew him up short, that an Amish woman
would maybe challenge his neat little lesson. But he
smiled to show even, white teeth. ''Precisely. Very
astute, Mrs. Mast, but I prefer to elevate our rural
Ohio past.''

''I'd like to hear what you have to say about the

barn, then discuss it with the leaders of my Church,"
she explained, trying to get him back on track. "So
if you can give me the pros and cons..."

He surprised her by leaning forward and whispering, "Actually, I would like to visit the barn so that
I can completely fill out the forms for my presenta-
tion. But I've got to tell you that one of my personal
pros for this is that I'm not only excited to be helping
you and that beautiful barn. I've been trying to get
Jennie Morgan out on a date for years, so I hope you
won't mind if I try to get her involved in this, too. I
was thrilled she asked me."

Now Rachel felt more comfortable with him.
Amish women were eternal matchmakers, and she
had worried that Jennie always seemed so alone.
Someone had said she was still in love with her former husband, but Rachel sensed it was something
else.

"Let me cook you and Jennie a nice dinner at
noon tomorrow, then we can all look at the barn,"
Rachel proposed, smiling back conspiratorially. "I'll
say it was my idea, because it was."

"Then I already owe you any help I can lend,"
Linc said, reaching over the arm of the couch for a
thin leather briefcase. "Now, let me just go over a
few things here, and you can ask Jennie about tomorrow."

The next day Rachel ended up also feeding Mitch,
when he stopped by to drop off a contract of agree-
ment for her to look over and possibly cosign with
him. It had been raining for hours and it was only
neighborly to invite him in. She saw him sniff the

scent of food and crane his neck at the buzz of guests in the kitchen.

"I'm glad you wrote it all out," Rachel told him at the door, "but I don't believe in signing agreements. My word—Amish word—is good."

"I believe that," he said, looking either embarrassed or annoyed. "I just wanted you to know up front what I proposed."

Their eyes met, and she nodded. "Then come in and sit down for dinner while you dry off. You can meet someone who is here to look around the barn you already know so well."

Rachel could tell Mitch was curious as he stepped inside the kitchen with her. "Mitch Randall, this is Mr. Lincoln McGowan," she began introductions. "And this is my friend who does my child care, Jennie Morgan. And these are Jennie's grandsons, Jeff and Mike, and my boys, Andy seated to the right of my chair and Aaron on my left."

"Two peas in a pod, that's for sure," Linc cut in as he stepped over to shake Mitch's hand. "Your name's familiar," he told Mitch. "I taught in the high school here for years and lectured at several local colleges. Currently, I'm on sabbatical from Ohio Southern University and with the State of Ohio Historic Preservation Department."

"Departments of government, local or national, is definitely not where we've met," Mitch said, his voice almost cold, "unless I was there bucking or suing them. I've read your articles in local papers. I especially recall one not far back where you said the sort of preservation work I do is defacement of the past and betrayal of the present." Crossing his arms over his chest, Mitch lifted his eyebrows in silent challenge. "And you used my name in the article, so perhaps that's why it rings a bell."

Uh-oh, Rachel thought.

"Ah, that's why it's familiar—precisely," Linc said, though he gave ground by going back to his seat. "Nothing personal. First Amendment rights, you know."

"Using names doesn't make it personal?" Mitch countered.

Rachel stepped between them. "Americans are good at a lot of things, including disagreeing," she said as she indicated that Mitch should take the last available chair at the kitchen table, unfortunately at the end of the table catty corner from Linc. "But they will still sit to break bread together—and not heads."

Rachel shot Jennie a rolled-eye look when the men continued to glare at each other as if they'd square off. Jennie annoyed her by mouthing with a nod at Mitch, *Gorgeous but dangerous!*

"At least we both care about preserving this barn," Mitch admitted with a nod toward the back door.

"Though we look at things completely differently," Linc insisted. "Disassembling an historic barn and moving it to a new site destroys its authenticity and character."

"Really?" Mitch countered, pulling his chair out from the table. "I guess we could have a very personal discussion on character. Putting a barn into the care of people who value it beats its being moved for a road or shopping center or just vandalized or left to rot or buried in academic or bureaucratic red tape."

"Well," Jennie put in, "what you two do have in common is a great Amish meal, if we can just eat it before it gets cold. It's not much of a lunch," she said with a little laugh as she swept her hand over the laden table. "Just bean soup, corned beef and stuffed cabbage rolls, homemade bread, hot German potato salad, applesauce and maple custard pie. Anyone wonder why I love hanging out with Rachel Mast?"

"'Cause she makes good food?" Andy piped up.

Blessedly, everyone laughed as Mitch sat and opened his napkin.

"That's *Daadi*'s chair," Aaron blurted.

Silence. Rachel felt her face flame, more than dishing up the steaming food or Mitch's arrival had done. She could have kicked herself for not seating anyone else there before today, even the twins, but the occasion had not come up.

"Yes," Rachel said. "It was *Daadi*'s chair but he would be happy to have Mr. Randall here visiting us today, along with Jennie and Mr. McGowan. All right, everyone please bow your heads for a prayer for peace in our world and at this table, then everyone help yourself."

"I apologize for my part in that little upheaval in there," Mitch told Rachel as she accompanied him to the back door after dinner. The rain had stopped, so he figured there was no reason for him not to go. He had already watched Linc McGowan take his briefcase and triplicate forms and go out to be big man in the barn. The four boys had been sent to play Frisbee in the side yard to get them out from underfoot for a while, and Jennie was starting to clear the table. It had turned out that she was Kent Morgan's mother, the guy who managed the lumberyard in town Mitch often used. Which meant Jennie was the mother of that teenager who was evidently abducted years ago.

"It's just," Mitch explained to Rachel, glad he had her alone for a moment, "that I'm doggedly dedicated to and defensive about what I do."

"I understand that, believe me," she said, her face so open. But it had occurred to Mitch that he was actually feeling jealous of the man in her barn. Rachel could decide to trust McGowan instead of him. But no, *that* line of thought would lead to considering *why* he was interested in her as well as the barn, and that would only lead to complications, big ones, considering she was Amish with twins. He needed to get personally involved with that sort of woman like he needed a hole in a barn roof.

"Your twins are great, and the meal was fabulous," he went on. "I haven't had a real home-cooked meal like that since my grandmother used to make them. I know you didn't fix it for me, but I was honored to be included."

"Someday I'll fix one for you," Rachel said, then bit her lower lip as if regretting being so forward. But his stomach went into free fall at what she'd said.

"And someday," he told her, "I'll take you to see Lake Erie."

She laughed. Her whole face lit, and the little lines of fatigue or worry around her fabulous green eyes softened. Wearing only her starched white cap and not that cavernous bonnet, she looked so natural and beautiful. Only someone with such balanced features could wear her hair parted in the middle and pulled straight back. The face that launched a thousand barn repairs he could not afford the time or money for, Mitch thought.

"Well," she said with a glance at the kids' game, then back to him, "I'd better go out and see what Mr. McGowan says about making things official. Then I'll have to ask my Church for permission—like for your repairs."

"Listen, Rach—Mrs. Mast," he said, propping one foot on a stone by the door where people obviously scraped their boots. "Just take what Linc McGowan says with a grain of salt, okay? He thinks he's got all the answers to everything."

"Mmm," she said, "then I'll have to read his newspaper articles. I could use the answers to a lot of things right now."

"If I can help, c—" He grinned and ran a hand through his hair. "I was going to say 'call me.' But I'll be back tomorrow. Right now, I'm going to talk to Jennie's son at the lumberyard in town about prices for replacement wood in the barn, just in case you give me the green light. You know, the go-ahead."

"You don't have to translate things for me. Linc said the Amish still speak the language of Luther, but I've got English down pat, too."

"Good," he said, staring into those eyes before his gaze wandered to her shapely mouth, "because that means we are starting to really talk the same language." He forced himself to walk toward his truck.

"About fixing barns at least!" she called after him.

Though he would have liked to turn back, he just grinned and kept walking.

Seven

——⚜⚜——

"Ah, there you are, Mrs. Mast," Linc McGowan said as Rachel joined him in the barn after Mitch drove off. "I must tell you I am certain the Historic Preservation Department will be greatly interested in this barn on several counts."

"And I am certain Jennie is very interested in you," Rachel said with a smile, recalling how Jennie had given a little thrilled shudder when she'd first mentioned Linc. "On several counts."

He chuckled, revealing even, white teeth. "You are a woman with good sense, not to mention your gift of hospitality. I'll just bet you don't stay a widow for long among your people. And then there is this great barn..."

"Someone will marry me for my barn, you mean?"

They shared a little laugh before he went back to taking copious notes. Rachel didn't know what was wrong with her. She felt almost giddy, like that time she was twelve and got into her grandmother's medicinal dandelion wine. Today, maybe it was the prospect of being able to repair this place without denting her meager pocketbook or the excitement of the coming barn dance. Or maybe it was that look Mitch had given her before he left.

Though the eaves still dripped rainwater, Rachel walked out the small back door with Linc and around where he could see the Mail Pouch painting better. Primitive art, Mitch had called it.

"This in itself is rare," Linc said, writing furiously, looking up at the barn, then back down at his notes. "Very few of these say 'Chewing Serves to Steady the Nerves.' Most say 'Treat Yourself to the Very Best.' Perhaps that will help me to date this painting. It's thrilling the barn itself is so clearly dated."

"Do you know who built the barn or owned it years ago?"

"I'll research that immediately," Linc assured her, still writing. "My current knowledge of it goes back only a little more than a decade."

He held the small, rear barn door open for her as she walked back inside with him. "It's dim in here today," she said. "I should have offered to light you a lantern."

"I'm fine. I've always had eyes that adjusted well to the dark."

"Like the cats in here," Rachel mused, nodding, "or the barn owls we used to have."

"I was just wondering if you've used that old pioneer root cellar I noted outside. It looks so overgrown with weeds, I imagine not."

"You're right. But," she said, walking into the bay where she kept Nann and Bett, "there is a trapdoor to it also, here by these stalls."

He came over, slightly hiked up each trouser leg

and squatted to look at the small door in the floor. "Do you mind," he asked, "if I glance inside? Perhaps a lantern would be of help."

Rachel fetched and lit one for him while he fumbled with the metal hook on the trapdoor and heaved to lift it. A smell of dusty dankness hit them, and they both sneezed. She held the light over the hole and, hands on the dirty floor, he glanced inside.

"Absolutely empty, as far as I can tell. Sometimes, you know, they are real treasure troves with old tools or crockery abandoned there. I knew one case where there was a real junk heap of the preserved past. Look out then, and I'll close it."

He banged the door shut with a puff of dust and straw. As she hung the lantern, Rachel realized it was three years since she and Sam had peered into the bowels of their barn and decided that cellar was useless for them.

"Forgive me for being so forward, Mrs. Mast," Linc said as he clapped dirt off his hands, "but I'd advise that you keep Mitch Randall just as shut off. If you need repairs here, get someone else, no matter what freebies he's promised you."

Rachel felt her hackles rise. "I could have guessed your opinion of him from your discussion with him inside." She wondered if Linc would apologize for his earlier behavior as Mitch had, but the man only nodded as he retrieved his notebook and went back to his writing. "I will, at least," she went on, "read your newspaper article on him."

"I'll be happy to provide you with a copy, but my warning goes deeper than opposing theories on American architectural preservation." He frowned intently, still not looking at her. "I don't consider it

gossip to tell you Randall's from a long line of trou-
blemakers, to put it nicely, and has, indeed, lived up
to his heritage.''

Her body stiffened. ''How's that, Mr. Mc-
Gowan?''

''I'd rather not say.''

''But your hints might be worse than the truth,''
Rachel protested. ''Just mentioning ominous things,
then not saying what you mean is hardly fair.''

''All right,'' he said, shuffling papers. ''His father
was a carouser and family deserter, and his grandfather literally shot up city hall over in the county
seat. Killed a man, wounded two others and ended
up in prison, where your handyman, Randall himself,
spent time, too.''

Rachel felt as if she'd been punched in the stomach. She wanted to know why Mitch had gone to
prison, but she'd ask him herself. And if it had anything to do with fraud or theft, especially of barns,
she'd show him the door.

''He's aggressive and belligerent to put it politely,
Mrs. Mast,'' Linc pursued when she didn't rise to his
bait, ''and not to be trusted on a professional level,
let alone a personal one.''

Gorgeous but dangerous, Jennie had mouthed to
her with a nod Mitch's way. If Jennie had known all
this about Mitch, why hadn't she said so? Still, her
friend had warned her about Mitch trying to cheat
her.

Rachel steadied the backs of her knees against the
ladder to the loft while Linc continued to take notes.
She felt deflated, because she had liked Mitch so
much. They had laughed together, and the way he'd
looked at her...

"I'm sorry to dump all that on you, Mrs. Mast," his voice sliced through her silent agonizing, "but it's best you not be deluded. You know, have the wool pulled over your eyes," he added as if he needed to translate his warning into simplistic, farmer terms. His condescension riled her more than Mitch's restating things for her had.

"Besides," he continued, scanning the rafters, "you're a friend of Jennie's, and I'm hoping that means I might be your friend, too. I've had my eye on her for years—ah, I mean from the moment her marriage broke up."

Despite her distress about Mitch, the way he'd said that made Rachel think he'd had designs on Jennie even before her divorce. He'd been watching this barn for years, so had he been watching her neighbor, too? She had to get him out of here and talk to Jennie about Linc and Mitch.

"Don't do too much preliminary work, Mr. McGowan," Rachel warned, escorting him toward the large open doors. "At least not until I get permission from my Church."

"If they don't agree, it will be a catastrophe for the place," he insisted, finally riveting his focus on her.

"It's already had a catastrophe," Rachel remonstrated, "that makes everything else seem small."

"Precisely. Oh—you mean your husband's demise." When she slowly nodded, he said, "Then the barn's had two major tragedies."

"What else? You said you don't know its history."

"I thought that Jennie would have said something," he floundered, looking embarrassed. He cocked his head. "You don't know, do you?"

"Know what?"

"Almost precisely ten years ago, Jennie's daughter was abducted from a high-school dance in this barn and never heard from again."

Doubly disturbed, Rachel went back into the barn to compose herself. Besides, she wanted to give Linc and Jennie a moment together before he left. She watched them through a large chink in the siding, then turned away, realizing it was wrong to spy on them. It lowered her to the level of whomever had watched her from the woodlot when she'd worked the field, and chased her through the corn...if someone had.

Rachel looked up and around, trying to see the barn through Linc's or Mitch's assessing eyes, but she always viewed it with her emotions and imagination. As ever, despite the light filtering in from the cupola, the heights were full of soaring shadows and the depths with shifting ones. The walls and cross beams seemed heavy with their burden. A floorboard creaked so distinctly overhead that, if she didn't know better, she'd think someone was up there.

She sighed as she recalled how Mitch had said that looking around the inside of the barn's skeleton showed so much about it. How she wished she knew more about him so she could reconcile what Linc had said with the man she thought she'd come to know, even if briefly. And she prayed she could help with whatever secret agony Jennie harbored about Laura's last known moments here, within these very walls.

* * *

Aaron had to chase the blue Frisbee far across the garden where Andy threw it. He waved to *Mamm* as she went into the house, then picked it up and threw it back to Andy. *Mamm* had been alone in the barn since that silver-haired man left.

"Hey, it's my turn!" their friend Jeff yelled. "You two can't hog it all the time."

"Do dumsy do," Andy said almost in a whisper, but Aaron knew what he meant. It wasn't too nice to say to their friend. So Aaron threw the Frisbee back to Jeff. He slipped on the wet grass, and the plastic disk sailed over his head.

Aaron watched Jeff chase it and Mike chase Jeff. Then he looked up at the barn. In the drop-down door high up, he saw a man. Then, like in the game peek-aboo, the man disappeared.

Who was that up there? The two men at dinner drove away a while ago. But maybe it looked more like an Amish man. He wasn't sure 'cause it happened so fast.

Aaron's mouth fell open and the Frisbee Jeff threw hit him in the knee. He tried to shout, "I got it," but no sound came out. It was just like the other night in the cellar when he was scared. Really scared, because that man who wasn't there now looked like *Daadi*, and *Mamm* said she didn't want to hear that anymore. So he better not tell her what he saw. Even if *Daadi* was really mad now that she let that one man sit in *Daadi*'s chair.

"Jennie, you didn't need to do all those dishes," Rachel told her friend as she went into the kitchen. "I thought you were just clearing the table."

"It's the least I can do after that great meal."

Rachel took the dish towel and dried the last pans on the rack. She had so many things to ask Jennie she didn't know where to start. Or if she should.

"Now that you've met Mitch Randall in the flesh," Rachel began, "what do you think?" She watched Jennie pull out the rubber stopper to let the soapy water swirl down the drain. When she said nothing, Rachel prompted, "Your calling Mitch 'gorgeous,' I can understand, in a rough kind of way, but 'dangerous'?"

"Linc said something, didn't he?" Jennie asked. She wrung the dishrag out so hard it reminded Rachel of what her mother used to do to chickens' necks.

"He said Mitch's grandfather shot and killed someone," Rachel blurted, "and that his father was a bad egg. I think it's wrong to blame people for what their family does, but do you know what Mitch went to jail for?"

Jennie sighed. "Kent said he beat a guy up really bad in a drunken brawl one night in Toledo. Nearly killed him with his bare hands."

"Oh, no!" Rachel sank into a kitchen chair. Not committing violence of any kind was practically an eleventh commandment to her people. Propping her elbows on the table, she put her face in her hands. And this was the man she'd agreed to accompany to see his new house tomorrow—with Jennie and the four boys along. And the man she was going to suggest to Eben and the deacons as worthy to work on her barn.

But the thing was, Rachel was having trouble squaring dark deeds with the Mitch she'd gotten to know. He'd shown some temper today with Linc, but she hardly blamed him. And she wasn't going to judge folks as evil without proof.

"I can't tell you how to live your life," Jennie said, her voice almost breaking. "But that's the reason I think you should stay away from Mitch Randall."

"At least," Rachel muttered, dropping her hands to the table as Jennie slumped into the chair next to hers, "he hasn't been cheating widows out of their barns. Has he?"

Jennie shook her head slowly. "Kent says he's a good builder—a rebuilder, he called him—but you obviously can't risk it now. Too bad, 'cause I kind of wanted to see his barn home."

"I'm still going to see it," Rachel stated matter-of-factly, smacking both palms on the table. "That would be the real way to get to know him, if you'll still go with me. Maybe you can phone him for me and tell him not to pick us up so we can leave when we want. If you can drive, I'll buy the gas and pay taxi, okay?"

The Amish insisted on paying what they called taxi fees if an *Englischer* drove them anyplace. Jennie had refused that arrangement before, but Rachel knew she was asking a big favor here.

"Look," Rachel went on, "I haven't even asked for permission for him to work here yet. If he seems shifty or shows a bad temper, I sure will drop him," she vowed with a nod. "But people can change, and above all, I've been taught to forgive and not just judge—even those who are not Amish."

"All right," Jennie declared adamantly, then jumped up and went back to the sink where she turned on the tap. But, staring out the window at the barn, she held the glass of water she filled until it ran over. Rachel saw it had started to sprinkle outside again, but she wanted to say more before she called the boys in.

Rachel stood and grasped the back of her chair. "Jennie, other than my sister Susan, I've never had a better friend than you. And knowing, *really* knowing folks is hard, and I don't want to pry. But why did you say you'd help me with the dance this weekend if it's got to bring back bad memories about that other dance ten years ago?"

Jennie dropped the glass. It shattered in the sink, though neither of them made a move at the sound. She jerked the water tap off, then propped herself up, stiff-armed. "Linc told you that, too," she choked out. "I really felt so good—safe—with you, because you didn't know all of that and so wouldn't ask or let something—" her voice was bitter as she began to pick up shards "—let something slip."

"I'm sorry," Rachel told her, stepping closer, undecided whether to touch her or not. "It's just that now I know why you never set foot in the barn even when you're right on top of it."

"And I don't plan to Saturday, either," Jennie admitted with a little shake of her head. "I told you I'd oversee the food here in the kitchen. I'll watch the twins and my two, then take all of them with me for the night, so you can put up more guests here."

Jennie's voice didn't sound like her own. It was small, soft and quivering, like a little girl's. And she kept taking big breaths between words.

"If it's too hard for you," Rachel whispered, "just because we're friends, don't feel you have to help with—"

"I *do* have to!" she choked out, still picking up glass. "I want to be here to see that things are all right now. I want to see kids go on—life go on—at a barn dance, the same place everyone—but whoever took her—saw her last."

Rachel touched her arm. "Jennie, I want to help."

"You can't. No one can. Well, at least just don't talk about it again and let me do things my way. Let me be your friend. Let me mother your little boys and help with those Amish kids at the dance."

"Sure. You know how much you mean to me, to us."

"I was here for that dance," Jennie went on as if she hadn't even heard her, "in this very kitchen, helping the Brickers with the food. Laura and Kent were out in the crowd. I didn't worry about a thing, at least not at first, even when she came up missing. I just knew she'd be all right at a high-school dance or sneaking off to a movie. I mean, this is the rural, upright heart of Ohio, for heaven's sake!"

"It's all right now," Rachel tried to comfort.

"It isn't!" Jennie turned her ravaged face partway toward her, a face Rachel hardly recognized. "Rachel, just let me even mother you if I can, because, God knows, I did something wrong with my—my..."

Rachel reached to embrace her. But as the boys clattered in the back door, Jennie dropped the shards of glass back in the sink, pulled away and ran into the other room.

The moment Rachel saw Mitch had made a play fort for the boys from sawhorses, boards and a huge appliance carton in his side yard, she was ready to call Lincoln McGowan a liar. No one could be this kind to kids and then be aggressive with adults. And she'd never smelled a bit of liquor on Mitch's breath.

Rachel stepped anxiously down from the van with the three oldest boys spilling out around her while Jennie got Mike out of his car seat. Mitch appeared from his old farmhouse to greet them, with a smiling, stocky man close behind. The tidy but small place also served as Mitch's office; he'd explained that his new barn house was set way back on the property.

"Welcome to Woodland," Mitch began, looking very pleased. He was in his usual black jeans, while the other man was in blue jeans, but both wore crisply ironed shirts. "Rachel, Jennie, this is my office manager, sometimes foreman of my construction team, and jack-of-all-trades, Gabe Carter."

Gabe nodded politely at each woman in turn as Mitch introduced them. Up close, the man looked not stocky but strong.

"Jack of all trades all right," Gabe said, "'cause I'm gonna ride herd on this bunch while you ladies get the twenty-five-cent barn-house tour."

As he spoke, Gabe bent to ruffle Jennie's grandsons' hair and tapped playfully on the flat black hats of her two. Andy grinned and knocked twice on Gabe's arm in return, while Aaron just gawked up at him. Rachel was starting to relax already.

"We don't want to inconvenience you, Mr. Carter," she told him.

"Call me Gabe, please, ma'am. Short for Gabriel—you know, like the angel, sent from heaven to do his master's work."

"That's a good one," Mitch put in.

"But," Gabe went on, "Mitch says Gabe's short

for gabby. And you're not inconveniencing me," he assured her. "I love kids, wish I had some of my own."

"Gabe's been known to play Santa Claus at malls and parties at Christmas," Mitch said. "Have beard and Santa suit, will travel."

Rachel noted Mitch suddenly looked as if he regretted saying that, probably remembering too late that the Amish had nothing to do with Santa Claus. Even Gabe's pale blue eyes were serious now, though his mouth and ruddy cheeks lifted in a smile. Since he had gray hairs woven through his unruly brown thatch, Rachel judged him to be several years older than Mitch's mid-thirties.

"You're both very thoughtful," she said in the brief silence, "and the boys will love that fort." That, at least, was obvious. All four were already peeking into the recesses of an empty refrigerator box tipped on its side.

"The fort's safer than the house just now," Mitch explained to the women as he walked them to his truck. "I don't have some railings or banisters up yet, and I don't want the boys hurt."

Sitting pressed between Mitch and Jennie while he drove them down the twisting lane, Rachel realized this was physically the closest she'd been to him. His well-muscled leg bounced warmly against her hip and thigh. She got almost dizzy at the hint of scent on him, tinged with tart, clean lime.

"Oh, it's huge," Jennie cried, and Rachel pulled her attention away from Mitch to squint through the sun reflecting off the windshield.

Mitch's new house *was* a wonder. A large, old barn weathered dove gray sat in a half circle of bright, autumn trees washed by recent rain. Curling slightly around the back and other side was a sparkling, L-shaped pond. Where once had been the double barn doors and higher loft opening now stretched a huge window to frame the new front door and let light into the house.

"This barn was going to be torn down for a suburban Toledo auto dealer who needed a bigger parking lot," he told them as he pulled to a stop. "I figured it would be better off as my dream home. I've been rescuing and saving structures for others, but this one whispered something to me."

As he turned her way, Rachel made the mistake of facing him. He might have even leaned slightly into her. Their profiles were so close. His breath smelled like mint toothpaste.

"It's beautiful," she said, her voice almost husky.

"I've always thought of it as a 'she,'" he said as Jennie got out of the truck to give Rachel more room to shift away from him, though at first she didn't budge. "I hope you'll like it inside, too," he added.

Rachel couldn't make herself believe that Mitch had ever been in a drunken brawl. *She* was the one who felt intoxicated near him, and she had to fight that feeling.

Mitch escorted them into his barn home, a mix of past and present, and started the tour. "It offers soaring spaces and cozy places, as our website puts it," he explained with a proud grin.

Made from the traditional Dutch barn design, the renovated structure had three levels. The first, which used to be animal stalls, now included a garage and storage area, a laundry room and large sunroom with an outdoor deck that faced the woods and pond in back. The next level, which had once been the threshing floor and haymows, had broad outside stairs down to the deck. This middle level also contained a spacious kitchen and a large, combined living and dining room. A sort of workroom or office with a bath—imagine, a bath just for one room, Rachel marveled—was also on this floor and shared a see-through fireplace with the den. On the third level were two bedrooms linked by a bath built around an open space that revealed all below. More small bedrooms for guests could be added under the slanted roof later, he told them. Scattered area rugs with color combinations that matched the few upholstered pieces drew everything together.

But the real miracle of the barn home was the balance of open and enclosed spaces. The huge pieces of country furniture did not overwhelm small touches, such as a framed collection of Indian arrowheads. As if they were abstract paintings, quilts graced the walls as well as the beds.

"Gorgeous quilts," Jennie observed, "but not Amish."

"Just country," he told them. "My grandmother made the ones on the walls and the one on my bed. She was the only mother I knew. She's—gone now, with a lot else."

Rachel was going to ask him more about his past, but it was awkward with Jennie sticking so tight. Mitch began pointing out the ceiling fans and the central-air ducts he'd put in. He explained about adding insulation, plumbing and lighting. Rachel felt his pride in this place, which she'd been taught was a sin. But his was a good pride for a good house. She felt so at home with the exposed beams shouldering the weight of the roof amidst shafts of sun. Two windows he called skylights opened up the roof to the heavens, as if to bless the place.

Later, Jennie strolled out by the pond to feed geese while Rachel and Mitch lingered on the deck. "Your new house is so attractive," she told him. "And big."

"But still intimate, I think," he said.

"Yes, it is. You believe it is your very best achievement, don't you?"

"Second place maybe," he admitted, scanning his little forest as if looking for something. "It still feels like a house and not a home to me for some reason. Actually, I'm my best achievement—that I survived at all."

Her head snapped around, and his eyes locked with hers. "A hard childhood?" she prompted when he offered nothing more.

"Bad, then good, then a nightmare."

Rachel bit her lower lip. She wanted to ask a hundred questions but she didn't want to seem nosy.

"I'm not blaming others," he confided, tapping a fist on the railing. "My grandfather told me that what a man makes of himself has nothing to do with lousy parents or circumstance, that I had to rise above that."

Rachel nodded. Their hands were so close on the railing she could feel the heat of him. She was beginning to tremble from deep inside, as though the deck boards underfoot were shaking.

"My mother," Mitch went on, so softly he almost whispered, "died driving drunk one night when she should have been home taking care of me—a mere toddler. I don't know, maybe she just took off for a few hours to get away from my father. Can't blame her for that.''

"So then it was just you and your dad.''

"Only until he could get to Ohio to dump me on his folks and take off. My grandparents were great, but when I was nine the state took their farm to build I-75, a national road that goes from north Michigan to south Florida. Who could fight that?'' he asked bitterly.

"But he did—your grandfather?'' Rachel said, starting to imagine how the shooting had happened.

Mitch turned to her, leaning his hip against the railing. "He believed you can and should fight city hall. He only shot at the ceiling, but a ricochet killed a clerk, and he wounded two others trying to subdue him. He died in prison of grief—that's my diagnosis—and my grandmother died of loss of the farm and him. Lawyer fees and her hospital stay ate up the money the government gave them for slamming that road right through their lives.''

Instinctively, she covered his hand with hers. Though she couldn't tell by just looking, he was shaking, too. "Mitch, I'm so sorry.''

His eyes glazed with unshed tears, but he frowned. "I'm glad to hear we're on a first-name basis,'' he said, but she didn't want him shifting the topic. She had to learn why he went to prison. And if they were going to be friends, she had to be certain he would not resort to violence again.

"But whatever I want from you, Rachel,'' he went on, his voice rough now as he opened his fist to take her hand, "it isn't pity. Anyhow, after I lost my grandparents and lived in a couple of foster homes, I set out to find my father.''

Another long pause. Rachel sensed how painful this was for him, and yet he was the one doing the leading, the bleeding, here.

"And did you?" she prompted.

"Yeah, I found him. He's dead now. End of story."

His face and mood had turned so dark that Rachel prayed it wasn't his father he'd beat up in some drunken rage. Mitch pushed away from the railing and started inside, but she snagged his arm.

"I don't think it's the end of your story," she dared. "I think you wanted to tell me more, to admit something—"

He swung back and grasped her upper arms in a viselike grip. "I know I started this, but don't dig too deep too fast, Rachel Mast, because that's when the walls cave in."

She wanted to challenge that, but she heard voices. Glancing over Mitch's shoulder, she saw Gabe had brought the boys down the road to the house.

The next morning, after another night of drizzle despite the previous bright day, fog lay so suffocatingly thick outside, Rachel couldn't even see the barn through her bedroom window when she looked out at dawn. Agonizing over how she felt about Mitch, she'd hardly slept and was groggy, but something had awakened her. Now she was certain she'd heard the barn door creak open, the jingle of harness and traces, the clomping of big hoofs.

She yanked up her window sash to listen. Yes, a snort and whinny swirling through this stew of gray mist. She was glad for once that Amish homes did not have storm windows.

"Chester!" she shouted.

The Percherons' distinctive neigh swam through the fog.

Someone was trying to steal her team!

Rachel didn't even stop for her shoes or slippers, or to pin her dress on. Yanking her robe from the chair, praying the twins would not waken while she was gone, she tore downstairs in nothing but her long, white nightgown and robe. Maybe Eben or Sim Lapp had come to borrow the team, but no one had asked. And if someone was here to feed or curry them as they had just after Sam first died, why would they be taking them outside?

Rachel unlocked and banged out the door, shouting first in German, then English, "Leave those horses in the barn!"

Her voice sounded muffled as if she were underwater. The cold dampness smacked her. Barefooted, she ran for the barn.

The open door loomed like a devouring mouth. Jonah swallowed by the whale, she thought, punished for not obeying the Lord's will for him. Surely, these strange occurrences were not warnings to her for fighting Bishop Eben or befriending outsiders like Mitch or Jennie.

The Percherons' stalls stood empty, their harnesses and rigging gone from the wall pegs.

"Chester, Cream, Gid!" she screamed. "Come here! *Komm!*"

From the other side of the barn, Nann and Bett shied nervously. Thank God, they hadn't been touched. But Rachel was sure the sounds the Percherons had made came from the direction of the fields, not from the road. She grabbed the long corn-cutting knife from its box near the door and tore out into the fog.

"Chester!"

No answering neigh this time but still the jingle of tack and trappings on the wind in a regular bouncing beat as if the horses were working a field. Fog made sounds seem closer than they were. Ignoring how cold and wet the ground felt against her bare soles, she began to run in the direction of the rye field she'd planted two days ago.

Panting, she stopped at the edge of the field. The harrower was gone, too, or else someone had moved it. This was insanity. Did Eben regret he hadn't sent his boys to help her harrow and plant as he'd promised and, not knowing she'd done it herself, had come over early to do it for her? If so, he'd make chaos of her careful job. But, then again, no one in his right mind would harrow a field muddied by the recent rain.

Still, she stepped into the field. Yes, under her feet, freshly furrowed rows had created worse clods than she'd broken up. Gripping the corn knife in both hands before her, she waded farther into the field, the mud up to her ankles. It was impossible to run toward the sounds. She'd stand her ground, call to whomever emerged from this soupy mist in the next rotation of the field, and tell him...

Rachel screamed, as looming from the fog, her own team almost mowed her down. She hurled herself away, tossing the knife free so she wouldn't cut herself when she rolled. Angry and scared, she looked up to see that there was no one running behind the hitched harrower, no one at the reins, which dragged along the ground, attached to a thick rope which was knotted where, perhaps, someone had held it far back from the team. Yet someone must have just been near, or the team would not be pulling like this.

"Chester, whoa!" she shouted. Her panicked voice bounced back from the fog, *Whoa, ho, oh...*

Confused and annoyed, the team halted and stood, shaking their shaggy manes. Tears of relief streaming down her cheeks, Rachel got clumsily to her feet. The three big beasts she'd washed and curried after she'd returned from Mitch's yesterday were a mud-splattered mess. But through that, their harnesses gleamed, with the leather newly oiled and each grommet and stud of metal polished.

Wide-eyed, Rachel approached the team. She had not had time to care for their gear and could never get it in the shape Sam used to keep it—this very shape.

Her gaze darted to the harrower. The horses were hitched to it exactly as Sam used to, the rope knotted as if he had done it. And there, with one iron spike of the harrower impaling it just like the heavy grappling hook had impaled his body, was Sam's straw hat she had hung back in the barn.

In her soul, Rachel heard her twins' whispers, *Mamm, Daadi's back, Mamm, he's mad at you...*

Her knees gave way and she crumpled, sobbing, into the muddy field.

Eight

The night of the Amish barn dance, Jennie Morgan kept as busy as she could in Rachel's kitchen. At least she didn't have the four boys underfoot right now, because her daughter-in-law, Marci, on break from the beauty shop, had come to Jennie's house and had taken the kids there.

So Jennie tried to concentrate on baking sheet after sheet of what the Amish called moon pies, which Rachel had already made. They were more like individual tarts, circles of dough folded in half and pinched together on the curved edge to encase their fragrant apple and cinnamon filling. Jennie was also in charge of refrigerating or storing whatever food Amish women handed in the back door on trays or in their beloved Tupperware.

Jennie did anything and everything to be useful here and to keep from having to think about *being* here. If she could just get through this dance, she told herself, it would be like giving up that first cigarette or drink on the road to recovery.

"Ouch!" Seeing her son in the kitchen door, she'd burned herself on the oven rack. "Oh, that's right," she said, thrusting her thumb in her mouth so her words came out muffled. "You loaned Rachel planks to make tables in the barn."

"Yeah," Kent said, shifting from one foot to the other. "She took the horses out and scrubbed the barn floor, then put down a big drop cloth. That's where she said to put up the tables for food. They're using only the threshing floor for the dancing."

Jennie nodded as she went over to the sink and plunged her thumb into cold running water.

"It wasn't my idea to come here tonight, Mom," Kent said, not budging from the doorway. "You still want Marci to drop the boys here when she goes back for her late appointments?"

"Sure," she said, looking at her thumb and not at him. "It'll give you two a quiet Saturday night once she's done. Go to a movie or something. Enjoy."

"With you here like this, trying to prove something to yourself or to me?" He slammed out the back door.

Jennie sighed as she stood at the sink and watched more Amish buggies arriving and Rachel running here and there to greet everyone. Rachel was going to burn herself out, Jenny thought. She'd looked frazzled all day. At least she had help from several young Amish couples, the Lapps, Troyers and Detwilers, as well as Sarah Yoder, Eben's girl, and Sarah's fiancé, Jacob Esh. That was another reason it wouldn't look odd if Jennie kept to the kitchen: it was pretty obvious that no one over thirty was attending what the Amish called a *rumspringa danze*.

Leaning against the sink with the water still running, Jennie Morgan felt herself drift back ten years, back through a torrent of terror and pain. It was not

Amish kids she saw but Laura and her friends running around out there, not buggies but cars coming in for the dance. A boom box was playing that soundtrack from the Patrick Swayze movie *Dirty Dancing* the high-school kids loved. She didn't overhear German, but English, teenage slang, talk from Kent about the Olympic basketball team in Seoul, Korea, or, earlier that day, Laura's chatter about that movie she wanted to see.

"You know I love those scary flicks, Mom!" Laura had told her as she came out of her room dressed for the dance. "If this is over early, I'm going with friends to see *Nightmare on Elm Street 4* in Bowling Green."

"Four? They made four of those awful slasher things?" Jennie had protested. "You know your father doesn't think you should see things like that."

"He lets Kent go see them!"

Everything Laura said seemed to be punctuated with exclamation points. Her life was quick and dramatic, and almost each event was a crisis.

"Lets Kent see what?" Jennie asked, realizing she didn't monitor what Kent did half as closely as Laura's doings.

"All those *Friday the 13th* movies! And there's seven of those!"

"I don't want you to see something so degrading. Have your friends choose something else, maybe that *Bull Durham* one with Kevin Costner that's about baseball."

"Mother," she said, her voice tinged with pity and patience, "that one's really a transforming love story. The baseball's entirely secondary except as a symbol of failings and redemption in life. That's what Mr.

McGowan said in history class last week. He's really smart and cute, all the girls think so.''

"We're not talking about Mr. McGowan, so don't change the subject. You and I will have to go to a movie together like we used to," Jennie suggested.

"Ri—ight," Laura drawled, hands propped on hips. "Like we'll both have time before Christmas vacation months and months away. But, no, really, I'd love to see a movie with you, hit the mall again. Thanks for the new dress and all." Laura darted over to give her a quick hug.

"Love you, honey," Jennie said and hugged her back hard. Moments like that had seemed fewer lately; Jennie recalled how Laura used to hang on her and want to be cuddled when she was younger.

"And about tonight?" Jennie prompted as Laura darted away and grabbed her purse.

"All right, I won't go to that movie! The dance may last forever, anyway," Laura had said as she'd sailed out the door.

And, Jennie thought now, that dance, in a way, had lasted forever. She'd never spoken with her daughter again. Time had stopped and yet stretched out, not only for the missing and presumed-dead Laura, but also for Jennie, eternally. What should she have done differently?

At the dance that fateful night, Laura and Jennie had made a deal that if Jennie helped the Brickers with the food, she wouldn't come outside to play chaperon during the dance. So she hadn't checked up on Laura as she should have or she would have realized her daughter was missing earlier and had not just gone to that forbidden movie or sneaked out in back to make out with Jim Thomas, the football player she had a crush on.

"Jennie," Rachel's voice jolted her back to the here and now, "are you okay? Are these moon pies okay?" Rachel rushed to take a tray of them out of the oven that was blasting heat into the room. Jennie saw she'd left the door open.

"Sorry," Jennie said, hustling to help. "I burned myself and had to run some water on my thumb."

Rachel placed the tray on the cooling racks on the counter. "If you'd like to go home..." she offered.

"No way," Jennie declared, forcing the remnants of her strength and control into her voice. Rachel looked as if she'd say something else, but someone called to her in German from outside and she hurried away.

"Go home?" Jennie whispered to the empty kitchen. "After that night, I can never really go home again."

Rachel kept running from guest to guest, from task to task, but she knew she was also running down fast. Whoever was playing cruel tricks on her—the straw hat, tampering with her horses—was not only taunting her, but haunting her, too. She had decided she must find out who was behind the events by discovering *why*.

Eben to force her to marry him? Some other Amish brother or sister who had known Sam's habits and either wanted this farm or thought they were doing her a favor by scaring her away? Someone who meant to make the point she was overstepping the line by working the farm herself? It had to be someone Amish—one of her own people betraying her—didn't it?

"Oh, almost forgot, Sam Rachel," the pregnant Sim Annie Lapp cried as she hurried past. "My bags of caramel popcorn balls are still in the back seat of my buggy."

Rachel smiled at Annie and said a silent prayer that her pregnancy went well. Annie and Sim Lapp had been desperate for a child, and a series of miscarriages had almost turned them bitter. But this pregnancy was so far along that surely it would come to fruition.

Rachel saw Sim Annie, hands on hips, then pointing, talking to Eben's oldest sons, Dan and Ben, who were unhitching buggies and tying horses, including Rachel's five, along the fence. Evidently Sim Annie had given the boys orders to find those popcorn balls *schnell,* because they darted off among the rows of parked buggies.

In the barn Sim Lapp and Amos Troyer set up plank tables and arranged bales of hay for seats around the threshing floor. Silently rebuking herself for turning so suspicious lately, Rachel recalled that Sim—Simeon, his name was—had once argued with Sam over whether the Lapps or the Masts would buy this farm and barn. It was the fact Sam had sons and the Lapps no children that had decided it, and the men patched up the disagreement by confessing it in church.

Before that single falling-out, Sam and Sim had been close friends, Rachel knew. When they were boys, people had teased them for their similar nicknames and called them twins since they so resembled each other. Since Sam's death, Sim had been nothing but helpful. Rachel had to get hold of herself, or she'd drown in her own distrust, even in the midst of such support from her people.

Also assisting her today, the newly betrothed Sarah and Jacob seemed to be everywhere. Other Amish who were not staying for the *danze* handed food in the back door to Jennie or carried it directly into the barn to the makeshift tables. In the best of Amish cooperation, they were all pulling as one team.

Rachel checked the table, groaning under the bounty of pickles and relishes, apple fritters, jumbles—the Amish's favorite cookie —and pyramids of moon pies. Rachel had no illusions that a few of the boys might not sneak Budweisers later, but barrels of homemade root beer waited in the barn. Spareribs, fried chicken, bowls of German potato salad and slaw, dropped off by other local Amish cooks, had yet to arrive. Though only seven of the guests were local, she was expecting to feed nearly fifty hungry young people and eight helpers tonight.

Rachel ran to meet a big van when it pulled in to the driveway. She didn't recognize it, not even as a local hired taxi from back home. For hours they'd been expecting some Maplecreek youngsters, including her two nephews, Sam's brother's kids, Josh and Ferd Mast. Now she saw, to her relief and surprise, that Josh was driving.

"Two other vans are close behind, but I just drove faster," the boy told her as he rolled down the automatic car window.

"Just look how big you are!" Rachel told him and patted his arm. She greeted Ferd and the four other kids from home, two she'd had as scholars in the one-room schoolhouse where she'd trained. She told them they'd get all caught up on news after they parked and freshened up.

Shaking her head, Rachel watched as Josh pulled the van away to park on the side lawn, revving up the engine several times before he killed it. Many of the kids in this rebellious period of their lives even drag-raced, when in her day, a souped-up buggy with a transistor radio had been the extent of Sam's *rumspringa* sins. Now Rachel wished she hadn't just gone along with Sam who had wanted to keep to the straight and narrow. If she'd rebelled more when it was allowed, maybe she could have gotten it out of her system.

"Lustige zeit!" Gid Fanny Detwiler called to Rachel as she got down from her buggy to hand a covered dish in the back door.

"Ja!" Rachel shouted back and waved as her friend let Dan Yoder take her buggy. "A merry time—I hope so!"

Rachel ran into her nephew Josh as he came around the corner of the barn. Josh and Ferd were the second and third sons of Sam's brother Zeb, from a family much like Eben's: big, well-to-do and respected in their community.

Now that he wasn't in his car with the others, Rachel was tempted to hug Josh but decided not to. The *junge leit* might look like long-legged kids, but they were trying to be grown-up. "Did you borrow that van?" she asked.

"Naw," he admitted, his shoulder hunched. "We went together and rented it so we didn't have to drag some adult along. Oh, almost forgot," he added, feeling in his jeans-jacket pockets. Most of the kids here tonight were dressed English, not Amish. He nearly spilled out a pack of Doral cigarettes, but hastily shoved it back down. "Here's a letter for you from my father. I heard him tell *Mamm* what was in it," he went on, seeming to swagger a bit as if he imparted forbidden knowledge.

"You sure you should tell?"

"Gonna read it, aren't you?" he said, his voice almost rude. "Father thinks you should either get married or give up this place and come home. After all, he owns near half of if," the boy added, craning his neck to look around. "And with me and Ferd coming on, *Daadi*'s still looking for good land for us to farm."

Rachel felt he'd slapped her. And not only because Zeb wanted this place for his own sons. Zebulon Mast had never quite approved of her. She knew he'd tried to convince Sam she was too flighty to marry.

Rachel stood silent, stunned. She hadn't thought about the possibility that someone who knew Sam's every habit of feeding and hitching horses, someone the horses knew and would instantly obey, someone who could want to make it hard for her to stay here, could be someone from outside their community. Like someone from Maplecreek.

"*Danke,* Josh," she told the boy as he handed her the letter and strolled off into the barn to look around, as his father had probably told him to. Could her own brother-in-law have asked someone here among the brethren to scare her away, thinking she'd run to Eben's arms or home to her family in Maplecreek? Could he have come here to do it himself?

When the two other vans of Maplecreek kids pulled in, she hurried to greet them.

* * *

Sarah saw Rachel was starting toward the barn after she'd greeted the other Maplecreek guests, and she went up to her. "You all right, Rach?" she asked above the noise.

Rachel jumped, then just kept folding and unfolding a letter. "Just excited from all this," she said, but Sarah thought her friend looked exhausted when the *danze* hadn't even started yet. At least Rachel had an excuse for looking gloomy since her husband had died here and she no doubt missed him, especially tonight, playing host all alone. Sarah felt swamped by guilt: here she was avoiding Jacob when her entire life with him lay ahead.

"Despite it all, you liked being married, right?" Sarah blurted, gripping her hands together so hard her fingers went numb.

Rachel's green eyes focused on her as if from far away. "Of course I did," she assured her so loud it seemed to Sarah she was trying to convince herself. "Sometimes," Rachel added, frowning, "it takes dedication, but the rewards are great."

"Didn't mean to interrupt if you needed to read that letter," Sarah said, noting that Rachel was still fingering it.

"That's all right. It will have to wait until I get my glasses. A note from family at home."

"Your mother?" Sarah asked, realizing she shouldn't pry and that she'd given away her own longings for her mother. Rachel had been the only one she'd ever poured her heart out to about how she still loved her mother when she was supposed to more or less hate her now. Of course, her father never said that, but it was as obvious as his other unspoken rules in the house.

"You're missing your *Mamm* again, the closer you get to your wedding," Rachel said as they walked out toward the barn together.

"Jacob—he just doesn't understand, not women's things," Sarah protested, but her voice broke. Lately, every time she thought about telling Jacob that they needed to get married soon, she almost hated him when she knew she really loved him. She felt so mixed-up. And when her father found out...

Rachel reached out and took Sarah's hands. "I know what's fretting you," she told Sarah. "Tonight's the end of your *rumspringa,* the start of a new life."

Sarah froze. The way Rachel had put that.... She was tempted to tell Rachel the truth. But she couldn't; she'd cry and everyone would see.

As the harmonica music started from inside the barn with "Turkey in the Straw" and others joined in with mouth music, Sarah nodded and went around the rear of the barn. Before Jacob saw her, she would sneak in the back door and climb a ladder to the haymow. It wouldn't take her long to get herself together, and then she'd come back down and have a good time. Later, somehow, she'd find the nerve to tell him, then her father. But till then it wasn't a "Turkey in the Straw" but a chicken hiding there.

At first, Rachel noted, the kids didn't seem to mix. Couples sat on one side of the barn, with the boys on bales, facing the girls, called *maidals.* But soon Amish teenagers began to take the floor in a hoe-down that the old-time pioneers could have joined.

Rachel thought of Linc McGowan; he'd love to see this living history in this historic barn.

The dancing became more exuberant as Dan Yoder's harmonica got quicker, louder, but after a while, everyone took a break to play ringtoss games and eat. *"Komm esse,"* Rachel told everyone. "Come eat." As darkness fell, the steady purring of the gas lanterns hanging on pegs and beams threw soft light throughout the barn. Some danced again, others drifted in and out, and everyone ate.

Rachel went back and forth to the house, partly to keep food flowing and partly to be sure Jennie was all right. Marci had dropped the boys off, and Rachel took them to the barn to see what was going on and to get them fed. The Maplecreek kids made a big fuss over their twin cousins, and the boys ate that up faster than the food. After she delivered the boys back to Jennie, Jacob, Sarah's intended, was waiting just outside her back door.

"Is she in there with you and the English woman?" Jacob asked.

"Sarah? No. I just assumed she was with you. I haven't seen her for nearly an hour," Rachel admitted.

"She was feeling funny, wanted to take a rest, so I said sure."

"Oh, I'll fetch her then," Rachel assured him, turning back into the house. "She's probably lying down inside."

But Sarah was not inside, including in the cellar, which Rachel checked on a whim.

"What's the matter?" Jennie asked, getting up from her chair at the now partly cleared kitchen table where she'd been watching the four boys devour jumbles and draw with crayons. "What did you lose? Not—someone missing?"

"It's all right," Rachel insisted, but her own voice betrayed her. "Jacob's just upset that Sarah's not feeling good and left him on his own a bit." Jennie opened her mouth to say something else, but no words came. "Don't worry," Rachel added, squeezing Jennie's shoulder.

But Jennie followed her to the back door and stood there like a statue. When Rachel hurried out, Jacob wasn't there, but she hadn't gone very far when she heard him shout, "Mrs. Mast, up here!"

She jerked to a halt. At first she thought she saw a stranger in the open loft door of the barn, but it was Jacob, leaning out, windmilling his arm.

"She's up there?" Rachel called to him. She had to cup her hands to her mouth because of the music and voices in the barn.

"No. Just wanted you to see me here," he shouted. "Can't find her anywhere here, either."

Behind Rachel, Jennie Morgan screamed.

To avoid panicking everyone, Rachel got Sarah's brothers, Dan and Ben, to help Jacob and her look for Sarah. The boys even made forays out around the barn and looked in all the unhitched buggies.

"It's not like her," Dan muttered when he passed Rachel during one circle of the yard. "Father will really give her what for."

Jacob's face looked set in stone, though no one was as worried as Jennie, who stood just inside the back door, calling to Rachel, "I could have told you she didn't come in here. This can't be, can't be."

She'd have to send Jennie home to phone for help,

Rachel decided—that is if she'd agree to take the boys and go. Rachel understood Jennie's fear, but it was only making things worse. Meanwhile, Rachel knew she had to stop the dance and get everyone to help search, while Dan went home for Eben and others. Would Eben be angry with her if she summoned the Clearview sheriff, too?

Rachel felt terror press its hands around her throat. She had been too distraught about her own concerns and problems. When Sarah tried to talk to her, she should have listened better or kept Sarah with her.

Rachel turned back toward the house to tell Andy and Aaron they'd have to go home with Jennie. All four boys crowded around her in the lighted doorway when Rachel saw Aaron point up toward the top of the barn.

"I know Jacob's up there, Aaron," she said.

"Is that the man again, Andy?" she heard him ask his brother. "Not in the barn, but on it this time?"

Rachel turned and looked above Jacob in the open loft door, beyond the overhanging peak to the cupola. Leaning against it, on the very top crease of roofline, a figure, a mere shadow, was leaning against the old cupola.

"Sarah?" Rachel cried and pointed upward to Jacob. His gaze followed her arm, and he disappeared inside the barn.

Rachel sprinted toward it, working her way around the moving, weaving square of dancers and others standing or chatting. She climbed the haymow ladder as fast as she could, then the next ladder up toward the cupola, trying to catch up with Jacob.

The barn roof was steep. What had possessed Sarah? Even in her darkest moments after Sam died,

Rachel had never so much as considered climbing up there to—to...

She saw Jacob was already straddling the loose boards inside the cupola just above her head. "Sarah, I'm coming out for you," she heard him cry.

Even over the harmonica and voices and laughter below, Rachel heard each word Sarah said: "If you do, I'll jump."

Nine

It had been an hour since Aaron had spotted Sarah on the barn roof, but it seemed a year to Rachel. Songs and laughs had withered to whispers. Guests had vacated the barn to stand on the lawn or sit in unhitched buggies. The audience grew as word spread that another tragedy—this one waiting to happen—was unfolding at the old barn on Ravine Road.

From a glance out the haymow door, Rachel could see Kent's and Jennie's silhouettes as they stood like sentinels in the back door of the lighted house. Jennie had taken the four boys and driven home to phone the sheriff, then Kent and Marci. Under protest, Marci had stayed next door with the kids, Rachel overheard Kent tell Jennie when he arrived. It wasn't that Marci thought her husband and mother-in-law couldn't get through another tragedy with a young girl at the barn, he'd admitted. Marci wanted to see her dad, the sheriff, in action here.

Tim Burnett, Clearview's longtime, popular sheriff, had driven in, lights flashing, bringing Eben with him. The sheriff had taken over, directing onlookers parked along the road to get back behind the yellow police tape his deputy strung across the driveway. In the crowd, Rachel briefly spoke with Linc McGowan, who said he was just driving by. She also noticed the two rude men who had stopped her buggy on the road. Walking past, she pretended to ignore them, but her insides lurched. Now they knew where she lived.

Sheriff Burnett had called for the volunteer fire department and ordered them to hold their canvas equipment covers like old-fashioned jumping nets on both sides of the barn in case they could get under Sarah to break her fall. An emergency squad had arrived from Bowling Green. The official vehicles' sirens summoned more folks from farms and from town.

Now the bar lights of the sheriff's and emergency vehicles pulsed beams of crimson against the house and barn. The potential catastrophe might be like Jennie's ten-year-old nightmare played out again, Rachel thought, but the scene reminded *her* of the night Sam died. Then, too, Sheriff Burnett and Bishop Eben Yoder had disagreed about how to proceed.

Tonight Eben wanted the crowd and officials to leave so he could order Sarah down, but the sheriff wasn't letting him get within talking distance of her. Instead, Burnett, a gaunt, gray-haired veteran of the job with a face like worn leather, was using Jacob Esh as the go-between to the distraught girl while a suicide negotiator from Toledo was on the way.

Jacob climbed down from the cupola to the top loft where Eben and Rachel waited with the sheriff. Flinching almost as if he expected a blow, Jacob said, "She won't talk to you, Bishop Yoder."

"Not to her own father?" Eben exploded. "Of course she'll talk to me. She'll get back down here so I can find out what possessed her." He sounded as stern as ever, but Rachel saw he was frantic.

The sheriff quickly raised his hands to quiet Eben's outburst. "What else, boy?" Burnett asked Jacob.

"She says," Jacob went on, a frown furrowing his brow, "she won't even talk to me anymore—only to Sam Rachel."

Eben turned to face Rachel. She had wrapped herself in an emergency-squad blanket over her clothes but she couldn't stop shaking. Though heights had never bothered her—she actually liked them—tonight this loft over the haymows, far above the threshing floor scared her. Rachel felt she was with Sarah on that peak of the steep, shingled roof, waiting to fall.

"What do you know about why she's up there?" Eben demanded of Rachel in German. "Here she is at a nice dance, got her own wedding coming. What in heaven's name is wrong with her?"

"Speak English," the sheriff ordered.

"I'm asking why my girl wants Sam Rachel," Eben muttered.

"All I know," Rachel replied, "is that the closer Sarah gets to her own wedding the more she worries. She's seen her own mother go missing and me lose Sam. She's scared of the things that can go wrong in a lifetime of marriage."

"And then she sees you put me off," Eben accused, slipping back in German, "and thinks something's wrong with me, wrong with marriage in general. She's acting like her crazy mother now. Besides, it's a sin not to trust the Lord.''

"I agree,'' Rachel said, ''but sometimes He gives us gifts and opportunities and expects us to make good on them without having to hold our hands each step of the way.''

"Are *you* preaching to me?'' Eben countered, aghast.

"Let's not argue,'' Rachel pleaded in English, despite the fact Eben wasn't heeding the sheriff's order to avoid German. ''Sheriff Burnett,'' she said, turning to face him, ''I'll talk to her.''

"The cupola walk,'' Jacob put in, ''it's real shaky.''

"Mrs. Mast weighs less than you,'' the sheriff told Jacob.

Rachel realized she was crying. The sheriff handed her a handkerchief. Nodding her thanks, she wiped her cheeks and eyes, then blew her nose. For some reason, Eben looked even more angry.

"I was going to get those boards in the cupola fixed soon,'' Rachel admitted, ''but I know where to step. I'll be careful.''

Silent but seething, Eben took her blanket as if he held her coat. Rachel recalled, as she climbed the small ladder to the cupola, that Mitch had made her promise not to come up here until he'd repaired it. She decided then to definitely have him work on it, maybe tomorrow, as soon as Sarah was safe.

Rachel braced herself on the narrow, curved boardwalk and shuffled over to the broken set of old louvers that Sarah must have squeezed through to get outside. The boards shuddered under her feet. Laura might have been lost from this barn and Sam, too, but Sarah would be saved, Rachel vowed as she clung to the makeshift handholds of the windowsill. Outside the wind picked up; she heard the horse weather vane scrape and spin on the dome over her head the way it had the day Sam died.

"Sarah, I'm here," she called out quietly. "Did you want to tell me something else earlier, and I just wasn't listening?"

Sarah didn't answer at first, then said, "Are you alone?"

"You bet I am. These boards can't hold more than one."

"More than one," the girl's voice drifted in so softly that Rachel had to stick her head out to hear. She gasped at the view and steadied herself again. Below the vastness of the pitch-black sky, the steady, pale house lights and red beat of emergency vehicles made her blink. At least with her nearsightedness, the crowd was a blur. Sarah sat, low enough to be out of reach, straddling the steep peak of roof, bracing her back against the cupola.

"I walked on those boards, and I'm more than one," Sarah said, craning her neck to look up at Rachel. Darkness swathed her face in shifting shadows.

"What?" Rachel asked. And then she knew. She'd been so busy, so obsessed, she hadn't seen or heard her friend. "You're carrying a child," she whispered.

"Yeah. Some wild *rumspringa,* huh?"

"Does Jacob know? I'm certain your father doesn't."

"Jacob—not yet. And the bishop?" She gave a frenzied little laugh. "He'd have thrown me off *our* barn roof by now."

Rachel leaned out, down, closer to her friend. "You don't mean that, Sarah. You know this happens sometimes among our people. It just moves the wedding up. Remember Leah Yoder back home, and she was your cousin. It was frowned on, but everyone forgave..."

"Don't try to sweet-talk me, Rach. Leah wasn't me. What Jacob and the bishop's daughter with the sinful mother did even before we were betrothed—it's wrong!"

"But it happens," Rachel tried to calm her, "just like other things in life. A new baby's a blessing, too. Sarah, it's not the end of the world if you don't let it be." The words tumbled from her. "And I don't mean just by taking the coward's way out to fall and kill yourself and that baby who's trusting you and didn't do anything to deserve dying without a chance to be born first..."

Rachel stopped. Maybe talking tough was a risk. "It's Jacob's baby, too," Rachel added, her voice more quiet now, "so he has some say in this, and he loves you."

"Yeah, but I thought, in her way, my mother loved my father. You know," Sarah said with a huge sigh the wind ripped away, "I understand why you won't be my stepmother, but I was wishing you would be. Then I could get through missing *Mamm*, loving her but hating her for going. That note she left us, left Father...I only read it once before he tore it up, but it was so strange, so—not like her."

"Why don't you give me your hand and stand up real slow, and we can talk inside?" Rachel suggested.

Sarah didn't budge. Rachel shifted her feet to ease her back, and the boards bounced beneath her.

"You know," Sarah went on, her voice slower, "for a while I was hiding inside your barn, in the hay."

"I've done that. A barn's a great place for thinking and dreaming."

"But then when I looked down at everyone, I just climbed higher," she explained, sounding awestruck. "Outside the cupola, it was so pretty with the stars and the fresh wind and silence."

Rachel held her hand out, down in front of Sarah's face as the girl stared out into the night. Rachel feared the way she'd said that last word *silence,* as if she'd like to just drift or fall away into it.

Sarah remained still as a statue. Then she shifted to one side and turned and reached for Rachel's hand. "I don't want to be crazy with fear, Rach, not like *Mamm* must have been," her friend said so quietly the wind almost snatched the words away.

"Then get in here and take care of Jacob and that baby," Rachel said. "And you move real careful, till I can help pull you back in."

Balancing with both arms out, bracing her feet, Sarah scooted her back up the cupola. Rachel, one hand on the sill, reached out to wrap her free arm around Sarah's waist. Yes, she was slightly swollen with the baby already. What a selfish, stupid idiot she'd been, Rachel berated herself, so tangled in her own terrors she didn't even notice. She had to start looking at things, at everything and everyone, more closely.

"You're going to have to sit back on the sill," Rachel coaxed her. Sarah eased inside the cupola, one leg at a time. As if everyone had been holding their breath on the ground below, muted applause rose to their ears. Rachel and Sarah stood inside the cupola, hugging each other for a moment, together on the trembling boards.

"I'm sorry about how dangerous it is even inside here, Sarah," Rachel whispered, holding her hand to lead her down. "This barn needs some fixing, but then, we all do."

Sheriff Burnett hurried down from the loft ahead of the others to send the crowd home before they brought Sarah out. Rachel heard engines start and horses neigh. Almost everyone left, except for the Maplecreek kids she'd told the sheriff could spend the night. He soon returned to insist Sarah be taken to the hospital in Bowling Green for an examination. And he wanted her to promise to see a counselor.

"My daughter doesn't need any of that," Eben declared. "She'll sleep in her own bed tonight and not a coffin, thank God."

"And thank Jacob and Mrs. Mast for that," the sheriff put in as he went out, shaking his head. Rachel had seen him do much the same when Eben and the deacons had told him Sam's death was God's will and they didn't need investigators crawling around the barn. Now Eben hovered over Jacob and Sarah, who sat on a hay bale on the ground floor of the barn amid the ruins of the dance.

"Father," Sarah said, her voice amazingly steady as she looked up at him, "I want to talk to Jacob alone first."

"Good. Fine," Eben said, surprising them all. He

steered Rachel out of the double doors and around the side of the barn.

"What did she say up there?" he demanded. "Why did she do that, following in her mother's steps by shaming us all?"

"She needs to tell you herself," Rachel said, pulling the blanket she'd retrieved tighter.

"Then you talk to me. I didn't mean to say anything to upset her or you these last few days." It was hard to believe, Rachel thought, but his voice was almost apologetic. "You see how much Sarah needs you," he went on. "I do, too."

She gaped at him in the shadows. This was a completely different tone and tactic from what she'd expected.

"I thought," she said, "you might be on a mission to show me how much *I* needed *you*."

"What do you mean?" Eben tugged her right hand into his big, square one. The blanket slipped off her shoulders and fell away.

"For one thing, telling me Dan and Ben would help with my rye field, then changing things, taking the horses. Eben, let me just say what's bothering me most about these indirect marriage proposals from you. Your first wife obviously rebelled about having to move here and ran away, and now you're trying to court another wife who won't toe your line?"

He looked shocked and squeezed her hand so hard she flinched. "It wouldn't be like that, you and me," he insisted, almost stuttering in his eagerness. "I've learned how to deal with that now."

Rachel decided to hit him with the other argument. She knew better, but she was so exhausted and still angry—God forgive her—with this man. "How can you be certain Eben Mary is really dead so you can marry again?'' she demanded. ''What if she just ran off but is coming back someday?''

Surprising her again, he looked relieved. ''*Ach*, is that all that's worrying you?'' He shook his head hard. ''You know I had her declared dead.''

''In the church,'' she countered, ''but you didn't have the sheriff try to search for her, and she hasn't been declared *legally* dead.''

''Legally? The sheriff? You believe the worldly government's sheriff has a—a say-so—power or given authority over us plain folk?''

''It's called jurisdiction,'' she supplied the word he'd fumbled for. Frustration roiled through her again. His own wife's disappearance aside, Eben hadn't let the authorities investigate why that grappling hook had let go to kill Sam, at least not after their initial report. ''How can you be so sure,'' she plunged on, ''that on one hand Eben Mary's run off, then you turn around and have her declared dead in the church when you can't know—''

''I do know, or she would have come back by now!'' he thundered. ''She has no means to make a living. She would at least contact me and the children. No way she would be gone almost three years if she wasn't dead. Rachel, if you feel I've been indirect or stubborn or not attentive, forgive me and let's start over with a real, proper courting.''

When he squeezed her hand in both of his again, she was shocked to see she'd let him hold it all this time. She tugged back and shook her head to clear it, but he evidently read denial.

''Don't say no,'' he insisted, his voice cracking. ''Our union will solve all your problems. You and the boys move in with me while Dan finds a wife and works this place and—"

"*I'm* working this place," she cried, stooping to retrieve the blanket and waving it in a circle to encompass the farm. "Not Dan, not my brother-in-law's sons, not even the brethren like Sim Lapp who sacrificed to save it for me after Sam died."

"Talk about me acting strange over losing Mary Eben," he scolded, pointing a finger in her face. "Sam's dead for sure, but you're still acting like you've got a man hidden around here!"

In that moment, she was almost certain it was Eben who had somehow found a way to sneak into her barn to tamper with hats and horses.

"My union with you," she said, crushing the blanket in her arms, her voice cold and calm, "might solve my financial problems but it would create personal ones. Eben, I want to inform you that I've decided to get some barn repairs done by a worldly man, a barn rebuilder, in exchange for his using pictures of the barn in his advertising."

"Not graven images!"

"It's been done before back home. In his ads, this man won't say where the barn is or who owns it. And, I'm going to register this place with the state as an historic building. It's my barn, an Amish barn now, but it's also a part of America which has been good to us Amish."

Rachel stood, waiting for him to digest all she'd thrown at him. In the back of her mind, she felt that, if he could just accept that she could have an opinion and make a decision for this place, it might show she'd been wrong about him.

"A worldly woman, that's what you've become,"

Eben declared and spit at her feet, just missing her. His eyes seemed to blaze in the darkness. "Trust the sheriff," he mocked, raising his voice like a woman's. "Let this barn where Sam died—and Sarah almost did—be used for advertisement and registered by the state. Not to mention," he went back to his own ringing tones, "how you've ignored my previous advice about the twins being handed over to a worldly woman during the day. And an *Englische auslander* barn builder...you mean that man at the auction?"

Rachel leveled a long look at him, trying to read some sign he was desperate enough to try to scare her away from her own barn and land. She could apologize now, say she was just under duress, take back all she'd just said. But this *rumspringa* she'd been feeling was coursing through her very bones.

"Yes," she said, lifting her chin, "that's the man and that's what I mean to do."

"Then stay away from my Sarah until you have permission to do otherwise. As your bishop, I must warn you that you stand in danger of shunning for such unsanctioned attitudes and actions. I will discuss these matters with the deacons and let you know our ruling on the matter. And you just remember, Sam Rachel Mast, that 'Pride goeth before a fall and a haughty spirit before—*utter destruction.*'"

Shortly after she'd fed breakfast and bid farewell to the Maplecreek youngsters who'd stayed the night, Rachel answered a knock on the back door. Mitch Randall stood there, newspaper in hand. She read his face faster than she could read the headline he held up.

"It made the paper?" she asked, wiping her hands on her apron.

He nodded. "Needed barn repairs and all. Thank God, the girl is safe."

"Then you believe in God, Mitch?" She could tell she'd surprised him with the question; it wasn't what he'd expected right now. Yet it didn't seem to faze him.

"I never could grasp how someone who sees the intricate, interrelated beauty of the world could not." He looked a bit sheepish. "I used to argue with God a lot, but you bet I believe in him."

As if he'd given the secret password, Rachel wordlessly pushed open the door for him. She was in so deep with Eben now, anyway, she didn't even care that she was alone in the house this early. The twins, who had spent the night at Jennie's, were still there. Mitch had so barely missed the Maplecreek kids that she wondered if he'd seen them leave.

"Would you mind reading the article to me while I fix us some breakfast," she said, taking two more eggs out of their cardboard cradles. "I've been feeding guests and was just going to make myself some sausage and scrambled eggs. I'll just do it by feel," she rattled on with a nervous laugh, "since I can't find my glasses again. I only knew it was you at the door by your voice..."

Her own voice cracked; she cleared her throat. As she broke eggs into a bowl, Mitch came up behind her and put his hands on her shoulders to turn her slowly to him.

"Mitch, I can't," she protested breathlessly, then realized too late she'd presumed he would kiss her.

"I haven't said or done a thing—yet. I just want

to show you my glasses and why I don't lose them."
His hands, light on her shoulders, felt heavy and hot.
No, *she* was getting warm.

"You wear glasses?" she asked, grateful to talk
about something mundane. "Oh, you mean those
kind that float right in your eyes."

"Contacts. Look close in the window light," he
said and leaned down slightly toward her.

Rachel knew it was a ploy, to calm her, to get
close to her. She didn't care. Tipping her head so
their noses wouldn't bump, she lifted her face to his
and saw the clear disks floating in his dark brown
eyes. This close, she could see every black eyelash,
thick ones for a man. He still looked sleepy, slightly
heavy-lidded, unless that narrowing of his eyes and
flaring of his nostrils meant something else. For a
moment they breathed in unison, and Rachel almost
felt she was hanging over the barn roof again, leaning
out into the stars.

"I hadn't noticed them before," she whispered.

"You never got close enough. I'm sure these are
worldly and forbidden, but you ought to try them."

"I can't. Won't."

"I understand, but you may change your mind. I
admire your mind, Rachel—too."

Like an idiot, she nodded. He did not pull her
closer, but seemed to be propping her up, or maybe
both of them. They weren't touching anywhere else
besides his hands lightly cupping her shoulders, yet
Rachel felt as if they were.

"You realize this is not a good idea," she told
him, her voice a breathy whisper. "Our—close-
ness...it's impossible."

"Obviously not. Only impossible that we're both standing here so restrained."

"*That* look and feeling is restrained?"

He laughed and, to her mingled relief and grief, set her back. She thought he would embrace her, but he reached past her, took the bowl of broken eggs and began to beat them with the fork.

"Go find your glasses while I fix breakfast," he said. "We're going out to that barn, and I want you to be able to see exactly what I want to do with the cupola for starters, then we'll discuss the other plans."

Rachel hurried into the dining room, then stopped. Other plans? And men didn't fix breakfast. The *Englische auslander* was taking over her kitchen, not to mention her barn and life, too.

Ten

"Won't you get in trouble for not being in church this morning?" Mitch asked Rachel as they entered the barn after breakfast.

She almost told him she wasn't even sure she'd be welcome at church, at least by the bishop. "Our people have church every other Sunday, and this is the off week," she explained, silently grateful she didn't have to face Eben today. "We take turns meeting in houses. When Sam and I had it here the week before he died, we used the barn since the house wasn't big enough. Did that take a lot of straightening and scrubbing! It looks like it could use a bit of that now, too," she added almost wistfully as they surveyed the remnants of the interrupted dance.

After Sarah was safe, the sheriff had disbanded things, and a circle of hay bales still remained. Rachel had, however, dismantled the plank tables and returned the horses to their stalls. Now, starting with the Percherons, she began to fork hay into their feed bins, grateful some phantom had not beat her to it or hitched them up. She considered telling Mitch about all that, but decided to keep him focused on barn repairs. As she worked, she kept shoving her glasses he'd insisted she wear back up her nose.

"Here, let me help with the horses," he volunteered. "I'll feed Bett and Nann." He walked across the width of the threshing floor to their stalls and gave each a pat on her flanks. "Remember me from the day the buggy almost went off the road, girls?"

Rachel smiled as she watched him stab the second hay fork into a bale to loosen the straw. "Amish buggy horses are retired harness racers, you know," she told him. "Hey, I see you're pretty good at hay."

He grinned. "Is that an Amish pun? And I'm a farm boy from way back, remember?"

Rachel shook her head and filled the third bin. When she looked up, he had finished and was squatting in the far front corner of the barn, peering at something. Rachel put down her hay fork and went to look over his shoulder. He was watching Mira, the crippled cat, sleeping.

"I suppose I should let sleeping cats lie," he whispered, "but this one's in danger, because this pile of stuff someone put here could fall over on her."

He moved the heavy apple-butter paddle and a few other tools, which leaned against the wall next to the cat. Mira jerked awake. Looking thoroughly annoyed, she glared up at them.

"That's Mira, my favorite barn cat," Rachel told him. "Her back legs and tail are partly paralyzed from an accident—Sam's accident. I nursed her back to health and wished I could have done that for him..." Her voice faded. She yearned to spill the details about Sam's falling on the kitten when the grappling hook fell on him. *Accident...hook fell on,* her own words and thoughts haunted her again. Or was it more like *murder?* But to let Mitch repair the barn was one thing and to ask him to help fix her frustration and fear another.

"Great antiques," he observed, evidently changing the subject to help her out. "What's this funny hammer?"

"It's a knocker to get snow out of horseshoes. It was back in the sleigh, clear in the corner of the barn, so I guess someone moved it—probably the men setting up last night."

Her voice began to quaver. Amish men, setting up, she thought, all friends of hers and Sam's, moving things around...

"And this?" Mitch asked, lifting on its old rope a heavy, four-pronged metal hook about a foot high. "If you're still planning to go with me to see Lake Erie," he said, obviously trying to cheer her up, "we'll go fishing and use it for an anchor."

"That's a well hook," Rachel explained. Suddenly, it reminded her of the bigger hook, though this one didn't open and close like that and its prongs pointed up, not down.

Rachel felt short of breath; she fought for every word. "When folks used to accidentally drop something in a well, if it was important they'd have to retrieve it, but we don't have a well anymore so..."

As Mitch looked up at Rachel, the frayed rope broke and the hook thudded to the floor. It missed Mira, and she took off as best she could, flopping in the middle of the threshing floor on the same spot Rachel had found Sam's body, the spot she'd sanded and bleached to get the bloodstains out. She looked up into the depths where the huge grappling hook still hung suspended, well used without problems at this year's recent harvest.

"Sorry, Mira," Mitch said and started toward the cat. He bent toward the annoyed animal, hand out, as if to pet her. "I didn't mean to scare you."

Covering her face with her hands, Rachel burst into tears.

Rachel did not protest when Mitch sat on a hay bale and pulled her onto his lap. Like Aaron had held to her last week in the dark cellar, she clung to Mitch. All the pent-up grief and rage at losing Sam and just burying her doubts about his death poured out of her.

"You mean you suspect foul play?" Mitch finally asked. His voice vibrated against the top of her head where she'd tucked it under his chin. She sat up, shrugged, then nodded. There, she thought, she'd finally admitted it to someone. Mitch steadied her as she stood, wiping her face on her apron. He rose, too.

"By whom and why?" he pursued. "I mean, I get it that the Amish believe in forgiving and forging ahead and not bringing in outside authorities, but you couldn't just let it go, could you? It's been haunting you."

She startled at his choice of words. "Yes," she admitted. "For more than one reason."

If he pushed her, she knew she'd blurt out the latest odd events, but if he accepted this much and told her she wasn't crazy, that would be enough for now. "I know you're here to work on the barn," she told him, "but if I trust you for that, I think I can trust you to be impartial and hear me out, help me see something I may have missed about that day, what really happened to Sam here.''

"I'd be glad to," Mitch assured her, gently grasping her shoulders, then rubbing them as if to let his strength flow into her. "I'm surprised you haven't asked Jennie to help by now."

"At first, I didn't know her well enough and lately I've learned she has her own problems with her daughter's loss here. But I want to walk and talk my way through it again. Does that sound insane?"

"Sane as can be. I'll bet you didn't use Jennie, too, because she's in-laws with the sheriff, and he should have pursued Sam's death even if your people were against it. Rachel, I was going to work on the cupola floor today," he said with a glance upward, "but…"

His voice trailed off, and she saw he was staring up at the grappling hook. "What's with all those big knots in the rope?" he asked.

"Oh, it's always done like that," she explained. "Sam started it and the men who used it here for the recent harvest did, too. Those are double-hitches to make sure the ropes hold."

"But they didn't hold," he said, frowning. "Not when Sam died. Okay, let's talk about it and investigate the evidence, starting with the hook."

Rachel and Mitch climbed to the highest loft, where the sheriff had established his command post for Sarah's crisis last night. Mitch carried up planks to build a makeshift scaffold. Laying the two-by-fours across big beams, he crawled out on them to examine the metal-track-and-rope rigging for the hook.

"This pulley system would have been fully mechanized if it had been installed from the 1920s on," he explained, "but if it was working, why replace it? It just took someone to handle the ropes."

"That's exactly how we've done it, and I'll save you time by telling you the ropes look good," she said. "It was last used this mid-August during hay harvest. If you look outside in the barn peak above the haymow door, you'll see the track extends out there. The team hauls the full wagon under it, then we unhitch the horses and use their power on the rope to hoist up the hay in the hook. When the load is swung inside and hauled to the right place along the track, we use a trip rope to make the hook open its prongs to drop it in the loft wherever we want."

"And, when it's in use, these knots obviously aren't here?"

"Right."

"Do those ropes need to be controlled outside the barn?" he went on.

"Not necessarily," she admitted. "Someone could be inside, even up here in the loft where the ropes are coiled and knotted when they're not draped outside for use."

"I saw hay lifted once that way, years ago," he called over to her after they were both silent for a moment. "The guy who showed me had been in the navy, and he called this hook a harpoon fork. Actually, it was Gabe's father, who once farmed."

Though Rachel's memories of Gabe were good, she shuddered at the image the words *harpoon fork* evoked: a body impaled with it...floundering, wanting to flee...Sam on the floor...

Hugging herself, Rachel watched Mitch inch

along, sometimes on his back to check the stability of the boards supporting the metal track.

"I know it's totally functional," Rachel insisted again, "even if it is old and rusted. I heard that was in the sheriff's report, brief as it was—old, rusted, with some loose boards, but functional. And the ropes were sound."

"It's a report we should read," he muttered. "If you made a statement to him, we could read that, too—to refresh your memory."

"Yes. I didn't think of that."

"I suppose this track could have been shaken by the wind, causing the ropes to go slack," he reported as he got off the scaffold and clapped dirt from his hands. "But if these knots were here, I don't see how the rope could slide through and fall."

He went over in the loft to examine the hooks and knots that held the main rope taut; he jiggled the smaller trip rope. "And," he said with a shake of his head, "even if a strong wind could have made it drop, I doubt if it was stored with the prongs open."

"Never," she said, wishing she'd thought of that long ago. "Their weight would just force them closed. So," she reasoned out loud, starting to tremble even more, "even if it dropped by itself, someone had to get the knots out and pull the trip rope to make its jaws open."

"Unless the knots weren't there at the time and the jaws opened on their own when it fell. We can test that. And, as you said earlier," Mitch went on, "if Sam was unhitching the work team, why would he suddenly walk around the stalls and into the middle of the threshing floor right under it?"

"I've agonized over that more than anything," she

said. "Maybe he heard a sound, something kicked loose in the wind that fell inside the barn, or he heard an intruder. Or maybe he just went over to pick up the kitten, Mira, there." She pointed at the yellow ball of fur, now complacently licking herself on the barn floor. "Sam never regarded the barn cats as pets, but maybe he thought he should take her back to her mother in the loft, since she'd obviously wandered from the others in the litter here in this mow," she added, pointing just behind Mitch, "and fallen down to the floor."

"Maybe that's what injured her back legs before he fell on her. He also might have walked under the hook to get a good look if he noticed the safety knots were out of it," he surmised.

"Let's remember it was probably too dark to see," she said. Mitch was making her realize she should have asked someone for help with this puzzle long ago. She was grateful she'd waited for Mitch. He was objective and didn't have a personal stake in Sam's death.

"I'll wash up, and we'll walk through everything, if you're still sure about wanting to look into this," he said, his face stamped with concern.

"Yes," she said. "I'm sure."

"Clouds were coming in for the storm," Rachel narrated her recollections aloud to Mitch. "The wind was up, the sky darkening early, but Sam hadn't lit any lanterns in here. That wasn't unusual, since he knew the place by heart."

Mitch sat on a bale of hay on the threshing floor while Rachel stood just outside the doorway as she had on that stormy night over a year ago. She prayed silently that she'd remember what happened and not mix it up with the many nightmares she'd had about it. Already Mitch's help made her feel a huge weight had been lifted from her shoulders. Thank God, she finally had someone she could really trust with all this.

"Anyway," she went on, "when I got to this point, I had just sent Andy back into the house from where he'd been looking at a dead—a dead animal, a mole—outside the barn, the side over by the root cellar."

"That wouldn't be a possible entry for an outsider, would it?" he asked suddenly.

"No," she answered, shaking her head. "I checked it more than once for that very reason. But the vines outside are intact. As far as I could tell, the straw dust and excess grain from Nann and Bett's feed boxes was untouched in the cracks on the floor until Linc McGowan opened it to peek inside last week."

"So you have been agonizing over this in detail. You've tried to think it through alone."

Rachel nodded, her eyes suddenly tearing up.

"You sure you're okay with this?" Mitch asked.

In answer, she continued, "Andy said his dad had told him to run tell me he was nearly ready to eat supper. But after he sent Andy away, out comes Chester still bridled, so Sam must have been distracted from finishing up, or dead by then, that fast."

"Have you asked Andy what he remembers?"

"No," she said curtly. "He doesn't need to relive any of that, and he wasn't even four. Aaron was watching from the house door, but the same goes for him. No."

"I understand. So did you hear anything *before* the horse came out, other than rattling barn sounds from wind blowing through cracks and chinks?"

She startled at the details he provided, but then, of course, Mitch knew this barn. "Yes," she said, still standing in the doorway. "I heard Chester shuffle around, snort and hit something. It was a thud."

"You're sure it was Chester? And a thud like what?"

"I thought it was Chester. I don't know, but it was a heavy thud."

"You mean he knocked against the wall of his stall like he did today or another sort of thud? *How* heavy?"

"I don't know!"

Pressing her hands to her temples, Rachel tried to remember. That thud could have been the hook hitting Sam, but she couldn't bear to admit that. She had taken at least another five minutes looking around for him when she could have helped him, saved him.

"I don't know," she repeated, "but maybe it wasn't Chester hitting his stall."

"Okay. And the three sounds were in that order?" Mitch asked, leaning forward with his elbows on spread knees, looking straight at her. "Shuffle, snort, thud?"

"I'm not sure. I've thought this over so many ways it's hard to keep things straight."

"Go on then."

"I was surprised to see Chester loose, but I grabbed his bridle and led him back in."

"Did you talk to Chester, like on the road that day the paramilitary guys stopped you?"

"What does that matter?" she cried, smacking her hands at her sides.

"Rachel," he replied, getting up and coming toward her, "if you think there's foul play, doesn't that mean someone might have been inside who shouldn't have been? If you made some sounds, he, or she, might have heard you and reacted."

"You mean heard me and ran out."

"Or hid until he could escape later. I don't know."

"I'm sorry I'm so on edge," she apologized. "I'll go on."

He sat back down on the bale while she pretended to lead Chester in. "Yes," she said, "I remember now. I may have clucked to Chester, but I called out to Nann and Bett to calm them in the rising wind. And right before that, I called out to Sam for the first time."

Rachel stared wide-eyed as the memories came roaring back. She took her glasses off and jammed one earpiece in the neck of her dress so everything would be more authentic.

"I said," she whispered, "'Sam, you here?' and told him Chester got out. I don't know why I said it that way, because if Sam was in the barn—and I thought he was—he would know Chester got out."

"But he wouldn't have *let* Chester get out," Mitch said. "So, that was a definite hint he might have been down already. And then?"

"I called Sam's name again, maybe twice. I remember thinking the storm, or the distress in my voice, had spooked the horses, but maybe it was that they'd seen what had happened to him—that thud. Or they saw someone in the barn who shouldn't be here."

Her voice broke, but she mimed taking Chester's harness off and putting him back in his stall. "Then, I thought," she went on, walking slowly toward the center of the barn toward Mitch, "maybe Sam went out the back door for something and would be right back in. The wind, or something, banged it shut."

"Rachel," he interrupted, "you didn't have your glasses on then, either, did you?"

"No," she admitted. "No, so that could have limited what I saw, let alone the fact it was dim in here. I know I made some bad mistakes."

"I didn't say that," he countered, but his voice was excited. "Go on."

"Standing about here," she explained, miming her actions that night, "I ducked when the barn owl came flying in and just missed my head."

"You have owls in here?" he asked. "I haven't seen any."

"The pair of them took off the day Sam died. They used to nest way up on that beam in the loft," she said, pointing. "They usually flew in and out the high haymow door when it was open. I thought it was the fact the sheriff came in here and tramped around and disturbed their nest—someone did at least—that was why they didn't rebuild. Owls fly silent, you know, so their talons can get their prey without warning."

She had choked out those last words. Her emotions were devouring her thoughts again. Fearful she would cry when she wanted to get through this, she held up her palms to Mitch who rose from his seat to start for her.

"No, I'm all right," she insisted. "I called out Sam's name and *Wo bist du?*—Where are you? Then

I found him sprawled under the weight of that hook, his body pierced by three of its six tines and Mira's hind end under him. I was standing in blood, and I screamed. I flagged down a car on the road to get help, and Jennie drove to fetch the brethren. And then the bishop and the deacons told me it was God's will and they'd asked the police not to pursue it further. I've felt like screaming ever since.''

"Sam Rachel bears the blame for some of this," Eben insisted.

"No, Father," Sarah protested. She had been holding Jacob's hand as he stood beside her during their confession, but now she dropped it and fully faced Eben. "None of this is Sam Rachel's fault," she insisted, "except the fact I'm still alive this morning."

Eben snorted as he rose from his chair. "Don't you sass me," he ordered. "I think you even learned that from Sam Rachel."

Bishop Yoder began to pace the polished floor in the front room of their home where Sarah and Jacob had asked to talk to him this morning. Last night the girl had collapsed from exhaustion, but Eben had made Annie sleep in bed with Sarah to be sure she did herself no more harm.

Yet this morning, he thought, Sarah seemed different. Stronger in spite of the fact she'd just admitted carnal knowledge to her father and her bishop and would have to confess it to the congregation in church before he read the marriage ceremony to the two of them next Sunday. The wedding had been moved up; no way was more time going by with his grandchild growing in her. At least their intentions had already been published, and the brethren knew they'd been promised since before her mother took off. He began to pace even faster.

"Sam Rachel's been fence jumping," he tried to explain, "working like a man, making decisions like one, too, breaking rules, ignoring the *Ordnung*." The *Ordnung* was the set of written rules that held each Amish community together. "My boy," he addressed Jacob, "you just be sure Sarah doesn't fall more under Sam Rachel's spell."

Jacob nodded, twisting his hat brim even more nervously in his hands. Sarah stood her ground, reminding him of Rachel when she'd faced him down last night, or of her own mother when she'd defied him about moving here to Clearview. Eben Mary had even challenged him that he wasn't acting on God's will for their lives but on his own.

"Whether or not," Eben went on, scowling, "Sam Rachel is a bad influence on you, daughter, I can't fault her entirely, since your own mother acted as she did. But I have told Sam Rachel to stay away from you, uh-huh. That includes she is not welcome at church at the Lapps' Sunday for your wedding, and you need not go near her to tell her so."

"She'll not be shunned!" Sarah cried, pressing her palms to her flushed face. "For what?"

"Jacob, I expect you to deal with this now," he ordered, shaking a finger in Sarah's direction. Jacob put his arm around her shoulders to steady her. "No, Sam Rachel Mast is not shunned," Eben explained calmly, rationally, "but I must counsel and consider some sort of sanction, perhaps the six-week warning for her to mend her ways."

Sarah looked so astounded or distraught, he wasn't sure, that she gaped at him like a fish sucking air. It was a good thing, Eben thought, that final justice

pronounced against Rachel Mast must come from the
brethren and from God, not only from him.

"Jacob and Sarah, I'll read your wedding ceremony after church on Sunday," he plunged on, "after your confession. The church supper will have to
do for your wedding meal."

"Fine," Sarah said, clenching her hands at her
sides. Jacob put a staying hand on her elbow, as if
he feared more was coming. "I will be proud to
marry Jacob on Sunday, Bishop Yoder," Sarah went
on, "as I should have done years ago when he first
asked me. As for Rachel at my wedding, since she
is not shunned but is still not welcomed there by my
father *and* the bishop," her voice rose in pitch, "if
I can't have my mother nor my best friend—"

"All right!" Eben exploded, shocking himself,
both that he lost control and was going to give in.
He frowned at his prodigal daughter. "So be it that
Sam Rachel will be there, Sarah. Consider it my
wedding gift to you on top of all the rest. Jacob, you
invite Sam Rachel, as your intended has plenty to do
before Sunday."

Eben tugged his shirt cuffs down under his coat
sleeves and took out his watch to glance at it. "Besides," he added, "it would do Sam Rachel good to
hear the sermon Sunday. But you can also tell her,
Jacob," Eben intoned, "that time is ticking. She's
been skating hard and fast on melting ice and, if she
persists in her disobedience to the *Ordnung*—not to
me, it has nothing to do with me—she's going to fall
right through."

"Let's make a list," Mitch told Rachel, "of things
we need to do. First, test this grappling hook to see
if, when it falls, it opens its prongs of its own accord."

She nodded, perched beside him on the bale of hay while he jotted notes on his clipboard paper.

"I'll talk to the sheriff and read his report," Mitch added.

"I'll try talking to Andy about what he remembers," she said, her voice almost a whisper, "but I hate to do it after all this time. I just hope it doesn't set him back."

"And you said Aaron was watching from the doorway of the house when you finally ran for help that night. Ask if he remembers seeing something strange, like someone who could have run out the back barn door heading for the road or woodlot."

Rachel's head snapped around to stare at him. Again, she almost told him she thought someone had been spying on her from the woodlot, but instead she protested, "But it was dark, and the boys were so young. Do you remember things that happened when you were four?"

"Only the traumatic things. I know you want to protect them, Rachel, but it's worth a try."

"All right. And I want to talk a little more to some of the brethren who were first to arrive here when word got out," she said, not mentioning she had those more recent incidents to probe with them. Sim Lapp, she thought, had been the first here and the first she should question.

"Good," he said, smacking a hand on his knee. "Then we have a plan. The other thing, of course, you need to do—if you think someone could have done this to Sam, and it looks at least probable—is figure out a motive. Rachel, who hated him or wanted what he had?"

Eleven

Mitch sat in his truck the next morning in Clearview, staring at the small sheriff's office across the street. Looking like a storefront, it was nothing like city hall in the county seat, where his grandpa had killed a man, but ever since, Mitch had felt an instinctive mistrust—actually, a roaring hatred—of government and law enforcement. Of course, three years in the state pen at Marion didn't help, either. But for Rachel and his own reasons, he was going to march in there and ask Sheriff Burnett to let him read the report on Sam Mast's death.

Mitch got out slowly and scanned the little town, all two business blocks of it. Some buildings were derelict; if he was into saving old commercial structures, he'd have a field day here. But thanks to the infusion of Amish into this area, Clearview was making a comeback. The plain people couldn't drive into Bowling Green or Toledo to shop, nor did they want to. Their growing presence would never revive the closed Rialto movie theater, the ladies clothing emporium, or the second gas station. But the lumber store, which doubled as a hardware store, was booming. A SuperMart and two restaurants had reopened lately, though Mitch couldn't understand, with great Amish cooking, why the Amish would ever want to eat out. He was sick of restaurants and, however many barns he saved, he was tired of loss in his life.

A bell jingled on the door of the sheriff's office when he walked in. *Mayberry R.F.D.,* he told himself, half expecting to hear that down-home, whistled TV theme song and see lawmen played by comedians. Maybe this wouldn't be as bad as he'd thought. This place was a pretty remarkable antique compared to the state-of-the-art prison he'd been entirely too intimate with.

He shuddered. Never would he be caught doing anything to get sent back there. He'd been real careful about that, but Rachel's plight was starting to make him feel reckless: the sheriff should have investigated Sam's death, no matter what the Amish leadership said.

Mitch greeted and shook hands with Sheriff Tim Burnett, the only one in the office. Two other desks sat cluttered but empty.

"So what can I do for you?" Burnett asked amiably. "Wondering who owns some barn site again?"

"No, Sheriff, though I'm working on repairs for the Mast pioneer barn on Ravine where that Amish girl almost jumped. I hope you can do me and Mrs. Mast a favor. She's asked me to read through the report on her husband's death for her."

"That right?" he asked, running a hand through his military haircut. Tim Burnett was as skinny as a scarecrow, though, Mitch noted, it appeared he'd been systematically going through a half-dozen powdered doughnuts at his desk. "The near catastrophe got her thinking about her own?" Burnett asked.

"Time's just cleared her head a bit."

"Hmmph. Amish are the reason I closed up the case so fast," the sheriff said, indicating Mitch should take the chair at the front desk while he stepped back to the rows of file cabinets behind his own. A computer sat on a back table, its screen dark. Maps were tacked on one wall, and a radio, probably turned to a highway patrol band, crackled in the background.

"Amish folk done a lot to bring Clearview back," Burnett went on as he opened one file drawer, banged it shut, then pulled out another. "So didn't want to rile them with a big-deal investigation when their leadership asked me to lay off. Don't question God's will and all that. And they sure as heck aren't going to press charges, anyway."

"But you did look into the death?"

"Some, sure. Actually, more than they knew, but that barn, as you oughta know, is rickety in spots and could have dropped that big old hook in the near gale we had that night. I looked around good out there and saw no proof of foul play, and like I said, the Amish are getting to be a force—a good force—'round here."

He fished out a thin manila folder and smacked it on the desk in front of Mitch. "You just tell Mrs. Mast if she wants this formally reopened, she needs to come in here herself. And tell her she'll have to handle her Bishop Yoder and that one deacon—ah, Simeon Lapp—if they get ticked off at me."

"It sounds as if you understand the Amish well, Sheriff," Mitch said, grateful at how the man was cooperating when he'd expected foot-dragging and arguments.

"Not really," he said with a sigh as he sat back at his desk and took a swallow of coffee. "It's hard to sympathize with folks who only educate their kids through eighth grade, won't serve in the armed forces, don't have to pay taxes and don't think they need legal authority. But they got all that squared with the government, so far be it from me to rock any boats. 'Sides, Sam Mast's death prob'ly was a freak accident. Tree limbs and wires went down everywhere that night. I got calls galore."

Which could have made the sheriff slight this investigation, Mitch thought. "I'm sure you feel you're caught between the Amish and some of the others around here, like those weekend warriors just over the county line." Mitch almost told him how the two paramilitary guys had harassed Rachel, but he decided not to muddy the waters right now.

Burnett snorted a laugh. "Yeah. Talk about opposite ends of the violence spectrum. Those guys think they're getting ready to fight a race war or barricade themselves in when all the computers stop at the millennium. See," he added, gesturing with a half-eaten doughnut toward his computer, "I got that solved. Just turn the damn thing off. But, yeah, some folks here'bouts don't think the Amish are so cute and quaint."

"Hopefully, the plain and gentle people will win them over," Mitch said, opening the folder.

"Yeah," Burnett said, finishing off the doughnut and talking with his mouth full. "Sounds like at least one 'a them done that to you."

* * *

The police file started with a detailed—and hand-written, for Pete's sake—report about the status of the death scene. Mitch also tried to decipher the scribbled interview the sheriff had had with Rachel two days after Sam Mast's funeral, when who knows what she'd forgotten or been told not to say. Yet, Mitch noted, it read in detail much like what she'd told him. Evidently, no one had thought to, or been allowed to, talk to the twins, and he wasn't going to bring it up with the sheriff right now.

Burnett's daughter, Marci Morgan, who worked at the beauty parlor down the street, had stopped in, as she put it, between cuts. Her voice was high-pitched and kept doing its own job cutting right through Mitch's reading and reasoning. Worse, she wore some sort of perfume or powder that fumigated the place.

Mitch shifted in the hard chair and tried to focus. The coroner's report was brief. He had wanted to perform an autopsy, but Amish outcry had kept that to a brief external examination of the body before it was handed over to a Bowling Green funeral home for embalming and was then sent to the Mast house for the private viewing and funeral. Samuel Mast had died of a crushed skull from the weight of the grappling hook—the coroner had even sketched the thing—and from internal injuries to vital organs from being pierced by three metal prongs. By the time the coroner had been called to the scene, the victim had pretty much "bled out," but he had obviously died instantly, the report said.

Newspaper clippings from various Ohio newspapers made up the rest of the report. Except for different headlines and leads, they were identical, borrowed, no doubt, from each other on-line.

Mitch looked up at the sheriff and his daughter. Perched on the edge of his desk, eating her dad's last doughnut, Marci was as wiry as her dad. She wore her brown hair long and curly. Her considerable makeup made her look older than she must be. Over black slacks, she sported a blue smock with *Marci, The Hairport* embroidered on the back, like that bowling shirt Gabe sometimes wore with his name and team.

"Excuse me, Sheriff," Mitch said. "No formal written request from the Amish to cease and desist the investigation?" He had wanted to see the way the request was worded and if it was signed by the bishop and that deacon the sheriff had mentioned.

"No way," Burnett said, looking up from a giggly story Marci was telling about her two-year-old. "Their word is their bond and mine is, too."

"Good enough," Mitch said, tapping the materials together and replacing them in the folder. "I really appreciate your help."

"A report about that girl almost jumping?" Marci asked, producing an emery board and attacking a crimson fingernail.

"Naw," her dad said. "That old case at the Mast barn, the farmer's death, not Laura's going missing."

Mitch rose but turned back at the door. "That's right," he said, looking at Marci, "Laura Morgan would have been your sister-in-law."

"I knew her in high school but married Kent after she died," Marci said, filing her nail faster. "But I wish Daddy could just keep looking for her, at least in his spare time, even if she disappeared years ago.

I mean, Kent would probably kill me for saying this because it would only get his mother all stirred up again, but a lot of cold cases are being solved these days.''

"Got the terminology down, don't you, honey?" Burnett asked proudly. "Marci's always been after my job, telling me what to do," he explained to Mitch and grinned when Marci playfully punched his shoulder. "She's my own little ambulance chaser.''

"I didn't read all those Nancy Drew books for nothing, and I just used to love Remington Steele on TV," Marci said, pocketing her nail file as she slid off the desk.

"Yeah, well," Burnett said, rising and shoving his hands in his pants pockets, "real life is not books and TV, honey. There was no trace of Laura Morgan, no ransom call, and we checked everybody out who so much as ever breathed in her direction, every kid and teacher in that high school. And her folks never pushed me any more on this than the Amish did on Sam Mast's case, so that's that. You just let your old dad handle everything here.''

Marci kissed Burnett's cheek, and Mitch held the door for her as she bounced past. Her fragrance nearly knocked him over. "Thanks again, Sheriff," he called, then lowered his voice outside on the sidewalk. "I've met your little boys," he told Marci. "I know your husband, too. He's been really helpful with advice on lumber.''

"Just don't tell him I'm after Daddy to reopen his sister's case," she said, rolling her eyes. "He's finally put her to rest, unlike his mom, though his dad never mentions it—well, all of them try to avoid the topic. Besides, if you don't tell, that way it won't get

around to the wrong people—people in plain black,''
she said emphatically, "that you're playing detective,
too.''

Marci Morgan sauntered away. He had, in a way,
he realized, just been threatened.

"Do you remember anything about the day *Daadi*
went away?'' Rachel dared to ask Aaron and Andy
as she tucked them in bed. She held her breath when
they looked at each other and didn't answer. "I don't
mean it has to be bad or scary things,'' she added.
"Good things, too.''

"I just want him back,'' Aaron declared, tugging
the covers up to his chin. "*Mamm*, Jennie says the
kind of beds we sleep in are called twin beds. Is that
why we have these beds?''

At least, Rachel thought, Aaron had just changed
the subject, whereas Andy now stared at her with that
all-too-familiar look that had so often shut her out.

"Andy…'' She said his name in a way that was
half command and half question.

"I don't want to talk now,'' he said and rolled
over with his back to her and Aaron. He muttered
something else.

Rachel touched his shoulder. "What did you
say?'' she asked.

"Nothing,'' Andy whispered. "We're 'sposed to
go to sleep. You said so.'' His little shoulder felt like
stone. Still, she ruffled his hair and rubbed his back
a moment, then Aaron's.

In the hall, moments later, Rachel leaned against
the wall and waited to see if they would get up to
look out the window toward the barn as she knew
they had other nights. Nothing. No sounds but house

noises. She was getting a little crazy, she scolded herself, suspecting her own kids, and of what?

Tiptoeing, she went downstairs. It was, she told herself, just this sudden passionate pursuit of Sam's death that had really rattled her. Monday evening Mitch had interrupted repairs on the cupola floor and they had run a test on the grappling hook by letting it fall into a scarecrow they'd placed on the ground. It had taken every ounce of self-control Rachel had to get through that. In three tries, the heavy hook had never once opened its prongs as it crashed into the dummy. The fourth time, from the loft, Mitch had opened it with the trip rope and it had thudded to the floor exactly as it had crushed Sam.

Rachel sat with a cup of hot chocolate at the kitchen table, trembling, trying to calm herself. There was no way she was going to try questioning her boys again. She gripped her cup tighter when she heard the lonely wail of the first evening train on the tracks out beyond the fields and woodlot. Each time the train went by, she thought not only of Sam's taking the boys against her wishes to see it pass, but of Elias Beiler, her childhood love from home.

If Elias had lived—if he had not been such a dreamer in the *rumspringa* he went through without her, for he was three years older—if he had not decided to hop that train to see the world and got his foot caught and been dragged to nothingness, while she screamed and screamed...

Rachel jumped up and slammed her cup down on the counter by the sink. Outside harassment was nothing compared to her own thoughts tormenting her like this. Arms straight, head down, she steadied herself at the sink.

After Elias's death, which no one but her sister Susan had ever known Rachel had witnessed after she had sneaked out to wave goodbye to him, she hadn't cared what happened to her. She'd lost herself in reading and agreed to be a teacher and worked hard enough at that to drown her loss, her own bad dreams. When Sam, her neighbor whom she'd put off for several years, had doggedly courted her and said he loved her, she'd said fine and was his wife almost before she knew what had hit her—like the train that had hit Elias.

As the whistle sounded again, Rachel looked out the window toward the tracks she could not see from here. She gasped. As if her longing or regret had summoned Elias or Sam, she saw a man silhouetted against the barn.

She stepped sideways out of view of the window, hurried to the back door and peered out. Yes, a man, and not one trying to run or hide. He was standing at the closed and latched barn door, but then he lifted his hand to the latch.

Her heart started to thud, her palms began to sweat. Her knees got weak. If it wasn't for the fact someone had tampered with her horses, she would have stayed barricaded in the house, but she had to do something to scare him off. What if he was the one who had taken the team out last time and run them in the field?

Rachel picked up a broom, then decided the bat the boys used for stickball would be easier to swing. God help her, she would do no violence, but she needed something to make him leave. For the second time in her life, she wished for a telephone in her house to call for help.

Not wanting to make herself a target, she left the lantern inside, opened the back door and peered out carefully. It had been eating at her that those two men in the Jeep had been here the night Sarah was on the roof. No, as far as she could tell, there was no second man. Could Mitch have come back for something he left and didn't want to startle her?

She didn't go far from the door in case she needed to run back to it. Lifting the wooden bat, she called out, "Who are you? That barn is closed for the night!"

"Mrs. Mast?" the voice, one she didn't recognize, said. "It's Mike Morgan, ma'am. I didn't mean to upset you. I know I'm trespassing, but I just had to come."

Jennie's ex-husband. Rachel had seen him several times in town with his new wife but had never spoken to him. He worked at the Willys Jeep plant in Toledo as some kind of foreman, so, with his hour commute both ways, he wasn't around during weekdays in town. She saw now he had parked his car at the bottom of the driveway.

"You did startle me," she said, peering through the dark at him as he slowly approached. He carried some sort of small sack.

"I see I did," he said, gesturing toward her raised bat with his free hand. "Sorry. I guess I was being sneaky, but I didn't want you to tell Jennie I was at your place. After I read about that girl almost getting hurt here the other night," he went on, his words tumbling out now, "I finally got the guts—sorry, ma'am—the courage to come back to where Laura was last seen."

"You haven't been here for a long time?"

"Since my—our—daughter disappeared. The place haunts me. But now, I had to face it."

Rachel nodded, feeling instantly sorry for him. Even in the gray swathe of night, Mike Morgan was a handsome, but sad-looking man. Rachel had overheard someone in town say Jennie still loved him, but she'd never said so, never said much more about him than she had about Laura, as if he had just disappeared, too. But Rachel knew Kent and his family saw Mike, and Kent and Marci's youngest had been named for him.

"If you'd like me to fetch a lantern for you, you can go inside," Rachel offered.

"I don't know," he said with a sniff, looking back at the barn. The paper sack crinkled in his hand and, from the way he held it, Rachel wondered if it was a bottle of liquor. "But I'm this far now after all this time. Sure, I'd appreciate that, ma'am."

Rachel handed him a lantern out the back door and waited while he went inside the barn. He left the door slightly ajar. She could see the light move through the big building, faintly etching the cracks in the boards. Mike Morgan evidently went across the threshing floor, then paused on the right side of the barn near where the Percherons were stabled. The light didn't move for so long that she wondered if he, like other strangers, was simply standing in awe at their size and strength.

Mike Morgan came out at last. He still had the sack, but it was wadded in his fist.

"She would have been twenty-seven today," he whispered. "I left some roses inside in Laura's memory. Is that all right?"

"Of course, Mr. Morgan. More than all right. And I won't tell Jennie if that is your wish."

"My wish..." His voice faded as he turned away into the night. "Thanks again," he called to her.

The next morning when Linc McGowan arrived and asked to see the barn again, Rachel was afraid he'd ask her who had left the roses. But she found Mike Morgan had put them too close to Cream's stall and the horse had chomped them down, thorns and all. Only a naked stalk and one crimson petal had survived.

"At least we won't have to apply for a grant if you're getting necessary repairs in trade for Randall's publicity shots," Linc told Rachel, though she could tell his feathers were still ruffled that she'd listened to Mitch instead of him.

"Then we are agreed," she said.

"Precisely. Especially since that girl climbed up there and could have fallen through those rotten boards, let alone from the roof. But all that aside, I've got some fascinating information to tell you after researching your barn." Linc sounded amazingly exuberant and looked so well rested he made Rachel feel as if she'd gone through her own washing-machine wringer. Lack of sleep and stress were wearing her temper thin.

"Do you mind if I water and feed the horses while you talk?" she asked.

"Absolutely not, go ahead," Linc said, looking a bit upset despite that denial. He pulled his creased pant legs up and perched gingerly on a bale of straw. "I've made a copy for you, anyway. Let me start with the pioneer family that owned the place originally, as far as my reading so far shows. Are you listening?''

''Yes, Professor,'' she said with a nod.

''All right then. The 1840 census records that the farmer, Thomas Wharton, did horseshoeing in the winter months and got kicked in the head by a horse and died.''

''In this barn?'' Rachel cried, sloshing water from a bucket, drenching the straw. Bett whickered and shook her head. Still holding the bucket, Rachel leaned back against the stall.

''My first fear exactly. I was starting to think there was a curse on the place, too,'' Linc said, looking smug, evidently pleased he finally had her full attention. ''But Wharton's demise occurred at the blacksmith shop in Clearview that eventually, circa 1928,'' he added, glancing at his notes, ''became the first gas station in these parts, but that's getting way ahead of my story.''

Thank God, Rachel thought, no one else had died here. She didn't want to so much as hear the word *curse* any more than she wanted to think this place was *haunted*. It wasn't, except maybe in her and Jennie and Mike Morgan's hearts.

''So, here's the part you'll really relate to,'' he told her as Rachel bent back to her work. ''The widow— one Varina Wharton—ran this farm by herself for several years until she evidently remarried and ran off with a local man, named Stephen Keller, whom some back then must have considered a ne'er-do-well.''

''A widow?'' Rachel echoed. ''Mr. Keller probably had wanderlust and she loved him enough to pull up stakes and go with him.'' She was thinking of

Elias Beiler again. "But why would she leave this fine farm? I guess she wanted the money more. Did she sell it to the Brickers' ancestors?"

"Yes and no," he said, frowning at her spate of questions. "Mrs. Wharton's departure was their entree, but strangely enough, she must have eloped without selling the place first, so it just fell to her distant relatives, the Brickers. Anyhow, I've got the rest laid out here for you, but let me run through a few things..."

He lectured on as though she were the most avid class of students. Yes, she did relate to a widow running the farm by herself and loving a man enough to risk changes in her life. But to run off and leave all this she'd fought so hard to keep...? Rachel wondered if the widow Wharton once had children to protect and felt alone and afraid. But surely she'd wed Stephen Keller because he warmed her heart and heated her blood and not because it seemed the smart, maybe the only, thing to do.

"Now to the timely things, considering Halloween's not far away," Linc droned on. "Amazing old superstitions, enough to get a good article for the local history magazines or even the paper."

"If you write it, just don't mention which barn," Rachel murmured, going back to carting water for the horses. If Linc kept up his spiel while she was out of earshot, that was fine with her, she thought. But he waited for her to come back in.

"Just two quick points," he added, jabbing his index finger on his notes. "Very few early barns were painted, but yours is done in homemade red paint. The recipe—iron oxide, milk, lime juice, and linseed oil. It sometimes contained glue made from cow hooves. But here's the thing. They also mixed animal blood with it to deepen the color. Sounds like something for an ancient sacrificial rite, doesn't it?''

"You know," Rachel said, her stomach churning, "I think for this early in the morning, I'd rather read this rather than hear it."

"Just one more thing. I know your Pennsylvania Dutch Amish relatives use hex signs on barns—*hexe* means witch in German, as you know."

"If you're going to say hex signs ward off evil, you're hundreds of years behind times," Rachel interrupted, putting down her bucket with a clunk. She wanted Linc to stop and go away. "Hex signs are strictly decoration now, Mr. McGowan, 'just for pretty' as the people say. And the Ohio Amish don't use them."

"Hear me out," he remonstrated, his voice almost condescending. "I read in German folklore that white lines around the barn door and trim keep the devil out. And you might know with this bloodred paint on your barn, some long-dead soul painted all your trim black. I don't believe in curses, of course, but if I did, this barn would be a prime candidate for one."

The unsettling nonsense about the barn wasn't the only thing Linc McGowan left her with when he got back in his car and drove away, proud of himself for all his research. Rachel glanced down at the copy of the information he'd left for her, but noted something else was paper-clipped to it.

She lifted the typed page to find two newspaper articles. The first one, Barn Rebuilder Pulling Down

History, was by Lincoln McGowan. Well, she thought, she'd asked him for that article about Mitch.

But the other, which had been copied in slightly blurry black ink, read, Local Man Sentenced to State Pen! Battered Toledoan in Bar Brawl.

Twelve

〜❦〜

"Intent to kill!" Rachel cried.

Hunched over the kitchen table, she read the article about Mitch's trial. The charges had been something called "atrocious assault and battery." At his trial Mitch was sentenced to three years in prison.

She read so fast through it that everything seemed jumbled. But what was clear was that Mitchel Randall had beaten up a State Department of Transportation official so badly that the man had fallen backward and hit his head on the corner of a bar and almost died.

"Three years for that," she whispered, horrified. She pressed her eyes tight shut. "If he had died, Mitch could still be in jail in the—" she opened her eyes and glanced down again "—the Marion Correctional Institute in Marion, Ohio."

Guilt crashed through her. Here she was, feeling for Mitch and not for that poor man he had hurt. And she'd been thinking selfishly that, if the man had died, she would never have known Mitch Randall. Born and bred Amish, she was acting every bit English and worldly.

Rachel skimmed the article again, making herself read slowly over the worst of it. *Drinking...fighting...bare fists...unprovoked attack...atrocious assault...intent to kill.* And Gabe had evidently tried to protect Mitch, so the state prosecutor had treated Mitch's friend, that smiling, sweet man, as "a hostile witness." Neither man was what he seemed to be.

Her mind darted to all those dreadful days Mitch had been locked up in a cell. Had he been able to picture the spacious barns he loved, to see on the blank wall an escape of clouds and waves on a great lake, as he had imagined in the grains and knots of her barn wood? At least this was an old newspaper article, ten years old, so he'd been out for a while, making his own way and perhaps mending his ways.

Though it didn't excuse Mitch, she figured she knew what had happened. That man he'd violently abused must have had something to do with his grandfather losing his farm, and after all, he was patterning his vigilante sense of justice after what his own grandfather had done so disastrously.

Jumping up, Rachel hid the article under the sugar jar and dashed upstairs to wake the boys. She didn't want to be here when Mitch stopped by this morning to check on the new pile of wood and make his plans to come back later. She couldn't face him right now and wasn't ready to ask him about all this. Besides, now more than ever, Rachel wanted to prove to herself she could solve Sam's death—his murder—on her own, without Mitch Randall.

She jerked to a stop halfway upstairs. Now that she'd finally admitted Sam had been murdered, she might as well admit her other fear. She was attracted to a potentially violent and definitely dangerous *Englische auslander,* and a relationship with him would mean shunning by and separation from her people. Rachel plodded the rest of the way upstairs and down the hall to the boys' room.

"Get up, lazybones of mine," she called out to rouse them. "After breakfast, we're going to tell Jennie you can't stay with her this morning. We have a little trip to make to town."

"To town?" Aaron repeated excitedly, sitting up while Andy opened his eyes but just stared at her. "Together, *Mamm?*"

"That's right. Just us, together."

"All right, here we go!" Jennie Morgan told her grandsons.

"Just like in that old cowboy movie, Gramma," Jeff shouted.

Rachel had ended up with Jennie and all four boys in the buggy. She couldn't turn her friend down when she'd asked if they could go along, not after all Jennie had done for her. Over the last, long year, Rachel had shared so much. Some folks needed a worldly psychiatrist; Rachel had Jennie.

Her friend sat on the buggy seat beside Rachel with little Mike on her lap and the other three boys in the back seat. It was brisk and windy enough today that they wrapped blankets around their legs.

"Just so Kent and Marci don't mind their boys taking a buggy ride," Rachel said as she giddyaped Bett and Nann.

"It's only into town. I'll deal with Kent, and he'll deal with Marci," Jennie assured her. "I've got to get a few things at the store and the boys can even pop in to see their dad at the lumberyard, maybe their mom at the beauty shop, too.''

General cheering swelled from the back seat.

''So you have a lot of errands to run?'' Jennie asked as the buggy rolled down Ravine Road toward town.

''Just one,'' Rachel said as she edged the horses over to let a car pass. ''I haven't been in the library since Sam died, but I think something to read will help me now.'' All that was true, she assured herself; she wasn't exactly lying. Besides, she'd confide in Jennie soon about looking into Sam's death. Rachel sure couldn't tell anyone Amish.

''Hmm,'' Jennie said. ''Is there such a thing as self-help Amish books?''

Rachel smiled tightly. ''The Bible is that for us, but I'm interested in a lot of things.''

''Not a barn-repair book?'' Jennie pursued as if she sensed there was something Rachel was hiding. ''Exactly what is Mitch Randall going to work on after the cupola floor and louvers?''

Rachel turned to look at her friend. During the whole conversation Jennie had been staring off into the passing fields, and Rachel couldn't see her face. But Rachel didn't want to discuss Mitch in front of the twins right now. Despite how they'd taken to Gabe, Aaron had been distressed more than once that Mitch had sat in *Daadi*'s chair or, despite the fact he liked to watch Mitch work, that he was spending too much time up in the barn where *Daadi* ''liked to be.''

''How did you know what specific repairs Mitch is doing?'' Rachel asked Jennie.

She shrugged. ''He'd have to start with that cupola after the near catastrophe,'' she said, still not looking at Rachel. "And Kent's supplied him with the wood, so I guess he must have mentioned something, too."

Rachel scolded herself for being overly suspicious of everything and everyone lately. Jennie was probably touchy because yesterday had been Laura's birthday and, unlike her ex-husband, who at least had done something to let his pain out, Jennie held everything in. Though Rachel had promised Mike Morgan last night she wouldn't tell Jennie he'd been to the barn to leave flowers in Laura's memory at the last place she was seen, she felt guilty about keeping things from her friend.

"Mitch is going to shore up a couple of beams," Rachel said. "He mentioned future roof and floor repairs, too."

Jennie's head snapped around. "If he does all that, he might as well be redoing the whole thing. And this is all in return for a few photo ops?"

"Photo whats?" Rachel countered, giving Jennie a little shake of the head while darting her eyes back toward the boys.

"Opportunities," Jennie muttered portentously.

"Here we are!" Jeff called from the back seat as Ravine Road met Main Street. This time the boys' excitement suited Rachel's desire to cheer herself up. After all, she was going to step back into a place she loved. Sam had resented her visiting the library, but since she was determined to find clues about who killed him, surely he would not begrudge her a little visit now.

"Rachel Mast," a familiar voice boomed from behind a library bookcase. "I haven't seen you in ages. About time you came back! Where are the twins?"

"I wanted to bring them in to say hello, but they voted to visit the lumber store right now," Rachel explained, smiling at the librarian through a hole in a row of books.

Once inside the narrow, two-room library, Rachel felt her breathing and heartbeat slow. She loved the smell of paper, even this sort of homey dust, the feel of books in her hands, the pages and pictures that could make her fly away from troubles and temptations—or lead her to them. Putting her glasses on, she closed the door behind her. As was common this early on a weekday morning, the place looked deserted. It had always been her favorite time here.

Pat Perkins, the librarian Clearview shared with another small town nearby, stepped out in view, arms cradling a stack of books. Twenty years older than Rachel, Pat was a widow like herself, but one who had returned to college to get her library degree. She was always telling Rachel she had a good mind and should go to college someday, too, which showed, Rachel thought, the well-read researcher knew zilch about the Amish. Though Pat was only the second librarian Rachel had known, she realized instinctively the woman was not the typical kind.

Pat Perkins was six feet tall and bigger-boned and stronger than most men in town; she made the women of the area, Amish or English, look bland and pale. Pat had once called herself an Amazon, then had to explain to Rachel that didn't mean she came from South America. Her severely cut, fire-engine-red hair framed four different jeweled rings piercing each earlobe. The colors of her clothing, today grass green and bright pink, were as brash as her nature and loud voice. And Rachel had heard, but not seen till now, she had a diamond stud right through her nose. Yes, there it was, though Rachel tried not to stare. It was a good thing she didn't have the twins with her, because who knew what they would have blurted out.

"I'm sure you know that things changed when Sam died," Rachel explained, floundering for an excuse why she hadn't been back for over a year. "I've been extra busy, but I'm glad to be here now, and I'd like a book on birds—barn owls."

"That's a twist from all those books on twin psychology we got from universities on interlibrary loan," Pat said. She put down her stack of books with a thump. "Anything specific about owls? Habitats, feeding patterns, habits? All I know about owls is that they used to be Greek symbols of wisdom— the goddess Athena had one—and in other cultures they're harbingers of death."

Rachel shuddered, but refused to let herself be spooked by that any more than she had by Linc McGowan's historical rantings. "No, nothing about other cultures," she told Pat. "I need to know why they would suddenly change their habits. For one thing, if their nest was knocked down, why they didn't just rebuild as they had every year before? And two, when they usually fly into a barn one way only, why would they change and suddenly fly in another?"

Pat narrowed her eyes a moment, then motioned for Rachel to follow her across the room. "I'll pull some books, but I don't think these old ones here would go much into bird behavior," Pat said over her shoulder as she steered Rachel to a chair beside a small television screen with a typewriter keyboard and gray plastic humped thing on a pad. Rachel sat next to her.

"For specifics like that, I rely on the Internet," Pat told Rachel, clicking the screen on. "And since we don't know a website offhand, we'll do a search to get addresses. Some ornithologist or professor or Audubon addict out there in cyberspace will know."

Rachel felt like a fool. This was a computer, of course, and *website* was the word Mitch used to explain where he'd placed pictures of her barn. Such a worldly thing as a computer was entirely off-limits for her, but if she had Pat make a call to the site or got addresses to write, then maybe she could see her barn on this screen.

Rachel fumbled in her bag for the card Mitch had given her that first time they'd met, just eleven days ago, and her life had been spiraling out of control ever since. She found the card and held it in her lap while Pat moved the plastic thing on the pad, which in turn somehow moved a mark around on the screen. Like magic, it sometimes turned into an arrow, a hand, or hourglass, as if to point out to Rachel that time was fleeting here. She had to meet Jennie and the boys at the SuperMart and then they were going to go get a hot dog and ice cream at the Dairy Queen before they headed back.

Pat explained things as she went. The plastic piece on the pad was a mouse, of all things. On the screen something called windows opened up and closed, just as they did, Rachel thought, in real life. She sat riveted as Pat typed her barn owl questions to some e-mail experts.

"I can let you look through a CD-ROM encyclopedia, too," Pat told her. "You know, it wouldn't take much for you to learn to navigate the web. You could use this machine when you come in."

"I'm having enough trouble navigating my own web in real life right now," Rachel told her. She realized most Amish would be insulted at the suggestion they use a computer, but she was intrigued. She handed the librarian Mitch's card and, feeling as if she was asking Pat to help blaspheme or covet or lust, she asked boldly, "Can you type in this website for me?"

"Oh, sure. A local guy, huh?"

Rachel only nodded, but at least, unlike Jennie, Pat did not pursue it.

Up on the screen popped color pictures and the big, barn-red words BARNS REBORN, REBUILT, RELOCATED. Pat moved the arrow around until it changed to other screens.

"There!" Rachel cried, pointing. "That's my barn!"

Pat clicked her way through photo after photo of a barn simply described as "Unique Pioneer Barn in Northwest Ohio." *Prototype, Not For Sale,* one page was labeled. At least Mitch had kept his word on not giving the specific place and not indicating it was for sale. She was certain he meant to protect her, not to hurt her, no matter what he'd done in his past. But here she was, checking up on him when she'd come in to work on solving Sam's death.

"Wait," she told Pat, leaning even closer. Rachel was surprised to see Mitch had even taken photos of her barn floor. She saw a split screen with close-ups that showed the planks of the threshing floor as being sound and the planks of a bay floor—it looked like the side with the Percherons' stalls—as needing work.

"Anything else?" Pat asked as she moved the mouse again. They both looked up as an elderly woman Rachel didn't recognize came in.

"Hello, Ms. Perkins," the frail, white-haired lady said. "I heard at church about an author who writes nice clean books about nice people in a little town. I think her name's Jan Caring."

"That's Jan Karon, Mrs. Rice, and I'll get one of those for you right now," Pat said. "Be right back," she told Rachel in her usual booming voice and tapped the mouse once more before getting up. Rachel nodded, just staring at a new, glowing screen that appeared, filling itself in again.

Rachel reached out and moved the mouse the way she'd seen Pat do. When she clicked it, the screen bumped up. Power, Rachel thought. Forbidden power and knowledge at her Amish fingertips. What came up into view at the bottom of the bright page was that quote from Goethe again, the one on the back of Mitch's card: *There is no Past we can bring back by the longing for it, there is only an eternally new Now that builds and creates itself out of the elements of the Past.*

Well, Rachel vowed to herself, staring at those words, she was done longing for the past. But somehow she was going to dig into it and solve Sam's death on her own.

When Rachel drove the buggy back after dropping off Jennie and her little charges, the twins saw Gabe Carter working on the cupola windows with Mitch and begged to watch them. Rachel let Andy and Aaron climb into a haymow, and, forced to keep an eye on them, sat there herself as Mitch and Gabe banged away. When the men took a break, she left the boys with them and went to get hot chocolate and cookies for everyone.

As she headed outside, Rachel tried to think of a way to tell Mitch she appreciated his help, but she really wanted to work on Sam's death on her own. No need to get him involved, she'd say, his contributions on the barn were fair trade for his publicity pictures. If she kept him at arm's length now, it was to protect her place in the Amish community, not because she couldn't forgive what he had done.

"Rats!" she said and went back into the house with the tray. She'd better leave Pat Perkins a note, telling her that if she stopped by with her information on owls, to look for her in the barn.

When Rachel had finished writing the note and started out with the tray, she was surprised to see Mitch and Gabe at her back door, while, over by the barn, the boys happily picked up handfuls of sawdust and put it in a bucket.

"Don't worry, mother hen," Mitch said, taking the tray from her. "I'll pay them minimum wage."

"Better'n you pay me," Gabe groused with a grin as Mitch carried the tray out to the barn. Rachel darted back to tack the note on her door and followed. "Mitch ever tell you," Gabe asked her, "that I'm the one first spotted your barn? I find most of them for him."

"I believe that slipped his mind," Rachel said. She felt two-faced, taking part in this light banter when she was going to tell Mitch to lay off trying to find clues about Sam's death.

"I got a confession to make, Rachel," Gabe said, lowering his voice. "Just wanted to be up-front with you, since Mitch says I'm gonna get to watch the twins someday when you two go to see Lake Erie."

Rachel's wide-eyed gaze met Mitch's. He looked like the kids when they were caught at something, but Gabe didn't notice and went on, "I used to be an alcoholic, Rachel. It was so bad my wife left me, but Mitch helped me get off the sauce 'bout three years back, and I haven't had a drop since."

"It's good you're not drinking anymore," Rachel told him. "And I'll pray you can patch things up with your wife."

"Naw, too late for that," he muttered, shaking his head. "Can't unscramble broken eggs. I used to lie and skip out on her and even wear disguises to sneak around on her in Fostoria where we lived. Your place here and your bringing us these cookies and all has really made me miss her. But I'm a new man, and it's Mitch I have to thank."

"That's quite a testimonial," Rachel said as the boys ran over for the food. "I appreciate your coming clean on your past, trusting me enough for that," she told Gabe with a look straight at Mitch.

That afternoon, while the men finished up, Rachel shooed the boys inside. She read to them about Noah's building the ark for all kinds of animals, then put them down for a nap. They'd been so exhausted lately that she sometimes thought they must be awake all night. When she came back downstairs, she saw Mitch's truck drive off without his saying goodbye, so maybe he did get her message—her cold shoulder, as Jennie would call it. Still, she owed him an explanation and he, not Gabe, owed her some sort of confession.

She made bread dough, let it rise twice, and started to bake it when she heard an engine and hurriedly washed her hands to go to the door. It was not Mitch back, as she had hoped, so they could clear the air. Pat Perkins got out of a small blue car and came to the back door.

"That was fast," Rachel told Pat as the librarian handed her two typed pieces of paper. "Won't you come in?"

"I'd love to, but I've got a dentist appointment in Bowling Green. Can I take a rain check?"

"Oh, sure," Rachel said, not quite certain what she meant. Did she owe money for this service? Surely Pat knew the Amish never used checking accounts.

"The bread smells great, but I'm late now," Pat told her. "Just come back in if I can help again."

As Pat pulled out, Rachel studied the pages. There were two answers from expert mail, one from a professor at the Ohio State University clear in Columbus, and the other from some person who was an officer in the Audubon Society and called himself only "Bird-watcher Bill." Both messages said pretty much the same.

Barn owls would just rebuild a ruined nest, even returning the next year or several years under ordinary circumstances. They would always fly in the barn through the same entrance if it was open, "come snow, sleet or hail," as Bird-watcher Bill put it. But both experts surmised, barn owls would avoid a habitual place and fly in another way to avoid a person who was too close to them or their nest.

"But Sam and I were downstairs when they flew in," Rachel muttered.

And then she knew. To prevent the owls from flying inside in their normal way and from returning later to rebuild, someone strange had been up in the haymow loft that night. And probably after that night.

The fact the twins were sleeping so long, Rachel realized, definitely proved they weren't sleeping well at night, any more than she was. Though it was late afternoon, she peeked in, then let them be, deciding she might try lying down herself. But as she moved toward her bedroom, she heard a bang from out by the barn, as if the men were working on the cupola floor again. That couldn't be. Maybe the back barn door had come loose in the rising wind. Wrapping a black shawl around her dress, she went out to hook it. Rather than going through the barn, she walked around.

She rounded the corner and bumped into Mitch.

"Oh," she cried in alarm. "I didn't know you were back." He put his hands on her waist to steady her, but she stepped quickly away.

"I had Gabe drop me off while he ran errands," he said calmly. "I noticed the wind had shifted straight from the north instead of the northwest, and that's the direction it was blowing the night Sam died, according to the sheriff's report. I'm trying to see if this door could have blown open, then banged shut on its own."

"That's all right," Rachel protested, planning to

go into her spiel about his not having to help her with this anymore. "I can do it myself..."

Her words trailed off as he opened the door slightly, and the wind banged it shut again. "See?" he said. He held it about shoulder width away from its frame. "Unless someone had opened it at least this wide, no way was it going to open or bang closed on its own. Rachel, someone was in the barn that night besides you and Sam."

"I—I think you're right. And I thank you for all the help, but..."

"But what?" he asked, turning to study her. "Don't tell me you're going to see the sheriff and reopen the case."

"Not exactly," she admitted. "That might be the last straw with my people right now."

"Meaning your friendship with me is the next-to-the-last straw?" he pursued, moving so that, when she stepped back, she stood against the barn with him facing her, trapping her. She could almost scent the rising tension in him.

"Meaning I'm just sorry I got you involved in all this, Mitch. Your contributions on the barn are enough, and I have no right to expect more." She started around the barn but he hauled her back by one arm.

"Don't!" She broke away and lifted both hands as if he would hit her.

"Don't what?" he demanded, throwing his arms out. "What have I done or said that has suddenly changed everything?"

"It's—it's what you didn't say—and yes, what you've done."

"Did you talk to the boys about that night? Did

they say something to upset you or make you decide to drop an investigation again?''

"I'm telling you I didn't—couldn't—really question them.''

"It's all right. I see,'' he said and put an arm around her shoulders.

"No, I'm fine,'' she said and moved away from him again.

"Rachel, yesterday, you were willing, even grateful, when I comforted you.'' He sounded edgy, angry. "You think my being here, sitting in their dad's chair that day or touching their mother is going to traumatize them? I know about trauma hurting a kid, setting him off, believe me.''

"You weren't a kid when you almost killed that man,'' she blurted.

He looked as if she'd struck him. Fierce emotions flitted across his face. She was afraid of what he'd do or say but she stood her ground.

"You'll never learn to trust me,'' he said, hitting his chest with his fist, "if you can't even trust your own boys. I'll just send Gabe to finish things here while I keep my damn distance.''

As if to make his words good, clenching his hands to white-knuckled fists at his side, Mitch walked way around her and went out onto the road until Gabe came to pick him up.

Thirteen

⁓⊷⊶⊷⁓

"We're going to pick pumpkins and get our stand set up," Rachel told the boys when she woke them the next morning.

She tried to look and sound excited, hoping the physical farm labor she loved might buck her up. After her argument with Mitch, she felt doubly devastated. She had not only handled it poorly, but she had gotten close enough to an outsider to hurt him and herself.

"After breakfast we'll walk over to Jennie's to see if she and Jeff and Mike want to help," she went on.

"But when is everyone coming to help cut the cornfield?" Andy asked. "At the *danze,* Sim Lapp said ours would be first, and then our Perch-ons would help do other fields."

"I know he said that," Rachel admitted as she stood at her sons' bedroom door. "I'm just not sure if that's still the plan or not. As soon as we hear, I'll have to get a lot of food cooked up."

"Sure," Aaron put in, "and when they cut the corn, *Daadi* will be watching from up above."

"That's right," Rachel said, surprised since she'd

never tried to equate heaven with the sky as she knew the *Englische* did. Aaron probably got that from Jennie, though it wouldn't have been in a discussion about losing Laura.

"I'm afraid Sam Rachel Mast is turning more and more to worldly influences and people," Eben told Sim Lapp and the other church deacon, Amos Troyer, as they met behind the Yoder house to make sure the community's harvester was in shape for corn cutting. Eben patted the now-silent, gas-powered machine as if it were a huge metal horse while Sim secured it to the work wagon. "Hate to say it," Eben went on, "but she needs a good jolt to get her on the right path with her own people."

"Been spending too much time with that woman who tends the twins," Sim put in. "Saw the *Englischer* fussing over the boys at the auction. Hear she and Sam Rachel gonna sell their pumpkins to anyone for any use, and after you warned her about Halloween and all, Bishop."

"It's worse than that," Eben muttered. "She's going to sign up her barn with a worldly government agency. And without asking for our guidance, she's got a male *auslander* fixing it up when it's her heart needs fixing up—and not from him."

"Would a stern warning be timely?" Amos asked from his circuit of the big machine, kicking each tire to see if it needed air.

"I've given her a personal one," Eben admitted, not looking at them now, but out past his house toward the road Rachel had come riding down the other day to boldly take her horses home. "And I've sent young Jacob to tell her to keep clear of Sarah, hoping that will make her realize she could be in danger of a sanction or even shunning.''

Both deacons froze and looked at each other. The shunning, or *meidung,* was a dreaded state, almost like death in life, where the brother or sister shunned could have no contact with any Amish. Worse, if the sinner didn't repent and get reinstated, the *meidung* led to permanent banishment and damnation.

"*Ja,* she was always close to Sarah, so that will shake her up," Sim finally said.

"Though I did decide to allow her to attend the wedding so she can hear the sermon that day," Eben explained, tugging down the front of his coat. "But, *ach,* we need to consider both those dire judgments if she does not…" He had almost blurted, *"Do as I tell her and marry me,"* but he caught himself in time. "If she does not return to the fold," he added hastily.

"You got my say-so to warn her or place her under it," Amos declared.

"Mine, too, Bishop. I will watch her closely—that is, when we go over to cut her field," Sim said. "The thing is, it's not only her life and future at stake."

"That's for sure," Eben said gruffly.

"Right," Amos added, "since the safety and souls of her boys are at stake, too."

Eben gestured them toward his house where he hoped Sarah had the coffee and cake ready. He felt only a bit ashamed he had not been thinking of the twins, but of his life and future with that passionate woman he needed to bridle and tame.

The boys picked and toted pumpkins, while Rachel lettered a sign and Jennie tacked some old oilcloth over their small sales table. But mostly the selling of their orange bounty would be on the honor system. Depending on the size of pumpkin selected from these piles or from the field itself, the buyer would leave between two to four dollars in a wooden box which Rachel would keep an eye on and empty frequently.

"Look, *Mamm*," Andy called out, pointing down the road at an approaching buggy. "Our first buyer, and it's Jacob Esh."

Rachel went to meet Sarah's fiancé as he climbed down in the driveway. Still holding the reins as if he couldn't stay long, he looked serious, almost stricken.

"Jacob, how's Sarah?" she asked him, clenching her work apron. "I wanted to visit but Eben said not to."

Jacob nodded slowly. "Doing better, much stronger, that she is."

"And your marriage is still on?"

"Sunday church at the Lapps'. We're to clear things with the brethren, then have the service after. We're both glad for that."

"Then I am, too," Rachel said. "You have waited a long time for her, Jacob, and I pray you will be happy—all three of you and more blessings to come."

"Folks have been kindly, mostly said the same. 'Cept I think Sim Lapp can't understand why the Lord lets Sarah get in a family way so fast when..." He cleared his throat. "You know they had troubles."

Rachel did know. Sim Annie's miscarriages had set her back physically and spiritually. Word was that the doctor at the Clearview Clinic had told Sim that Sim Annie should not get pregnant so soon again. But she was, and this time, God willing, the signs looked better.

"You'll be at church then," Jacob said, his voice somewhere between statement and question. "Sarah asked for you to be there."

"I will, of course. She's a dear friend."

"It won't be much the usual wedding," he explained with a little shrug. "No fancy bride's table and all, but it will have to be enough. And," he said, tilting his head so the morning sun shot into his eyes before he shifted it again, "Bishop Yoder says you're to remember the *Ordnung.* Well, all of us are, as my Sarah and I skated on thin ice and fell through, too."

The young man twisted the reins. Rachel could tell Eben had set up poor Jacob to deliver his veiled warning just as he'd sent Sarah to tell her to shape up once before. And she wanted to, had to, didn't she?

"Please tell Bishop Yoder," Rachel said, choosing each word carefully, "that I don't even like to skate, but I do like to work my own farm."

"Oh," Jacob blurted, "that reminds me. Tomorrow everyone will be here to cut your corn first thing in the morning, so have your team ready to pull the big harvester. Then it's on to the Lapps' fields that afternoon, Friday Yoders', Saturday ours."

Relief flooded her, then regret at her former defiance. The brethren were still willing to help her. She was yet part of her beloved family of believers. But she had so much to do to prepare all that food.

"I'll have a good dinner for everyone," she told Jacob as he climbed back up in the buggy. "And, of course, Sim can care for the Percherons when the team works the other fields.''

As Rachel waved Jacob away and ran toward the twins to tell them the good news, she realized she had overstepped lately but was being given another chance. She needed and loved her people. She was a part of them and the *Ordnung* and would always be. Her fascination with Mitch Randall must be put aside, and she must accept that a freak accident could look like murder but be God's will. Or, though she hated to admit it, Sam could have been careless, walking under that heavy hook when he might not have secured the ropes right. Barn owls, open prongs, and banging doors aside, she was still Sam Rachel Mast, and she and her beloved boys were still full Amish.

Rachel was as thrilled and excited as her four-year-olds when the workers arrived, pulling the gas-powered corn harvester behind a work wagon. An antique that ran on a diesel engine, the machine was sanctioned by the *Ordnung,* since no electrical wires linked it to the outside, nor was it a vehicle one could drive to stray far into that world.

Although Rachel had spent hours cultivating her rows of corn in the summer sun, something Eben and Sim Lapp had said she should not do, she knew it would be impossible to cut and shock this big field without their help and that communal machine. Of course, her Percherons helped, too, but she supposed a big team of other horses could have handled it.

"Hurry up, *Mamm,*" Andy called impatiently from the back porch where Rachel had made the boys promise to stay until the men had gone out to the field. She knew the twins would love to dart here and there, but she needed to know where they were, with horses plodding and wagon wheels rolling. She had invited Jennie and her charges to come watch, too, but Jennie had refused to let them near the barn in all this confusion. She said she'd let them observe with binoculars from the back of the pumpkin field.

"I am hurrying!" Rachel cried as she struggled to attach Cream's wire-mesh muzzle, called a *mahlkorply,* to the bridle. Though she hated to impose these on her team, she knew if she didn't, they'd sample every ear of corn they could get a nose near. She'd already put Gid's on him and was saving Chester's until last.

Eben and Sim Lapp arrived in the same buggy and climbed down before the other men. "How's Annie doing today?" Rachel asked Sim.

"Real good of you to have your English lady friend drop off some pumpkin pies for our feeding folks when you had all your own work to do," he said instead of answering her question. He walked past her to tell the men where to pull the harvester for hitching up the team.

Eben took the last muzzle and put it on Chester, though the big horse shied away and Eben had to pull him back. "With some of the things I've said to you lately, feel like I should put one of these on myself sometimes," he told Rachel. "I want only the best for you and the boys." He nodded his head toward the twins. "I hope you can find it in your soul to forgive my harsh words, Sam Rachel."

Stunned, she nodded. Eben was becoming an enigma. When she was certain he'd condemn her, he always gave her another chance. But if he thought she'd agree to wed him, he, too, would be surprised.

"Your kind words are much appreciated, Bishop Yoder," she said and pulled the team over to get them hitched.

"Gunshots," Rachel whispered to herself and froze like a startled doe. Now that she and her kitchen helper, Amos Leona Troyer, had the large meal waiting for the workers, Rachel had begun to make the rounds with the big thermos full of cold water for the men.

But, standing at the side of her half-cut cornfield, she strained to listen. The distant crack of rifles even pierced the chugging sound of the harvester. After all, it was deer season, she reassured herself. She could only hope the hunters weren't in her woodlot, because it abutted the back of the cornfield near the ravine, and a stray shot could harm someone today. At least the twins were safe, sitting on the growing pile of ears in the makeshift corn crib in the barnyard with Eben's boy Ben, whose job it was to help pile each wagonload.

Watching for the flash of orange vest or cap that would indicate a hunter, Rachel headed for the back of the cornfield, stopping as she went to offer a cup of water to anyone nearby. Though the air was chilly, this was hot, dusty work as the maw of the monster machine crunched dried stalks and leaves into fodder and fine dust.

Rachel kept moving, edging around the fringe of newly cut field. Sim had volunteered to hand-cut the last four rows that contoured the ravine by the woodlot, where the harvester could not go without tipping.

As she got closer, Rachel recalled her panic when she'd fled through the uncut, whispering shocks last week. She had thought someone was after her, but she must have been wrong, just as she'd surely been mistaken that someone Amish had meant to harm Sam. But she still wanted an explanation for who was tampering with his straw hat and her horses. Though Simeon Lapp didn't want to talk to her, she was determined to talk to him.

Her pulse pounding, she was out of breath when she saw Sim whacking through stalks, then gathering them into standing, bound sheaves the Amish called *stooks*. Sim's two-foot bladed corn knife, which had been Sam's, flashed in the sun with each powerful swipe. Since Sim's coloring and size was similar to her husband's, she halted for a minute, stunned at the scene.

Suddenly Rachel recalled Mitch's asking her, "Who hated Sam or wanted what he had?" Sim and Sam, though friends, had argued about who would buy this place with the big barn. They had patched the quarrel up, but the sore point was that the brethren had decreed the Masts should have it because they had sons and Sim and Annie did not. She began to walk again, slowly.

Almost as if he sensed her presence, Sim looked up. "Annie's all right, isn't she?" he asked, stopping in midstance.

"As far as I know," Rachel answered. "You didn't exactly say how she was when I asked you earlier." She regretted her words and tone; she had meant to do this gently, cleverly.

"Then you didn't need to come way back with

water. I've drunk out of the little stream here more than once."

"Today or other times?" she asked, then silently scolded herself again for her tart tongue. She didn't want to spook him.

"Today and on other harvest days," he told her with a shrug. He took off his hat and wiped his forehead. Despite what he'd said about the water, he took the proffered cup from her and gulped till it was empty. Some ran down his beard and sinewy throat.

"I appreciate your doing this harder cutting," Rachel said, taking the cup and retreating several steps. Her stomach knotted tighter, especially when she heard the distant wail of a train whistle and realized they'd have to talk louder over its approach.

"Any young buck can swing this thing," Sim said, lifting the long-bladed knife upright between them. "It's working with the ropes that baffles them."

She watched as he hacked through a cornhill of stalks with one blow, then stooped to gather them, heavy with ears, in his left hand and arm. Hurling the knife ahead of him so it stuck in the ground, he balanced the heavy load on his hip and dragged it to the shocks he'd already gathered.

Grabbing a precut length of rope from the ground, he bound the *stook* with a double-hitch knot and shoved it upright to stand with the widely spaced row of others. Rachel had seen her husband do this, but now she just kept staring at Sim's hands—big for a man his size—as they re-coiled what rope he didn't need, hacked it off with the retrieved corn knife and dropped it to the ground.

"So, what's the problem?" he asked as he bent to slice through more stalks. "I'll take good care of

Sam's Percherons at the other farms while we harvest. I always do."

"You know, speaking of them, I was just wondering if you could help me figure out who has been a sort of—well, an Amish angel for me."

"Like what?" he asked as he dragged stalks and shocks to make a new pile.

"Sam's favorite straw work hat turned up just like a miracle a while ago and, more than once, someone has secretly helped me with the horses, fed and watered them, even hitched the Percherons once when I wasn't in the barn."

He dumped the armload and stood to face her. The train was at its loudest now, and she stared at his lips to read them, as if he were whispering when he was almost yelling.

"I once wanted to work this farm, Sam Rachel, but it went to you and Sam. Except for helping like now, I'm too busy to be your Amish angel. You think you can keep this place, keep it, then."

They stared at each other as the train noise faded so that she could hear the harvester again, even the distant *pop, pop* of a hunter's gun.

A hundred things flitted through her mind to say to Sim. That she was sorry he still resented Sam's getting the place. That she wished him and Annie well with their child. But instead, as she turned away, she said, "Whatever it takes, I will keep it, Sim Lapp."

In her bedroom after everyone left, Rachel stretched her arms above her head and arched her back. She ached all over, but it was a good ache.

She'd been so pleased to place big pumpkins in each departing Amish buggy or wagon when they left.

Her corn was cut, and most of the stalks would become fodder or stall bedding; the ears in the makeshift crib in the barnyard would soon be husked, if she worked away at it bit by bit. Lastly, she would use Nann and Bett to drag in the *stooks* that Sim had bound. Even if deer, coons or mice got to some of it first, her corn harvest was bountiful. If only the shots from the hunters' guns wouldn't keep coming closer, she could lie down on her bed, fully dressed like her little boys, and for once, fall dead asleep.

The *bang, bang* of the gun suddenly became *ping, ping,* a strange metallic sound close by. Rachel looked out her bedroom window. Two men in mottled brown clothes and caps with no orange hunters' vests had come into the far edge of the barnyard, carrying a dead doe with her feet tied to a tree limb. Putting the carcass down, they lifted their rifles and took a shot at the horse weather vane atop the cupola.

As she watched, aghast, the fine old piece spun wildly until it was almost blasted to bits. And then, as they whooped in delight and one took off his hat and threw it in the air, she saw who they were.

The two men Mitch called paramilitary, her harassers on the road. She had hated how they'd stood in the crowd last week, watching to see if Sarah would kill herself.

Unfortunately, they saw her, too, just as she jumped back from the window.

"Hey, honey, come on down!" the one who'd been driving that day shouted. "Not gonna turn us down a second time, no way!" Another whoop followed the crack of a gun. Dog-drunk, both of them,

Rachel thought. She got down on her hands and knees, crawled past the window, then darted for her door. Should she lock the boys in the cellar? But that would terrify the twins. She looked in on them: they both slept. At least they were on the safe side of the house. She closed their bedroom door, turned the old key in the lock and shoved it in her deep apron pocket.

At the small window on the landing as she went downstairs, she saw the men had now turned their shots to Mitch's renovated louvers in the cupola. At least her Percherons were at the Lapps', but Bett and Nann would be panicked.

A fierce anger flooded Rachel. If she had a gun right now, she was not certain what she would have done with it, Amish *Ordnung* or not. And she'd been wrong not to report these men before. She'd been not only forgiving but cowardly to tell Mitch they'd come after her if she reported them. They were worldly men, so let the world deal with them.

Praying they would keep their shots to the top of the barn and then go away, Rachel systematically closed all the bright blue curtains that hung at her downstairs windows. Agonizing over what to do, she kept low, upset by their shouts and shots. She wouldn't try to face those two down, nor risk running out the front door with the twins. Her close neighbor, Jennie, had never seemed so distant.

When she heard a second-floor window shatter, Rachel threw herself flat on the kitchen floor. Scrambling on her hands and knees, she tore upstairs, fumbling in her apron for the key to the boys' bedroom. The sound of breaking glass seemed to go on forever.

"Hey, Amish honey! Come on out and party!"

The shot-out window, thank God, was in the guest bedroom. She was shaking so hard she could not get the key to turn in the lock of the twins' door. If she could only hide them somewhere, then lead those madmen away.

She heard a huge roar. At first she feared they had set something afire, but it sounded like an engine, a motor. Tearing to her jagged-jawed window, she darted a look out. Mitch's truck had turned into the yard, scattering the men, nearly pinning one against the barn. She watched in awe and horror as the scene below exploded.

The one trapped against the wall lifted his rifle and shot at the truck. Its front window shattered and one front bumper struck the barn, just missing the hunter. The car's engine still running, the truck stopped, Mitch's door opened, and she saw him half roll, half fall out.

Was he hit? she thought. Dead?

But he rolled again and crouched behind the corn crib while the man came at him, maybe out of ammunition now, swinging his gun like a club. Mitch leaped to his feet, aiming for the man's midsection, taking him down. The hunter's head struck the side of the truck, and he lay still.

It must be like that time Mitch almost killed a man, she thought. She stood frozen in fear. She tried to scream and run to help, but as in a nightmare, her feet were leaden and her voice snagged. The other hunter crept up on Mitch, who stood there, half-dazed, bleeding. The man lifted his rifle barrel toward Mitch.

"Mitch, gun behind you!" Rachel screamed out the window. She tore downstairs, ignoring her boys pounding on their bedroom door and calling her name. "Stay there, stay there!" she called to them in German as she held up her hems and took the steps two at a time.

When she got outside, neither Mitch nor the man were in sight, but she heard them inside the barn. Someone banged against a wall, someone grunted, shouted. Fists. When men fought, she realized in horror, you could actually hear their fists on flesh and bone.

Rachel picked up both rifles and dropped them in the full water trough, then stepped in the door of the barn, grabbing the iron snowshoe knocker. Mitch was pounding the man with his fists, then began to bang his head against the post by the buggy horses' stalls. Rachel gripped the heavy iron piece in her hand. Rage roared through her and she knew she could have—would have—beat that man's head in to protect her boys, even Mitch.

"Mitch," she cried. "Stop! Remember what happened before!"

Mitch stopped in midpunch, his fist drawn back. Throwing the hunter flat on his face, he yanked his hands behind him.

"Get me some rope," he ordered, panting. Rachel dropped the iron and ran to obey.

"I've got to get to the boys upstairs," she said as she handed him the coil of rope. She sprinted for the door, then turned back. "Mitch, I understand what you did before. I've been taught force and violence are always wrong, but this time, it was right."

"You should have reported that someone was threatening you," Sheriff Burnett scolded gently, then took another swallow of the coffee Rachel had poured him.

He had returned to the farm about an hour after his police car had hauled the two hunters away and another squad car had taken Mitch to the emergency room in Bowling Green. His truck, with its shattered front window and scraped side, still sat out back as evidence, along with the dead doe. Marci had driven in right behind her dad and had taken the twins over to Jennie's.

"We've got laws to protect you, Mrs. Mast," the sheriff went on, thumping a fist on her table, "and I promise those two are going to trial for trespassing and destruction of property. But the new law on the books that's really going to fry them is ethnic intimidation. Been used to protect the Amish more than once in the Midwest, and I'm gonna throw it right at the bozos."

"I do appreciate your help, Sheriff," Rachel said, passing him the plate of cookies again. She had finally stopped shaking. "It will be a relief to know they won't be coming back, but I cannot go into court to testify."

"Understood. Fortunately, Mitch Randall can do that, though if those two get themselves any kind of decent lawyer, he'll probably drag out Randall's past in their defense."

"But Mitch was just protecting me and the boys," she protested.

"And his new barn work. I see those idiots shot it all to heck. Sometimes I almost think there's a jinx on this place. Sorry if that offended you, Mrs. Mast," he added hastily.

Rachel nodded and sighed. She was tempted to tell

the sheriff the other things that had been happening in her barn lately, things she was certain two "bozos" couldn't possibly have managed to pull off. She'd love to blame them and believe she was safe now, but their style was hardly sneaky and subtle.

The sheriff wiped his mouth on a paper napkin and stood. "Like I said, I'll get that tow truck out here to haul Randall's truck into a repair shop. Anything else I can do for you before I head on back to town to finish up the paperwork and get those two transferred out of here to a permanent holding tank? Want me to radio over to Jennie's and have my Marci bring your boys back now? Or can I do anything about the earlier investigation into your husband's death?"

Somehow, Rachel thought, she'd known that last question was coming. She had a good notion to ask him to reopen Sam's case, but she couldn't and still be true Amish.

"No, Sheriff Burnett," she told him, meeting his hard, assessing gaze, "though, again, I am grateful for your kindness."

"Let the dead rest in peace, huh?" he said as he took his hat from the table and headed for the back door.

Rachel nodded, but she knew now that however much the Amish helped her and supported her, *she* would not rest in peace until she found and faced down her other harasser. Even if—especially if—it was someone who had hated and hurt Sam.

It was an hour before sunset when Mitch came back, driving Gabe's old car. A tow truck had taken away his vehicle and the dead deer, when Rachel said she didn't want the venison. At least she wouldn't have to bury it out back. Poor Mitch looked more scraped and bruised than his truck had been. His right eye was going black and blue, and cuts on his face and fists were daubed, bandaged, even stitched.

Rachel knew she should just thank him and pay him, though she did not have the money, for his early barn work and his truck repairs. She should ask him not to come back—not because she was afraid of him, but because she was beginning to be afraid of herself. Though she had wavered, she still wanted to solve Sam's death and to cling to this outsider. She knew something bad, that felt so good, would happen, and it did.

Between the barn and Gabe's car, they came together in a mutual embrace. Her arms wrapped around his back, his went around her waist to clamp her tighter. Her face fit right in the hollow of his throat; she could feel his pulse pounding there. Her breasts pressed to his hard chest, and her knees leaned into his, so rock steady after that fight. For one moment, the two of them seemed to become one being, breathing in unison.

"I didn't thank you earlier," she choked out. "I may not have an Amish angel, but I have a guardian one in you."

Looking puzzled, he set her back slightly. He seemed to have tears in his eyes, but she couldn't be sure. For one moment she thought he would kiss her, but his lips looked puffy and one was split.

"Rachel, I was coming back to say I was sorry for stomping out of here before," he explained, squeezing her hands. "I'd driven by earlier and saw everyone here harvesting corn, so I stayed away. But when

I went by again and saw those bastards shooting up the barn, I just lost it.''

"Like you did with that man who had taken your grandfather's farm when you finally found him?'' she asked.

"I guess it's time to explain all that,'' he whispered. "Are the boys here?''

"Next door.''

"Let's go assess the damage before it gets dark,'' Mitch said with a glance at the blasted cupola. "After, we can board up that upstairs window they shot out, then go get the twins. I promised the sheriff I'd come in to make a statement before I went home, but I've got a statement to make to you, too.''

"All right,'' Rachel said, running back to pull the house door shut and lock it. She knew she should send him away, but instead she let him take her hand and pull her toward the barn as she stretched her strides to match his.

Fourteen

❧❧❧

The damage was devastating. Rachel and Mitch stood shoulder to shoulder staring out through the blasted louvers of the cupola at the bloodred sinking sun. At least the solid boards under their feet had not been harmed.

"We can still build on the past," Rachel quoted his own favorite words to him, "even if we have to do it over."

"Yeah."

He sighed and leaned against one of the six supporting posts that still held the cupola roof up, though the proud, old weather vane above it was pretty much gone.

"That man I beat up years ago," Mitch said, obviously struggling for words, "and my going to prison—was it Linc McGowan who told you?"

"More or less," Rachel admitted. "He gave me the article he wrote about your tearing down barns and one about your trial."

"Rachel, I swear to God, that seems like a different person to me. But I figured if you knew any of that, you'd never let me near you, let alone near the barn."

"So the man you fought was the one who, you felt, turned your family out of their farm?"

"Right."

His jaw clenched, unclenched. Rachel could tell he was still having trouble getting the words out. Yet, she knew it could only help. She turned to him and grasped his upper arms. "After today, I can understand your fury at your home being taken and your family being hurt. Those men just ruined a small part of my farm, and I could have hit them with that snowshoe iron, or if I'd had a gun..."

"Then try this," he clipped out. "I beat that guy up but I was really beating up my father."

"What? Your father is the one who—"

"No, but I was lying to you when I told you I searched for my father after my grandparents were dead and didn't find him. That was not the end of the story."

He pulled gently away to lean his elbows on the sill, the broken louvers framing him. His voice sounded so raspy, almost a whisper, so she leaned closer, not touching him again.

"After high school—staying with foster families—it took me almost a year to trace my dad through a couple of his old friends and a former employer," he explained, his voice a monotone. "I found out he was living in a little burg called Trenton, Missouri, working at a Nestlé's chocolate factory there. That's a good one, isn't it, since I always pictured that as a kind of comfort food? My grandmother always fixed me hot chocolate after I'd come in tired and wet from working with my grandfather."

His bruised fists tightened on the windowsill, as if he was oblivious to the splintered wood.

"But you found your father," she prompted quietly.

"Oh, yeah, I found him. I had worked up all these TV family show–type reunions in my mind with excuses for his desertion. You know, scenarios like he didn't mean to leave me and never call or come back. He'd just been trying to work hard to get enough money to build a house to make me proud of him when he came looking for me. Or he was so ashamed he'd left me, but the moment he'd see me he'd break down in tears…"

His voice snagged and he turned away, then squared his shoulders and plunged on, "But he had a decent house. And a wife, who resembled my mom, hanging up clothes in the backyard, and two boys about seven years old playing in *Star Wars* outfits out in front."

Rachel had no idea what *Star Wars* were, but she knew better than to ask. "Mitch, I'm so sorr—"

"The bastard had just replaced Mom and me, thrown us away like trash."

"Did he say that when you talked to him?"

"I didn't talk to him. I hid and watched him come home and the kids hang on him and the woman kiss him. I stalked him for nearly a week, thinking I'd confront him, kill him, I don't know," he whispered, shaking his head. He had his eyes shut tight the way the twins did to close out something they disliked or feared. "But I kept seeing the way those boys hung on him, and I knew how they'd miss him."

He turned to look at her. To Rachel's surprise, his eyes were dry, but the setting sun bronzed his face, making it look like a mask—a frightening mask. She took a step back until she bumped into the wall.

"See, that's why I didn't want to drag all this out," he said, turning slightly away again. "I've scared you."

"No. It just made me realize how hard it's been for you. That's why you said you were really striking out at your father when you happened to find the man in the bar."

"I didn't *just* happen to find him in the bar," he admitted, his voice even more bitter. "I traced the guy who had not only evicted but taunted my folks. At first, I just told him off, accused him of ruining farms and lives. He said farms like the one my grandparents had ought to be trashed and replaced with new roads, new things. His face merged with my dad's, and I hit him..."

"You deserved justice but you were wrong to beat him," she declared.

"My little Amish conscience," he muttered, reaching for her. Though that sudden move surprised her, she did not resist as he hauled her close to him. "Are you going to pass further judgment on me, shun me, as your people say. Kick me out of this barn that needs help, kick out a man who hasn't felt at home in all the beautiful homes he's built for people, not even my own?"

"I didn't say that, Mitch Randall. Don't you start telling me what I think. Sometimes I think I've had enough of that."

His stiff expression broke into a tight smile, though he winced at his bruises. "My lips are a mess," he whispered, "or I'd kiss you. My hands aren't much better, but they're going to have to do the kisses right now.''

She stared up into his eyes, seeing the sun set there. She supposed, if she wasn't careful, it could rise there, too.

He slowly lifted his hands, swollen knuckles and all, bandage on his left palm, and skimmed his fingertips from her lips along the slant of her cheekbones, up into her temples. His touch feathered through her hair, lifting her stiff cap away, snagging her hairpins that kept the bounty of her tresses close to her skull.

"Does all this come loose like that first day I saw you?'' he whispered.

"Only at night in privacy,'' she murmured, deciding not to tell him that an Amish woman's freed hair was only for her husband's eyes. With Mitch, *that* was more impossible than this, and this was *verboten* enough.

"It's private here and almost night,'' he said. To her amazement, when she shook her head to deny him, her heavy top braid tumbled free as if it was a sign. When she shook her head again, she heard a pin hit the cupola boards and another bounce clear down to the barn floor. Her heavy hair tumbled loose on one side, then the other. It brushed her brow, sliding forward, falling back, bouncing on her shoulders.

Mitch held her to him, burying his face in her hair.

"Is that *Mamm* up there with *Daadi?*'' Aaron asked Andy in German as Marci, who was kind of Jennie's daughter, drove them into their driveway and back toward the house and barn.

Andy squinted upward, looking through the same

window, following Aaron's gaze. He looked bug-eyed when he saw. "Must be," he whispered, using German, too, so Marci wouldn't know what they were saying, "'cause her hair's down. You were right about he's back. But he's a spirit, a soul, like *Mamm* says. He doesn't need to eat, so it's okay if *Mamm* doesn't save his seat at the table. He comes and goes and does what he wants. And he wants to see us."

"What are you two jabbering about?" Marci asked as she jumped out and tapped her car horn. "I swear, how you've learned two languages and some of your own twin talk when you were younger blows my mind. Hurry up now, or I'm gonna be late to get Kent his extra car keys."

Aaron and Andy saw their mother jump away from the window. The man was gone, too, just like he'd disappeared other times.

Marci honked again, then started for the house, which showed Aaron that Marci hadn't seen *Mamm* and *Daadi* in the barn.

"She's up there," he told her and pointed.

"I'm here, Marci!" *Mamm* called down. It was getting really dark but Aaron could see she had her hair fixed now, kind of messy, and her white *kapp* back on. They didn't see *Daadi* at all. Maybe Gabe was somewhere here, though, because his car sat in the yard.

"Kent called, and he's locked himself out of the truck," Marci called up to *Mamm*. "I'm in a hurry to take him another set of keys. Jennie has a headache, so I said I'd bring the boys back."

"I'll be right down. Go ahead to Kent. The boys will be fine."

Mamm disappeared from the high-up broken window. Marci got back in her car and drove away while Andy and Aaron started for the barn. Without talking to each other, Aaron knew they'd take a quick look inside to see if *Daadi* could have come downstairs. Maybe he didn't always like to look out high-up windows. At least now *Mamm* wouldn't get mad at them next time they told her *Daadi* had been back, because she'd been with him, hugged him, too.

Aaron gasped. There was *Daadi* outside the barn, so he must have come down the ladders ahead of *Mamm* and stepped out the back door.

Aaron grabbed Andy's arm, and they both stopped and stared. They heard *Mamm* yelling something inside the barn, but they weren't sure what. *Daadi*'s face was in darkness and night was falling fast, but when he motioned them to follow him behind the barn, then toward the woodlot, they went in a hurry.

"Mitch," Rachel cried, wanting to hurry down to the boys, "the ladder to the loft isn't here!"

He kneeled and looked over. "I didn't hear it fall. It's getting so dark in here, but I don't even see it. Watch out. I can drop as far as the loft."

"Be careful. You're already bruised enough for one day."

She heard him thud to the floor of the haymow just below.

"Did the ladder slip?" she called down to him. Her eyes were adjusting to the darkness but she wasn't wearing her glasses.

"I don't see it anywhere. It must have fallen down one more level. I'll have to nail the thing down.

Meanwhile, I'll pull up the one to the ground floor to get you.''

Rachel darted back to the broken cupola windows and peered out. She didn't see the boys, so they must have come into the barn. Her first guilty impulse in case they had seen her hugging Mitch had been to keep him hidden, but that was ridiculous now.

She went back to where the ladder should be and leaned over the black expanse. "Call down to tell the boys to stay put," she said.

"I don't hear or see them below. Or that other ladder."

Rachel's heart began to pound harder than it had when Mitch had touched her. She had told him less about the odd occurrences in the barn than he had told her about his past. And she was terrified there was no time to explain now.

"I'm coming down," she told Mitch as she sat on the edge and swung her legs over. "Help me."

"Rachel, just wait."

But she hung as he had and dropped. It had been years since she had hated her long skirts. He helped break her fall.

"Andy! Aaron!" she shouted into the darkening well of the barn below. "Where are you?"

Only Nann and Bett answered, shifting in their stalls.

"I've got to get down there," she said, smacking her palms on her skirts, then pressing them to her forehead as if to keep her thoughts from exploding. "They're not here and not outside."

"Of course they are. And you're not jumping again. That next drop is too big for either of us."

"We've got to rig the ropes then. Please, Mitch!"

He worked quickly, pulling and knotting the ropes, the same ones that operated the grappling hook. "The hook won't drop, will it?" she asked.

"No, but it will give us the leverage to swing down. Me Tarzan, you Jane," she thought she heard him say, but nothing made any sense. She would be furious with him, the twins, too, if they thought this was some joke. Maybe the boys were just hiding. When they were younger, they'd hidden in the barn.

"Here, let me try it first," he insisted, but she took the rope out of his hands, tugged it once, then spiraled down, ignoring the burn of hemp against her palms.

"Andy! Aaron!" she cried, running across the threshing floor, looking in the dusk of both bays, then tearing out into the barnyard. The house stood locked and black. *"Andreas! Aaron! Kommt hier schnell!"*

Mitch ran from the barn, rubbing his raw hands. "They can't have just disappeared like that," he said, but she ignored him, running back toward the barn. She stopped and peered into the gathering blackness.

"Rachel, I know you're thinking of that night you found Sam, but they're here somewhere," Mitch insisted, running up behind her.

"Please help me find them then!" she cried. "Could you go around the house, maybe walk the pumpkin field in case they headed toward Jennie's for some reason?"

"All right. But don't go back into that barn without a lantern. Open up and light the house, and maybe they'll get hungry and come in. You know boys."

He squeezed her shoulders and took off at a near

jog around the front of the house. And then she heard the distant train whistle and realized it was fairly close. It must have blown a time or two before, but for once she'd been too frenzied to hear it.

Rachel looked toward the silhouette of the black woodlot against the even blacker sky. She'd forbidden the boys to go there, but their father had taken them more than once despite her protests.

Rachel began to run.

Daadi stayed a little ways ahead of them and that bugged Aaron, and Andy, too, he could tell. Now they were taking too long through the trees. *Daadi* turned back to them and held his arms open, like he'd hug them. Then they hurried again, even if they were getting kind of tired, but he'd just move on. Maybe spirits were like that, souls which had gone to heaven, then came back to check on things, Aaron thought, trembling.

The twins held hands now, something they didn't do much anymore. It was scary out here, even with *Daadi* just ahead. They could see him, his Amish suit, his dark brimmed hat and beard, but not his face too good.

Andy stopped and so did Aaron. If Andy wasn't going closer, he wasn't, either. Andy always did things first and that was okay with him.

"What?" Aaron asked his brother.

"Hear the train? That's where he's taking us. He wants to lift us up and let us see the train go by like we used to. I remember that about *Daadi*. Now I see why he doesn't want *Mamm* here."

"*Ja,* she never liked when he did that."

The train tracks ran behind the woods on a little

man-made hill of stones. It was funny that *Daadi* liked trains when *Mamm* didn't. She liked some other worldly things.

"*Daadi*'s stopped, too," Aaron said. "He's looking at us."

"Maybe he saw we're too big for him to lift us both up like he used to," Andy said, still holding back.

"It's too dark to see if he's smiling," Aaron said. He had to make his voice loud over the noise of the train. He could see its light coming down the tracks to make the earth shake. It was coming very fast.

"I think he's smiling since he likes trains and likes us, too," Andy shouted close to his ear. "And he hugged *Mamm* back in the barn."

They clung together as *Daadi* walked toward them, windmilling his arm to tell them to come closer to the tracks. Andy wondered why he didn't talk, but maybe it was just because the train was so loud. The big front light was bright on the engine, and the cars roared closer. *Daadi* always let them watch from the woodlot on this side of the tracks, not go across. But Aaron guessed that's what he wanted them to do now, even with the train coming.

Shaking, holding hands, Andy and Aaron walked closer like *Daadi* wanted and climbed the steep hill of stones to the wooden pieces that held the iron tracks. The train's front light came at them, glowing like a big eye, making them blink and close their own eyes. The whistle screamed at them and screamed again.

Rachel raced toward the woods. She gasped for breath, feeling a stitch in her side, and tried to shove her horrid thoughts away. Elias hit and dragged by that train. Her boys, drawn by their father's fascination with the noise and motion and power...

Plunging into the woods instead of going the longer way around, Rachel sucked in breath after breath. She knew better than to waste her strength shouting their names. The clatter and continued crash of noise was deafening. The entire universe reverberated, shaking her to her core.

She fell once, tripped up by a vine or root, then scrambled to her feet again. The lights on the engine and in its cab stabbed into the blackness ahead. She wanted to just stop and throw herself on the ground and scream out all the fears that had been smashing into her since Sam left her with the boys. The boys...

The rhythmic rattle-clang of huge metal wheels on the tracks went on endlessly. Rachel tore up and down beside the elevated bed of stones, one way then the other, then fell to her knees as the rest of the train screamed by. Could she have passed the twins in the woodlot? She hadn't seen them there, but they'd never go across the tracks.

And then she knew: the boys weren't out here at all, but back in the pumpkin field or sitting on the front porch, and Mitch surely must have found them. The feeling of being watched, Sam's death, her conflicts with Eben and the brethren had all gotten to her. She had to go back, go back now to find her boys.

But as Rachel sat sobbing and the rumble ebbed and the tracks went silent again, she heard a sound. Scattered stones? Sobbing that was not hers?

Still kneeling, she froze as Andy and Aaron, coming from the other side, climbed onto the tracks above her. Both were bareheaded, holding hands, white as sheets. For one moment, she gaped as if they were ghosts.

"Did *Daadi* bring you here, too?" Aaron choked out. "We think he jumped on the train, 'cause he just disappeared."

Somehow, Rachel carried both boys all the way back to the house, clasped in her arms, with them holding on to her so tight she could hardly breathe. None of them would let Mitch help when he ran up, asking questions.

"Please, I'll just see you tomorrow," she told him and put the boys down long enough to unlock the back door and push her sons inside. Without further explanation, she closed the door on Mitch's stunned face.

She sat the twins, still quivering, at the kitchen table and banged around in the cupboards to get hot chocolate and cookies, even as she heard Mitch drive away. She washed the boys' flushed faces and hands and made them eat and drink. Neither of them had said one word since that outrageous, lame excuse about *Daadi* taking them to the train. Rachel shook with rage, but also with relief.

She sat at her place between them.

"Why did you go out there when you shouldn't have?" she asked. Her voice trembled; it was not her own. She gripped her hands around her own cup of cocoa, but even that did not warm her.

The two of them looked at each other. "But you saw him, too," Andy said.

"Who? I—it was Mitch with me. Did you see

someone else who could have moved the ladders from the barn when we were up in the cupola?''

Both wide-eyed, looking like mirror images, Andy and Aaron shrugged in unison.

''At the tracks,'' Rachel tried again, ''you mentioned *Daadi*. I know he used to take you out to see the trains, but he's not here anymore.''

''No, he took the train but he'll be back,'' Aaron said with such conviction that Rachel's insides cartwheeled.

''I know you believe *Daadi* is still with us, and he is in our hearts and minds always, so I can understand what you mean,'' she said, choosing her words carefully. She realized she was gripping her hot mug so hard her hands felt scalded. She put them in her lap so the boys couldn't see how they were shaking. ''But in the real world we have to live in, *Daadi* is gone now, gone for good and not just on a train.''

''Gone for good,'' Andy echoed her words. ''He wasn't very good to make us cross the tracks. The train went by so close the wind from it made us both lose our hats!''

She stared at them, and they stared unblinking back. Promising herself she would try again with them after they had a good night's sleep, Rachel put them to bed. But she didn't sleep and wasn't sure she ever would again. Especially when, the next morning, she found both boys' hats hung on pegs in the barn next to Sam's straw one and the missing ladders back in place.

Fifteen

❦

"Look, *Mamm*," Andy cried, pointing down the driveway as he ran into the backyard. "Here comes Kent with some wood in his truck for Mitch and Gabe."

Rachel looked up from sweeping the back porch. "You must call Kent Mr. Morgan," she told Andy. "You honor even your worldly friends' father by saying mister."

Andy stopped in his tracks so fast Aaron almost ran into him. "But Jennie calls him Kent," Andy protested. "She said we could call her Jennie, and she's a grandmother."

Gabe had posted both boys by the pumpkin-sale table to watch for their wood delivery from the lumberyard in Clearview and to keep them temporarily out of the way. It was barely nine o'clock in the morning after the nightmare with the train, and Rachel was relieved to see it had not seemed to leave any lingering terrors, at least for the twins. She was still shaken but was determined she would not let it do her in, despite the fact the torment had now turned to threat: her beloved boys' lives had been endangered.

Since Mitch and Gabe were still up in the cupola, attaching new louvers, Rachel put down her broom to greet Kent as he pulled up in the driveway. Andy and Aaron got even more excited when they saw Kent had Jeff and Mike with him.

"You're making a lot of your own deliveries lately," Rachel noted as Kent climbed down from the truck cab. He swung his sons down, then unloaded the new piece of glass for her upstairs window.

"It's just that I like to get out of the office and warehouse sometimes," he explained, lifting his baseball cap, raking his thick hair back, then shoving the cap down harder on his head. "Especially in this great autumn weather before the bad stuff hits. It gives me a chance to be with my boys and not have them underfoot at the warehouse where they could get hurt."

He looked past her at Gabe, who had come to stand in the open haymow door. "Got your big pieces for the beam repair!" Kent yelled up to him. "And glass for that shot-out house window."

"We'll be right down," Gabe shouted.

"You could back the truck up to the barn door," Rachel suggested, "and unload it inside in case it rains. Forecast says it might tomorrow, despite how pretty today is shaping up. I've got to get hustling to get my other shocks inside and husk that pile of corn—and get that boarded-up window replaced."

"Yeah," he said, not looking at her. He watched the four boys begin to play tag on the frost-dusted grass, leaving their tracks there. "Nothing personal,

Rachel," Kent went on, "but I'm not too fond of making deliveries here, so I'll just let Mitch and Gabe carry the lumber into the barn." Even as he spoke, he began to unload it beside his truck.

She nodded, remembering that when he'd unloaded her planks for the barn dance he hadn't gone inside, either. Mitch had told her that Marci had said Kent accepted Laura's loss, but it hardly sounded that way now. She wondered if it would help or hurt Kent to know his father had gone into the barn and left flowers in Laura's memory.

"I'm sorry," she told Kent. "I've made peace with the place and thought you had, too."

"Amazing," he said, shaking his head, "that with everything that happened here..." He bit off his last words and looked embarrassed he'd said that. When his oldest son ran up to them, Kent stopped unloading wood and turned to him.

"Dad, can Aaron and Andy go with us, please?" Jeff asked and tugged on Kent's jacket.

"No," Rachel put in. "We can't impose on—"

"Sure," Kent said. "I was going to ask, anyway. Mom's flitting around today," he explained to Rachel, "all nervous about having a date with Linc McGowan tomorrow, her first since Dad left."

"Yes, I think it will be good for her. But you do so much for us already," Rachel protested gently.

"Hey, I've got my own two, I might as well have four," he said with a laugh as he went back to hauling off the big boards. "Let me take them on my rounds, then drop them at Mom's and you go over and get them when you're ready. She'll be back soon, and you know she loves the noise and action instead of a quiet house. Really," he went on as

Gabe and Mitch walked up, "no problem. Besides, I hear you're taking care of the four of them tomorrow when Mom goes into Toledo with McGowan."

Rachel noted that Mitch's head jerked up at the mere mention of Linc's name. She knew bad feelings still festered between them. Sometimes she felt she was doing a balancing act to keep Mitch and Linc happy, both with stakes in the barn and her goodwill.

"All right," she conceded, "but I need to talk to the twins first. Andreas and Aaron, come over here."

While the three men worked with the wood, Rachel lectured the twins about behaving. She sent them to the outhouse and to wash up while she quickly packed Kent and his charges cookies and moon pies for snacks. It heartened her to see Andy and Aaron, peering and waving importantly out the back truck window, as Kent drove off.

"Now I'll fetch my two other favorite kids a snack," Rachel teased Mitch and Gabe as she started back into the house.

"Wait a minute," Mitch said, catching up with her. "If you don't have to worry about the twins all day, why don't you let me come up with the treats for once? Gabe will be better off doing the finishing work with a little elbow room. And I know where we can get a decent antique replacement for your ruined weather vane, even if it does have a ship on it instead of a horse."

"Where?" she asked, suddenly breathless.

"In a derelict barn about a mile from Lake Erie," he said, smiling. "I just bought it—the barn, not the lake."

She laughed.

"I'm serious," he said, taking her hand. "You can ride along to yea or nay the weather vane. As for the weather itself, I'd say this might be our last great day for a while. And don't tell me you have to stay to sell pumpkins, because Gabe can check the money in that box on the table. You said you always wanted to see the lake. I'll put in your new window while you get ready. Let's go."

Rachel knew she shouldn't go, not if she was going to get all her work done here and get back in the good graces of her people. But when she opened her mouth to explain, she said, "Yes. Let's go."

Mitch said they could take the Ohio Turnpike east out of Toledo, but they opted for old Route 2, which skirted the south shore of the lake. They stopped at the barn near Oak Harbor, where Mitch had the weather vane already off the roof. He said the rickety edifice would be dismantled, power-cleaned, moved and reassembled next month. She loved the weather vane's old, greenish copper sailing ship bent into the wind on a row of sculpted waves. But she loved the vast expanse of real water more.

"I knew it would be wonderful," she said as they sat side by side with their deli sandwiches and soft drinks on a massive boulder. This rocky, white-stone promontory called Marblehead jutted out into Lake Erie north of choppy Sandusky Bay.

When the wind yanked her bonnet back, Rachel let it bounce on its ties around her throat. Despite her stiff *kapp,* her hair began to tug loose and whip around her face as she surveyed the scene.

The water was the cobalt blue of her house curtains. The whitecaps seemed to mimic the racing clouds overhead. The stiff breeze smelled of adventure. Despite her problems at home, Rachel had never, at least for the moment, felt happier. She even put on her glasses to see it all better, though they were soon fogged with spray. She was getting wet, too, but she insisted they sit where the waves crashed instead of at a more sheltered picnic table back in the grassy park.

"Now that you've been bold enough to come away with me, without Jennie," Mitch told her as he heaved a stone out into the waves, "the next step is for me to make an appointment with the ophthalmologist who prescribed my contact lenses. You know, for someone as young and nearsighted as you, they also have a laser operation where you don't ever wear lenses again."

"Contacts? Laser surgery? For me? Oh, no," she said with a little laugh. "Impossible."

"As impossible as letting your hair blow free or coming away with me?"

"That was a poem," she said, desperate to change the subject.

"I feel poetic today," he said, leaning back on his elbows and letting the wind rip through his short, black hair. "How's this? You are the most fascinating woman I have ever known as well as the most beautiful, even windblown."

Rachel felt herself go suddenly shy. He was teasing and yet so intensely serious. Those worldly compliments were about shallow things, but still they warmed her heart. She knew she would always remember this escape to such wild, vast beauty and the lovely things he had said.

If only, she thought, their lives were different,

there might be a future for them. But she came from a world where widows didn't clamber over boulders with their skirts hiked up nearly to their knees. A world where it was prideful to speak of physical beauty and sheer insanity to talk of fascination, however, well—female it made her feel. She came from a world where work and duty called, not the desire to fly with the screeching seagulls or set out over the horizon with those distant specks of sailing ships bent into the wind, just like on her new weather vane. Or the need to throw oneself into a man's arms and hold on forever.

"Rachel, I didn't mean to upset you," he said, leaning closer. "Do you want to talk about what happened with the boys last night? I promised myself I wouldn't pry, but something strange went on, especially with those ladders being back in place this morning and the look on your face when I asked you how and why."

She told him then, not only about the boys saying their dead father had led them back to and over the tracks, barely missing being hit by the train, but about their lost hats showing up in the barn. And then about Sam's hat turning up and then in a rush of words, all the rest that had been going on.

"But, even if I do believe in spirits, I mean eternal souls, I don't believe in ghosts," she concluded. "A flesh-and-blood person wants me scared away."

Mitch had edged even closer and put his arm around her shoulders. She leaned into the solid strength of his ribs and arm, letting her tears mingle with the fine mist as the wind kicked up even more.

"Rachel," he said quietly, "are you thinking that whoever killed Sam is now after you and the boys?"

It was one of the questions she had not wanted to hear or face.

"I don't know," she admitted, shaking her head. "Several among the brethren believe I should leave the farm for one reason or another, men who would then have different plans for the barn and the horses—or for me. But all that is Sam's and my heritage for the twins!"

"Right, I understand. Then there's only one thing I can think of to do. I'll bunk in the haymow for a few nights to see who or what turns up."

"No, I couldn't ask you to do that, couldn't allow it," she insisted, shifting slightly away from him.

"The barn, Rachel, not your house or bedroom, although…"

He didn't finish what he had started to say, so she replied, "I am grateful, but absolutely not. It might be dangerous for you, but for me, it's forbidden, such a thing from an outsider, a man. You know that."

"I think it should be done. All that's happened recently took planning and cunning. And if you think one of the Amish brothers might be behind it, you can't use them to set a trap. Besides, Eben Yoder's answer would probably be that you should just move out."

Rachel nodded. "I know. Move out and marry him." She felt his body stiffen.

"I'm glad you've ruled that out, but who do you think it could be?" he demanded, his tone going as tense as his muscles. "If Eben is only candidate number one, who else could be behind all that?"

Rachel bit her lower lip. She had considered Sim Lapp, of course, and even, when she was at her most distraught, her own brother-in-law, Zebulon Mast, despite the fact he lived clear across the state in Maplecreek. But she dare not get Mitch directly involved in this. She knew he could explode into violence and, if he became her champion, even a calm one, against the Amish, she'd be shunned for sure.

"Mitch," she said, taking his free hand in both of hers, "if you are my friend, you will let me handle this my way."

"Which is?"

"To show my tormentor I am not leaving, am not afraid. That the farm is mine, and I will make it prosper and keep it for my sons."

"In other words, the same way you're working on the possibility your husband was murdered—to stall and then back off and do nothing." His voice rose, accusing. "Of course, you don't forget, but you forgive and just forge ahead, the accepting, obedient Amish woman, which you're not. I repeat, your tormentor could be the one who killed Sam and is, therefore, deadly dangerous."

Dangerous—Jennie had called Mitch that, too. And he was, for she was coming to care for him too deeply. She pulled away and jumped up, crinkling her sandwich paper in her hand. Starting across the pile of boulders, she nearly slipped but continued onto the stony beach, then the grass of the little park. He caught up with her, swinging her around to face him.

"If so," she said, "my tormentor will tip his hand and then I'll have him dealt with—arrested—like those paramilitary men."

"When he's got you cornered, maybe worse than they had? And you'll call who for help on your non-existent Amish phone?" he goaded. "Will you just pray for him or grab some kid's baseball bat or that snowshoe knocker to defend yourself?''

Rachel gaped at him. Surely he didn't know that she'd carried a stickball bat outside to face down Jennie's ex-husband. She hadn't told him that. But, of course, he knew she'd almost brained a man with the knocker and he was just imagining the rest.

"I am not your concern," she said, tossing her trash in the wire basket, then struggling to shove her hair back and retie her bonnet. "I will find a way, so your hard work in my barn is enough."

"Whether you like it or not," he countered, "you've become my concern. All right, I won't camp out in your barn, but you get word to me if anything goes wrong."

"Yes, all right. You've been a tremendous help already," she admitted. They were halfway back to Gabe's car, which they'd borrowed, before she realized how true that was. More than once, Mitch had miraculously been there for her. When he took her hand and swung it slightly, she squeezed his back.

"What else shall we see on our way home?" he asked, obviously trying to lighten the mood, maybe even change the subject.

"Actually," she said, "if we could stop at a few grocery stores, I'd really appreciate it. I'm going to a wedding on Sunday and I need about three hundred stalks of celery."

He looked surprised, then laughed. "Celery it is. The entire supply for northwest Ohio for the lady," he shouted as if he had to be heard above the wind and waves.

She smiled then laughed, too, at how crazy he

was acting, how alive—and electric—he suddenly seemed.

"And what are you going to do with all that celery?" he asked, leaning close to her.

"I don't dare make creamed celery for a traditional wedding, because it isn't going to be that," she tried to explain. "But I'm going to make some huge displays, you know, bouquets. I'll probably get in trouble, but my friend Sarah deserves to be honored and happy no matter what her father says and does."

"Sounds like another Rachel rebellion," Mitch said as they walked together, only their hands touching. But to her it was such a sweet delight. No, maybe not sweet, for it made her feel sensations in her belly and thighs that were so foreign. She felt almost dizzy but exultant, as if she rode those waves out on the lake.

Rachel noted an elderly couple walking their dog and a police officer looking out of his cruiser window, staring at them from the parking lot. They were probably intrigued by the way she was dressed. Though she felt warm in the bracing wind, she shuddered. Even here, she had not escaped the dread of someone watching her, just waiting for something to happen.

While Rachel baked pumpkin pies to sell at her and Jennie's stand, she let the boys sit out front, supposedly guarding pumpkins on display, but she kept a sharp eye on them. Jennie and Linc were to drop off Jeff and Mike on their way into Toledo for the day on their infamous first date. Rachel had already cleaned hundreds of stalks of celery she now had crisping in water-speckled plastic sacks in the refrigerator.

But as busy as she kept her hands, her mind was busier as she agonized over what to do about her dilemma. Someone, maybe the same person who had killed Sam, was trying to ruin her and the twins' lives. Though she felt she had no right to deny Sam's sons their Amish heritage, if her headlong pursuit of this cost *her* the support of her people, it was a risk she must take.

When she peeked out and saw Pat Perkins among their customers, she went outside with a freshly baked pie for her.

"I hope it doesn't rain on your parade," Pat called cheerily to her and glanced at the gloomy, midmorning sky.

"Farmers can always use rain," Rachel replied. She liked the way Pat talked, bringing in all sorts of pictures in her language. The Amish were very factual; there was hardly a real parade, though she saw her twins were looking up and down the road as if one was ready to roll by. Rachel had looked up Pat's use of "rain check" in the dictionary, too, and learned what it meant. Today, Rachel thought, would be better weather for a rain check than a parade.

"Selling pies, too?" Pat asked, looking up from the pile of biggest pumpkins.

"I'm going to be, but this one is for you for all your help," Rachel said. "I'll put it on your car seat, as it's still hot."

Rachel saw the boys were staring at Pat's pierced ears and nostril. At least they talked to each other in German about "the nail in her nose."

"They're darling and they've grown so much, Rachel," Pat told her as she picked out a pumpkin and paid for it. The boys, still staring, thanked her in English and put the money in the box. "Oh, great," Pat muttered, looking over Rachel's shoulder as another car pulled up. "My favorite person."

Rachel knew from her tone of voice she meant just the opposite. But she saw it was Jennie in the car.

"You don't like Jennie Morgan?" Rachel asked.

"No, the guy with her," Pat said as everyone got out of Linc's large car.

There was no time to find out why. Rachel went to greet them and assure Jennie the boys would be fine with her until Marci or Kent picked them up later. Linc looked as elegant as ever, and relieved, Rachel thought, either to be getting rid of the boys or because Jennie was finally going out with him. They had tickets to a matinee of *Phantom of the Opera,* which was on tour in Toledo, and then they were going out to eat. Jennie looked both excited and strangely resigned.

"I wanted to get tickets to that show, Mrs. Morgan," Pat piped up across the table, "but all the good ones were sold out and I'm not sitting way back. I can listen to the music all I want but I'd be paying for those special effects. I've seen the production twice, but I always thought it would be fun to be right on the main floor when that chandelier swings down to crush—well—" she interrupted herself, evidently realizing she'd said too much "—hope you enjoy it."

"I'm sure we will," Jennie said. "Linc has a beautiful voice, and sang in a few musicals himself, didn't you?" she prompted.

"The lead in *South Pacific* in college, but I decided a career in musical theater or acting would be crazy," Linc admitted almost sheepishly. "I like the finer things in life too much to starve."

"I suppose you could have taught high school or college vocal music instead of history," Pat suggested.

"Tell them about that Amish part you had in *Plain and Fancy*," Jennie went on. "Rachel would be interested in that. He's much too modest," she added, when, for once, Linc said nothing. "He sang that famous song 'Young and Foolish' in the play."

"And now we're middle-aged and foolish," Linc said as if to conclude Jennie's chatter. He looked slightly embarrassed, though Rachel had never seen him flustered or modest before. The last thing in the world she could imagine was the self-confident, suave Lincoln McGowan playing an Amish part on stage.

Everyone waved to Jennie and Linc as they got in and drove away. "Why don't you like Linc?" Rachel asked Pat as she walked the librarian to her car and held the back door open while she put the pumpkin on the floor.

"You mean, besides the fact he's a pompous ass— sorry."

"Pat, the Amish know what asses are. Stupid and stubborn, but I don't think he's that."

"It just annoys the heck out of me that he has the nerve to look down his nose at the library Clearview's struggled so hard to get," Pat accused, fishing in her purse for her car keys as Rachel put the pie on the back seat. "He's always carrying on about what university libraries are like."

"If ours is so inadequate, why does he even use

it?'' Rachel asked as Pat got in and put the key in the ignition. She rolled the automatic window down before she closed her door.

"You know, I never could quite figure out how he could get a sabbatical after just teaching at Ohio Southern for two years," Pat said, frowning and not really answering Rachel's question. "Usually sabbaticals come after you earn them, and his getting off, with pay, to publish those little articles he writes can hardly be the cause. I swear, I'm going to check that out about him."

"On the Internet?" Rachel inquired.

"Yeah, that's a start. And as for your question about why he uses such a country-bumpkin library and why I don't like him…" She paused a moment. "He puts on a big show with the high-school girls who come in to do their papers, especially history ones he helps them with," Pat said. "Frankly, I'm glad to see he's dating someone his own age, because he's got at least a couple of those high-school honeys hot for him. Oh, Rachel, I didn't mean to—"

"Stop apologizing. If I look shocked, it's only partly what you just said," Rachel said, gripping the lower part of Pat's car window. "He's always made me a little uncomfortable, too," she admitted, "but not that way. More like, because he's so condescending to me. Then, too, sometimes I think he's been watching the barn."

"Watching the barn?" Pat repeated. "You mean watching *you,* don't you? I'm only saying that because I've seen him follow one of the girls to see when she came into the library. Actually, the guy gives me the creeps," she added with a shudder.

Pat said she had to get going but Rachel's stunned

mind was racing as fast as Pat's car. Mitch had told her that Sheriff Burnett had checked out the students and teachers at Laura Morgan's high school when she disappeared. Linc McGowan had been Laura's history teacher. Maybe Linc had been close to Laura, closer than people knew, closer than he should have been.

But what really came back to haunt Rachel was, when she'd first met Linc, he said he'd had his eye on her barn for years and that he'd had his eye on Jennie for years, too. Monday morning, maybe she should join Pat in looking into Linc's past. He'd been pretty upset just now when Jennie blurted out that he had played an Amish part in a musical. Maybe he still had the costume, even a beard.

But that very afternoon, Linc McGowan came to her: at least his article on her barn did. Carloads of people drove by, some stopping to buy pumpkins, several who asked to see the barn, and a few who boldly walked back toward it before she chased them out.

"I read all about it in the article," one woman told her. She had white-blond hair with black roots. Since rain was threatening, she wore a raincoat, a bright green one that almost hurt Rachel's eyes as much as the woman's high-pitched voice grated on her ears.

"Are there ghosts in the barn, too?" the woman demanded. When Rachel just gaped at her, she added, "I'd love to rent it for a Halloween party. I mean, I think this is the place where a man got crushed to death, isn't it?"

Rachel gestured the woman off to the side, away

from the boys, though they'd obviously heard. "Where are you getting all this about the barn? Where is everyone getting it?" Rachel demanded.

"The weekly *Clearview Chronicle,* of course," the woman said. "It just came out this morning. Don't you Amish read the papers?"

The blonde-brunette pulled it out of her purse, and Rachel, unAmish-like, snatched it and squinted to read it. A Haunting Place: Folklore in the Heartland, the article was titled. Lincoln McGowan had written it.

Rachel skimmed it, seeing he'd included most of the things he'd told her about the barn's history. He hadn't given her exact address, nor had he specifically mentioned Sam's death nor Laura's disappearance here, but he had included the pioneer-farm information and the blood-red and devil-black paint descriptions. And he'd said the barn was a Ravine Road remnant of Americana that would forever haunt local hearts.

"This is a big PR break, since you'll sell all your pumpkins now," the woman's voice sliced through Rachel's rising fury. "You ought to give barn tours, too. I know the Amish look poor, but with all those restaurants and knickknack stores, not to mention the rich farmland you have, you're probably rolling in—"

"Get off my property," Rachel said, first to the woman and then in a louder voice so the others at the pumpkin table or heading back into the driveway would hear. Lincoln McGowan had betrayed her, maybe betrayed her friend Jennie, too. Rachel felt herself lose the reins of her control. "If you've just come to buy a pumpkin, fine,'' she shouted, ''but the barn is off-limits. Yes, I'm asking you to leave!''

Rachel was actually grateful when Eben pulled up with his two eldest sons in the buggy and helped herd everyone back into their cars.

Sixteen

Over the bent heads of the bride and groom, Bishop Eben Yoder looked directly at Rachel, sitting on the women's side in the congregation.

"'Listen to what I tell you,'" he recited the traditional wedding ceremony from the Apocryphal book of *Tobit* in the Amish Bible. "'Listen and I will show you over whom the devil has power, namely over those who enter upon marriage without respecting God in their hearts. But rather they follow the desire of the body like the mule and the horse, who know nothing else. Over such the devil has power.'"

That indirect warning and accusation jolted Rachel. When Eben looked and sounded like that, she became convinced he was behind the frightening events her farm. But she also knew it would be fruitless, maybe even dangerous, to ask or accuse him. Besides, when she saw him minister to the brethren or when he helped or encouraged her, she wasn't sure he was responsible at all. Eben and his boys had kindly spent yesterday afternoon and evening at her place, helping the twins sell pumpkins and keeping gawkers away from the barn.

The rain increased outside, rattling against the windows and drumming on the roof, but Rachel forced her attention back to Sarah and Jacob's service. Despite the shame of having just confessed their sins, this wedding should be for dedication and rejoicing. Rachel tried to concentrate on how sweet Sarah looked in the white bridal apron and cape over her blue dress. After today, the white garments would be tenderly put away in a dowry trunk to be worn again only in her coffin.

Despite the warmth in the crowded Lapp living room, Rachel shuddered as Eben's deep voice intoned, "'What God hath joined, let no man put asunder.'" Eben had helped her out yesterday, but he had also lectured her about cutting all ties to worldly men, lest she face shunning, the dreaded *meidung*. She had listened properly and politely but knew she could not let go of things now. Not with Mitch or Linc, for very different reasons, though she had not openly objected to Eben's warning.

"Are there any objectors," Eben went on, "before our final blessing on this brother and sister as man and wife in holy wedlock?"

Wedlock, Rachel thought as the silence stretched out and Eben gave the final blessing. Poor Sarah feared she'd be locked in an unhappy marriage as her mother must have been. And, Rachel realized, as they all turned the pages of the *Ausbund* to a wedding hymn, her own marriage had been broken by death. And if that death was murder, she was dedicating herself to finding out the truth, even if she wasn't certain how to proceed or whom to investigate.

"Oh, I can't believe my eyes," Sarah cried, beaming as Rachel and her boys went out in the rain to carry in glass jar after glass jar filled with stalks of leafy celery from a carton in their buggy.

"I can't, either," Eben muttered ominously behind her. But that didn't stop Rachel from bustling past to cluster jars on the *eck,* the corner bridal table. The fresh scent of celery filled the air to vie with that of cold-cut meat and cheese sandwiches that were the standard after church fare when there was not a wedding.

The regular meal was, Rachel had heard several of the other women whisper, part of Sarah's penance. But everyone felt they were being punished, too, for the Amish loved weddings. It hadn't stopped the women and children from bringing the traditional, small, handmade gifts of candy and gum. Tied or taped together, there were small buggies, tables, houses and barns for the bride and groom. The usual apples, candy and flasks of cider crowded the *eck* right along with Rachel's bounty.

Again, her love flowed out to her people. She did not want to grieve them with her defiance, and when she did, she only upset and hurt herself. Sometimes, she felt torn in two over wanting the best of both worlds.

Breathing a sigh of relief that she was not alone in her quiet protest today, Rachel began to distribute the extra jars of celery to the other tables set up in the same living and dining rooms where they'd just had their four-hour church. Unlike the bigger Amish communities, which would have to eat in shifts at a wedding, the Clearview Church was small enough to partake together.

Rachel relaxed even more when she saw some of the sisters had brought the usual kitchenware or household tools for wedding gifts. People, even Eben, applauded as Sim Annie Lapp, as hostess today, presented the blushing Sarah and Jacob with the traditional gift of a new kerosene lantern from the congregation.

Everyone laughed when Sim Annie gave Sarah a clothesline that was playfully knotted. "Sim tied it in his fancy harvesting knots!" she cried, displaying the maze of snarls and tangles. "At least it didn't get thrown up a tree like at our wedding."

As people sat at the tables to eat, they passed around the lantern and clothesline for inspection and comment, as if everyone had not seen such items a hundred times before. The moment Rachel touched the looped and knotted rope, she knew something about it was disturbingly familiar. The knots were indeed Sim Lapp's double hitches, the same ones that were still around her extra *stooks* in her cornfield.

But now she knew they were also just like Sam's knots and the very ones she'd seen two other places: on the rope dragging behind the team's hitch that foggy morning in the field, and in the rope that worked the big grappling hook that had killed Sam—knots she'd never seen Eben make. Perhaps she had been wrong to suspect Bishop Yoder and should be watching Sim instead. Or they could both be working together.

It was tradition that Amish newlyweds not set up housekeeping until several months after their marriage. Until then, they would visit relatives and friends, including some kin in Maplecreek. So, as

Rachel prepared to bid Sarah farewell for who knew how long, she let the twins sit in the buggy, holding Bett and Nann's reins while she hugged Sarah good-bye on the back porch. Blessedly, the rain had let up.

"I'll never forget what a good friend you are to me," Sarah told her and grasped her hands. "You saved me when I could have—could have been killed."

Rachel startled at the way she'd put that. "I just want you to be happy," she insisted, looking intently into Sarah's blue eyes.

"That's what I want for you," Sarah said. Her voice dropped to a whisper. "And I understand that doesn't mean with Bishop Yoder. Someone else will come along," she vowed, holding Rachel's hands even tighter.

"You are all right today? See how everyone pitched in to make it special for you?" Rachel encouraged her. "No second thoughts now."

"Only something that I forgot to tell you on that night," Sarah said, still whispering. She spoke quicker now, probably because others were coming up to bid their farewells.

"The night of the *danze?*"

"*Ja.* It slipped my mind because of everything that happened after, but there was a kind of nest up in your haymow when I was hiding up there."

"A nest? You mean, my barn owls are back? I haven't seen th—"

"A nest hollowed out in the hay, body-shaped, the size of a man. Maybe a bum off those trains has been sleeping in your barn."

A chill raced through Rachel, brushing her skin to

goose bumps. "I've taken a rest up there," she told her friend, trying to convince not Sarah but herself. "Just a couple of weeks ago, on the fresh hay, right under the haymow door so I could look out to see who was coming if I heard a sound. It was me for sure. Or else someone else during the *danze* went up there and—"

"No," Sarah said and shook her head so hard her *kapp* looked skewed. "Not unless you've been cutting your hair up there, and I know better. I saw some hair, a reddish-brown, and a Mars bar wrapper, and a piece of paper that I couldn't see real good because it was getting dark. But it looked like a form to fill in about Ohio historic buildings."

"That explains it then," Rachel said. "Linc McGowan must have been climbing around up there and took a rest. You know, the man I was listing my barn with as a historic site. That is," she said glumly, "until he wrote that article for the local paper that put me under siege yesterday. Now I'm going to cancel out on him."

"That may annoy Mr. McGowan, but it will please the bishop," Sarah said with a roll of her eyes. "So Mr. McGowan's reddish-haired… I'm glad it's nothing." Sarah and Rachel hugged again, then Sarah turned to her sister, Annie, who had waited patiently while they talked.

Rachel knew she had misled Sarah so she wouldn't get her upset on this special day. Looking at her buggy waiting in the long line of them to depart, Rachel saw Andy and Aaron sitting so proudly, both holding the reins, whispering. Her fears whispered to her, too.

Maybe Linc McGowan did have it in for her and

wanted her barn. And if he had a liking for young women like Laura, he could be involved in all that, too. Perhaps her tormentor could be the brilliant Linc, who had once played an Amish man in a musical and perhaps still had that costume and beard— maybe a reddish one—to disguise his elegant clothes and silver hair. He was a skilled researcher and interviewer; he could have learned how Sam used to wear that straw hat and hitch a buggy. But, decked out in Amish clothes and beard or not, she couldn't picture him lying down in the hay.

Determinedly, Rachel climbed up into the buggy, wedging herself in between the twins.

"We're going to play a game," she told them as she giddyaped the horses toward home. "I'm going to ask you one at a time about something, and you don't get to talk it over or even look at each other before you answer, okay?"

"Okay," Andy said, his voice wary.

"I say okay, too," Aaron put in.

She hated to play this their way, but she was getting desperate. And if she let them be together but not confer, maybe she'd get a straight answer. When she'd tried to separate and question them, they'd clammed up. When they could confer, only Andy had given answers, and precious little of those.

Her voice shook as she said, "I want to know how *Daadi* looked the other night when he took you for a walk to the train tracks."

Rachel saw Andy lean back in his seat, probably to shoot Aaron a glance or word behind her, but she leaned back, too, and looked down at him. "Andy, you go first. Tell me just one thing you remember."

"He was like before," he said, sitting stiffly on the bouncing seat and looking straight ahead.

"Tell me one thing that shows that."

"He had on his regular clothes."

"His work clothes—straw hat?"

"His good black ones and hat like this," he insisted, touching his hand to his wide, black brim.

"Good. Now, Aaron, tell me one more thing about how he looked."

"Holding out his hands if we went slow in the trees."

"Or stopped," Andy put in.

"Yeah, to make us hurry."

"Did you want to go with him?" Rachel pursued.

"Sure," Aaron replied, "but it was getting dark, and he didn't carry us like he used to."

"He had his regular-color hair—like ours," Andy said. "Red. And his beard."

Rachel's insides cartwheeled.

"But not bright red, 'cause it was dark," Aaron finished the thought for him.

They were almost thinking and talking together again, but at least they were talking to her about it.

"And he wasn't smiling, but wanted us to hurry up," Aaron added.

"So you could see his face?" she asked. "And it looked just like *Daadi?*" She wondered again how good their memories of their father could be. For once, she wished her people approved of photographs so she could have refreshed the boys' memories.

"Like him when he's mad at you," Andy said, still staring straight ahead. She felt both boys lean in toward her and stretch their little arms across the buggy seat behind her back, not to embrace her but to touch each other as if they could communicate with that alone.

"Why," she dared, her voice catching, "would he be mad at me?"

"We thought you hugged him in the barn but it was Mr. Randall, wasn't it?" Andy asked accusingly. "So he wanted us to come with him, but then he got on the train and left us, maybe because you came running, too."

"Yeah," Aaron piped up. "But he's up in the barn a lot. We've seen him, and he'll be back."

At home Rachel made the boys go with her up into the haymow. The gray day was getting darker, so she carried a lantern. Earlier she had thought they were making up seeing their father, but since everything from the barn owls' departure to Sarah's seeing the shape of a body in the straw suggested someone *had* been in the barn, she knew better now. And she remembered things—innocent things, she'd thought—the twins had said. That *Daadi* would be watching from above. That *Daadi* liked to be up in the barn.

She stopped and stared. The indentation of a body was discernible just to the left of the drop-down haymow door. It was near the place she'd lain on her birthday when Eben then Mitch had come to see her. But she couldn't find the candy-bar wrapper, reddish hair or blank form about historic sites anywhere.

"So that's where he sleeps," Andy declared, crossing his arms. Aaron nodded, wide-eyed. "But he should come in the house at night when he's not working in the barn and fields. It's cold and dark out here."

"And the barn roof might have some leaks,"
Aaron put in. "But if we all want him to come in
the house," he went on, looking up at Rachel hopefully and taking her hand, "I bet he will."

Tears stung Rachel's eyes. She didn't know
whether to play along or scold them or just scream.

In the house, across Rachel's pristine linoleum
kitchen floor, were a set of muddy tracks, men's
tracks. But every time she'd seen Mitch and Gabe
come in, they'd dutifully scraped their boots on the
rock outside. Though the back door had been locked,
the footsteps were positioned as if they had come
through it. Without breaking stride, the prints went
directly under the kitchen table and into the hall toward the stairs to the second floor, then faded.

Rachel gaped as her mind raced for explanations.
Could she have accidentally left the door unlocked
and Mitch or Gabe had come in? No, she'd just had
to unlock it. Someone had gone to great lengths to
make it appear the person walked right through the
door and then the big table. And why would the steps
head upstairs?

"We didn't do that," Andy protested before she
said a word. "It's too big for our feet, see?" He
dangled one of his small ones next to a footprint.

Blood pounded through Rachel so hard she barely
heard or saw him. These prints were blunt-toed, not
like the shoes or boots that Mitch and Gabe wore.
Blunt-toed, like Amish work boots. She'd heard the
two paramilitary men who'd shot up the barn were
out on bail. Did their boots have toes like this? Or,
if it had been Linc in the barn, could he have donned
boots as part of his disguise? Whoever it was had

gone out of his way to make her think the intruder was a spirit or a ghost.

Trembling, ignoring the fact the boys were whispering, she lit a lantern and closely examined the prints as they faintly etched the rag rug in the hall, then disappeared on the hardwood floor of the stairs. But, Rachel realized, they were definitely headed up.

She racked her mind to recall who had ever had a back-door key. Eben and Sam Lapp had had one each, after Sam died, though they'd given them back. Still, they could have had copies made. When the Maplecreek kids stayed here for the *danze,* a door key had gone missing, but she'd just thought she'd been distracted and misplaced it.

Shaking, trying to keep the twins from seeing her panic, Rachel told them to wait in the kitchen while she carried the lantern upstairs. It was raining again, and the late afternoon had gone darker yet. In the dim rooms, she peered under beds, in closets, behind doors, then searched the first floor and finally, her heart in her throat, the cellar.

Nothing. Absolutely nothing amiss but those mud prints.

The twins sat strangely subdued at the kitchen table. They probably didn't realize it was impossible for a man's prints to go *under* the table. Andy was yawning and Aaron had his head down on his hands. Thank the Lord, her mad search had not panicked them.

"Did you find him upstairs?" Andy asked.

"There is no one in the house but us, boys. The tracks are just an—an accident. There has been someone sleeping in the barn, but it was not *Daadi.*

I'll just mop these up," she said, trying to steady her voice so she didn't explode in a fit of sobbing.

As she fetched the mop from the corner of the pantry, she heard Aaron's muffled voice. "His shoes are clean now. And he'll stay where it's warm."

Rachel hustled out to insist they stop such talk, but her brain didn't seem to be working with her mouth. Before she could stammer a word, Andy put in, *"Ja,"* then turned to look at her instead of Aaron. "Those feet," he said, pointing at the prints under the table, "are not an acc'dent. Now you know about him, too, *Mamm,* he won't sleep in the barn but in your bed."

Seventeen

❧

"Not even time for a cup of coffee, Rachel?" Jennie asked Monday morning. Her lower lip thrust out in a pout as she poured herself a cup. "I thought you'd want to know all about my day with Linc. You were pleased and excited about my seeing him."

"I was—am," Rachel replied. She was making a disaster of this deception, but she didn't want to tell Jennie what she'd come to suspect about Linc, at least not yet. Nor did she want her to know she was on her way to get evidence that he was not only the man who'd been tormenting her for some reason, but had perhaps been closer to Laura than he'd admitted. "It's just I'm in a hurry to get some things done in town," she explained lamely.

"I can see that, since you forgot to kiss your kids goodbye."

Shaking her head at herself, Rachel hurried back in to hug the boys. They seemed all right this morning, not upset about last night, not—thank the Lord—talking about *Daadi* coming in the house again. When she bustled back out into the kitchen, Jennie had poured a half a cup of coffee for her.

"Not that you need this to get revved up this morning," Jennie observed, nodding toward the cup, "but I want you to stand still long enough for me to tell you something."

Rachel stopped and took the coffee.

"I know," Jennie went on slowly, "the night of your Amish dance you realized I can't bear to talk about losing my daughter. And I said I felt good with you because you knew nothing about it and so didn't ask or pry."

Holding the cup halfway to her mouth, Rachel nodded. Surely Jennie couldn't know she was meaning to do just that. She felt like a Judas.

"So," Jennie went on as Rachel forced herself to sip the hot liquid, "I made a deal with Linc, since he knew Laura. He was one of her favorite teachers, actually. She had a real crush on him."

Rachel nodded to encourage her. She had several people in mind to interview about Linc and Laura, but she'd never expected Jennie to be one of them.

"Linc and I are not going to talk about the past at all," Jennie rushed on, "not that past, anyway. Which, for a man who loves history, is a real concession. That is, until I'm ready someday—if I am."

"I see. That shows he thinks a lot of you."

"I figure it's like he's doing with your barn, honoring, preserving, but not tampering, not—digging."

Rachel almost told her that she was going to cancel out on dealing with Linc on the historic preservation of the barn. He'd used it and betrayed her just to get a good article in the local paper, or, for all she knew, try to get the house next to Jennie's. At any rate, Jennie evidently hadn't read the article and had no idea the farm and barn had been besieged by curious gawkers. And Rachel wasn't going to tell her right now, because she wanted to be on her way.

Rachel took a last gulp of coffee. "I'm glad you enjoyed your time with Linc, Jennie, really I am." She put the cup down and edged toward the back door. She regretted rushing after all the times Jennie had listened to her pour her heart out about Sam's life and loss. But, even if it hurt her fragile friend, Rachel had to know the truth about Linc and then make Jennie listen to that truth.

Since Pat Perkins had said she was going to look into Linc's sabbatical from Ohio Southern University, Rachel's first stop was the library. Early Monday morning, except for Pat, it was blessedly deserted.

"I'm really upset that Linc McGowan did that article on my so-called haunted barn," she told Pat right out, "so I was thinking I might just do a little research on him."

Pat smiled smugly. "Turnabout's fair play, you mean? Doesn't sound very Amish, but pretty American."

"I know," Rachel said and heaved a sigh. "We're to turn the other cheek, but on this, for several reasons, I can't let it go."

"And you knew I was checking up on him, too," Pat replied, making no effort to keep her booming voice down. Rachel only hoped that if someone came in, she would.

"The man should be writing fiction, not history," Pat declared, gesturing Rachel over to her cluttered desk, "because he's evidently a great liar. I found out he's not on sabbatical from Ohio Southern at all, though if cornered on it, he'd probably say we were mincing words. He's on, ah, where is that?'' she muttered as she scrabbled through several piles of paper. ''Oh, here.''

Rachel leaned closer to look over her friend's shoulder at a printed page. ''He has taken,'' Pat continued, pointing a blue fingernail at a line of print, ''a leave of absence. It was like pulling teeth to get the campus librarian to say why, but it's evidently pending some sort of disciplinary hearing. A personnel matter,'' Pat said, lifting her eyebrows.

''But that could be anything.''

''Considering how he's carried on with several young ladies in here,'' Pat went on, finally lowering her voice, ''I played a hunch and asked for the e-mail address of the campus newspaper and did a virtual chat with a student on staff.''

Rachel held her breath. ''And?'' she prompted.

''Professor Lincoln McGowan evidently got in trouble for having an affair with a student, so don't tell me you can't tell a skunk by its smell.''

''Oh, no!'' Rachel cried. She began to agonize about whether or not to tell Pat that Linc had been the favorite teacher of a girl who'd strangely disappeared from a dance he'd been supervising, a dance in Rachel's barn. But that would be accusing him of too much, too soon. Before she told anyone her suspicions or faced down the man himself, she needed to talk to some others about him.

''You know,'' Pat was saying, though, after the previous revelation, her words hardly sank in, ''I had a friend who was stalked by a guy, so I looked up the personality traits of a stalker, thinking that might give more insight into McGowan. And listen to this.''

She grabbed another piece of paper from another pile. ''Stalkers are often quite intelligent and some hang around universities. They can be charming, cunning and seductive. Sound like anyone we know so far?''

''He does fit those traits,'' Rachel admitted. But if Linc's tastes ran to high-school or college girls, why would he stalk a widow with two kids? Since she was Amish, did she come across as innocent or gullible to him? He did love to lecture her and flaunt his knowledge.

''And the worst news is,'' Pat plunged on, ''when a stalker is thwarted, his behavior escalates. Even if told or officially ordered to stay away, he comes closer and closer, and mere harassment can turn to threats and violence. You've got to admit some of this profile could fit McGowan, though I don't know about these other things.''

''Like what?'' Rachel asked, but she wasn't listening anymore. Rachel's stalker had not just watched her boys but had tried to lure them in harm's way. Now he'd been in her house. Shuddering, she recalled Andy's words that he'd be in her bed.

''A stalker,'' Pat went on, ''sets up situations where the victim will turn to him for help, then rides to the rescue. Has he done that?''

''What? Oh, yes, trying to help with my barn, then scare me about it,'' Rachel said, not even sure she was making sense. She edged toward the door.

''A stalker has an intense need for control,'' Pat continued, still reading from the paper. ''I know McGowan always expects me to listen up when he bestows his pronouncements, let alone the high-school honeys he's had in here. And last, a stalker has something called an attachment disruption. In other words, he lost someone he loved early in life and fixates on never being hurt again by a love object rejecting him—or else he gets violent, sometimes even committing murder.'' She looked up, surprised. ''Rachel, are you leaving already?''

''I've got to get going. Thanks again for your help.''

''Are you sure you're okay, girl?'' Pat asked, jumping to her feet. ''Have you heard a thing I just said?''

''Sure,'' Rachel insisted, though she knew Pat's last words were one big blur. She had to do a little more checking on Linc, then sever her ties to him. She'd have to decide whether or not to tell the sheriff so Linc could be questioned, even if it would doubly devastate Jennie and maybe put Rachel in jeopardy with her own people. Mixing into worldly things with worldly men would surely get her shunned faster than anything.

In Clearview Consolidated Junior-Senior High School, Rachel pressed herself against the wall as a bell rang and students exploded from their rooms to change classes. Locker doors banged, voices rose, then faded as kids disappeared and only silence echoed again in the high-ceilinged halls. Despite her long black skirt and bonnet, no one had given Rachel a second look, but there were a few Amish scholars attending here. Did she appear so young they'd thought she was one of them? Maybe she'd looked that way to Linc if he really was the sort of predator Pat had called a stalker.

Rachel passed several glass cases displaying trophies and photographs of winning teams in various worldly sports. She found Kent Morgan in one picture, AAA State Basketball Semifinals, 1988. Surprisingly, Kent was frowning in this picture, where most boys looked either serious or outright proud.

But it would have been his senior year, she calculated, for he was one year older than Laura had been. Basketball concluded in March, so this photo would have been about six months after Laura disappeared. Rachel wondered what he was thinking then to cause that sad look. Maybe he had blamed himself for not keeping a better eye on Laura, since Jennie had said he'd also attended that fateful barn dance. Or was he just worried about something small like homework that wasn't done, or a basket he'd missed that could have taken the team to the finals? Or was this about the time his parents' marriage had begun to fray?

Rachel found the main office and asked the secretary if she might speak with the principal. Franklin Mercer was evidently an institution within this institution. She'd heard he'd been here for years, so he must know if there was any connection between Linc and Laura.

Butterflies fluttered in Rachel's stomach as the secretary came out a door down the short hall and said, "He's busy but he will take a moment for you. Mr. Mercer always likes to keep up good relations with our Amish parents."

Ordinarily Rachel would have corrected the misconception she was a parent of someone in this school, but she wanted to see the man and now. Yet she scolded herself that she was starting to blur or hide the truth, first with Jennie, then Pat, and now this woman. And she could hardly tell the kindly, white-haired man who greeted her that she was trying to link his former history teacher to sins and crimes.

Nervously, she began to explain and was amazed at the skewed story that came out of her mouth.

"So," Mr. Mercer said, "Lincoln McGowan has done a story on your barn and now you think the paper would like a story on the man himself." She noted he more or less repeated whatever she said to him, maybe to be sure he had it right or to give himself more time to think of his reply.

"Yes, and I realized you'd be the best person to ask what sort of teacher he was—strengths and weaknesses."

"Ah, yes, everyone, even the most popular, which he was, has strengths and weaknesses." He steepled his fingers before his mouth as he faced her across his desk. "Lincoln McGowan was very bright. And he was best, actually, with bright students. He challenged them to go beyond themselves. Ah, aren't you going to take notes?"

"I have a good memory, but yes," she said, fumbling for a pen and paper in her canvas bag that served as purse and sack. "Why did he leave here then?" she asked. Mercer's hesitation and nervous shifting in his chair told her she was on to something.

"Indeed, why did he leave? No doubt, partly because we are a rural high school," he said and cleared his throat. "And that was too narrow a venue for Lincoln's many interests."

"I see. I'll bet since he was so popular, his students, at least his favorite, bright ones, gave him a real going-away party at the end of the year when he left.''

"Actually," Mr. Mercer said, "Lincoln made his decision to pursue a degree and career in higher education midyear, so he departed rather suddenly. It was all handled internally and was a real shock to some of the students."

"I imagine it was especially unsettling for them since he left shortly after the mysterious loss of one of your—and his—pupils, Laura Morgan. He did leave that same year, didn't he?"

Mr. Mercer's steepled fingers lunged together to grip each other. "Where is all this going, Mrs. Mast?" he demanded, suddenly not sounding so kindly. "Perhaps you'd best interview Lincoln himself. I am just not at liberty to—"

"I will see him myself, sir, and I thank you for your time. You see, I'm coming to learn that there are some things that can't be handled internally, whether you're in charge of a school or an Amish community or just a barn."

"A barn? Mrs. Mast..."

But she was already sailing out his door.

Though no one was in the sheriff's office but Tim Burnett himself, Rachel felt awkward entering. It most certainly was not the Amish way to darken the door of worldly government or law officials.

"Mrs. Mast, what can I do for you?" Burnett said, hopping up from reading a paper called the *Toledo Blade* at his desk. "Not had second thoughts about reopening the investigation of your husband's death, have you?" he asked as he indicated she should sit in the chair beside his desk. Taking a deep breath, she perched on the edge of the chair while he re-seated himself behind the desk, but turned his rotating chair toward her.

"Not at this time, Sheriff, but I do have a question. As you may know, Lincoln McGowan, whom I understand lives on the other side of town, so is in your jurisdiction..."

She wasn't sure how to word this. He was leaning toward her, hanging on her every word. When she paused, he spoke to fill the awkward silence. "I read the article and heard a slew of folks came calling, Mrs. Mast. But I can't warn or arrest a man about using free speech."

"Oh, no, not that. It's just that he's asked me to trust him as an advisor for my barn, listing it with the government historical society. What I'm asking is if, as far as you know, Sheriff, the man's to be trusted."

"You know, Mrs. Mast," he said, rocking slightly back in his chair, "if you'd asked me that about Mitch Randall, I might have had something to say."

"I realize that, but Mitch was protecting me, not attacking someone, Sheriff. And I know about his past."

He frowned, shifting in his chair. "I see. Well, about Lincoln McGowan then, all I could really say is the man's a bit flighty when he takes on projects."

"Leaving his high-school job suddenly midyear and the same evidently with his college teaching?" she asked.

"Done your homework, haven't you? Has McGowan done something illegal or amiss?" he queried.

"That, Sheriff," she said, "is what I was hoping you could tell me. So you've never had to investigate him for any reason?"

From somewhere in the back of the building, Rachel heard a muted toilet flush and a door open. Marci Morgan came into the office, wiping her hands on a paper towel.

"Oh, Rachel," Marci said, obviously very surprised. "Nothing's wrong at home, I hope—Jennie's house and the boys, I mean."

"No, everyone's fine," Rachel said and rose.

"Hey, honey," Sheriff Burnett swung around in his chair toward his daughter, "you knew Linc McGowan when he taught here. He seem trustworthy and all to you?"

"Daddy, you're the one who looked into him when—"

"I know," he cut her off, "but I can't talk official business, now, can I? So what did *you* think of him?"

"He had big-time self-confidence," Marci muttered, "but then I guess anyone stuck on himself like that must."

"Oh," Rachel said, wondering if the sheriff was using Marci to warn her about Linc. But then, if Marci, and maybe Kent, too, didn't like him, why didn't they try to keep Jennie away from him? Maybe they were just so glad she was seeing someone socially. Rachel didn't want Marci telling Jennie she was checking up on Linc, not until she figured out what he was doing and how to break it to her friend.

"You know," Rachel prompted when Marci just

glared, "I'd heard Linc McGowan was a very popular teacher."

"Yeah, but he can't please, or fool, all the people all the time," Marci said, shooting her wad of paper towel into her dad's wastebasket. "Frankly, I detested him because he had teacher's pets and the heck with the rest of us average, nonworshipful kids—teacher's *pests*. But if you're checking up on him to see if he's okay for Jennie to date, I'd give anything to see her happy."

"Me, too," Rachel said, hoping Marci and the sheriff thought that was the real reason she was checking on Linc. And if she came here again, she told herself as she thanked them and headed out to her buggy, especially if it was to report that Linc McGowan should be questioned again about Laura's disappearance, she'd make sure Marci wasn't hiding in the bathroom.

Though it was starting to rain, Rachel drove the buggy out the other side of town toward where Linc lived. She had no intention of stepping into his house, but she wanted him to know she'd changed her mind about putting her barn in his hands and she wanted him to keep clear of it and her. Then she was going to talk to Mitch about what to do next. Though he didn't like Linc, she trusted him to give her advice about whether to talk to Jennie first, especially since she only had strong suspicions, or to go back to Sheriff Burnett and ask him to look into Laura's disappearance again. And in the back of her mind, Rachel was hoping that would halt Linc's haunting of her barn.

She passed the Clearview Care Nursing Home

where Linc's mother stayed. She'd heard the old woman wasn't well or Rachel would be tempted to stop to see her, she was that desperate. She passed Mike Morgan's new place—his name was on the roadside mailbox big as you please—and wondered if he'd made peace with losing his daughter by placing roses on the spot she'd last been seen. It startled Rachel to realize that, although a big field stretched between the houses, Mike Morgan and his wife were next-door neighbors to Linc.

The McGowan house, which Jennie had described to her when she was trying to talk her into trusting Linc with the barn, was a renovated slice of history. Surrounded on three sides by someone else's fields, the old farmhouse was painted white down to the lacelike trim Jennie had called gingerbread. An L-shaped porch with white wicker, a swing shifting in the increasing wind, and hanging plants—actually now-dead geraniums, Rachel noted—framed a big bay window. When she saw two cars in the driveway, she slowed the team down along the shoulder of the two-lane road.

One car was Linc's; the other was a beat-up, older model with cardboard taped in the back passenger-side window where the glass was gone. The car's rust spots and a variety of bumper and window stickers made the thing look like a patchwork quilt.

Rachel didn't want to face Linc on his front porch if he had company. She'd go back home, talk to Mitch, then return with him. If she told him what she suspected about Linc, she couldn't be sure Mitch wouldn't lose his temper, but she had no one else to turn to. She didn't want Eben involved in this, nor did she want him to think she was giving him control of her life. And she needed to know more before she told Jennie. She could try the sheriff again, but she had no real proof of anything—she couldn't accuse a man of *maybe* stalking her, *maybe* harming Laura or Sam. She had nothing but doubts and suspicions and a growing lump inside her that was fast becoming not just fear but frenzy.

The rain was starting to fall harder. Rachel looked for a place to turn around, then pulled into a dirt lane where a local farmer evidently had access to these fields. Though confrontation was not the Amish way, she had to get rid of this man. Or, maybe she should leave him a note, she told herself, digging in her bag for the pen and paper she'd used in the principal's office. She tied the reins to an apple tree in a copse that didn't hide them from the road but probably did from the two houses. Tugging her bonnet forward and her cloak closer, she trudged along the shoulder to Linc's driveway.

Since Rachel didn't want to be spotted through the big front bay window and was used to going in back doors, she wrote a note, pressing her paper against the wooden house under the shelter of the small back porch roof. She sniffed at a distinct odor here, not the wet smells of the rain, but maybe fresh paint. She saw a cellar window was open in the brick foundation of the house beside the porch, so maybe the paint was down there. Still, she checked to be sure the house hadn't just been painted before she leaned her elbow on the wall. She wrote,

Lincoln McGowan—
I do not want someone supposedly preserving my barn who only wants it for his own uses,

which threaten the barn and me. Cancel my request for historic status. And do not visit my place again or I will ask the sheriff to question you about why.

                              Rachel Mast

She folded the note, once, twice, and wedged it in the storm door.

Through it she heard a distinct feminine giggle. The lace curtain covering the window of the door moved, then smashed flat to the glass as if something or someone pressed up against it. Rachel heard another giggle and then Linc's voice, slow and seductive, saying something about not telling anyone. And then, "And not telling anyone how quickly you learn everything I want to teach you, sweetie."

Rachel jumped back and ran. The rain was pounding now; evidently he—they—hadn't heard or seen her.

She had wanted to peek in, but she just couldn't. She'd sunk low enough today, lying to several people. She wasn't going to dig down to Lincoln McGowan's level and spy on someone.

Rachel kept her head lowered, holding her skirts up as she ran along the road, then up the lane back to her buggy. She felt soaked clear through and racked by both chills and heat. As she untied the reins and clambered up, she glanced back at Linc's house.

Through the slanting sheet of rain, Rachel saw him step out onto his back porch with a woman. She was young and slender with long, straight blond hair. They kissed, melding to one gray form, her arms lifted around his neck, his holding her hard to him.

They would be out of sight of anyone passing on the road. Linc smacked her on her blue-jeans rear as she darted to her old car.

Rachel watched aghast as, before Linc turned to go back in, he stooped and retrieved something from his porch.

It must have been her note.

As soon as the girl roared by, heading back toward town, Rachel snapped the reins and followed as fast as Nann and Bett would trot.

"At least his house doesn't look so forbidding when it's not raining and I'm not alone," Rachel told Mitch as he drove her and the twins into Linc's front driveway late the next morning. Last night Rachel had told Mitch about her suspicions of Linc and about what she'd seen at his house, and she'd made Mitch promise he would not interfere if he accompanied her to Linc's. Strapped in the back seat of Gabe's car, Andy and Aaron were acting like angels since they'd been promised hamburgers and shakes at McDonald's afterward.

Linc's vehicle was still parked in the same place she'd seen it the day before. "He's evidently here," Mitch observed and surprised Rachel by honking twice.

"At least if it's the only car, there can't be more tutoring going on," Rachel murmured.

When another long horn blast did not bring Linc out of the house, Rachel said, "I'll just go as far as the front porch. You boys sit here, and I'll be right back. And Mitch—Mr. Randall—is in charge."

She got out and went up the three steps. Perhaps Linc was a late sleeper, though it was nearly

11:00 a.m. It was just tough, she thought, if the suave, sophisticated Professor McGowan wasn't presentable yet. She was getting this over with now before she talked to the sheriff. Then it would be up to him to reopen Laura's case, though Rachel knew she'd feel terrible if this hurt Jennie or her family.

Rachel lifted her fist to knock; the door swung open at her first rap. Perhaps it had been ajar and the wind had partly closed it. She stepped forward to peer inside a small foyer.

"Hello? It's Rachel Mast. I need to talk to you."

She looked back at the puzzled Mitch and shrugged. He said something to the boys, got out and came up on the porch.

"McGowan?" he bellowed so loud she jumped.

No answer or sound came from inside except muted music of a big orchestra, a piece with lots of drums and brass.

"I'll bet he's stepped out into the backyard or garage," she said.

"Yeah," Mitch agreed, nodding, but he sounded wary. "I don't lock doors when I'm home, but then I don't leave them standing open, either. Let's walk around in back."

"Could you drive around—with the boys in the car and all?"

"Sure. It's best we keep them in sight and safe, I know that."

He went back to the car while Rachel closed the front door and hurried around the outside of the house to the back porch. Again, she smelled fresh paint through the cellar window that stood ajar. And the back door was propped open with an old, glazed clay crock.

She exhaled a sigh of relief. Of course, she reasoned, Linc was in the basement painting something with music on loud and hadn't heard them. And the doors were propped open to dissipate the smell.

The moment Mitch pulled the car in sight, she stuck her head into the kitchen. "Linc! Linc McGowan!"

Suddenly, she shuddered. Calling for him, looking for him, however bright the day, reminded her of the stormy one when she'd searched for Sam.... She began to shiver, but she summoned her courage and anger at what Linc had done.

While Mitch and the boys waited in the car, Rachel marched off the porch and knelt in the wet grass to poke her head nearly in the open cellar window. The aroma of paint struck her again and then another, unnameable smell.

"Linc McGowan, are you down there?" she cried.

Shading her eyes from the morning sun, she could see bookshelves freshly painted white. And above that, below her eye level but way off the floor, were Linc's polished, fringed leather loafers partly covered by that sharp crease in the cuffs of his trousers, just hanging there, somehow suspended in midair.

Eighteen

❦~❦~❦

"Sorry, ma'am," Sheriff Burnett told Rachel as he leaned in the back window of his squad car, where she'd sat for two endless hours. "Too bad you had to find him—after the other—your husband," he stammered, then cleared his throat and looked away to survey the scene again.

Still stunned, Rachel only nodded, leaned her head back on the seat and closed her eyes to shut out the sight of highway patrol officers going in and out of Linc's back door. At least Marci had come to take her boys away from this, though Rachel got the impression the sheriff's daughter would rather have stayed here. Mitch had held Rachel's hand while they'd waited for the police, so that had helped, too. If she opened her eyes, she'd see him now, answering questions from a Clearview deputy just outside of the fluttering bright yellow crime-scene tape.

They had fingerprinted Mitch, just to eliminate his prints, the sheriff had explained, in case he touched anything in the house. After Rachel had seen Linc's body hanging, Mitch had rushed inside to see if he could help, but Rachel could have told him the feet were motionless. No kicking or turning. No life left.

Yet she had forced herself to peer inside again to see Mitch standing horror-struck, staring up at the corpse before he ran back out to call the sheriff on his car phone. When Sheriff Burnett came roaring in, Rachel had told him everything she knew about Linc and his female students, even her suspicions about Laura.

But she had not explained her personal complaints against the man. After all, they were unproven and paled next to Laura's disappearance and this sui-cide—unless, by some chance, Linc had killed Sam. But she just couldn't see Linc messing with ropes and a grappling hook. Anyway, if Linc had invaded her barn and house, that was all over now. *Vengeance is mine, sayeth the Lord,* she thought.

Rachel jumped alert at the sound of the sheriff's voice. "Gonna be a lot easier on everyone if it's a suicide," he said.

"If?" she repeated, sitting up straighter to look out the window at him where he'd propped his el-bows. "What do you mean, 'if'?"

"Just gotta be careful, that's all, 'specially after what you said you saw here yesterday. A man se-ducing young girls has enemies, and that sure opens up a can of worms about possible suspects for a mur-der, don't it?"

Wide-eyed, hating to agree, Rachel nodded. "You mean," she asked, "some girl's father found out and took justice into his own hands?"

"A top possibility," Burnett said, taking a little notebook out of his shirt pocket, "though I guess revenge and crimes of passion are something that you Amish wouldn't understand.''

His eyes lifted to meet hers. The sharp undercurrent to his controlled voice made the hair on the back of her neck prickle. She had never taken the sheriff for one who professed to admire the Amish while secretly detesting them. Above all else, perhaps Tim Burnett was just a practical man, and she could understand that. He had not questioned her about the note she'd left for Linc, so either they had not found it yet or Linc had destroyed it—or if there had been an intruder, that person might have taken it for some reason.

''Actually, Sheriff,'' she said, ''since Sam's been dead, I believe I do understand having a passion for answers and justice.''

''That right? You know, if you weren't a slip of a woman and Bible-believing to boot, I'd have to put you on the list of suspects, 'specially after your visit to me yesterday trying to dig something up on him. But then, who would be crazy enough to come to me about that just before or after murdering him, huh?'' He kept scribbling notes with a ballpoint pen as he talked. ''So I'm betting you been real up-front here and your beef against McGowan's a minor one. His writing an article about a haunted barn's not much, 'least in my book. 'Course, your guardian angel Randall over there's strong enough to give someone like McGowan a good boost-up into a noose, and I know him and McGowan don't get along from way back. McGowan was real good at alienating folks with his articles.''

''But you said Linc had climbed up on a stool, then knocked it away. And Mitch would nev—'' She cut herself off. Despite his heartfelt confessions about his past, how well did she really know Mitch Randall? She herself wasn't being as up-front as the sheriff thought, but she couldn't see going into all the things that had happened in her barn.

"Then, too," he went on, still writing, "part of police work is psyching people out. That sexy good-bye you described McGowan gave the girl yesterday sound like a distraught or despondent man to you, Mrs. Mast?" His hand poised on the page, he looked up at her. "There's a bruise on the deceased's head, too, though with bending, and painting those new bookshelves he's been building from a stack of boards down there, that bump could've happened lots of ways. But why new bookshelves when you're gonna hang yourself? Why start a new romance with Jennie Morgan? And why bother with fancy knots in the noose, too?"

Her head jerked. "Fancy knots?"

"Double hitches. A man of many talents, maybe one that got him killed. Don't look so shocked now. I just gotta cover all the bases, then we'll let the coroner and forensic guys throw in their two bits. You're not under suspicion, Mrs. Mast, so don't get all het up now."

He looked away as one of the highway patrol men in brown uniforms with broad-brimmed hats—almost Amish style—came out of the house. He gestured to the sheriff, who stepped over the tape to talk to him. Their words carried to Rachel as the trooper showed the sheriff a piece of letter-size paper in a clear, flat plastic sack. Rachel saw the man wore white plastic gloves, too.

"Sitting right there on his computer screen ready

to be printed up, huh?'' the sheriff said, squinting at the paper. ''A real *mea culpa* suicide note, but why didn't he print it out then? Be sure and dust the keyboard for prints.''

Rachel didn't know what *mea culpa* meant, but she breathed a sigh of relief. At least it *was* suicide then, so no one else could be blamed and she wouldn't be questioned anymore. But then, why was the sheriff checking for prints? Maybe if someone else besides Linc wrote that note, the culprit knew how to type but not how to work the printer. But, in that note, had Linc McGowan blamed himself for tormenting her or for doing far worse with those young girls?

'''Deeply ashamed of myself for betraying a trust, for seducing them—including Laura Morgan,''' she heard the sheriff's voice crack out as he read through the note.

Rachel pressed her clasped hands to her lips. Her instincts and proof about Linc had been right. But she knew Jennie might take her meddling all wrong.

''Would you mind checking the house and barn with me before we pick up the boys next door?'' Rachel asked Mitch as they drove down Ravine Road toward the farm over an hour later. ''Now that Linc's gone, I want to see that everything is—well, as it should be at home.''

''Sure, we can stop. You really think it could have been him trying to scare you out of here then?''

''I know that Eben or Sim Lapp, maybe both of them taking turns, are the most likely suspects,'' she admitted, gripping her hands in her lap. She shook her head. "But I still can't believe an Amish man would do such a thing."

"But a worldly man would?" he asked, his voice on edge.

She sighed and her shoulders slumped. "This whole thing is getting to be such a nightmare, one I'm trapped in and can't get out of."

He put his hand over hers on her lap until just before he turned into the gravel lane toward the barn. When he stopped the car, he hurried around to open her door for her, a practice that still felt so strange to her. However deeply she was coming to feel for him, she knew Mitch must soon go back to being a stranger to her.

"Shall we check the barn or house first?" he asked.

"House, I guess, since that's what was tampered with last."

Rachel unlocked the door, and Mitch followed her in. She scanned the kitchen floor for prints and saw nothing. "I'll fix us something to eat," she offered, "but I'd like to check upstairs and in the cellar first."

"I'll do it," he volunteered.

Rachel busied herself making him a thick, fried bologna and cheese sandwich on rye, though she just got out crackers and cut cheese for herself. Besides not sleeping, she wasn't sure when food would look good again. She was queasy from finding Linc like that and could still smell fresh paint and death in the pit of her stomach.

Rachel heard Mitch walking in each room overhead, opening and closing closet doors. Ordinarily, she'd never have a worldly man go through her private domain, but she was only grateful now. Still, it sounded so strange to have a man's heavy footfalls in the house after all this time.

"Looks fine up there!" he called to her as he came back down. While Mitch took a lit lantern from her and went down to the cellar, the sight of Linc's feet so still, just hanging in his basement, flashed through her mind. But she steadied herself and made a circuit of the first floor, looking under and behind furniture and doors where someone could hide.

"First thing tomorrow I'm getting your house locks changed and buying ones for the barn doors, back and front," Mitch declared as he came into the kitchen and washed his hands as if he belonged here. "I'll take the cylinders out of your locks and pick up all the necessary hardware at the lumberyard."

"No Amish lock their barn doors," she protested quietly, "but I agree. Linc's gone but it would be good for peace of mind."

"And tonight I'm coming back to make a bunk in the loft near the haymow door to keep an eye on the barn and house. And never mind arguing this time," he declared, sitting next to her at the head of the table. Last time he'd sat there, she had almost panicked; now it seemed nearly natural.

"Mitch, if someone saw you..."

"Someone Amish? I'll hide the car in the old apple orchard that's just across the far field heading toward town," he told her, speaking so quickly it seemed he'd had all this planned long ago. "I'll walk in along the back of your property and approach through the woodlot and use the back barn door. No one—including you—will see me come and go, but I'll be there. And if you need me inside, since I see your bedroom faces the back of the house, just keep a lantern lit and simply part the curtains. Or if the lantern goes out, I'll know that's a sign, too.''

"All right," she agreed. "It seems you've thought of everything." She had not told Mitch that someone had been sleeping up in the hayloft, but now she must. "But after we get the locks," she added as she folded her hands for prayer on the edge of the table, "it will be best you don't stay there. And I'm not going to tell the boys. I just can't bear to hear any more about their father sleeping out there and being cold."

She thought Mitch was reaching for his napkin, but instead he covered her clasped hands with one of his and bowed his head, too. Usually, the Amish blessed their table food silently, but she said, her voice almost a whisper, "Please, dear Lord, come and be a guest at our table and in our hearts. And keep us safe from others who would enter in and do harm. Amen."

Mitch squeezed her hand, then devoured his food while she picked at hers. Every time he touched her, she thought, she felt safe from everyone but him, for he made her want him permanently in her house and in her life. And none of that could ever be.

Daylight slowly faded toward dusk as they went out to the barn together. Nothing looked amiss on the first floor. They opened the big double doors for light and air, then fed and watered Nann and Bett. Perhaps, Rachel thought, Linc McGowan had indeed been the one behind everything and her troubles were really over.

"I want to get the Percherons back soon, now that everyone's corn is cut," she told Mitch, hoping Eben and Sim Lapp would not try to keep the team longer as they had before. "Andy and Aaron always call them the 'Perch-ons,'" she admitted with a little smile, "as if we rode them."

"Before you get the 'Perch-ons' back, how about I repair those few sections of floorboards that the horses are about ready to step through? You don't need them breaking a leg. Gabe and I can finish that one big tie beam after I fix the flooring, but he has no patience working on his hands and knees. I'll just have him cut the oak planking for me this afternoon, but I'll finish the floor myself."

"All right," she agreed. "As soon as the flooring's done, I'm asking for the horses back. By then, I'll bet I can return to a normal life, too. Mitch, if nothing happens for a few nights, I'll know it was Linc trying to get me to leave this house and his precious historic barn so he could swoop in and buy it from me—and maybe be close enough to keep an eye on Jennie. The first time I met him he let slip that he'd been watching her for years."

Mitch only nodded as they climbed up into the cupola to see Gabe's finished repair work. "Good as new," Mitch said, a tinge of pride in his voice as he looked around and cranked the louvers open and shut.

Nodding, she let him put an arm around her shoulders. She placed her left arm around his waist, over his thick leather belt. "'There is no Past we can bring back by the longing for it,'" Rachel recited his favorite quote. "'There is only an eternally new Now that builds and creates itself out of the elements of the Past.'"

They stood, hips and ribs pressed together, and

looked out from the heights as they had four days ago, when Andy and Aaron had seen them hugging. An awkward silence stretched between them.

"But when," Mitch whispered, "that Now creates itself, are we bold enough to face it, to embrace it, no matter who gets angry, or shuns us?"

Despite that dire reminder of their differences, it scared her how much she longed to throw herself into his arms, to cling to him, to ask him to stay and protect her and the boys forever. But that was not her way. She had been striving to stand on her own and would continue to.

"Some of us," she said, "like the Amish, must rely on our pasts to guide our futures."

"Even when you're with them," he insisted, his voice becoming challenging, then urgent, "are you really a part of your people anymore? Sure, the ties run deep, but you're different, Rachel," he went on, turning her to face him. "You've got a rebel's streak, an imaginative, wayward heart that—"

"Don't," she protested, gently hitting his hands away and taking a step back until she was pinned against the small, curved cupola interior wall. "So much is going on for me now, I can't handle that, too. Just don't start. Come below with me. I want to show you something," she said, pushing past him and heading down the ladder.

On the haymow floor below, she preceded him to the hollowed-out place where someone had lain in the hay near the open loft door. Mitch squatted to look closer at the indentation.

"You're not trying to imply I stayed out here already after you asked me not to?" he said, looking up at her.

"No, I know you weren't here. When you look at me, it's a different feeling from that other one I have of being watched—you know what I mean."

"Rachel," he said, standing slowly, his lips set between a grimace and a grin, "if you're trying to hold a man at arm's length like you do me, you really shouldn't tell him that his just looking at you makes you feel unique or special."

"I didn't say that," she protested much too loudly.

"You didn't have to, but then, I feel the same whenever you so much as look at me."

"This isn't the time..."

"Of course it is. Anytime two people instinctively feel this way about each other and no other person stands between them, it's the perfect time."

Rachel meant to lead him down the ladder to the first floor, but her feet wouldn't move. She meant to thank him for all his help and insist they go to Jennie's to get the boys, but she dreaded facing her friend. So instead of moving and talking, Rachel stared back into the depths of Mitch's dark eyes.

Then she threw herself into his arms.

It surprised him. The impact bounced them against stacked hay bales he leaned on to support them. He clamped her to him and his kiss became so demanding and devouring it took them to their knees, facing each other, holding tight.

The kiss deepened, careening wildly out of control, racing through her limbs, her very veins. Her body fit against his so perfectly as he shifted closer, as if covering her with his big frame like a protective roof against the harsh world outside.

However dizzy she felt, reason returned to slap her sober. The boys. She had to get the boys and try to help Jennie. She had to get her life and her right mind back.

Mitch must have seen the resignation on her face, because he sighed and pulled away only to rake his fingers through his short hair. He got up, helped her to stand.

"Mitch, I didn't mean to start that."

"And you certainly didn't mean to finish it," he said, his voice raspy. "That's all right. When this is solved—over—there will be another time then."

"Do me a big favor," she whispered.

"Anything."

"Just let me off at Jennie's but don't wait for me."

"I want you and the twins back here safe."

"I'll get Kent or Marci to drop us off. That way, you can be in place before we get here, so no one will see you."

"All right," he said as they went down the ladder to the ground floor. "I'm going to call Gabe to come cut the beam boards before it gets dark, but that won't take long. After that I'll leave, then circle back. You just remember to feel safe tonight, because I'm going to be right up there watching after dark."

As was her habit, Rachel went in the side door at Jennie's, opened it a crack and started to call to her friend. But Kent's angry voice drowned hers out. Deciding she'd better step back outside and knock, she turned away. They weren't in the kitchen, Rachel realized—for their voices to carry like that, they must be in the dining room or the hall to the bedrooms. She started to shut the door behind her, then stopped.

"You're going to have to face it, deal with it now, aren't you?" Kent said, his voice sounding desperate but goading. "I'm sorry about Linc's leading you on, Mom, but the question is, did he lead Laura on, too?"

"He's dead, he got what was coming to him, so what does it matter?" Jennie cried, her voice hoarse. "And how dare he make me think he cared about me, then imply in a suicide note that he had—relations with—someone not here to defend herself."

"He seduced her, you mean. I told you that holy virgin shrine you've been worshiping at is nothing but—"

A sharp smack stopped Kent's voice. "I should have known you'd never understand, not you!" Jennie cried. "Like father, like son!"

Kent gave a harsh laugh. "You don't know the first damn thing you're talking about, Mom!"

A loud clunk followed and then the sound of feet hard on the floor, coming closer. Rachel barely got the door closed behind her before Kent yanked it open to step outside. He looked shocked to see her.

"She's so shook," he said, his expression and voice hard, "that Marci took all four boys to our place. I'll go get them for you, so see if you can do anything with her."

He stomped out to his truck. Rachel darted after him. "If you're this upset, Kent, I'll have someone else come pick them up. Don't you drive this way or be driving my boys, either."

"All right, all right," he said, getting into the driver's seat, then slamming the truck door. She thought he'd cut her off, but he rolled his window down. "I'll have Marci drop them off," he added, his voice quiet but still bitter. "Wouldn't want young kids to get hurt, not like I did when Laura was taken and everything revolved around her, even worse than it did before. It's like I was never there again, like I was nothing while they argued, then split, blaming me for—for something or other..."

Kent gunned his engine and backed out of the driveway. Trying to steady herself, Rachel walked slowly back toward the side door of Jennie's house.

Nineteen

ᕯᕯᕯᕯᕯ

"Jennie, it's Rachel!" she called into the silent house.

She waited just inside the door as muffled footsteps came down the hall. Her friend wore a long black pullover and black tights. Though the day was damp and cold, she was barefoot. She looked as if she'd been out in the wind, but she'd probably just been raking her hands through her hair. Her face was drained of all color.

"The twins are at Marci's, but I can call her to bring them over," Jennie said, stopping on the other side of the kitchen table and gesturing Rachel in.

"I know. I saw Kent on his way out. He'll tell her."

As Rachel faced her across the width of the table, Jennie leaned her hands on it, as though they had something to negotiate. She looked both exhausted and energized.

"What else did he say?" Jennie asked.

"That you were upset, and I should see if I could help."

Jennie snorted. "How sweet of him." Her voice

dripped sarcasm. "And did you tell him you've already helped enough by tying Linc to Laura and bringing it all up again?"

"Jennie, I'm so sorry you had to get hurt in this, but I started thinking it might be Linc doing those things in my barn to shake me up, that maybe he even coveted my place."

"Oh, he did *covet* it," Jennie said, as if mocking the way she'd said that. Jennie did not sit down as Rachel expected but folded her arms over her chest and leaned in the doorway to the hall as if she was guarding this house from an intruder. "He would have loved to play lord and master of that historic barn. And he'd have been closer to more easily seduce me as he evidently did Laura, as if that would amuse him. Tim Burnett told me about the suicide note. I should be used to being betrayed by now, but it doesn't get easier."

"You don't mean by me?" Rachel asked, and her voice broke.

"Not intentionally. Of course, you didn't mean to."

Rachel nodded, thankful for that much. Despite her unease at how Jennie seemed ready to explode, Rachel felt enormous relief, not only that Jennie wasn't blaming her but that now she knew for sure Linc's motive was scaring her out of her historic barn and off its land.

Who else but Linc could have so cleverly contrived all that had happened? He had tried to convince her the barn was haunted and must have known, when he got that information printed in the newspaper, that would draw gawkers to rattle her even more. Who else could research Amish ways and things about Sam and pull ruse after ruse, including footprints of boots right under her kitchen table as if a ghost had been there? Yet she could see there was no relief in her friend's heart.

"Jennie," she said, gripping the back of a chair, "at first I didn't know Linc was tied to Laura, but when you said she had a crush on him, and I saw him with a young girl yesterday, I—"

"You what?" Jennie screamed so suddenly Rachel jumped back. "You thought besides stopping Linc from messing with your barn you should solve what happened to Laura? I thought the Amish weren't supposed to get—get involved."

Rachel recovered and went slowly around the table toward Jennie, holding her hands up as if to ward off blows. "I know you can't bear to remember, but wouldn't it help to have Laura's disappearance more settled? Maybe when they go through Linc's house they'll find some hint of what happened or where she went."

"'Closure,' we worldly folk call it, Rachel—closure. Having the answers is supposed to heal everything, but it can't—it can't!"

Jennie didn't really cry but heaved huge, dry sobs that clenched and shook her shoulders. Rachel shuffled closer, her arms out, until Jennie took a step away.

"Do you have closure about Sam?" she demanded. Up this close, Rachel could see her friend's eyes were dry but her lashes were clumped and her mascara had smeared into now-dried half moons above her cheeks. "Do you?"

"Yes and no. But I had a body to grieve over and bury, so I realize it was—easier for me."

"Exactly. And Linc McGowan betrayed me now and maybe in the past. But whatever the bastard did or didn't do to Laura, I don't have her body because she *is not dead!*"

Rachel's eyes widened and her stomach cartwheeled. "Jennie, it's been ten years," she said gently. "I'm sure it hurts to face the possibility, but you know Eben's wife hasn't been gone one third of that time, and he's certain she's dead because she hasn't contacted them."

Jennie turned and grabbed both of Rachel's wrists. Rachel's first instinct was to yank free, but she felt her friend shaking.

"But you're Amish, so you just don't know," Jennie insisted. "You haven't seen the TV shows or read the books about people who have amnesia and don't know who they are for years before they remember or someone finds them. There are hundreds of kids temporarily lost in this country. You've seen those milk cartons?"

"Yes, of course, but the odds are great. Jennie, this isn't right for you to keep hanging on. You're suffering, and poor Kent—"

"Kent? He doesn't understand, either!" she cried. "But I'll bet you don't even know who Patty Hearst is, do you?"

"W-what?" Rachel stammered, taken aback again. "Patty Hearst?"

"See? She got kidnapped by criminals who brainwashed her not to want to go back to her family. But she's back now, married, normal, has a family of her own. And then there are those crazy religious cults where they screw up kids' minds and you have to practically abduct them back to get them deprogrammed.''

Rachel didn't move, but her mind raced. She could think of a hundred arguments against Laura's being out there somewhere after ten years, but she realized she had no right to ruin Jennie's hopes. Gently but firmly, Rachel twisted her wrists free, then held her friend's hands. But Jennie obviously was not ready to calm down yet.

''Come with me,'' she said, pulling Rachel down the hall. ''Come down here to her room, and you'll understand better. Did Andy tell you about her room?''

''No, should he have?'' Rachel asked, annoyed at him if he was supposed to tell her something. ''Sometimes, since they have each other, the twins don't tell me things.''

''It isn't just that they have each other, Rachel,'' Jennie said, her voice controlled and quiet now, as if the old Jennie had slipped back inside this desperate woman's skin. ''That's just boys. Kent didn't tell me half of what he should have.''

She swung open the door to a darkened room and hit the light switch. At the sight of a teenage girl's room so perfectly preserved, though wilted and faded, Rachel stared, then sneezed.

''I try to dust it every day,'' Jennie said, folding her arms over her chest, ''but it just kind of hangs here, anyway—the dust.''

And Laura's spirit, Rachel thought as she scanned the trophies and mementos. Besides posters of people from the movies or music, a big picture of Jennie and Laura, both laughing, was stuck in the mirror. For one moment, Rachel thought it was Marci in the photo because Jennie was doing some strange thing to Laura's hair, but she could not be curling it. Rachel recalled from the other picture she'd seen Laura's hair had been as curly as lamb's wool.

As Rachel's gaze wandered the room, she knew that her friend had to find a way to let Laura go. But, like Jennie, Rachel, too, could only let the past go if she settled once and for all.

"I'm so sorry," Rachel whispered, putting a hand on Jennie's shoulder. And she was sorry that she'd never quite trust her neighbor again to care for the boys, not when she could turn so distraught and unbalanced, and when she knew Andy had somehow been in this bizarre, empty tomb.

"If you're still apologizing about tying Linc to Laura, forget it," Jennie whispered. "At least he's killed himself for betraying all of us. Tim Burnett said he even had his last will and testament laid out on his desk."

"Oh," Rachel said, "I didn't hear about the will." Obviously the sheriff had not wanted to upset Jennie more by hinting that Linc might have been murdered, and she certainly wasn't going to tell her.

"You understand now, don't you?" Jennie asked suddenly. "You kept things of Sam's, you told me, and I don't just mean the barn and house you've fought so hard for."

Rachel turned to look into Jennie's eyes again as they stood in the doorway of what Kent had called the holy virgin shrine. "Yes, I understand better now. And, of course, I kept some personal things," Rachel admitted. "Besides tools and his equipment, I saved clothes and his pocket watch for whichever of the boys is married first. Jennie, I do understand, but you know Laura wouldn't want you to keep all this if it's a burden instead of a blessing to you.''

"I'll take you home," Jennie insisted and reached to close the door. Rachel followed Jennie down the dim hall back into the kitchen.

"I'll be fine walking across the field," Rachel said. "It's barely dusk and you don't need to be out driving. And as soon as Marci drops the kids off, I'll tell her to stop by to see you. Or do you want me to stay until Marci gets here?"

"No, I'm better now, and she already said she'd come over, partly to handle any phone calls from reporters."

"Newspaper reporters?" Rachel asked, instantly alarmed.

"Television, whatever. You're just so sheltered," Jennie said, shaking her head—the old, concerned Jennie again. "Even after that little article Linc did about your barn, I heard you were bothered by people. Believe me, Rachel, they'll jump on this, especially with the seduction of high-school and college girls."

"As long as reporters just call, they won't find me," Rachel vowed, trying to convince herself. "Besides, you've already made me feel safe," she assured Jennie, squeezing her hands at the back door. "Thanks for telling me that Linc was interested in my place, because I'm sure he was the one watching me. Too bad the brilliant mind, the master researcher had to turn out to be a manipulator of women he thought were gullible. I'm going back to being unafraid."

"I'm glad you wouldn't ever sell," Jennie said with a sigh. Strangely, the first tears Rachel had seen from her tonight sprang into her eyes. ''I hope to still be your neighbor when your twins are farming the fields, and maybe I can tend their babies, too, someday.''

Rachel regretted her earlier doubts about Jennie watching the boys. She seemed so normal now, and it would really hurt her and the boys to separate them. She owed Jennie Morgan a great deal. Maybe she should rethink letting Mitch spend the night in the barn. If he and Gabe were still there cutting wood, she'd tell him not to worry about her anymore.

At the side door, the two women hugged, then Rachel cut straight across the now-emptied pumpkin field toward her house, silhouetted against the darkening sky.

It felt so good not to be afraid, Rachel thought as she strode along. She had always loved to be outside at night. She couldn't tell if the stars were out yet, but if she had her glasses they would probably look like clear pinpoints. She inhaled fresh, crisp air. The remaining pumpkin vines were shrunken now, like her problems, and didn't trip her up. She'd go in, light the house without searching every nook and cranny and wait for Marci to bring the boys back. She felt delivered from destruction.

She saw the barn doors were closed, so Mitch and Gabe must be gone already. Mitch had told her not to watch him or give away his presence in the barn, but he didn't know all she did about Linc now. As she stood with her keys in her hand, ready to unlock the back door, she glanced up toward the barn loft. A gray form stood in the opening. So he was in place and had seen her.

''Mitch,'' she called. ''I'm not worried about

things anymore. It's okay. Come on down, and I'll explain!''

She squinted to try to make him out better. The form disappeared into the black barn as if the darkness had devoured him. He was probably coming down to talk to her. Leaving her keys in the door she moved across the small porch to start across the yard, then saw a piece of paper tacked to the post.

A note from Marci?

She pulled it off and stepped into the washhouse to light the lantern there. The note read:

Gabe cut his hand bad on the saw. Taking him to hosp. Back as soon as can. Same plan as before.

M

She crumpled the note. Then who was that in the barn?

Eben realized he had to go down to face Sam Rachel. He had wanted to see her, and he had a good excuse for why he was in her barn when she wasn't home. His eyes were well adjusted to the dark by now, so he climbed down the ladder to the threshing floor and started for the back door, the way he'd come in.

He avoided the piles of lumber and the electric saw and generator he'd seen set up here. The saw and boards had been messily, hastily abandoned, and he didn't think much of that worldly barn builders's work habits. Sam Rachel's buggy horses whickered as he passed. They were, he thought, better behaved than those beautiful Percherons she hardly deserved to own, the way she'd been acting lately. The woman did not deserve how much he wanted her, even after the tragedy with his willful wife.

And tonight, Rachel had expected him to be, no doubt wanted him to be, that worldly *auslander,* Mitch Randall. She had called his name and said he should come down and it was okay. But nothing was okay between them anymore, though he'd give her one last chance. And if she would not let him take care of her one way, then he'd just have to take care of her another.

The back barn door creaked as Eben went out, then banged closed after him in the wind. He walked around almost clear up to where Rachel was opening the front barn doors, before she saw him.

She screamed and jumped back, her eyes wide and white in the dark. Gaping, she stared up under his wide hat brim.

"Eben?"

"I know you thought it was him, Sam Rachel," he accused.

She blinked at him like an owl. "You—scared me. That was y-you up there?"

"I came calling," he said, gesturing toward his son's courting buggy he had left on the driveway side of her house, "and you weren't home. I thought I'd just check the barn, see if things were fixed since Sarah almost had an accident up in the cupola."

"You must know the barn quite well to be inside without a lantern," she said, her tone hard and wary.

"It wasn't that dark at first. I came also," he added, "because I heard you found a man dead today, and I wanted to comfort you, to tell you that if you need to be among your people, I could have

Annie and the boys stay with you for a few days or you could come visit us at the dairy farm.''

"I appreciate your kindness," she replied, her voice clipped, "but I will be fine here at my house."

"*Ach*, maybe your Mitch does that, eh, comfort you, so you don't need your people, don't need me. Another worldly man of all those who are your friends when you argue with and disobey the leaders of the brethren like me, Sim Lapp and Amos Troyer. But you see what ruination can follow. You go looking for a worldly male friend and there he is, dead at the end of a rope."

Her head jerked as she stared at him, but she didn't answer right away. She took her time closing the barn door again. "I'm waiting for a friend to bring the twins back," she said, moving away from the barn. Her voice was still shaky, and she hugged herself as if for warmth. "If you want, we can sit on the front porch and wait for them."

"Fine," he said. "Wouldn't be proper for us to go inside."

He hurried to catch up with her so he could see her face when he said that, but she walked faster, not looking at him. He patted his horse's flank as they walked by his buggy and climbed the porch steps where he had sat to propose to her barely two weeks ago, though it seemed an eternity. They sat in the same rocking chairs, but today he was glad it was dark with no lights in the house to silhouette them on the porch. The blackness suited him.

"I am here, Sam Rachel," he began, wiping his sweating palms on the knees of his trousers, "because 'My eyes fail with tears and my heart is troubled. My anguish is poured on the ground because of the destruction of the daughter of my people.'''

"I hope that is not your idea of another marriage proposal," she dared to retort. "Is that dire judgment from Isaiah?"

"Always defiant comments and questions, eh? It's from Lamentations, and don't go shifting subjects on me. I grieve for your house, and barn, and you," he went on when she continued to stare at him. "You have been warned but still transgress. You chose worldly friends instead of our people—"

"*In addition to* our people, Bishop Yoder."

"Do not Bishop Yoder me, Sam Rachel!" he cried, leaning forward so fast his rocker almost tipped him out. "Let me be to you all I would, your help and comfort, your earthly salvation."

"Earthly or heavenly, someone's salvation is quite a tall order for a mere man, bishop or not," she said. "I'll just adore the Lord, not you as lord and master."

He bristled but fought to keep control. In the end, Eben Mary had dared to challenge him, too. Sometimes, God forgive him, he was grateful she was gone, but, like his wife, if this woman would not bend, she must be bent—or broken.

"I mean," he amended, trying to bridle his temper, "I am here to save you from yourself. Sam Rachel, unless you choose one or the other of two narrow paths, broad is the way which shall lead to your destruction."

She jumped up from her rocker and stood at the edge of the porch, one arm around the post, facing out toward her piles of pumpkins in the yard. Curse the woman, he had advised her not to grow and sell those, too.

"That's the second time you've threatened me," she replied.

"Warned, not threat—"

"Threatened me with destruction, Bishop Yoder. Are you going to explain to me the two narrow paths you've chosen for me or shall I recite them?"

"If you know my mind, then say so," he challenged, getting up to face her. He longed to seize her in his arms, to shake some sense into her stubborn spirit, but all that might have to wait.

"One," she plunged on, "I must renounce my worldly friends and ways and toe your line. Or two, I leave this house and barn and land and let someone else buy and work it, such as your sons, or Sim Lapp, while I marry you."

He knew he looked shocked and wondered if she could tell in the thickening night. He was suddenly terrified she could see into his soul. Quickly, he lowered his gaze. "*Ja*, that's it," he muttered. He looked up again, narrowing his eyes at her. "Choose one of those paths or else I'm here to tell you that the elders have decided that a six-week taste of the *meidung* begins tomorrow. And then, until we decide if it is permanent, there will be no comfort from your people. There will be nothing from your people, as if you did not exist."

She sucked in a sharp breath and put both arms around the post when he wanted her to hold to him. What else could he do to scare her enough to hold to him?

"I suspected it might come to that," she whispered.

Ach, now he had her, he thought, for she sounded breathless. "Riding about in Mitch Randall's car," he pushed his advantage, ticking things off on his big fingers before her face, "then going to a worldly house to find that other man's dead body. Getting yourself and your barn in the newspapers. Entrusting your precious children to worldly women. Preaching God knows what defiance to my Sarah. Being in the barn and house alone with Mitch Randall, taking a day trip with him and leaving your boys with Kent Morgan, that lumber man in town, however much he is kind to us Amish, then—"

"Quite a list of sins," she dared to interrupt. "Have you a swarm of spies, bishop, or did you gather that information yourself by hiding in my barn? Are your boot soles like your soul, dark with mud to track through my floor and my life so that—"

"What?" he shouted. "I was in your barn tonight but that is all since the *danze*—no, since the day we cut your corn. Sam Rachel, I do care for you and would be honored to make all I have yours, for you need a husband's firm hand of correction. The twins, too, need a strong, steady hand you cannot give, and I know my children would come to love you as I do and..."

She lifted both hands to her face and either cried or laughed. He stood appalled, then enraged, at her. Hysterical, that's what she was. He'd hoped to force her into trusting him, but saw it would take more than all he had done so far.

He seized her wrists and pulled her hands down, then shook her. "Stop that!" he shouted. "Are you demented? Rachel!"

Before he could control himself, he slapped her

across the face. His palm stung. She gaped at him silently, as shocked as he. Not since his and Eben Mary's last argument had he struck a woman, and he'd vowed he never would again.

Rachel yanked away as a vehicle's headlights turned in her driveway and slashed across them. Someone honked twice. If that was Randall and he came up here, Eben Yoder knew that he'd want to do much more than slap him.

"Rachel, can I let the boys out here?" a woman's voice called from what looked like the lumber delivery truck.

"Sure, Marci. Thanks. And your mother-in-law needs you!"

Such defiance—the strength back in Sam Rachel's voice—infuriated him even more.

"Right! I'm going over there," the woman called.

Eben stood horrified at the violence he'd just done and what he must yet do. "Six weeks," he hissed, pointing a finger in Rachel's face, "and then if you don't submit, the *meidung* could be forever."

He thudded down the porch steps as the twins hurtled out of the car toward their mother. Eben turned back to her. Headlights lit her tear-streaked face as the car backed out and turned away.

He didn't even try to talk to her sons as he strode back to his courting buggy and climbed up on the narrow seat. One way or the other, he'd be back for her.

Rachel tossed and turned that night. She was first chilled, then so hot it almost felt as if Sam was back in bed putting off his body heat. She prayed she wasn't coming down with something, with something, that is, more deadly than the shunning her people called the *meidung*.

She kept seeing Linc's covered body when the medics had finally brought him out of his house. That memory merged with Sam's form, sprawled in a red nightmare on the barn floor. Was there a tie between the two deaths—or murders? Were they not a freak accident, not a suicide? Those double-hitch knots, maybe like those of Sim Lapp's on Linc's noose and Sam's ropes to the hay hook, tied them together. Maybe it had not been Linc McGowan scaring her lately. Why, why when she was so exhausted, she thought, punching her pillow, couldn't she sleep?

Maybe, she reasoned as she sat up in bed and threw the quilts off, it was just that she wasn't used to sleeping with a lit lantern in the room. She wasn't sure that Mitch had made it back from the hospital to keep watch tonight, but she assumed he was out in the barn. If she doused the light or opened her curtains to take a look, he might think it was a sign for him to come running.

Her pulse pounded, but she kept thinking she heard muffled ticking. She was glad she didn't have a clock by her bed to stare at in the night, to know time was passing. Jennie kept one in Laura's tomb of a room, glowing by the untouched bed.

Rachel flopped onto her stomach and stretched out her arms, hoping to get comfortable. Her right hand struck something cold and hard, not under her pillow but under the one that had been Sam's. Getting on her knees, she carefully lifted it and just stared.

Sam's pocket watch, right where he used to keep it. Wound and ticking. But she had kept it untouched in the drawer since he died.

Twenty

Rachel closed her eyes, then looked at Sam's pocket watch again. She crushed her pillow to her belly and hunched over it, stifling her sobs.

She could not bring herself to touch the watch.

What person, who had access to this house, had Sam told he kept the watch here at night? Eben or Sim Lapp? Or, before he died, could Linc have sneaked in here and moved it? Yes, she'd get the locks changed first thing tomorrow, make sure it was done herself while Mitch worked on the new flooring in the barn. She was afraid to trust anyone, maybe even Mitch.

Her stomach plummeted. Andy's words about *Daadi* soon being in her bed racked her. The twins had known about the watch. Sam had played games with them about hiding it, but they could not have wound it—could they? Unlike with some watches, the stem had to be pulled out one click to wind it and two clicks to set it. Could the twins have recalled and managed that? They had seen Sam do it, but they were so young then. And when had they been upstairs without her so that they could take it from the drawer, wind it and place it here?

She wondered if it was set correctly, but she still couldn't touch it. "Correctly," for Sam meant not right on time, but five minutes ahead because he never liked to be late. He had always set this watch and the one on the wall downstairs as precisely as he had shined and oiled the Percherons' harnesses. He had argued with Eben once that a timepiece—for Eben often consulted his watch, too—should be set ahead, not right on the button.

Rachel heard the old clock downstairs chime two. Slowly, she reached out, lifted the watch, and, turning it toward the light, pushed the release that sprung the cover. The face of the watch, which she hadn't looked at for a year, read exactly five minutes after two.

She dropped the watch. Lying there, with its thick chain coiled around its flat head, it suddenly seemed a serpent in her bed. When she shifted away, its cover sprang open again like jaws ready to strike.

Rachel scrambled back, trying to get up, caught in the covers. She knocked against the nightstand. The lantern toppled off; its chimney smashed on the floor. She heard kerosene splatter. At least with the light out there would be no fire. In the sudden dark, to avoid shards of glass, she jumped back up in bed.

She huddled there again, breathing hard, her heart pounding to drown out the louder ticking, ticking of the watch. After the brightness in the room, it was profoundly dark.

Rachel sucked in her breath and held it. Floorboards in the hall creaked. Footsteps came toward her open door. Aghast, she stared into the blackness.

Someone stepped inside the room, she could hear it, feel it.

"Who's there?" she whispered.

"Us, *Mamm*. What broke?" Andy's voice, all quivery.

"Oh, thank God it's you. Don't come in here. *Mamm* broke a lamp, and there's glass on the floor."

"Did *Daadi* get up and cut his feet?" he asked.

Rachel felt the reins of her control slip. Her eyes slowly adjusting to the dark, she lunged across the bed, away from the broken glass. Before she could stop herself, she gripped Andy's upper arms and lifted him off his feet, pressing him against the door so he stared directly into her face.

"I told you not to say such awful things!" she screamed. "Did you two put his watch under his pillow? And don't you tell me he did it himself!"

Silent but scared, the child stared at her, wide-eyed.

Horrified at herself, Rachel put him down the same moment she heard a thumping on the back door. She tried to pull both boys into her embrace, but Andy ducked away.

"He wants in," Aaron cried, darting back, too. "He was in the barn, but he wants to come sleep here with you and his watch."

She dug her nails into the palms of her fist to keep from shaking him. Forcing calm in her voice, she told them, "That's only Mr. Randall." She prayed she was right. "He's staying in our barn just this one night to be sure no one bothers us. I have to go down and tell him we're all right. Just stay out of that room!"

She dare not go back across the glass and kerosene

for her wrapper or shawl, so she pulled a quilt from the hall linen closet, wrapped it around her night-gown and started downstairs in the cold dark. Behind her, the boys were whispering to each other. She was still so distraught that it took her a moment to realize they were not speaking *Deutsche* or *Englisch.*

Rachel stopped a few steps down, straining to hear their voices over the increased pounding on the back door below. She gripped the banister so hard her hand cramped. Her boys were speaking the nonsense words she hadn't heard for nearly two years, words that shut her out. Now it was as if her own flesh and blood wanted to shun her, too.

Rachel shook so hard her teeth chattered as she peered out to see a distraught Mitch at the back door; she unlocked it for him.

"I was ready to break it down," he said and hauled her into his arms. "What happened?"

"I accidentally broke the lantern," she murmured, pressing against him. His hard embrace felt so good, but she knew she had to do this alone. Caught be-tween Mitch's world and that of her own people, she would live in neither until she could decide to which she belonged. But she did not step away.

"You're all right then?" he asked, tipping her back and turning her chin up with one hand. "No, you're not," he answered himself when he saw her face this close in the dark. "Rachel, what hap-pened?"

"Is Gabe all right?" she asked instead of answer-ing him.

"A lot of stitches, and he won't be doing manual

work with his right hand for a while, but he was lucky. Tell me what happened.''

"I know I should ask you in and fix some hot chocolate or coffee, but I just can't,'' she explained. "I need to get back to the boys, clean up that mess in my room and get some sleep. If you don't want to stay in the barn, that's fine. I think,'' she added, almost choking over her own words, "nothing worse can happen tonight. Join us for breakfast tomorrow morning and then finish what you need to do in the barn, because I'm going to have to work things out alone these next six weeks.''

She saw his frown lines deepen, even in the dark. "Why six weeks?'' he demanded. "And when I've fixed those floorboards, it doesn't mean that I'm done here.''

"Mitch, I'm on probation with my people, and I need time to think. I found Sam's watch under his pillow tonight where he used to keep it, set just the way he liked. I suppose it's possible Linc could have put it there before he died and that someone told him Sam always set it early. So after breakfast, I'm going to take the twins to the key shop in the lumber store and get my locks changed myself. I've got to spend time alone with the twins. Besides, Jennie's really on edge and...''

Rachel let her voice drift off amidst her nervous torrent of talk. Her legs felt weak. She tried to soak in his strength. Mitch had always been there for her, and it would kill her to keep him away. But the moment that barn was done, she must. Unless, that is, she learned in these hard weeks to come she could not do without him. That thought terrified her even more than the prospect of a formal, permanent *mei-dung,* which could follow.

"They haven't shunned you?" he asked, as if he'd read her mind.

"Just for six weeks, a warning, a trial period." Her voice came muffled against his shoulder. "Time for them to decide—and me, too."

His embrace tightened and his voice came hot in her ear. "I love you, Rachel. I know it sounds too soon, too crazy, but I was intrigued from the moment I saw you staring down at me in the barn with your hair loose and your feet bare—like now. And that became attraction, then concern, then—this need and desire—to help you, not just to possess you."

She tried to speak, to tell him not to say these things, but instead she clung to him, though the quilt slipped free from her shoulders to be caught between them. Somehow his arms and hands were under the quilt anyway, and his hard body radiated heat.

"That's what real love is," she whispered. "Not wanting and taking, but giving."

His voice got deeper, rougher. "You just filled some place inside of me that's been so empty and dark, sweetheart. You made up for all the losses, and I won't let you be hurt. I swear, Rachel Mast, I'll follow you to the ends of this worldly world or any Amish one you try to live in without me to help you and the boys."

Though her resolve softened at his words, Rachel stiffened in his arms. Something someone had said to her about losses and emptiness and following someone raked at her memory but would not come clear. Was it something Pat Perkins had said about Linc?

Carefully, reluctantly, Rachel stepped back from Mitch. "I need to get upstairs," she told him. "I care deeply for you, too, but you will have to give me time and distance to resolve some things in my mind and in my life. Until I find out where the next few days take me, I can't promise more for later."

Raw emotions raced across his face, but he pressed his lips together in a hard line. His eyes narrowed as if he'd be angry, but he said, his voice quite calm, "Breakfast is still on?" When she nodded, he added, "Afterward, I'll show you how to take the cylinders out of your door locks so you can get them rekeyed. I was thinking tonight that I'd never be able to rush to your rescue because I don't have a key to the doors. Sorry I got you all shook, pounding like that."

"That's all right," she said, still trying to recall what Pat had said. Those words "rushing to your rescue" triggered unease, too, but she couldn't think why.

"I can never thank you enough for all the times you helped," she told him.

"We'll think of something," he said, but his stiff smile did not reach his eyes.

As Rachel stepped back farther to close the door between them, her bare feet felt nearly frozen to the linoleum floor. They'd been standing in an open door with the cold wind sweeping in, and she hadn't noticed until now. But she knew she'd be so very cold without him—or without her people.

"Remember what the rules are, boys," Rachel repeated as she snapped the reins to head the buggy toward town the next morning. "If you cannot talk either German or English to each other, just do not talk to each other at all. If you cannot talk German or English to me, don't talk to me, though then I won't know what you want to eat or when you want to play. But remember I love you and want to talk to you.''

She had been trying to recall all she'd learned from worldly books about what the *Englische* called "tough love." It had caused great upheaval between her and Sam when she'd treated the boys this way to break them of their twin talk before, but it had worked, and it was going to have to work again.

"What about talking to Nann and Bett?" Aaron inquired. Rachel was so relieved to hear something she understood that she smiled and put an arm around him. Last night, she'd sat in a chair between their beds, forbidding them to talk that nonsense until they all finally fell asleep.

Now, despite how she'd lost control last night, this new day gave her hope. She was taking control of her life and of theirs. During the next six weeks, she would do two important things. She must find out who killed Sam and then decide which world she belonged in. Things *had* to get better, she vowed to buck herself up.

"To Nann and Bett we talk horse talk," she answered him. "*Gee* and *haw* and *giddyap* and *whoa,* and they talk back to us in their own words because horses only know horse talk."

"Well, we're twins with twin talk," Aaron declared smugly.

"Da, dumdy morma nos de fam," Andy said, and Aaron nodded.

Rachel gritted her teeth and headed into town traffic. "Stop it!" she ordered in such a loud voice that

Bett and Nann threw back their heads and halted in an intersection. "No, not you. Bett, Nann, giddyap!"

Rachel turned the buggy down the alley behind the row of stores where the Amish tethered their vehicles. One big buggy and a wagon were tied to the hitching post here. The lumberyard itself stretched a good distance behind its facade on Main Street, but what she wanted was in the combined lumber-hardware front section of the store. She gathered up the two lock cylinders and led the boys toward the back door.

It opened nearly into their faces as Frederick Esh, Jacob's gray-bearded father, came out. Rachel had just seen him at Sarah and Jacob's wedding two days ago, and she knew he'd appreciated her bringing the celery. Now he looked at her, then away, and said, "Good morning, boys," before he went on.

Rachel's heart fell to her feet. So they all knew already. This was what it was like to be shunned.

The twins obviously noticed the snub but were stubbornly saying nothing to her. Rachel headed toward the far aisle where Mitch had said the locksmith worked. Like their father, the twins looked instantly intrigued by every hardware or lumber display they passed.

As Rachel turned into another aisle, she nearly bumped into Jennie's ex-husband, Mike. Since it was a weekday morning, she wondered why he was not at work, but she knew worldly folk believed in things like personal days and vacations.

"Mrs. Mast," he said, grasping and bobbing the bill of his baseball cap, "you know, I'm sorry you got mixed up with my neighbor, McGowan, but glad you turned up something that may lead to news about Laura's disappearance.''

He spoke quietly, maybe so her boys or so his own grown son wouldn't overhear if Kent was around this morning.

"I appreciate your kind words, Mr. Morgan," she told him. "As you can imagine, Jennie doesn't feel the same."

"Ah—no, she wouldn't. She refuses to let Laura rest in peace, wherever she is, yet won't let anyone grieve—well, this isn't the time or place," he added, looking nervously around.

"I know Kent is upset, too," Rachel whispered.

For one moment, Mike Morgan looked deep into her eyes, as if trying to read something there. She saw in his stare much more than curiosity about her, which was something the Amish were used to. It was more like he wanted to ask her something about Jennie or even Kent. But that probing looked passed swiftly, and he gazed down at the twins.

"Do you two know my son, Kent?" he asked, leaning slightly down. "I know you play with my grandsons, Jeff and Mike."

Rachel held her breath, wondering if the twins would use their secret code. Instead, amazingly without looking at each other to plan it, they both nodded and smiled. She felt somewhat relieved, however doltish it made them seem.

Rachel had started to move on when Mike Morgan said, "And thanks for your kindness about the flowers. I'd like to do that again. Just once a year on that day from now on. It made me feel—well, a little better."

Rachel looked back at him and nodded. Though

she was grateful he had not blamed her for stirring things up as Jennie had, she wondered two things. Why, since he lived just across the field from Linc, had Mike Morgan not noticed girls at the other man's house over the years and wondered if Linc had been too close to Laura? And why, unlike Jennie, since Laura was only still officially missing, had he been so sure for years she would not be back?

Rachel shook her head as she hustled the boys on. But blocking her way, looking at door hinges, stood the Amish Zooks, all six of them, their four little girls ranging from ages three to ten. Ella, the five-year-old, had often played with the twins after church services.

"*Mamm,*" Ella said to her mother and broke into a big grin at the sight of the Masts. "There's Andy and Aaron and Sam Rachel."

Their mother glanced up, bit her lip and looked away. David Zook didn't even turn his head but said something about the hinge he held. When Ella and the eight-year-old Naomi started toward the twins, both parents pulled them back and steered them all away. The hinge David had hastily discarded clattered to the floor.

The twins stared up at Rachel. She hadn't explained to them about the six-week taste of shunning being forced on them, but obviously she would have to. She hadn't guessed it could be this cold, this hard to face. And it would only get worse.

"Here," she said, thrusting the two cylinders into the boys' hands. "Since *Daadi* is not coming back, you two are going to have to help take care of the house and barn and me now. Come with me and tell the man, in English, that we need to have these locks rekeyed, and we want to buy two locks for our barn, one big and one small. Come on."

Stopping only to replace the hinge David Zook had dropped, Rachel marched the boys up to the counter that said above it, Keys Made While You Wait. Behind were arrayed racks of shiny new but uncut keys in all colors and shelves with larger locks. No one was staffing the counter now, so she rang the bell once, then again. She held her breath. Would her new tactic with her sons work? They were so young, but maybe they could learn to help her, not fight her.

Both boys reached up to place their cylinders on the counter on either side of her. "Just a sec!" Rachel heard a man's voice call out from nearby. Now she would at least know if the twins would obey her.

"Hi, guys," a jaunty, familiar voice behind them called out as Kent hurried behind the counter. "What can I do for you?"

Rachel looked down at Aaron then Andy. "*Mamm* needs rekeys," Andy told Kent. "We're not going to see Jeff and Mike today, 'cause we have to stay with *Mamm* till we talk better."

"Sounds like you talk okay to me, right, Rachel?" Kent said and smiled as she sheepishly shrugged and nodded. The distraught man of last night was not in evidence, but Rachel couldn't worry about Jennie's son's moods right now. She was so relieved about her own boys she almost burst into tears, that is until Kent started a loud machine to carve the new keys. Then she saw the twins whisper something to each other, and she was sure there was not one word she knew.

Mitch installed Rachel's new locks the minute she got them home. She decided to wear the new keys, both pairs of them, around her neck on a string under her dress. After fixing everyone sandwiches, she delivered Mitch's to him in the barn without asking him in again. She couldn't bear to have him see the way her twins were acting. When they could manage to briefly turn their backs on her, they began talking in what the books she'd once gotten from Pat Perkins had termed "cryptoglossia." Rachel had learned it was not uncommon, especially for identical twins, to make up their own baby talk as if they needed no one but each other.

Rachel told the twins they couldn't play or work together since they weren't really talking, so she put Andy to work raking the garden and Aaron sweeping out the washhouse. She could see them both from the front door of the barn from where she stood, building up her determination to talk to Mitch, who worked inside. What she had to tell him made her just as sick as forcing the twins to stay apart.

Rachel stood quietly for a moment just watching Mitch. He moved with determined, angular grace. He was muttering measurements to himself and had his back to her while he stretched out his metal tape on the floor over the spot near the Percheron stalls where the wood was starting to weaken. He had already strapped on knee pads over his black jeans and donned work gloves. Behind him was the circular saw Gabe had cut himself on and a stack of floor planks Mitch was going to nail in place after he tore the old ones up. He'd said he might have to go down several feet to the old fieldstone foundations.

Rachel thought briefly about that widowed pioneer woman, Varina Wharton, who had owned the barn so many years ago. Why had she run off with Stephen Keller and left this place she must have loved and fought to keep? Rachel wondered if she could ever do that, even if she loved a man beyond all reason.

"Hey, you startled me," Mitch said when he saw her standing there. With a mere touch of a button, he made his measuring tape retreat into its metal case. "Everything okay?" he asked. "I mean, other than everything that's wrong?"

She wanted to smile at the way he'd put that and to run to his arms and hide. Instead, she glanced back out at the twins, then said, "I hope and pray you will understand why I need some time with just my boys to sort things out, things between me and the Amish and between me and you. And I need to once and for all know what happened to Sam."

"I understand," he said, stuffing the tape measure in his back jeans pocket, "but I don't understand why I can't help you." To her surprise he kept busy while he talked, maybe so he could take out his frustration on something besides her. On his knees, using a big claw hammer, he began to tear into and yank up floorboards.

Rachel raised her voice to talk over the racket. "These coming six week will be time for me to answer a lot of questions," she said, though he kept at the floor with a vengeance. "Besides, if I was seen around with you now, I'd be permanently shunned for sure. But I wanted you to know, if you feel I should pay you for this work, instead of doing it free, as you have been, I can sign an I.O.U. It's against the Amish way not to pay for things up front, but I can't ask you to keep taking care of me in case there is no future for—for your wishes.''

He continued to rip at the wood. ''Rachel,'' he said loudly, still not looking up, ''I'd love to cut you some slack, but I'm afraid someone may still be around who wants you hurt. You're a strong, stubborn woman, but if you won't let me help, I'll be forced to hide just off your property to keep an eye on this place. And then, once we're sure you're safe, we can decide together what happens to me in your life.''

He placed boards behind him against the pile of new-cut planks. Rachel noted that some of the new wood had red stains that might be Gabe's blood from the accident last night. As if Linc haunted this place now, Rachel remembered he'd mentioned that animal blood, like a sacrificial ritual, had been used to darken the barn paint. She shuddered as Mitch bent low over his work and whispered, not angry but awed, ''What in the heck...''

Rachel shuffled closer as he pulled and yanked at more boards to open a space between them about three feet by two. Only indirect light from the open door reached here, and her skirts shadowed the opening. She stepped behind him and peered over his shoulder.

''What's that?'' she asked, trying to keep her voice steady, though she felt fierce foreboding. ''Bones!''

''Light a lantern,'' he ordered, but her feet felt nailed to the floor.

She gasped as she leaned closer. Mitch tried to touch the thing, but a white shroud of some sort shredded in his gloved hand. Below this original flooring in a scooped-out, shallow grave lay a human skeleton, its skull faintly framed with what was left of long, straight, chestnut hair.

Twenty-One

Rachel fell to her knees beside Mitch on the barn floor by the makeshift grave.

"Look, scattered arrowheads," he whispered. "Maybe it's an old Indian burial."

"Why wouldn't the hair be even darker then?" Rachel asked. "More likely it's Varina Wharton. Don't touch it again. I'll get the light."

"Who's Varina Wharton? You mean, that pioneer woman McGowan talked about in that article?"

"Right. The widow who supposedly fell for some ne'er-do-well then suddenly disappeared, supposedly ran off with him. But maybe she didn't. Just a minute."

Rachel darted away to peek out at the twins. Both were still working. She lit the lantern with her shaking hands and turned up the wick. Kneeling by Mitch, she lifted the light above the bones.

"See those scraps of an old-fashioned dress or apron under the rotted quilt or shroud?" Mitch said, pointing.

She leaned closer to see several layers of white

cloth over the chest of the skeleton. Rachel drew in a sudden breath as Mitch took the lantern from her.

"What?" he asked, tearing his gaze from his grisly discovery.

"Eben Yoder's missing wife had long hair about that color. And we bury married women in their bridal garb of white cape and apron."

"But you said she ran off."

"That's what Eben told everyone."

"What about—it can't be Laura Morgan?"

"Her mother's convinced she's still alive," Rachel said, gripping his arm so hard with her free hand that the lantern wavered. He put it down. She wrapped her arms around herself and rocked slightly on her haunches. "Besides, it would have been really difficult and stupid for a killer to bury her here where everyone was looking for her. The Brickers lived here then, and we lived here when Eben's wife took off. This has to be a pioneer era burial, but why under the barn floor?"

"She's not under the foundation, so it can't be that the barn was built over her grave somehow."

Their eyes met, and she nodded.

"As much as I hate to keep saying this," Mitch muttered, "we've got to call Sheriff Burnett. No, I left my phone home, so we'll have to ride in for him. I'm not leaving all of you here. I'll cover this up, and you tell the boys we've found the body of the day."

Still stunned, she protested, "That isn't funny. I've been trying to shelter them, keep all these terrible things from them. I haven't told them about Linc, and I'm not telling them about this."

"You probably haven't explained the temporary

shunning, either, have you?'' he challenged. ''Maybe you shouldn't try to keep things from them, even upsetting ones.'' He took new boards to begin to lay across the opening.

''Mitch, they're not even five years old!''

''I know,'' he said, looking up at her as she got to her feet. ''But I know how screwed up I got when people whispered around me, and I knew something was wrong and thought it might be my fault.''

She recalled that Kent had said much the same when he'd stormed out of Jennie's house last night. With all his family's talk and guilt about losing Laura, he came to feel something was his fault and now bitterly resented it. But she was desperate to protect her twins at any cost, Rachel vowed as she ran toward Aaron and Andy.

Mitch followed her out and closed and locked the barn doors, front and back. He jogged toward her, car keys in his hand as she locked the house and explained to the boys they had to take Mitch's repaired truck into town together. ''Now that it's fixed and he doesn't have to drive Gabe's car anymore, let's see how it rides,'' she told them, ignoring the warning look she got from Mitch for her latest cover-up.

''Shall I wait here with the boys or will you?'' Rachel asked as Mitch parked in front of the sheriff's office. She'd never gotten to town so fast.

''We'd better both go in,'' Mitch said, turning off the engine.

''Then everyone out,'' Rachel ordered. ''I don't want them left alone.''

''After my messed-up childhood and the years I

spent in prison," he plunged on, ignoring her sharp look to keep quiet, "I'm not any happier about dealing with the police than I was yesterday." As he swung the boys down to the curb, she glared at him, realizing he was purposely challenging the way she handled her sons. Yet, as if they were a family, they went in together.

"Sheriff, you're not going to believe this," Mitch greeted Tim Burnett just inside the door as he held it open for Rachel and the twins, "but we need to talk to you privately."

The deputy who had interviewed Mitch yesterday was there, as were two highway patrolmen. Everyone stopped what they were doing and looked up. So much for trying to keep this quiet, Rachel thought. Despite Jennie's mistaken predictions that the worldly press would bother her over Linc's death, she had no illusions she'd escape gawkers over this find, especially after Linc's haunted-barn newspaper article. Word spread fast in a small community, even among the Amish. At least, she noted, the sheriff's shadow, Marci, wasn't here right now, so maybe Jennie wouldn't have to be upset by this, if they got the body looked at and quickly declared a historic one.

"Let's step into the back room, Mitch, Mrs. Mast," the sheriff said, gesturing, "and Deputy Jaye can mind the twins for a bit. Maybe show them a map of where they live and all. Now, something else about McGowan?" the sheriff asked as he closed the door behind the three of them. They were in a small room with file cabinets, shelves stacked with office supplies, even some weapons and holsters on wall pegs.

"I was repairing some rotting boards in Mrs.

Mast's barn floor,'' Mitch began without answering the man's first question. "In pulling them up, I found an intact, female skeleton buried in a shallow grave under the flooring. Looks like an old pioneer or Indian burial to us.''

For one moment, the sheriff sucked air. "You gotta be kiddin' me!''

"The corpse is obviously old but the bones are in decent shape, with some hair,'' Rachel put in, gripping her hands around her own apron, thinking again that the corpse's apron could have been Amish. Since Eben had struck her, he could certainly have hit Eben Mary. Sarah had always been so shocked that her mother had run away and never contacted her children. Was Eben skilled enough that he could have carefully taken up those floorboards, buried his wife, then replaced them? He'd had the Percherons to his place that week, Rachel recalled, then brought them back when she wasn't home.

"Mrs. Mast?'' the sheriff was saying, leaning close to her. "You're not gonna faint on us, are you? What's that hair look like?''

"Oh, no, I'm fine. The hair's long, straight and brown—maybe chestnut brown.''

"Whew,'' Sheriff Burnett said and wiped his forehead. "At least it ain't Laura Morgan. All the missing photos we used of her showed her hair was real naturally curly. Let's go. You all head back in your vehicle, and I'll get the forensic team outta Toledo for the second day in a row, then follow.''

The sun had shifted higher to pour in through the drop-down haymow door on the second floor, dazzling their eyes with dancing, whirling flecks and dust motes as they unlocked the barn door and walked in with Sheriff Burnett.

"Go ahead. Uncover it," he told Mitch as they stood over the boarded-up grave site. "Historic barn, historic skeleton, I'll bet. After the forensic guys take a look-see and it goes to the coroner, we'll get us some university anthropologist to check it out."

Mitch quickly uncovered the grave; the boards he threw behind him clattered to make the only sound in the barn. But there was nothing in the grave except a scrap of white cloth and a half-buried arrowhead.

Rachel gasped. Mitch swore.

"It was there," they chorused. Rachel pointed, and Mitch bent low to stick his face in the opening until the sheriff yanked him back.

Rachel fell to her knees beside the empty hole. She collapsed, not at the horror of the missing bones, but at the terrible knowledge that someone was still watching this locked barn—watching her.

"Sheriff, please," Rachel pleaded as he and his deputy wrapped her barn in a long string of yellow police tape that read over and over, KEEP OUT. "Can't we keep this private? No skeleton is here now, and we're telling you it was buried with scattered arrowheads and was dressed in some sort of historic garments."

"Right," he muttered, narrowing his eyes, "like you're wearing right now. Clothes, arrowheads, nothing but the bones can prove they were old. There's too much we don't know, and I'm not going out on a limb—even for you Amish—by not checking this out to the nth degree."

Rachel shook her head and led Nann and Bett

away from the barn to tether them to the porch post. Behind her she heard Mitch take up her futile argument.

"Sheriff," he said, and she turned back to see him glance at the two forensic pathologists inside, "the grave has obviously not only been—well, robbed, but scraped clean."

"So maybe we've got theft, murder and abuse of a corpse," the sheriff insisted. "It's up to them to find out."

As if the pathologists had overheard them, one came to the door of the barn and called to the sheriff, "We're going to impound both shovels and the spade we found in here and the work gloves Mr. Randall wore. This may get down to dust spores or DNA and that takes time."

"Sheriff, this is a working barn for a farm," Mitch said.

"And I'm gonna post a guard here day and night for a while to make sure no one bothers it so it can be returned to Mrs. Mast as fast and intact as possible," the sheriff told Mitch, punching the air with an index finger.

Mitch walked over to Rachel and the horses. The twins' faces were pressed to the back screen door behind her. She kept looking between them and Mitch.

"I do understand how you feel," Mitch said, flexing and unflexing his fists, held stiffly at his sides. "This is exactly what happened to my grandparents' farm with the public domain controlling it, tossing us out when they had no right to."

"Again, I'm grateful for your help and support, but I don't want you to get all caught up in this—

more than you already are. I see I have no choice but to cooperate.''

"All right," he said, staring straight into her eyes. "On the condition that I don't lose my chance to help you through this."

She glanced at the boys in the doorway. She could tell they were chattering their talk. "I've got to go in and tell them something or other about all this," she said.

Mitch seized her wrist as she turned away. His grip was unbelievably strong. "How about trusting them with the truth for once?" he demanded. "You can't keep protecting them like this. Believe me, it won't work. Why don't you just lock this place up for now, bring the horses—the Percherons, too, if you can get them back—and stay at my place? I can bunk in my office at the bottom of my lane by the road so you'll have the house to yourselves."

"No need," she said, tugging her wrist free. "This is my home, and it's time someone learned that I'm not running, no matter what."

But that night, Rachel wished she had run. When newspaper reporters from Bowling Green and Toledo knocked on her door, she told them she did not give interviews. People paraded their cars past and some parked along the road and even blocked her lane until Deputy Jaye, whom the sheriff had left on guard, made them leave and stretched more police tape across her driveway. If the deputy had not been on her property, she had no doubt people would have swarmed her barn. Somehow, though the news had missed the newspaper, it had gone out on local TV and the radio. Still, she worried the most about what poor Jennie had learned and wondered about the body. Again, she desperately wished she had a phone.

Rachel tried to calm herself as she fixed and shared a chicken dinner with the twins, but they were still defiantly using twin talk, so she had forbidden them to speak. That meant the sporadic slam of car doors outside, and the buzz of voices close to the house were the only sounds. Occasionally, Deputy Jaye would yell at people to clear them out.

After dinner Rachel let Andy and Aaron throw a beanbag around in the living room, which she never allowed. She had told them that an article in the paper had talked about the barn and they'd found some Indian arrowheads and everyone was wanting to see them.

"Why?" Andy asked. "Lots of places and people around here have arrowheads. Gabe showed us some. We saw some at Mr. Randall's barn house. Jennie has some and even Bishop Yoder's boys got them plowing."

She hated to admit that Mitch might have been right about not trying to shelter her kids, Rachel thought. She wasn't exactly lying to them, but neither had she trusted them with the truth.

"Besides the arrowheads," she tried to explain, "there were also some old bones, probably Indian bones."

"Neat! Why can't we see them?" Aaron asked.

"When we went to tell the sheriff, someone took them away," she admitted.

In the string of nonsense words that passed between the twins in rapid fire, the only word she could pick out was *Daadi*.

"Well, that's it," she scolded them in German. "I told you if you talked nonsense again, you would have to sleep in separate bedrooms tonight. Let's get ready for bed."

It wasn't dark yet and people were still prowling around outside; Rachel could hear voices. Once she thought she heard a buggy horse go by at a good trot, but she knew the Amish had abandoned her to her fate.

As they passed the front living-room windows that overlooked the porch on their way upstairs, someone tapped on the glass. They all glanced up to see four demonic faces staring in at them. Both boys jerked and shrieked.

"It's just those Halloween masks," she told them, "just kids trying to scare us."

Rachel sent the twins upstairs, opened the front door and called out, "You go on now, or I'll get the deputy out back!"

The boys scattered but she saw her own smashed pumpkins all over her porch and front walk.

Rachel closed the door, turned down the single lantern and sat on the bottom stair, where the intruder's footsteps from under her kitchen table had disappeared. Not only her house had been invaded and violated, but the very foundations of her beloved barn, her livelihood and her life.

She heard whispering and realized it was her boys upstairs this time. "I'll be right up!" she called and darted into the kitchen to glance out to make sure Nann and Bett were all right. Either the deputy or the trespassers had evidently loosed their reins or scared them enough that they'd pulled free of the porch post. Both were standing by the pile of *stooks*

Sim Lapp had cut and bound, stuffing themselves with corn.

Rachel lifted both hands to her head as if to keep it from exploding. Then, to her dismay, the deputy's car lights sprang on, he started his vehicle and drove out, first stopping to clear then replace the tape across her driveway. He surely wasn't going for help, because he had a phone in his car. Was someone supposed to replace him and they had not? She wished she had not insisted Mitch leave. It wasn't just the fact that she realized she needed him for protection but that she needed him even when things weren't this desperate. And that really scared her.

Rachel returned to the kitchen to be sure the back door was locked. It was and the keys still hung around her neck. But glancing out through the door window, she saw a note taped to the glass. Perhaps the deputy had wanted her to know where he'd gone. The last time a note was on her porch, it was from Mitch, so maybe he'd been by. She fumbled to unlock the door, snatched the note off, then relocked it.

She ripped the note open.

YOU REAP WHAT YOU SOW. REPENT NOW, COME TO ME, AND I CAN SAVE YOU.

It was unsigned and in block letters as if to avoid being identified but surely the note was from Eben. She wadded up the paper, tossed it in the trash and ran upstairs just as a deafening sound split the air, vibrating the house to its cellar.

Andy and Aaron were already glued to the windows in their room. Even before she got to them, she could see a sweep of a blinding beam outside.

Rachel lunged for the boys and pulled them back between their beds where the three of them huddled on their knees. The light slashed through the room, which instantly plunged into darkness again. She clenched the boys to her, picturing the roar of that train and its lights that had almost devoured them. Then, as the light seemed to circle away and roar back again, she knew what it was.

"One of those airplanes!" she shouted to the boys. "With the round blades—a helicopter!"

"Chopper!" Andy yelled, then told Aaron, "De dom *Mamm* gettun foba."

Ignoring that, Rachel left them peering over a mattress and darted from one window to another on the second floor. Out the newly replaced guest bedroom window, which had been shot out, she saw Bett and Nann running around the barnyard in fear, then, seeing the barn doors were closed, they came back and huddled together near the buggy.

Out the side window of their guest room, she saw the plane, like a big, glowing plague locust, land in her pumpkin field. Whether it carried the police or TV reporters or just more gawkers didn't matter. She sprinted back to the boys.

"Get some clothes together," she ordered. "Just pull things out of your drawers and put it all in your pillowcases to carry like a sack. We're going to sneak outside and go for a night ride away from here. Hurry now."

As a news team with a bright light connected to a camera perched on a man's shoulder knocked at their front door, Rachel and the twins ran out the back.

She swung them up into the buggy, then frantically tried to get Bett and Nann hitched. When the buggy neared the yellow tape stretched across her driveway, she had the team going at such a good clip that the horses plunged right through it.

Ignoring the shouts of their uninvited guests, they made it to the phone booth by the gas station before Rachel saw the lighted helicopter in the sky again, probably trying to follow them. She blessed the light in this glass booth though, because she had to squint to read the phone book's small print to find the number she wanted, one she'd only dialed before in her dreams.

Twenty-Two

When Rachel woke, she was so groggy she felt drugged. Rain rattled on the roof and thunder rumbled, coming closer, getting louder. Keeping her eyes shut tight, she stretched, then froze. This pillow and mattress were harder, the sheets softer than hers. They did not smell of fresh air from being dried on the outside line. This was not her house, not her bed.

She sat bolt upright. Mitch's barn house. In his bedroom and in his bed.

Everything came tumbling back. Late last night, she had phoned him, and he and Gabe had come with a pickup truck and a horse carrier to bring them here.

The twins. She had to wake her boys and get dressed. The glowing clock on the bedside table said ten o'clock. Was it this dark from just the storm? Surely, she had not slept till midmorning.

Rachel flew out of bed before she remembered she wore only Mitch's T-shirt. She had left her house so fast she hadn't even taken a nightgown.

She darted through the bathroom into the adjoining bedroom where Andy and Aaron had slept in what Mitch called bunk beds. It amazed her how deeply she'd trusted Mitch to shelter them. So she could hear if the boys called for her in the night, she'd left the doors open. Could they have slept so late, too? Or if they were up already, maybe their voices didn't carry from the living level below.

In the guest bedroom, the twins' clothes were gone and their beds were mussed but empty. The door to this room was opened to the hall, and she smelled coffee and bacon. Feeling somewhat relieved, she told herself that the boys might as well go down to eat if they had a mother who had turned into a slug-a-bed.

Retracing her steps, she used the toilet, washed her face, then caught sight of herself in the huge mirror on the bathroom wall. Just seeing her full, life-size reflection startled her. Her hair was wild and loose, her legs bare from midthigh down. She looked too thin and too frazzled.

Leaning her shoulder on the tiled wall, Rachel lifted her hands to her face and tried to keep from sobbing. She should be grateful, she lectured herself, that Mitch had taken her in. But that was her problem, one of them at least. Mitch and his seductive world *had* taken her in. And she was terrified he was right that she had been overly protective and too secretive with the twins. If she had misread her own flesh and blood, who else had she misjudged? Someone was still out to harm her.

Rachel jumped when nearby thunder rattled the house down to its very bones. The shower door and mirror vibrated, making her image seem to quiver.

She hurried back into the bedroom. Mitch stood in the doorway. She gasped as his steady stare brought her to a halt.

"I thought I heard you up," he said, extending a cup of coffee, but not stepping into the room. He had slept on the couch downstairs while Gabe stayed at the other house. Rachel became so aware of her body; she couldn't decide whether to run into the bathroom or jump in bed to cover herself. Mitch wasn't budging. She walked quickly to the closet, took out his terry-cloth robe she'd seen last night and pulled it on.

"Maybe you don't want the caffeine," he said. "You probably just got the only good night's sleep you've had in weeks, and a rainy day's always good for sleeping. I can bring you breakfast in bed."

"That's only for invalids, and I'm not sick," she protested, her voice too strident. But having him so close, blocking the door of his bedroom, was making her light-headed. Her belly was empty, except for the butterflies when he looked at her like that.

"Rachel," he said, pausing to sip the coffee himself, "it's not a sin to relax sometimes, to just kick back, rest and enjoy before facing the world again."

"I can't now, not until I get my barn back and find out what's been going on with that woman's death—and Sam's."

"And maybe Linc's," he put in, his tone turning ominous.

"I'll just get dressed and join the boys at breakfast."

"They ate about eight and are down at the other house with Gabe. I figured you'd follow your nose to have breakfast with me so we can make plans. The storm's getting so bad outside I'm afraid the electricity might go out and you'll end up with nothing but cold toast."

His eyes were intense, darker than she recalled. He seemed larger than usual, like that first time she'd seen him when he'd suddenly appeared and said, "I want your barn." Now, she knew, he wanted her, and she wanted him, too. Yet something was holding her back, something more than her Amish sense of right and wrong. He had said she was hoping she'd follow her nose, but in a way it seemed he was always following her, always ready to rescue her. It could be God's will he'd sent Mitch to her, or it could be Mitch's will to control her life. And didn't someone who controlled a life also control death? Her heart started to pound so hard, competing with the thunder.

"The breakfast sounds good," she told him, her voice breaking. She gripped her elbows as if to hug herself. It was just this man's tremendous magnetism that was rattling her like this, wasn't it? Thoughts that he could be her enemy were demented.

"I'll just wash up, get dressed and come down," she went on. Something Pat Perkins had said snagged in her thoughts. There was a phone in this room. Maybe she could call Pat for help. "Then I want to rescue Gabe from the boys," Rachel added, talking faster and louder.

It helped to fill the air with words, even if she had to vie with the storm. "I need to settle some things with them to stop that twin talk," she heard herself say.

"Don't worry about Gabe and the kids," Mitch said. "You know he used to play Santa Claus, and he can carry on in crazy voices and faces with the best actor you've ever seen—which, I'm forgetting, you haven't seen. Relax, Rachel. We'll work this out together. I'll have breakfast waiting." Taking another swallow of coffee as if he hadn't a care in the world, he turned and walked away.

The moment she heard him start downstairs, Rachel darted to close the door behind him. Grabbing her clothes from the closet, she scrambled into them but left her hair free. Praying the boys were safe with Gabe and that Mitch wouldn't pick up a phone downstairs for a call of his own, she looked through the drawers on the bedside table for a phone book. Would phones work during a storm like this?

No book here. She lifted the top part of the phone from its slender box and punched O. It buzzed for an interminable time before it was answered.

"Operator."

"I need the number of the Clearview Public Library."

"Can you speak up, please?"

"The Clearview Public Library's number!"

Rachel grabbed a pencil and wrote on the small paper pad beside the phone, then punched in the numbers with a shaking index finger. She almost cried in relief when Pat Perkins's loud voice boomed in her ear to beat the thunder.

"Pat, this is Rachel."

"You aren't still living on the farm, are you?" she asked. "The TV and newspapers are going wild with—"

"I think *I'm* going wild. Listen, Pat, can you tell me the signs of a stalker again?"

"You know, I thought you'd be calling about Indian and pioneer burial practices. Rachel, since Linc McGowan is dead, is someone else after you? Sorry for being so nosy, but one of the Toledo stations even had views of the barn from a chopper and used quotes from that stupid article McGowan wrote before he died, about that pioneer woman or someone haunting the place so—''

''Please, Pat!''

Rachel gripped the phone harder as Pat apologized for rambling and enumerated things she'd told her about stalkers before, things she'd missed because she was so fixated on Linc McGowan then. Each characteristic smashed into Rachel like a cold, hard wave of Lake Erie water.

''In other words, a stalker,'' Pat continued as if she were reciting word for word, ''has an intense need for control, which stems from something called an 'attachment disruption.' He lost someone he loved early in life and fixates on never being hurt again by a love object rejecting him. He won't allow it and gets increasingly controlling until he can explode with violence. Rachel, tell me what's going on. Where are you? I just want to help if—''

Rachel jumped at Mitch's voice on the line. He cut off Pat in midword.

''Rachel, what are you doing on the phone?'' Mitch demanded. ''I was going to call Gabe to see if the boys are okay in the storm, but you should never use a phone long with lightning this close. Get off!''

The phone went dead. The bedroom lights flickered once and died. In a moment's pause in the wind and thunder, she heard Mitch slam down the phone. He must be coming back upstairs. Confused, disoriented in the dark, she felt her way into the black bathroom to the gray room where the boys had slept.

How could Mitch have been so prophetic about the lights? Had he cut them off himself?

Suddenly, fragments of thoughts and impressions clicked into place for her. Gabe was good at dealing with kids and disguises, and Gabe would do anything for Mitch, including, perhaps, imitate a dead Amish farmer and father to scare her away from her land and into Mitch's arms.

Mitch had lost his parents, then his grandparents, lost the only home he'd ever known. So many attachment disruptions could surely warp someone into being controlling and violent. Mitch had let slip that, when he'd found his father, he'd stalked him. And he'd followed that man who'd taken his family farm to confront him.

But what was she to Mitch that he would swoop in to save her, that he would spy on her to know when she needed him? Was she the symbol of stability for him, the comfort of the farm home he had lost, or did he just, as he'd said at first to her, *want her barn?* When she'd turned down his lucrative offer, he'd decided to get it another way.

Rachel screwed her eyes shut and shook her head as pictures of him beating up those two paramilitary men flashed at her. Yes, Mitch Randall could explode into violence and had already gone to prison for it.

She pressed herself to the wall as she heard Mitch pass the guest room in the hall. Waiting until he knocked on his bedroom door, she peeked out at him. He had no flashlight, but was moving easily around in the dark.

When she didn't answer at the bedroom door, Mitch opened it and stepped in. Rachel darted out into the hall, which was open on one side but for a banister overlooking the great room with its lofty ceiling. Some light seeped in from the large window where the haymow door had once been. She rushed down the stairs, but her mind raced faster. Nann and Bett were stabled in the shed between the houses. She had to rescue the boys and get out of here. But in a buggy she'd never outrace Mitch, so maybe they'd have to hide—if Gabe would even let her have the twins.

"Rachel?" Mitch's voice echoed. "Rachel!"

She heard him take the stairs down after her two at a time. Sprinting across the flagstone entry, she tore toward the front door. He vaulted after her and pulled her back, swinging her around hard into his arms as her hair fanned out like a huge cloud between them.

She tried to fight him but his strength was steel and stone. He picked her up while she kicked and flailed.

"Put me down! Let go!"

He sat on the broad leather couch with her sprawled across his lap, but when she kept struggling, he spilled them onto the deep rug between the couch and low table. His big body pressed her down, his hands held her wrists over her head, and one leg stilled both of hers.

"Rachel, you're going to hurt yourself and me. What's the matter?"

"Pat Perkins knows I'm here," she lied. "Just let me go!"

"I can't. I can't let you go."

"It was you, wasn't it?" she demanded.

His voice was raw with anger. "*What* was me?"

"Hiding in the barn, spying…"

"Are you crazy? I didn't know the first thing about Sam to try to use his habits against you," he yelled.

"But all those times you were there when trouble came."

"And you'll blame me for that? Listen to me," he ordered, his face so close to hers. "The only time I ever spied on you was last night with your permission. And if this is truth or consequences time, once I climbed a tree with binoculars just off your land to check out your roofline I couldn't see from any other angle. I saw you come out the back door and walk through the pumpkin field."

"But you didn't follow me through it?"

"Sweetheart, I'm starting to think I'd follow you to the ends of the earth, but no, I didn't."

Her heartbeat began to slow. "You were checking my roofline?"

A hint of smile softened the taut corners of his mouth. He loosed her wrists. "Rachel, at that point, you were hardly letting me check out your other lines. I was deciding about cupola repairs, and yes, I decided to work on the barn to be near you as well as near the place itself. I didn't want to admit that to myself at first, but it's true."

He leaned on both elbows, his mouth inches from hers. "I know you're under a lot of pressure," he went on, tenderly brushing her hair back from her eyes, "and I'll admit I can be a bit obsessive. I can't explain how you've—well, haunted me since I first saw you. I don't believe in love at first sight, Rachel, wasn't even sure I believed in love at all anymore until I got to know you. But if I'm overly dedicated, determined, protective and damn stubborn, so are you, woman, so are you."

She lay stiffly under him, trying to hold herself away, but his words, tone and expression convinced her. All this had gotten to her. Her frenzy had become raw fear, but no more. Looking deep into his eyes, she knew for certain she could love—and trust—Mitch Randall.

"Come with me, boys," Rachel said. Getting out of Mitch's truck, she took one of Andy's and one of Aaron's hands to pull them along. "Mitch is going to wait for us here."

"Mata dornan fa *Daadi*," Andy told Aaron.

"Da fum *Daadi* monna gan," Aaron replied.

"That's right," she told them as she led them along the fringe of the old Clearview Cemetery to the far corner where the Amish had purchased several plots, though only Sam's was taken now. "We are going to see *Daadi*'s grave."

She ignored the surprised looks that passed between the boys at the fact she had understood their comments. Her skirts were soon sodden from the grass, and the shoulders of the huddled blue spruces still dripped water from this morning's rain. The chill wind sliced right through her. Still, she led the twins on when they tried to pull back. Whatever happened to her in facing down Eben and Sim Lapp later today, she would at least have done her best with her and Sam's boys.

She stopped at the small, flat headstone which read only, SAMUEL MAST, 1969–1997. Tears of rain had washed the stone and filled its sharply incised words. She realized now she should have brought the boys here more often, but this last year she'd buried herself in work, trying to ignore that Sam had been murdered and that their people could accept that when she could not.

"Do you remember when we all came here to put *Daadi* in the box in the ground?" she asked. Still holding their hands, she stared at each of them until they nodded.

Suddenly, Andy pulled away to lean down and put his small hand on the stone. Aaron did, too. Despite the sopping grass, Rachel knelt and pressed one hand flat between theirs.

"*Daadi*'s body is still in this grave," she began, choosing her words carefully, "but his heart and mind—that's kind of what we call his soul—lives with the Lord in heaven now. But he has a different, heavenly body there. That means he won't come back in his earth body to visit us again. So he doesn't need to hang his hat in the barn anymore, he doesn't leave footsteps in the house, and he doesn't take you two toward the train tracks anymore. He doesn't need a watch and he does not sleep in *Mamm*'s bed. I am telling you the truth."

"Mora fam *Daadi!*" Aaron protested.

Rachel turned to him and took his chin in her hand. Turning his face to hers, she could see him clearly under the wide brim of his hat. "No, you didn't really see him," she said, her voice as quiet and as calm as she could manage. "Is that what you just said? But you *think* you saw him."

"*Ja,*" Aaron answered for his brother in German, then added, "Yes."

"I didn't want to scare you boys, but I know now I should have explained all kinds of things to you. I was trying to take care of you, and now I see I need you to take care of me, too, like you did when you ordered the new locks for me.''

Aaron nodded earnestly. He darted Andy a glance as if asking for permission to trust their mother.

''Mr. Randall—our friend Mitch—convinced me,'' she went on, ''that I should tell you some things, and he's right. He once lost his *Daadi* too, so I think he understands how you feel.''

Without so much as a blink, they both nodded, and Rachel realized that Mitch had already told them that. God knows, the twins needed a man in their life, and she blessed Mitch for reaching out to them. The fact that they were listening raptly to her showed that Mitch had not overstepped: he had expected her to tell them this on her own.

''Someone bad,'' she went on, ''but not *Daadi*, has been in our barn and is trying to scare us away. And that person has been in the house. He is dressing like *Daadi*. I know that's scary, but none of this is your fault, and I was hoping you could help me be brave in all this.''

Her voice and words rolled on faster, though she tried to keep control. ''And the reason the people, our Amish friends, have not been speaking to me is because they are angry with *Mamm* for being close to worldly people like Jennie and Mitch. They don't want me to try to find out if someone hurt *Daadi* in the barn. But I'm going to find out who did it and why.''

She looked at each child again. Andy frowned; Aaron nodded.

''And yesterday,'' she concluded, ''though a barn floor is not a cemetery like this, Mitch and *Mamm* found a body of a woman buried under the planks near the team's stall, probably from a long time ago, and that's really why everyone is going there, not just because of arrowheads.''

"But," Aaron said, "there was a man in the barn who took us to the train tracks. So if it wasn't *Daadi,* who was it?''

It amazed her that of all this that consumed her, only their *Daadi* really mattered to the twins. "I don't know yet," she said, blowing her nose. "Do you think it could have been Bishop Yoder or Sim Lapp, maybe, trying to look like *Daadi?*''

Both boys exchanged lightning glances she could not read. Aaron shook his head and Andy shrugged.

"Or do you think," she pursued, "this bad person looked anything like Kent's dad, Mr. Morgan, we saw in the hardware store yesterday?''

"Don't know," Aaron whispered. "But we saw someone," he said louder.

"I should have listened better to you before," she assured them. "I have to find out who it is and see he's stopped and punished."

"Good," Andy said. "Don't cry more, *Mamm,* 'cause you're already wet enough. Tell her, Aaron. Maybe she can look in there and guess who it is."

"Look in where?" Rachel asked. Did he mean the barn? Surely not Sam's grave? She watched Andy turn to Aaron. Her knees were aching from kneeling so long, but she didn't budge. Suddenly, her quieter, shyer twin looked as frightened as he had that night in the cellar when she'd found and comforted him.

"One day I saw *Daa*—I mean, the man, staring out the haymow door at us," Aaron said, speaking slowly. "So I tiptoed in and saw him put on a hat and frock coat where he hides it. Not where *Daadi* kept his on the wall pegs. High up, near where the owl nest used to be. We can't reach that high, but I'll tell you and you can look. Maybe his name will be in his coat like you sewed ours.'' As if she needed to be reminded, he unbuttoned and opened his black coat where she had stitched his name.

"'Cept *Mamm* can't get back in the barn now,'' Andy put in, "'less she just sneaks in like that bad man did.'' He leaned down to pat Rachel's knee in reassurance the way Sam used to do to them.

Rachel was going to break into her own barn. The twins were safe with Gabe, but she wanted to get in and out quickly. At least she'd have the blessing of a silent night, not one all thunderstruck and wind- and rain-whipped like the last one.

She and Mitch, both in black, parked his truck in the old orchard just off her property line and hiked into the woodlot. From there, they felt their way from tree to tree in the moonless dark. They both wore what Mitch called fanny packs, with the purse part turned around in front of them. Rachel carried Mitch's big flashlight and he toted a trowel and a sharp hunting knife for cutting their way in through the vines choking the unused cellar entrance. The sheriff had taken her keys to both barn doors.

Rachel and Mitch had already planned to enter the barn to look for the Amish clothes Aaron said were wedged in a beam, but a call from the sheriff had triggered this haste. He'd tracked Mitch down with a message for Rachel that, starting tomorrow, the rest of the barn floor would be torn up to look for more remnants of the unidentified corpse or even other bodies.

Now, Rachel and Mitch hunkered down behind a screen of lilac bushes just behind the barn until they spotted the sheriff's deputy. As the man made a circuit of the barn, Rachel grabbed Mitch's arm. She wore her glasses and was certain what she saw.

"That's Burnett himself," she whispered, her mouth close to his ear. "Maybe he's just taking a shift, giving the other man a break."

When Burnett walked down the driveway toward the house, they made their move. Rachel held a beam of light on the cellar door while Mitch tried to slice quickly through the tangle of vines. They were so thick he had to saw through them.

"At least the phantom didn't come in this way," she whispered. "I didn't think so since this can be partly seen from the house. I still say he's been getting in and out the back door somehow."

"Does this creak?" he asked as they bent together to heft the cellar door. It lifted silently. Rachel entered first, feeling her way down the steps.

Shouldering the weight of the door, Mitch started down behind her. It thudded shut above them, she thought, like a coffin lid to entomb them.

Once they were safely in, they breathed easier until dust and a moldy smell hit them. Rachel sneezed and jammed her finger under her nose. She heard mice scurry away, but she'd steeled herself for that, as the cats couldn't get down here. They had decided they would use their light as little as possible. Rachel remembered only too well that the night Mike Morgan laid flowers in the barn she could see his lantern through the boards from outside.

Rachel leaned closer to Mitch, who was ahead of her. "I just thought of something," she whispered. "If those bones were Laura's and her father knows it, that's why he didn't complain about Linc and those girls he must have seen next door over the years. He was letting sleeping dogs lie by not stirring up a new investigation that could point to him."

"But if he knew where she was," Mitch whispered, "he'd have something to do with her death and that's inconceivable. You said he seemed a sensitive, nice guy who thanked you for finding out about Linc. You're just afraid to find out it's Eben Yoder. Come on. Let's check out what Aaron saw, see if we can tie it to anyone, then get out of here. You're still going to have to confront your Amish friends tomorrow, but with me as backup, even if they have a fit about that."

Cobwebs laced themselves across Rachel's flushed face as she went a ways in before clicking on the flashlight. Above them, they located the trapdoor that opened into the barn floor. Its ladder wasn't in sight, but that could have been gone for years. Mitch used his knife to quickly cut around the outline of the door.

"Dirt fell in my contact lenses," he told her. He sniffed hard, blinked, then let both eyes water.

"I'll finish it," she told him. "Let me have your knife. Careful!"

When they turned off the flashlight again and pushed the trapdoor open, grain and straw cascaded in on them.

"Your eyes?" she whispered.

"I'll live."

''See, drawbacks to modern miracles like contacts.''

She laced her hands to give Mitch a boost, and he shimmied up. Lying flat on the barn floor, he reached down for her. She quickly put the flashlight back in her fanny pack. Her eyes finally adjusted to the blackness, allowing her to discern the silhouette of his hands and wrists.

He pulled her up. Scraping her stomach and thighs, she wished she had agreed to wear worldly men's clothing, but she would have had to cinch in the waist and turn up the pant legs of Mitch's jeans. So she'd worn her dress without the white apron, cape and hat. She pictured the corpse they'd uncovered just across the threshing floor. The remains of an apron and maybe cape crossed over the breast had been in evidence but not a cap or bonnet. No way that could have been Eben's wife. The quilt placed over the body had seemed so old and it wasn't a real Amish pattern.

She thought she heard Mitch shuffle away as she took out her flashlight again, cloaking it with her skirt and one hand so it wouldn't throw a big beam. But he must have thudded into something and tripped, because he pitched toward her, taking her down to her knees.

''Mitch, are you all ri—'' she began, but he was dead weight. She dropped the flashlight to the floor. It clattered and rolled away but she could see blood glinting on his head.

She tried to cradle him, but a hard hand pulled her to her feet. Someone shone another flashlight in her eyes, blinding her, but not before she saw a rifle barrel.

"Look what you made me do to save you," a deep voice whispered. "Now we're going to settle everything for good."

Twenty-Three

Rachel recognized the voice. "Eben," she cried. "What are you doing here? You've knocked him out!"

She tried to put a lot of volume in her shaking voice so the sheriff would come running, but she heard nothing. Not a breath of wind outside, only Eben's heavy breathing in the silent barn.

"He deserved it, seducing you like that," he muttered. "It's judgment on him."

Rachel saw Eben was holding a rifle in nervous hands. Not only had this Amish bishop, this man of nonviolence, struck Mitch, but he had evidently done it with a gun. Rachel knew Eben, like other Amish, had hunted years ago to supplement his table with game, but why...

And then, as he pulled her away from Mitch and pushed her across the dark threshing floor toward where they'd found the makeshift grave, she went limp with fear. Eben must have killed his wife and buried her in this barn. But had he killed Sam, too, fearing he'd find the grave? Or because he coveted his neighbor's wife?

"We've got to get help for Mitch," she insisted, trying to yank free from Eben's fierce grip.

"I was tempted, God forgive me, to shoot him. *Ach,* enthralling you like that, taking advantage of you and the boys."

"It wasn't like that. Put the gun down and let me go!"

Rachel wondered if she should pretend to go along with him and grab the rifle. Then she could scream for help. She hadn't heard a car pull away, but when she and Mitch had driven by, she'd seen the police vehicle down at the end of the driveway. Burnett would have a phone, and she needed the emergency squad fast. Mitch's knife—she'd given it back to him. His trowel could be a weapon, too, but it was still in Mitch's pack.

"All right, let's settle everything," she said, trying to sound calm, "but put that gun down first. And that light's in my eyes, so I can't see you."

Rachel sensed him waver, though he thrust her down on a bale of hay. He sat on one facing her, their knees touching, his gun still ready to be swung or fired. He lowered the beam of light from her face to their feet. She prayed that, seen dimly through cracks in the barn, it would bring the sheriff. Her eyes adjusted steadily to the dark so that she could make out the gaping grave a few yards away and realized that the sheriff—or maybe Eben—had enlarged it. Before, it had been a window to a tomb; now it could swallow a person whole.

"Confession time," Eben said. "Are you guilty of fornication with that worldly *auslander?*"

"If it's confession time," she countered, adjusting her glasses on her nose to stare back at him, "tell me what really happened when Eben Mary disappeared.''

"She left me, and I swore on my soul that such shame would never happen again.'' He hacked and spit on the floor in bitter contempt. "Betrayed her marriage vows, took leave of her senses and took off for damnation.''

"I can't believe you didn't try to stop her, like you're doing to me, only worse,'' she protested, struggling to sit still, to reason with him so she could get that gun and get back to Mitch.

Eben had slightly lowered the barrel, and his finger was not on the trigger. If she moved fast, grabbed and knocked away his flashlight as he had hers, maybe tossed the rifle in Nann and Bett's trough that still must have some water in it, she could at least scream for help before he grabbed her again.

"She only left me a note,'' he intoned, "just like you did.''

Despite her panic, that snagged Rachel's attention. She sat up even stiffer. Her stomach cartwheeled.

"What note?'' she asked. "*You* sent me a note tacked on my back porch post, but I sent nothing to you.''

"*Ach*, turned liar, too?'' he demanded, bouncing the barrel in his palm. "A note writ in your hand, tacked on my back door just after dark tonight, and I had to come fast to get here. Don't know who you got to deliver it, but it said come to the barn 'cause the *auslander* was going to take you away and you knew you had sinned with him and wanted me to save you.''

Rachel shook her head, uncertain if he was lying. She was sweating so hard her glasses slid down her nose, but she shoved them back up. "You—then you don't know anything about the woman's body found here?" she stammered, gesturing toward the grave.

"Know what I read, that she was a pioneer woman and all. Look, you heathen fence-jumper," he went on, his voice hardening, "you don't think that could have been Eben Mary?"

As he jerked his flashlight in surprise and leaned slightly forward, his features distorted like those grotesque masks that had stared in her house window. But Eben looked so genuinely appalled, she believed him.

"Then how did you get in this locked barn?" she demanded, lowering her voice to a whisper.

"Just the way your note said. You'd open your new lock on the back door for me so's I could get in and be waiting for you to come with the *auslander*."

Rachel pressed her clenched hands to her breasts as the terrible possibility hit her. She hadn't been set up because she'd come here on her own, but someone had lied and lured Eben here and for what? And had she and Mitch just stumbled into that lie or had whoever wanted to trap Eben known she'd end up here?

"Eben, turn off that light!" she whispered as her eyes searched the blackness of the barn beyond its wan glow.

"So's you can slip away?" he said with a snort. "I want to know if you're ready to come back to the fold now, ready to repent and then we'll get help for your *former* friend over there."

"I'm afraid not," another voice came from the darkness just beyond the grave. Something—someone—rose from the other side of Mitch's circular saw that still stood nearby.

When Eben jerked around to shine his light and lift his rifle, a deafening blast rattled the barn to its beams. Rachel sprawled on her face on the floor as Eben fell over her, onto her.

She cried out from shock and fear, although his weight punched the breath from her. Stunned, dizzy, she lay still as someone stepped forward to drag Eben off, then jerked her to her feet and slammed her back against a stall.

Jennie Morgan jumped straight out of her chair when the side doorbell rang after dark. Her heart thudding as hard as her headache, she peered out, dreading to see who'd be standing under the porchlight. When she saw it was Kent's father-in-law, Tim Burnett, that only made it worse. Sheriffs didn't bring good news.

She fumbled with the dead-bolt lock and yanked the door open.

"Are Kent and Marci okay?" she cried. "And the kids?" His police radio was squawking a woman's voice with a lot of loud static. "Did you find Rachel?"

"Jennie, sorry to startle you this way, but nothing's wrong. 'Sides, you got to realize Rachel's an adult, Amish or not, and doesn't need you mothering her. She's staying with Mitch Randall, so you can read into that what you want."

He was trying to humor her. His voice sounded like you'd lecture a four-year-old, and his open hands gently lifted as if to calm her. "I just wanted," he went on, "to drop by to see how you're doing after all the upheaval at Rachel's barn again. I was watching the place because my deputy took sick, but I gotta 'nother call of a robbery up by Kent and Marci's neck of the woods."

"It wasn't their house?"

"No, but if I don't get there directly, Marci'll beat me to it and solve the crime for me. You know how she is," he ended lamely when she just stared at him.

"I hope Kent didn't tell you I'm doing poorly and to check on me," she said, folding her arms over her chest. "I'm not exactly dancing in the streets, but I'm a survivor. No, you go on to your robbery, Tim, and don't think you've got to spend time with someone who's already lost everything."

"You see now, Jennie," he said, shaking his head, "that's the kind of talk that worries Kent and Marci—worries me, too. You're close as can be to our grandkids and have lots of happy memories about Laura and the old days that—"

Though she could tell no difference in the chatter or cadence of his radio, the sheriff stopped in mid-thought and cocked his head. "I'll be back later, when I give the Mast place its next look-see," he called to her as he turned and sprinted for the car. "Seems the robber took some guns from a firearms collection, and we don't need this spreading to armed robbery next. I'll have Marci call you."

"Not tonight. I'm going to bed," she yelled after him. "I said, don't worry about me."

Maybe he didn't hear her. He had the light bar throbbing but did not turn on the siren as he swung around and roared out of her driveway. But Ravine Road was deserted at this hour, so who needed sirens

screaming? She didn't because her head was making
its own noise.

Jennie relocked the door in the silent house and
shuffled down the hall toward her bedroom. But she
stopped at Laura's room, opened the door and entered. Except for Andy Mast when he'd peeked in,
no one but her and Rachel had been in this room for
years. That is, until she'd caught Kent in here yesterday and really laid into him. Now she'd best check
once more to be sure he hadn't disturbed anything.

She clicked on the light and blinked at the brightness. Her insistence on keeping things the way they
were had been one reason Mike left her. Like her
and yet in a different way, he'd never been the same
after Laura went missing. He'd not so much as been
able to look her in the eye, let alone touch her after
that. He'd seemed not only to blame himself for
Laura's disappearance, but blamed Jennie, even
Kent, for not watching her closer, not protecting her.

Jennie moved slowly around the room, surveying
each area to be sure Kent hadn't taken some me-
mento or moved something. Noticing how yellowed
and brittle the invitation to the barn dance looked
where it lay on Laura's desk, Jennie picked it up and
pressed it in the biology book lying there. Her family
couldn't say she was obsessed with keeping everything the same. To preserve the invitation, she'd
moved it.

Jennie stared for a long time at the last picture of
her with Laura. A Polaroid, it was yellowing, but she
didn't move it from its place in the frame of the
mirror where Laura had left it. The very day of the
barn dance, in their pre-Marci era, Jennie had helped
Laura straighten her curly hair. Imagine, a girl with

that bounty of curls wanting long, straight hair. She had worn it that night with a white, almost Victorian-looking dress—the perfect way to make herself look older, Laura had said. Though lost that night, Laura had never changed, never aged a bit in Jennie's mind or heart.

As she turned to go, Jennie saw the bedspread looked mussed. Had Kent dared to sit or lie down on this bed, or had the spread been pulled awry some other way?

Jennie got down on her knees and saw the fringe of the spread was ruffled inward as if something had been shoved under the bed. Laura used to hide here as a child with her dolls or other clutter, but Jennie had insisted it be kept spick-and-span after Laura had been bitten by a spider. But now the room did smell musty and a bit moldy. Tomorrow, she'd have to dust and clean again.

She lifted the bedspread then bent to peek under the bed. She screamed and screamed until the silent house screamed back.

"You—you shot him!" Rachel cried as the man pressed the gun against her chest to hold her to the big beam. She had lost her glasses but she knew that voice and that face, so close to hers, even in the dark.

"Very observant, Rachel," Kent Morgan said. "You know, the blinkers you Amish wear like some of your horses used to make me feel safe. Then when Sam died, I could tell you were changing, you would ask questions and challenge everything. A bright, too-clever woman who reads worldly books, Sam once described you. You know, I think that was the same day he asked me lumber prices for redoing the barn floor, at least half of it. And I couldn't allow that.''

"Sam—told you things?"

He'd moved the gun barrel upward, almost choking her. Why didn't the sheriff come running? Could he and Kent be working together?

"Your father-in-law, Sheriff Burnett, is in on this, too?" she asked.

"No way," he clipped out. She could smell garlic on his breath. "Let's just say he's been called away by a crime where someone stole a rifle. You know, I'll bet it's a lot like this gun that Mitch shot Bishop Yoder with after Yoder hit him over the head with that old hunting gun of his. Mitch has a jail record, you know. Breaking and entering to get a gun would be kid's play for him and an outburst of violence par for the course.''

"You're the one who summoned Eben here," she whispered. "You meant to use him to kill Mitch and me, like Amish justice on two lovers."

"You know, I like Mitch, and I'm real sorry he got mixed up with all this," he said as if they were having a heart-to-heart chat. "And I hardly knew you two were going to show up tonight. I was originally planning to drive Eben in his buggy to see you at Mitch's where Eben could shoot you both there, but, once again, Rachel, you've screwed up my plans.''

"Was that your sister in the grave there?" she asked. "Laura?"

"Very good. Let's just say it was my mother's daughter, the golden girl, the favorite, the chosen one. Hell, once Laura showed up, she might as well have been an only child. At best, I'm the prodigal son.''

"But the prodigal son was loved and welcomed back."

"Then I'm nothing to Jennie Morgan. At least my father understood and stood by me."

"You dressed Amish and spied on me and the boys," Rachel said, fighting to keep her voice calm. Although she feared making him tell her everything, she wanted to know. Besides, she had to keep him talking. "Kent, you've proved that you're the one skilled at breaking and entering."

"Your kids really fell for that *Daadi* bit. I'm sorry, Rachel, sorry they have to lose their mother, too, now, but some of your people will take them in. I hear Simeon Lapp wants this place and they want lots of kids, so maybe they can have the twins, because I intend to outbid them for this place."

"You talked to Sam and learned all about him," she said, feeling awed at the magnitude of what Kent had managed. Words she couldn't hold back spilled from her. "But he wouldn't have told you all of it, not Sam."

"Sure he did, with coaxing. I liked Sam, too, though that pompous ass McGowan deserved to die. But I had to protect Laura's resting place at any cost. At least, till you messed things up, I was able to do that. Can you imagine how much worse my mother would be if she knew I'd hidden Laura so close?"

Rachel gasped, but only partly because he pressed the barrel to her throat so hard. Was it possible that his father—God forbid, Jennie, too—knew that Kent had killed Laura but not where he'd buried her? And some of the things Kent had known about Sam had come from things Rachel had told Jennie. Did that mean Jennie had helped Kent try to scare her away from here? Surely Jennie could not have known what Kent had done and decided to cover for him so she didn't lose a second child.

"What happened to Laura?" she barely breathed.

He pressed the barrel against her throat. "That slut," he spit out, flecking her face with saliva, "not only had a boyfriend but was taken in by McGowan. McGowan this and that, just like it was Laura this and that at home. Mom was blind to anything she did wrong, blind to anything at all I did, but losing Laura got her attention!"

Bitterness and pain roared from him to chill her as, wide-eyed, not seeing her now, he went on. "After the school barn dance that night, it only started out back in the woodlot as an argument between me and Laura. She actually wanted me to cover for her while she went to a movie, and I told her no. And then Miss Perfect Bitch slapped me, and I hit her back. She screamed she'd tell Mom I'd roughed her up, and I just wanted to keep her quiet so I put my hands on her damn throat..."

He pressed the barrel harder against Rachel. She gagged and gasped. Her whole life of training to turn the other cheek, to do no violence flashed before her eyes, then faded as she felt breathless, light-headed.

"You'd like to lie in this barn you love, too, wouldn't you?" Kent goaded, his eyes focusing on her again. "Maybe after they rip up the floor, when I rebuild it and everyone goes away again, I'll plant you there, too."

"Kent," she choked out. "Sam. What about Sam?"

"I figured Sam would like to die here, so I threw

the kitten down from the loft and, when he came over, I just dropped the hook.''

''But why? *Why?*''

''I told you, to protect Laura's grave. Then when it looked like you'd get people in here to dig up the floor, you had to go, too—at least be scared off. Then I'd get Mom to convince you to sell the place to us, not to the Amish who weren't standing by you like we were.''

Rachel's mind raced. Then Jennie couldn't be in on this, too, since she'd been the one to bring in Linc McGowan. Or did she think she could control what Linc did?

''So sorry, Rachel, but it's your turn now...''

Steadily, he pressed the gun barrel closer. Fearing her throat would collapse, Rachel kicked at Kent. She felt her knee connect between his legs. He gasped, dropped the flashlight and gun. The light went out and rolled, then dropped somewhere, maybe into Laura's grave. When Rachel heard him retching, she felt for the gun on the floor and staggered away to drop it in the partly filled water trough. She knelt where Mitch lay, but when she reached for him, her hand came away wet and sticky from his head and the floor.

Blood. Both he and Eben could be bleeding to death or were even dead. She felt for Mitch's neck pulse. When she heard Kent run at her, she tried at first to turn Mitch over to get the trowel he carried, but realized she had no time. She darted for the back barn door.

Kent tackled her. They hit the floor hard, rolling, thrashing until he pressed her under him.

''You'd have loved my Amish *Daadi* imitation,''

he goaded. "Maybe I'll do it for you. I heard the twins talk about *Daadi* getting back in your bed. I'd have liked that."

"They trusted you, you traitor! Everyone trusted you!"

She fought him like a madwoman. He was much stronger, and she'd never lifted a hand to a human being before, except to *bletch* the boys if they misbehaved.

Her boys...misbehaved...Kent could have killed them with that train.

Strength she didn't know she had flooded her. Though he held to her skirt until it ripped in his hand, she shoved and scrambled away, dizzy and disoriented in the dark barn. The back door. He'd come in through the back door he'd made the keys for and fled through on the night he killed Sam. Where was the back door?

Rachel felt the rough wood of Bett and Nann's stall and ran for the tiny crack of gray in the darkness. But she saw his silhouette there, blocking it, anticipating her next move, as he had for far too long.

She veered away and climbed the ladder to the first loft. If she had to, she'd go clear up on to the roof the way Sarah had. She'd sit there until dawn, screaming for help. Would anyone hear her but Jennie? Would she help?

She heard Kent on the ladder behind her, felt the rungs bounce with his weight. But he didn't have a light or a gun now. However much he'd hidden in the barn, used the barn, she knew it better.

Rachel forced herself not to run for the next ladder up to the cupola as she had planned. Trying to quiet her breathing, she hunkered down behind a row of hay bales where she had sometimes rested. She heard him stop, could feel him look around.

"Stop playing games, Rachel," he said, gasping for breath. "I've got a lot to do tonight before the sheriff gets back here. Don't you want to go for a ride with Mitch and your bishop? Each time I took you or the twins for a ride, I saw that look of longing in your eyes, for adventure, for worldly things as you plain people say. I may have gone astray, but it was my mother's and Laura's fault. You've gone astray from your people and have no one to blame but yourself."

Wishing desperately that the sheriff had not confiscated the barn shovels—a big one had once hung on the wall here and would do for a weapon—Rachel thought of the grappling hook. Kent had killed Sam with it. If she could just loose it and handle its ropes by feel, she could swing it at him and pin or knock him down.

She took off both shoes and aimed one toward the front of the barn so it would hit under the drop-down haymow door. Hating to admit cold weather was here, she had not closed and latched it for the winter yet.

Rachel heaved the shoe and heard it hit. Kent moved swiftly past her toward the sound. Barefooted, amid loose straw, she moved quickly toward the guide ropes for the grappling hook on the wall.

She fumbled with the knots, realizing Sam must have showed Kent how he did his double hitches. The rope was tightly knotted now because she'd feared the hook would fall again. She picked frantically at them.

When Kent figured out she wasn't where the sound

came from, he started back across the loft, his feet whispering through the hay. If she could only loose the ropes now, she could see him to swing the heavy hook.

"I've got a shoe here and I know I ripped your dress. Going to undress for me, Rachel? You know, I can understand Mitch's fantasy to strip all those layers of starch and black away. You do know the more you cover a woman's body, the more it tempts, don't you, and those black stockings I've seen bobbing on your clothesline..."

The ropes loosed; the hook started to rattle on its track. Kent saw or sensed her and charged. She yanked the main rope and the hook lumbered along its path. But it was going too fast to hit him; she couldn't swing it over far enough into the loft, nor had she untied the rope that could make it drop. It would go along the entire track and out the haymow door as if a wagonload below awaited its jaws.

It was then she decided. She flung herself at the hook, grabbing its long, curved prongs, praying it would not drop or open. She swung free over the threshing floor far below. It took her past Kent, between the two lofts, along the entire spine of the roof and out onto the peak above the front doors where it jerked and swayed to a stop.

Rachel hung outside the barn, twenty feet in the air. Kent saw or heard what she had done and rushed to the open haymow door. Her hands cramping, she hung there, exposed against the gray sky.

"Let go," Kent taunted, his voice close as he stood in the haymow door four feet from her. "It will be better for you than what I planned. That hook took Sam. Let go and just fly away. If you don't, I'm going to swing you back inside right to me.''

Her arms ached. Her sore body screamed. She heard his feet on the loft floor as he ran for the ropes. If she let go, she'd break both legs, maybe her back, too. Scanning the dark yard below, her house and driveway beyond, she realized that the sheriff, indeed, had gone. The only lights she could see were distant ones at Jennie's and those were a blur without her glasses.

If Jennie heard her scream, would she help her or Kent? It all depended on how much she would let Kent kill to protect their family secret that one child had murdered the other. But surely Jennie could not have known that. She must want Kent stopped or punished. But maybe, for the sake of her grandchildren, she would not let their father leave them, especially not to go to prison.

The hook shuddered and jerked, then started back inside. Rachel knew she had to let go now, take the chance. She pictured her twins and Mitch earlier today, talking about trucks and bunk beds and building barns. She recalled the view from the cupola and the roar and rock of the waves on Lake Erie.

And then she realized the hook was not moving her back in but was dropping, plunging. Kent was going to kill her under the hook the way he had Sam.

Twenty-Four

Rachel screamed, kicked her feet and let go before the grappling hook thudded to the ground beside her. Hitting on her bottom, she lay back, staring at skies of stars flying through her head.

Kent shouted something, and she heard him run across the loft for the ladder. Aching, limping on one twisted ankle, Rachel scrambled to her feet. She saw no car lights on the road. Where were the gawkers and the helicopters when she needed them? Jennie was her only chance to get help fast for Mitch and Eben. If not for them, she'd lock herself in the house. But Kent probably had a copy of that key, too. Those must have been his footprints on the floor, and he'd put Sam's watch in her bed.

Praying Jennie would help and not harm her, Rachel hobbled into her black, bare field. The pumpkin vines had rotted to nearly nothing, but they still tripped her up. She had to drag her right foot, and she was so dizzy.

She kept hearing the thud of that gun barrel against Mitch's skull; she felt his blood, warm, sticky. Eben had been shot and all the time she'd spent struggling with Kent was gone without her getting help for them. She could only pray Kent had not gone back inside the barn to finish them off.

To get him away from them, she dared to turn back and lift her hands to her mouth. "Your mother's going to hear what you've done, Kent Morgan! No wonder she loved Laura more!"

She hated herself for that, but he had to come to her bait. This time she was making herself his prey instead of being his victim. Panting, a stitch in her side, she pushed herself faster, glancing back, even stopping to listen for a pursuer.

Nothing. Rachel wished—she willed—him to come after her to get him away from those wounded men. When she'd run through the rustling corn that day, Kent must have been the one who'd chased her, so why didn't he come now?

These fields had given up the scattered arrowheads she and Mitch had found in Laura's grave. If Kent had buried his sister, especially ten years ago when he was still young, he had probably not put those there to make someone think it was an Indian or pioneer burial. He had put them there as tokens of his jealousy and anger.

A night train rumbled down the distant tracks as Rachel emerged from the field and hobbled across the familiar driveway. The side porch light was on as usual, but it looked both welcoming and ominous. The train seemed louder, louder.

Rachel pounded on the side door. "Jennie, help me! It's Rachel. Help!"

The train roar became the sound of a truck as Kent screeched to a halt in the driveway. He had driven without his lights, and the train had cloaked his engine noise.

Rachel prayed she was right about Jennie. Surely, her mourning for Laura had been so great she could not know Kent had killed her. Even if she had, Jennie had said she cared for Rachel like a daughter, and she'd believed her. But would Jennie choose to save her over Kent?

"Jennie!" Rachel screamed.

She had no idea what time it was. Jennie could be in bed. Kent could have his mother staying at his house.

"Jennie!" she shouted again. "Kent killed Laura and he wants to kill me, too. He's says it was an accident, but he's afraid you loved her—love me—more and he just wants to get rid of us!"

A few yards from Rachel, Kent jerked to a halt, staring aghast. But when a light clicked on in the kitchen, he lunged at her.

He tried to pull her into the darkness behind the house, but she went limp, and he had to drag her on the ground like dead weight. At the corner of the house, she grabbed the drainpipe. He cursed and kicked at her.

The side door banged open. Rachel cried out, but Kent fell on her, one hard hand over her mouth, the other choking her.

She tried to scratch, to kick him again, but she couldn't breathe, couldn't think. She felt herself falling, then floating. She'd never know if Mitch was alive, never know how her boys would do without her.

Darkness came closer. Was that Sam or Elias in that big-brimmed hat and frock coat motioning her toward the tracks? A bright train light blinded her, noise roaring at her, but it was beautiful, even though it was screaming, shrieking in her ear.

"What did she say about Laura? Get off her!"

"She's crazy."

"No, you are! It had to be you who put Laura's bones under her bed. You took her from Rachel's barn, didn't you?"

"What are you talking about? Laura's bones?"

"It's her. I know her hair and you were in her room."

"Sin of all sins to enter the shrine! But you always wanted her back, didn't you? Well, you've got her now."

"You're the crazy one. If you knew Laura was the one in the barn, you must have put her there. Did you? *Did you?*"

"It was an accident, okay? Everything since then has been for you. To protect Laura, like you always wanted. I had to get rid of Sam Mast, that lying seducer McGowan, the men Rachel dragged into this. Now she knows too much. You want my boys to be without a father like I was because you couldn't keep Dad here, hardly knew he was alive? At least he understo—"

"Get off her! You're not killing Rachel, too!"

The heavy weight lifted from Rachel, but both voices pressed her down.

"Still all for Laura, right, anyone but your only son? Thank God for my father, but the way you are, I can't live with it. Never could."

More jumbled cries, shouts. Then just someone sobbing. Rachel knew it was probably her because she wanted to save Mitch and hug her boys. She sucked in long, deep breaths of sweet, chill air.

The light from the train faded as someone cradled her, hugged her, lifting her head. But headlights slashed through her brain as an engine started nearby. Was that train still going to hit them? Her head cleared. It was Kent's truck. She was in Jennie's arms. Rachel tried to point, to shout that Kent could kill them, too, run his truck right over them.

But he backed out and roared away.

"He's gone," Jennie cried. "Rachel, are you all right?"

In the wan light from the house, Rachel saw Jennie's face was slick with tears. "I knew you'd help me," Rachel tried to whisper, but it hurt so much to talk she could only wheeze. "Even if you knew Kent killed Laura," she gasped out, then began to cough.

"How could you—believe that?" Jennie cried. "I—I know there was sibling rivalry. But isn't it natural that the mother favors the daughter and the father the son?"

As Rachel struggled to sit up, Jennie rocked back on her heels and sucked in a huge breath. "His father," she whispered. "He said his father understood. So then—Mike must have known."

Rachel pressed her hands to her head, fighting to clear it. "Jennie, call the squad—sheriff," Rachel whispered. "Mitch and Eben are hurt in my barn."

Jennie seemed to snap alert. "You mean by Kent. Then we've got to get over there to be certain he didn't go back—but I think he's running. God forgive me, I hope he's got enough of a start."

When Jennie drove Rachel into the hospital in south Toledo, the emergency-room nurses would not let Rachel farther than the waiting area. Both gravely injured men had been med-flighted and, besides not being family, there had been no room in the helicopter for her. How the boys would have loved to have seen that chopper, she thought exhaustedly as she phoned Gabe to tell him what had happened. He said he'd wake the twins and drive to tell Eben's family. Finally, a doctor came out to explain that it would be several hours until they really knew the status of either patient.

"I'll be back in a couple of hours," Jennie told her suddenly, grabbing her purse and fishing for her car keys. "I don't want to leave you alone but I have to see someone."

"You're going to Marci to explain what happened?"

"Her father can handle that right now."

"You're not going after Kent?"

Rachel saw her purse her lips. "Jennie, what good will it do to face Mike now?" Rachel pleaded, guessing what she intended. "It's going to be light soon, and you're as strung out as I am—"

"Yeah, it's going to be light soon, and I'm finally going to face him. He's going to look me in the face and tell me why he left. Because I think he must have known about what Kent did all these years."

"I'm going with you then," Rachel insisted, jumping up. "If Mike's innocent—and obviously what Kent says can't be trusted—he could be furious if you accuse him of something like that. Or if he covered for Kent—"

"That would probably make him an accessory to murder, even if it wasn't premeditated."

"What? I just mean if Kent can be this—unbalanced—Mike could be, too. Jennie, I do think Mike could have known, but I'm not sure. I should have told you, but on Laura's birthday he brought roses to the barn and lay them right on her grave, but I had no idea that was her grave, and he asked me not to tell—Jennie!'' she cried.

Rachel chased her friend down the hall and through the double doors into the chill, faint dawn.

Rachel lifted her skirts to keep up with Jennie across the mostly empty parking lot. "I have to do this alone, Rachel,'' Jennie said, but Rachel opened the passenger-side door and got in, anyway.

"No,'' she told Jennie. "You've helped me through things and I'm going, too. I'll stay out of your way, but you're not going alone.''

Jennie just nodded, slammed her door and jammed her key into the ignition.

Rachel saw Mike Morgan step out onto his front porch rather than asking Jennie in when she rang the bell. Being just across the field from where Linc McGowan had been killed made Rachel even more nervous. Mike glared out toward her sitting in the car in his driveway. Recalling that he should at least have tipped everyone off to Linc's preying on young girls, Rachel put her face to the windshield and glared back. But, of course, there was a wide field with that copse of trees in the middle, so maybe Mike hadn't seen girls at Linc's house. And Linc, like Kent, was good at pulling the wool over everyone's eyes. Arms crossed, she slumped back in her seat.

Mike and Jennie walked off the porch and across the yard away from the car, but Jennie had cracked their windows on the way back to Clearview and their voices, at first low, then raised, carried to Rachel.

"No, I haven't seen him and wouldn't hide him," Mike was insisting to his ex-wife. He sounded worried, not defiant.

"I don't know why not, since you've covered for him for years about Laura. Haven't you? *Haven't you?* He killed her and hid her and you knew!" she cried, flinging gestures at him but not striking him as Rachel had feared.

"If you'd been tuned in to him instead of so obsessed with her, you'd have known, too," Mike insisted. Their tracks were dark on the frosted grass, and puffs of their breath flew in each other's faces. "He was racked with pain over it—so was I. But you just built that shrine to her and shut us out. Even when you must have known that she was lost—dead somehow—you couldn't help the living, could you? Well, someone had to help the boy. I wasn't going to lose him like we'd lost Laura!"

"We didn't 'lose' Laura. Our own flesh and blood killed her, then—"

"He hit her, and she struck her head, Jennie." His voice rose to match hers. He seized Jennie's shoulders and stared right into her impassioned face. "I believe that. He didn't mean to kill her. It was a catastrophic accident, and I saved him from prison even if I couldn't save Laura—or our marriage."

"No wonder you couldn't face me," she accused, pulling back several steps. "No wonder you ran away, just the way Kent has now. Like father like son. But I realize you don't know he's killed others since then."

"What? No way he—"

"Sam Mast, Linc McGowan. He needs more than help, Mike, he needs to be stopped—"

They quit shouting and turned to watch the sheriff's car pull up in front, then coast in the driveway to block in Jennie's car. Thinking the sheriff needed more information, then fearing he had tracked her down to tell her Mitch or Eben had died, Rachel got out of the car, shaking. But he only lifted a hand to her to stay back and walked straight to Jennie and Mike. Mike's wife, looking frazzled in robe and slippers, evidently wakened by the shouting, came out on the front porch with a coffee mug in her hands.

"When I heard you weren't at the hospital," Tim Burnett said, "I had no idea you'd be here, Jennie, so I just came to see Mike." He took off his hat and held it before him, turning it in his hands. He cleared his throat and sniffed so loud Rachel could hear him where she stood.

"Have you found Kent, Tim?" Mike asked, taking a step forward. Jennie did the same. All three of them stood frozen in place.

"I'm afraid so," the sheriff said and his voice caught. "He's my loss, too, with Marci, the kids and all. Sorry, but Kent put that truck right into a tree near Fremont, folks, at about eighty miles an hour. No skid marks, the patrol says, so 'fraid he meant to do just that. He's—gone, Jennie, Mike. And since I've been putting two and two together on this—" he glanced over at Rachel, then back to the shocked parents "—there's no way everything past and present isn't gonna come out now."

Rachel started toward Jennie, and Mike's wife hurried off the porch toward him, but neither of them were needed. In a fierce embrace, Mike and Jennie Morgan clung together, stunned and sobbing, holding each other up.

Epilogue

"Rachel, there's a buggy coming up the lane," Mitch called to her. He'd been wrestling with the boys on the wet April grass and all three of them were a mess.

Rachel shaded her eyes with her hand, before she remembered her sunglasses were almost as good as an Amish bonnet had been. And her new contact lenses were a modern miracle, one among the many she'd enjoyed the last six months since Kent had tried to kill her.

"It's Jacob's buggy, with two people in it!" she called excitedly to Mitch. "It must be Sarah, come all this way, but I can't tell if they have the baby with them."

Rachel lifted her ankle-length denim skirt and started to run. She seldom wore slacks still, though she liked them well enough when she did. But some changes she just couldn't stand to rush. The boys had taken to T-shirts and jeans, though Andy sometimes stubbornly wore his broad-brimmed hat. And Rachel still drove the buggy from time to time and fully intended to plow these fields with the Percherons. They were sharing the back meadow with Bett and Nann until their stalls were reassembled after the wedding ceremony tomorrow. The new barn floor Mitch and Gabe had built after they'd moved the barn was so pristine and smooth it looked as if they'd sanded it by hand.

When Rachel got closer to the buggy, she saw Sarah was beaming, though Jacob looked as nervous as a sinner on doomsday. Sarah was waving something at her, holding it up in a big basket. Surely not the baby.

Celery!

Grasping her hands in excitement, Rachel ran beside the buggy.

"Turnabout's fair play, Rach," Sarah cried. "You know I can't come tomorrow, so I wanted to help you set up today. I've got about a barrel of this in here and other things for your bridal table. I didn't want to bounce little Mary all the way out here, so Annie's taking care of her at home."

Sarah jumped down and hugged Rachel before Jacob even had the reins wrapped. "Are you really getting married in your old barn?" Sarah asked, wide-eyed.

"It's a new barn now to celebrate the boys' and my new life," Rachel said, pointing at the pioneer building. Its skin and skeleton had been taken apart, power-cleaned, then resurrected on the other side of the pond from Mitch's barn house. However different their pasts, the two barns looked perfectly mated, Rachel thought.

When Mitch had pulled through his concussion and trauma, she had made good her promise to give him the barn. In return, he had given her and the boys his barn house. He had moved into the older house on the property with Gabe and proceeded to court her and, in another way she'd never fully understand, to counsel and court her boys, who adored him.

Rachel had left her farm and the Amish faith, though she'd asked if her sons could spend some vacations visiting among them, living with Sarah and Jacob. She had made her choice freely after knowing both worlds, but she wanted her sons to be able to do the same.

She greeted Jacob, and the three of them walked toward Mitch together.

"Gabe and the twins are fishing at the pond," Mitch told Rachel, then nodded to Jacob and smiled at Sarah. "We're honored to have you stop to see us. Sarah, how's your father?"

"Ornery as ever. No wonder that bullet went right through him. And, Mr. Randall—"

"Mitch, please."

"Mitch," Sarah went on, "Father is grateful you didn't press charges. Though he's been forgiven by the people, he's still ashamed for having to resign as bishop. In public confession he said he was a failure as head of his household and head of the church, but I actually like him better now, *ja.* But he did tell me to say a good hello to both of you, that he did. I'm sure that meant a good wedding, too."

Mitch nodded solemnly, almost Amish-like, Rachel thought. "Men who recover in the same hospital room," Mitch said, "get to understand each other, at least a little bit. Besides, Eben and I decided it's as wrong to hold a grudge against a dead man as a living one."

Rachel wondered if Mitch was thinking of how he'd come to terms with his tough past or just about Kent. The four of them kept silent for a moment. Kent had died instantly, but the story of Laura's murder and the others Kent committed to protect her resting place and his crime had still come out. But Jennie Morgan had never told a soul that Mike knew what Kent had done all those years ago.

Rachel had sold her house and land to her brother-in-law, Zeb, to settle her debts with Sam's family. That had allowed more Maplecreek Amish to move to Clearview. Jennie had sold her place to an Amish family so she could move in with Marci to help her with the kids. Marci was home less than ever since she'd left hairdressing for training at the police academy in Toledo. Mike helped a lot with the kids, too. As a matter of fact, he'd spent so much time with Jennie and those kids that his wife had left him, and who knew what was on the horizon there? But above all, Rachel thought, Jennie and her grandsons were coming for the wedding tomorrow.

"Come see the barn," Rachel said to her Amish friends, linking her arm in Mitch's. "You won't believe it, but a pair of barn owls are nesting there already." In the spring sun, her engagement ring glinted, startling her. After all, she had never worn any ring before, let alone one that flashed fire.

"Oh, the barn looks just the same," Sarah said, still cradling the basket of celery. "And I'll bet the

view's still fine from that cupola. Oh, didn't mean
that like it sounds, no.''

"You and Jacob should go up there together," Rachel said. "It's our favorite place for smooching."

Sarah laughed, and Jacob grinned.

"The barn has a good, new life here," Rachel
went on, "but it's still the same sturdy barn."

Mitch's arm slipped around her waist and
squeezed hard. Along the fringe of the pond, Aaron
pulled up a flopping fish on his line while Andy
cheered. And in the rippling meadow just beyond,
Nann and Bett munched grass and the golden Percherons ran free.

Author's Note

My special thanks to a variety of people who helped me find information for this book. First, as ever, my husband, Don, for our trips through Amish country, both in Ohio and Pennsylvania.

Also, I'm indebted to Paul Locher, barn expert, writer for the *Daily Record,* in Wooster, Ohio, for advice on Ohio Amish barns. Amish barn builder and timber framer, Joseph Miller, Jr.'s, sketches on barn building were of great help. I am grateful to the Amish farmer, who will remain anonymous, who so kindly let us look around his barn when we simply asked to do so.

Thanks to a special four-year-old, Zachary Brett Cross, for giving me a glimpse into the world of a guy his age. Zachary is not a twin, but he has enough ideas and energy for two. And to my sister-in-law, Evelyn Harper, for her advice on pumpkin patches and for letting me know her and her husband's small, lovely Ohio farm over the years.

As I drive through Ohio and the Midwest, I do mourn the loss of so many barns and farms and the way of life they symbolize. Perhaps someday the

Amish will preserve America's only "small" working farms. My great-grandparents were northern Ohio farmers, and most of us could find ancestors who tilled the land and loved their barns. I'm pleased to say there are growing numbers of rebuilders and restorers today who, like Mitch in this book, preserve America's vanishing barns by living in them or using them for studios or getaways.

Also, my great appreciation goes to the "team" that encouraged me to write this Amish story: Meg Ruley, Amy Moore-Benson and Dianne Moggy.

Karen Harper
September 1999

Her family, her career, her life.
Mariah Bolt is trying to save them all...

GUILT BY SILENCE

TAYLOR SMITH

On the cobbled streets of Vienna, an accident nearly kills
David Tariff and severely injures his daughter.

On a deserted highway in New Mexico, a leading scientist
disappears in a burst of flames.

Mariah Bolt—CIA officer and David's wife—is one link
between the tragedies. And as the unanswered questions
grow, so does Mariah's determination to prove that neither
was an accident. But as she probes deeper into what really
happened, she begins to realize that she can trust no one.
Not the government, not her mentor...not even her husband.
Because now Mariah is the next target.

On sale mid-July 2000 wherever paperbacks are sold!

MIRA®

Visit us at www.mirabooks.com

MTS537R

The sweet smell of…revenge.

ELIZABETH PALMER

Charmian Sinclair runs her own PR firm, is close to her family and has a regular series of married lovers for each day of the week. This very satisfying lifestyle demands order and routine to run smoothly…and chaos is lurking around the corner.

When Charmian's brother-in-law is fired from his high-powered job, she resolves to avenge him, and launches a campaign to infiltrate the ranks of the corrupt corporate elite. But the stakes get higher when she meets her match in Toby Gill, a man with his own agenda for revenge. Can their relationship withstand the innuendo and betrayal that is a part of this game each is determined to win?

Flowering Judas

"Engaging characters and lush atmosphere add up to delightfully fresh and frolicsome fun."
—*Publishers Weekly*

On sale mid-July 2000 wherever paperbacks are sold!

Visit us at www.mirabooks.com

MEP593

The house on Sunset was a house of secrets...

SHADOWS AT SUNSET

The house on Sunset Boulevard has witnessed everything from an infamous murder-suicide to a drug-fueled commune to the anguish of its present owner, Jilly Meyer, who is trying to save the house and what's left of her wounded family.

Coltrane is a liar, a con man and a threat to everything Jilly holds dear. Jilly has to stop Coltrane from destroying everything she cares about—including her heart. But to do that, Jilly has to discover what Coltrane is *really* up to.

ANNE STUART

"Anne Stuart delivers exciting stuff for those of us who like our romantic suspense dark and dangerous."
—Jayne Ann Krentz

On sale September 2000 wherever paperbacks are sold!

Visit us at www.mirabooks.com   MAS571

MIRABooks.com

We've got the lowdown on your favorite author!

☆ Read an excerpt of your favorite author's newest book

☆ Check out her bio and read our famous "20 questions" interview

☆ Talk to her in our Discussion Forums

☆ Get the latest information on her touring schedule

☆ Find her current besteller, and even her backlist titles

All this and more available at

www.MiraBooks.com
on Women.com Networks

MEAUT1

Down in Louisiana, you can count on family.

New York Times bestselling author

JENNIFER BLAKE

And in the delta town of Turn-Coupe, the Benedicts count on Roan. As town sheriff, people call him whenever there's trouble—which is why he's at Cousin Betsy's the night her convenience store is robbed.

It isn't like Roan to make mistakes, but that night he makes three. The first is shooting from the hip when one of the robbers tumbles from the getaway car. The second is letting the other two escape while he disarms the one he's downed. The third is falling hard for the woman he's just shot....

ROAN

Jennifer Blake will "thoroughly please."
—Publishers Weekly

On sale mid-July 2000
wherever paperbacks are sold!

Visit us at www.mirabooks.com

MJB630

KAREN HARPER

66520	THE BABY FARM	___ $5.99 U.S.	___ $6.99 CAN.
66433	LIBERTY'S LADY	___ $5.50 U.S.	___ $6.50 CAN.
66278	DAWN'S EARLY LIGHT	___ $5.50 U.S.	___ $6.50 CAN.

(limited quantities available)

TOTAL AMOUNT	$_____
POSTAGE & HANDLING	$_____
($1.00 for one book; 50¢ for each additional)	
APPLICABLE TAXES*	$_____
TOTAL PAYABLE	$_____

(check or money order—please do not send cash)

To order, complete this form and send it, along with a check or money order for the total above, payable to MIRA Books®, to: **In the U.S.:** 3010 Walden Avenue, P.O. Box 9077, Buffalo, NY 14269-9077; **In Canada:** P.O. Box 636, Fort Erie, Ontario, L2A 5X3.

Name:_____
Address:_____ City:_____
State/Prov.:_____ Zip/Postal Code:_____
Account Number (if applicable):_____
075 CSAS

*New York residents remit applicable sales taxes.
 Canadian residents remit applicable GST and provincial taxes.

MIRA

Visit us at www.mirabooks.com

MKH0800BL